Titles by Maisey Yates

Silver Creek Romance Novels

UNEXPECTED
UNTOUCHED
UNBROKEN

Silver Creek Romance Novellas

UNBUTTONED
REKINDLED
UNWRAPPED

UNDONE

MAISEY YATES

BERKLEY ROMANCE
New York

BERKLEY ROMANCE
Published by Berkley
An imprint of Penguin Random House LLC
1745 Broadway, New York, NY 10019
penguinrandomhouse.com

Book design by Kristin del Rosario

ISBN: 9780593952962

First Edition: October 2025

Unbuttoned was originally published as an ebook in 2013.
Rekindled was originally published as an ebook in 2014.
Unwrapped was originally published as an ebook in 2014.

Printed in the United States of America
1st Printing

The authorized representative in the EU for product safety and compliance is
Penguin Random House Ireland, Morrison Chambers, 32 Nassau Street,
Dublin D02 YH68, Ireland, https://eu-contact.penguin.ie.

Contents

UNBUTTONED . . . 1

REKINDLED . . . 105

UNWRAPPED . . . 209

EXCERPT FROM *UNBROKEN* . . . 311

UNBUTTONED

CHAPTER

One

Lucas sometimes wondered if Carly Denton reserved that facial expression particularly for him. He'd never seen her make it at another person. She smiled at most people, even complete strangers. But not at him. With him, those normally lush, pink lips were pulled into a tight line, blue eyes glittering with a kind of cool disdain that warned him to keep his distance.

In her defense, he'd just walked into her office unannounced and late in the day. He hadn't even given her a chance to fake being okay with his presence, which she did a decent job of sometimes.

Not today, but sometimes.

"I was just about to leave, Lucas. You don't have an appointment, do you?" She straightened, shoulders back, fine brows arched. She looked like a strict headmistress. Which, he had to admit, a part of him kind of liked.

The office was just as severe as the woman. A showcase for just how neat and orderly she was, and lacking in any personality. Pictures on the wall of places he knew she'd never been to. A bookshelf filled with books that were probably just there because the leather bindings and gilded lettering looked nice, not because there was anything interesting in them. Because for Carly, it was all about image.

Given the image her family had presented to the community during her childhood, he couldn't really blame her. But it didn't mean she couldn't stand to be loosened up, either.

He took his hat off and set it on her desk, palms flat on the glossy surface. He knew invading her space like that would annoy her. Knew that cluttering up that pristine surface would get her back up. But he considered attempting to loosen Carly up a bit of a hobby. Though she always resisted.

"Nope. But I had some important things to talk to you about concerning the Ride for Hope."

"What does that have to do with you?"

"I'm representing the Rodeo Association for this project."

"What? No. You aren't. I mean, it seems like someone would have told me."

"Warned you?"

She spoke in a monotone, overly calm voice. "It's just, you don't normally do charity things, do you? I mean, unless it's a bikini car wash."

"I didn't organize that. I did get my truck washed though, but in my defense, my truck was dirty."

She arched one brow. "Was it?"

"Your brother went too, so unless you raked him over the coals for his attendance, I think you need to let it go."

"I absolutely did rake him over the coals for it. That is simply not the kind of image we want Silver Creek to have. This town is about family." She cleared her throat and sat back in the chair, her hands folded in front of her. She was so damn prissy.

She hadn't always been. He could remember her, thirteen,

barefoot, with mud up to her knees and her hair a tangled mess behind her. She'd had freckles then. She might still, but it was hard to tell with that coat of makeup spread over her face. It made her too perfect. Too clean.

Like her office, everything about Carly was a bit too something. Too clean, too perfect, too orderly. Her pink lipstick matched her pink nails. Her gray suit jacket was tailored perfectly, as were her gray pants. The pink shirt beneath, of course, matched the nails and lipstick. Blond hair sleek, shiny and not one strand out of place.

She looked pretty disturbed by the mention of the car wash, and he wondered if he'd actually pushed her too far this time. Pushing her too far wasn't his aim. If he did that, she might boot him out of his office, and then he couldn't play with her anymore.

"Ah, yes, sorry, I had a lapse. Well, when you're done playing morality police, maybe we could get back to the business at hand."

"I don't particularly want to do business with a man who considers dress clothes to be a pair of Wranglers that don't have a hole in them."

"And a bigger belt buckle."

"Thank you for reinforcing my point."

"I don't really like having to deal with a woman who probably irons her socks, but this is about the charity. Do you think the other members of the Silver Creek City Council will be happy to know you chased the liaison for the event out the door with your special brand of meanness?"

She frowned, and for a moment, he wondered if he'd actually hurt her feelings. "I'm not mean."

"You aren't sunshine and light where I'm concerned, sugar. Never have been."

"That's because you're . . ." He was sure she was about to spit out a particularly vile insult, but then thought better of it. Her lips puckered in tighter, and she looked like she was chewing on her words. Like she was trying to demolish them before they burst into the room and kneed him in the balls. "You and I don't always see eye to eye."

And he'd never been certain why. Or what had happened. All he knew was that the first time Carly had come home from college, she'd started avoiding him, and when he did see her, there was no more warmth, no more genuine smiles. All he got was frosty reserve and distance. No matter what he did, no matter what he said, he got a sour-apple face and a tart response.

He missed the freckles. And the smile. But he doubted he was going to see either today.

"That's putting it mildly."

"But I'm sure we can get along for a while. It's for charity, after all." She smiled at him, smooth as glass. She really was pretty when she smiled.

"Admirable," he said. "I'm here to drop off donations." He held up the blue bank bag, and she extended a delicate hand and took it from him, careful to make sure her fingers didn't touch his, he noticed.

"Great. How much is in here?"

"Enough to cover the cost of the food," he said. "We still need to get donations of either money or time to get the rest of the events up and running."

"Well, I've got Delia to cook, and the wait staff from the restaurant are coming and serving for free. So that's labor. We still need someone to man the hayride. And . . . you know, provide the wagon and the hay."

"I'll put in a call to the Mitchell ranch and see what we can get. They always give." The Mitchell family was a pillar in the Silver Creek community. If something needed to be done, everyone knew they could count on them.

"Well, that's . . . nice of you."

"I can be pretty nice, Carly, if you'd just give me a chance."

"Does that wounded act usually work on women?"

"Always."

"You're shameless."

"Always have been."

"Always will be?" Her expression tightened again, some of the chill returning. Suddenly, he didn't find it quite as funny.

"Every time you see me, you look at me like you just sucked a lemon." He reached out and put his thumb on her bottom lip. "Relax a little."

He felt her grow completely stiff beneath his touch, her lip tightening. Her shoulders curled in, her eyes like chips of ice. "I can't relax with you touching me like that." She pulled away. "And this is why I don't like to deal with you."

"Why? Because I call you on your attitude?"

"Because you walk around like you're God's gift, and you expect every woman to want to open the package." Color flooded her cheeks. "I didn't . . . That came out . . ."

"Package, huh?"

"Lucas, this is what I'm talking about," she said, her voice turning stiff and formal. It shouldn't turn him on. But it did a little. That, come to think of it, was probably why he liked needling her.

"Oh, I'm sorry, I forgot. Business, right? No room for jokes. Not in Carly's world."

Carly almost corrected him. But she didn't. Because in a lot of ways, he was right. She didn't have room for jokes. Not with him. Not with a man who had the power to get under her skin like he did. It was especially bad when he ambushed her with his presence, like today. If she had time to prepare, she could deal. She could even act kind of normal. But she needed to be warned.

Lucas Miller had long been a burr under her saddle. He and her older brother had terrorized her constantly when she'd been a teenager. And then her annoyance with him had started turning into something else. And she'd done her very best to turn it back to annoyance. Especially once she'd realized that he was just the kind of man she ought to avoid.

She didn't have time for a man like him. She had ambition instead.

More than that, she wasn't wasting her time on the kind of man she knew would never settle down. She'd watched that drama play out in her parents' marriage, and she'd been more than happy to learn from their mistakes.

"Well, you're here for business," she said. "So maybe that's what we should stick to."

He smiled, that cocky, irritating smile of his that made him look so damn hot, she felt the need to start shedding clothes. To cool off. Not for any other reason. No. Certainly not so she could be skin to skin with him.

No. Not that. Never that.

Still, it was impossible, even for her, to ignore how sexy he was. Tall, broad chest, lean waist and hips. Jeans that were just tight enough to give hints to some serious assets—not that she'd looked.

He was always a little disorderly. Dark stubble coloring his jaw perpetually, like he was constantly a few hours past due for a shave. His hair always a little too long, looking like a very intimate acquaintance had run her fingers through it while receiving the gift that was currently tightly wrapped by those jeans.

She wasn't sure how he managed to not have hat hair, like most of the cowboys she knew. No, Lucas Miller never had the decency to look so unfortunate.

Another annoying thing about him. But he had enough women waiting around to fawn over him. She didn't need to join the herd.

"I think we covered all the business. Unless you had something specific you were wondering about?" Lucas said.

Oh, shoot. She did. She really wanted to just say no and send him on his way. "How many riders do you have for the saddle bronc event?"

"Five or six. I think I can get more; I just need to make some calls. The Pendleton Round-Up is happening just a couple weeks after this. I'm thinking I can find out who might be in the area and see if they want to pop over and raise some money for a good cause."

Why did he have to be efficient and helpful? "Great, thank you." The words nearly choked her, especially when they earned her one of his smiles.

"You're very welcome." That smile lingered, and she felt the impact down to her toes. If she wasn't wearing restrictive heels, she would have curled them. "Can I go now, ma'am?"

The way he said that sent a shiver down her spine that she tried very hard to ignore. He was being patronizing. She should be annoyed. Not . . . shivery.

"Yes," she said, trying not to sound too much like she was giving him permission, because for some strange reason, he seemed to enjoy it. And a part of her, a traitorous, evil part of her, enjoyed him enjoying it.

"All right then. I'll see you later."

"Yeah," she said. *Hopefully much later.*

And when he walked out, she most definitely didn't look at his butt. No, she did not.

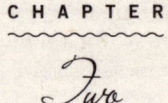
"Oh . . . Mac. Why didn't you mention that he was coming?" Carly peeked out the kitchen window and watched the navy blue pickup roar down the driveway and stop in front of the house.

Mac looked up from his place at the dinner table, his expression bland. "Who?"

"Lucas." Carly practically growled the name. But she'd already seen him today and that was one dose of Lucas too many in her opinion.

She'd avoided him quite nicely in the two years since she'd returned from college. But now that the fundraiser was forcing them to cross professional paths, avoiding him wasn't going to be quite so simple.

It didn't help that Mac was being spontaneous, rather than sticking to his usual guys' night schedule, which also played a big part in her ability to avoid Lucas.

"He comes over for a beer all the time. I didn't think I needed to mention it. Anyway, he wants to see the finished kitchen."

"You still might have mentioned it."

"Did you not make enough food or something?"

She was ready to brain her brother with the saucepan she had on the burner. It would knock him cold, and scald him. It was a happy thought, but not one she'd follow through on. "I made enough," she said carefully, "but it should have been, you know, leftovers, for your work lunches."

"I can make my own lunch. You don't have to be such a hen."

"I like taking care of you."

"I'm your older brother. That's supposed to be my line."

She crossed the room and set a bowl of salad on the large, mission-style dining table before going back to the stove.

Everything was open in her brother's home, the kitchen, living room and dining area all part of one expansive area. She liked it, usually. It was certainly nicer cooking here than in her little house. But today that meant that, no matter what, she would be sharing space with Lucas Miller.

Sharing space with Lucas Miller made her cranky. And edgy. And fluttery. She disliked all of the aforementioned feelings, which, really, was mainly why she disliked Lucas.

"Yes, well, until you get a new housekeeper to cook and clean up after you, I worry that you're going to expire from starvation beneath a pile of laundry."

"And we all know Mom's not going to drop by with any chicken soup," Mac said, pushing his baseball cap back and running a hand over his hair.

"No, she's too busy keeping a tail on Dad, watching him meet up with bimbos at sleazy hotels. Who says you can't go home again? Our childhood lives on."

"Yay us."

The front door swung open and Lucas walked in, all broad and tall and grinning. It made Carly's stomach curl in tight.

"Hey," Mac said.

"Hey. Place looks great, Mac. They did a hell of a job."

"Yeah, no more yellow tile," Mac said.

Then Lucas's focus landed on Carly. "Well, isn't this a pleasant surprise?"

He didn't mean it. She could hear that in his tone. And maybe she couldn't really blame him for not being thrilled to see her. She hadn't been very friendly with him earlier. She never was.

But that was more about her than him, and she knew it. If she was friendly, they might end up spending time together, and more time with Lucas meant . . . What she needed was sanity. Self-protection. His ego didn't really come into it.

"Isn't it?" she asked, dumping her pasta from a pan into a bowl. If he was going to play civil, then so would she. She was hardly going to fire barbs at him over Mac's head. Not that that usually stopped either of them. "Have a seat, dinner's almost ready."

She spent dinner watching Mac and Lucas BS about everything. Women, horses and Lucas's rodeo rides past. There was something vaguely comforting about it. Something normal.

It had been so long since they'd all sat down together. But there had been a time when Lucas had been a fixture at their dinner table. She'd lost track of the times it had been just the three of them for dinner.

Lucas's dad never noticed if his son was home or not, the haze of alcohol he preferred to be under keeping him from seeing much of anything clearly. Mac and Carly's parents had simply been too involved in keeping Silver Creek supplied with new episodes of their live soap opera.

That had meant more than one dinner like this. Pasta, salad, and three people just looking for a little bit of normal in a world full of crazy.

She'd hero-worshipped Lucas a little bit back then. He was big and tall, strong. And in her opinion at the time, he'd been a better bronc buster than any cowboy on the pro circuit. And he was the handsomest man she'd ever seen. And to her thirteen-year-old eyes, the seventeen-year-old had been a man.

She'd actually fawned over him, rather embarrassingly, until she graduated from high school and got a giant slap of reality where he was concerned. Some might have even called her past feelings for him a crush. She didn't. Nope. It was just youthful . . . whatever.

That was before that summer day just before she'd gone off to college. The memory still had the power to make her shake with anger, and she wasn't sure why. She'd gone over to his brand-new ranch, the one he'd secured with his already respectable rodeo earnings. And she'd seen him. Lucas, with some hot brunette, pressed up against the side of the barn.

And given the other woman's state of undress and the flush on her face, her skin, there was more than kissing going on. Carly hadn't stopped to look for details.

Her face had prickled like she'd run head on into a cactus, her throat burning with a rash of heat, tears stinging her eyes. Even now, it was easy to remember how acute the pain had been. Which was silly, then and now. Lucas had never asked for her admiration, and he'd never owed her anything. And it had served as a warning. One she'd held close to her heart, down deep, ever since.

By the time she'd come back for Christmas, Lucas was walking around town with a redhead wrapped around him like tinsel. When she came home in spring, he'd traded the previous one in for a shiny new blond model, and that was when she'd had to face reality. It was who he was, what he did.

And men like that didn't change.

Those memories were the biggest reason she treated him like she did, why she held him at a distance. They'd given her a window into Lucas Miller's attitude on life. The kind of attitude one hid from one's best friend's younger sister.

From then on, it was eyes wide open for her.

Mac picked his hat up from the kitchen table and rose from his chair. "I'm going to run out and make sure everything's all secure."

Her brother's ranch was the most important thing in his life. A small operation catering to people who wanted extra-lean, natural beef. Mac had built it up from scratch, with a bit of start-up money from Lucas. Which she had to admit was decent of him. She hated to admit that.

Lucas nodded from his position at the table, making it very clear he was sending his friend off and not going with him.

Oh no.

She really didn't want to be alone with Lucas, most especially with the memory of him, and just what he could do to a woman, fresh in her mind. That image still made her face hot and she was afraid the heat didn't come purely from humiliation.

As soon as the front door closed behind Mac, a smile spread over Lucas's face. "Twice in one day. What did I do to earn the honor?"

She stretched her lips into a fake smile. Anything to avoid being told she looked like she'd sucked on a lemon. "You could have gone with Mac."

"I'd rather talk with you, actually. Is that so hard to believe?"

"A little surprising, is all." She stood up and grabbed her plate, and Mac's, walking across to the kitchen area and putting them both in the sink.

"Why is that?"

"Well, somebody told me earlier today that I'm mean. I would think you might want to avoid me, all things considered."

"You aren't *that* mean, sugar."

"Until today I didn't realize I was mean at all. That news flash came straight from you."

"So it's just me then," he said, taking the bowls that had contained the pasta and salad, standing and making his way over to where she was.

"What do you mean?"

"You really do reserve the attitude for me specifically." He set the bowls on the counter. "And that means one of two things."

"Oh, good. I'm about to get some cowboy wisdom. Let's hear it." She crossed her arms beneath her breasts and rested her hip against the countertop.

"Either you like me a whole lot less than you like most people . . ."

"Good. Deductive reasoning. Very sharp."

"Or you like me a whole lot more."

Her chest tightened. "Are you serious?"

"I don't know, Carly," he said, his voice curling around her name like a caress and making her feel more than a little hot and bothered. "That's the part you'll have to fill in for me."

She started to tell him just what she thought. Why not? It would be satisfying to take a little of that attitude out of his hide. He deserved it.

But then he shifted, moved so that he was standing in front of her, one of his hands on the counter behind her, the heat of his body in front. And she caught the scent of his aftershave. Clean. Masculine. Just like him. Like leather and soap. And beneath that, his skin.

And something in her, something she'd tried to suppress, more than suppress, beat into submission, every day since she was eighteen years old, woke up. And it woke up hungry.

That part of her had wanted to be close enough to Lucas Miller to smell his skin for ages, and it was making itself known big-time now.

"I don't—" she said, the words coming out more as a squeak than a beginning to a confident and witty insult that would take Lucas down a peg or two.

"You don't what?" he asked, angling his body toward hers.

It was like magic. Or like a magnet. She found herself angling toward him too. Into his heat. Her heart was pounding fast, her head spinning. She had to bite her bottom lip to keep it from trembling.

Then, for the second time that day, Lucas extended his hand and brushed his thumb along her lower lip, his touch hot and rough, sending an arrow of pure want through her, hitting a target in her stomach, the impact vibrating through her.

Her eyelids started to flutter closed, and that was when she knew, even as she surrendered, that she'd lost this battle. And she was going out white flag waving, giving up of her own free will.

The sound of boots knocking against the front step, and the warning provided by the rattle of the turning doorknob, broke her out of her trance. She sidestepped Lucas and scurried to the center of the kitchen, her heart thundering in her ears, her entire body trembling.

If she hadn't been so desperate to hide what had just happened from everyone in the entire world, including herself, when Mac walked through the front door, she might have thrown herself at his feet and kissed those muddy boots in thanks.

"Thanks for having me over, Mac," she said, crossing the room and pulling her brother in for a hug. She felt like she'd just had too much caffeine. Her words were coming out too fast, her body still trembling from the inside out.

"You aren't going to stay to do the dishes?" She shot her brother an evil look. "I mean for dessert," he amended.

"No to both. I think you can do it all without me."

"All right."

"I'm going to take off too," Lucas said, pushing off from the counter.

"Beer tomorrow?" Mac asked.

A half smile curved Lucas's lips and something tightened in Carly's stomach. If Mac and Lucas were going out tomorrow night, they were probably going to try to pick up some women. And if they tried, they would succeed.

And after what had just happened . . .

No. Nothing had happened. Nothing at all. And being annoyed about Lucas and other women made even less sense now than it had six years ago.

"Well, I'm off. I have work in the morning," Carly said.

"Someone in violation of the Historic Colors Ordinance?" Lucas asked, referring to the town regulation that ensured all historic homes and buildings were painted colors that were accurate to the time period they were built in.

"The Historic Protection and Design Regulation?" she corrected. Lord, she even sounded prissy to herself. "That rule has been around since long before I have been. And no. That's not it. I'm going to the elementary school to help with the launching of a summer art program."

"Well, it's not baling hay, but it sounds like damn hard work," he said dryly.

"Art is important," she said.

"Not arguing with you."

She let out an exasperated breath, feeling suddenly much more Lucas-impervious than she had a moment earlier.

"Well, anyway, see you later, Mac. Lucas." She breezed out the front door, gulping in the crisp evening air as soon she was outside. She had to clear her head. Had to get her control back.

She wasn't going to be like her mother. Not ever. She wasn't going to be the idiot who fell for a charmer and then was shocked when he didn't change. She doubted her father had been faithful to her mother at any point in their relationship, but her mother had always wanted him too much to give him an ultimatum.

And Carly hated that. Hated the scenes it created. Hated that her mother had so little pride.

She hated what her father did too. But her mother enabled it by staying. She gave it a stamp of approval. At this point, there was literally nothing her father could do to make her mother leave, and he knew it.

So he philandered. He did it publicly. He did it often.

And her mother was always on standby to make a tearful, shrieking scene.

Carly could just imagine what would happen if she ever did something like that. Councilwoman Carly Denton shouting down a bar while her husband made out with a busty brunette in the corner, totally unconcerned with her heartbreak.

She shivered and cast a glance back to the house. No. That would never be her. Not ever. Which meant Lucas Miller wasn't getting within touching distance of her lips ever again.

CHAPTER
Three

Lucas hadn't had such a bad night of sleep in years. He'd had the hard-on from hell, and every time he'd taken it in hand to relieve himself of it, Carly and her pinched lips entered his mind.

And then, shortly after that, her expression softened, the way it had in the kitchen at Mac's when he'd touched her lip. She'd softened then, but more than that . . . there had been heat. Serious heat.

And then he'd realized he was about to engage in a heavy sexual fantasy about his best friend's little sister. His best friend's little sister who, if she knew, would probably treat him to a stare so cold it would freeze his erection clean off.

Which was when he'd pulled his hand away and consigned himself to a night of discomfort because, dammit, he was not going there.

It wasn't just that Carly was Mac's younger sister, although that played into it. But Carly and Mac, and the dinners at their house, dinners a lot like last night's, had been a part of his sanity growing up. Before he'd made friends with Mac, he'd been drowning; an isolated kid whose drunk of a father spent half his time passed out, and whose mother had disappeared completely.

Carly and Mac had become like family. At least until Carly had decided she hated him. In the two years since she'd been back from school, he'd hardly seen her, but the memories remained. The importance of what she and Mac represented remained.

And that meant no fantasies about her. And most definitely no acting on them.

He liked to harass her, no question about that. But that was a far cry from screwing her.

Of course, what had happened last night had gone a bit beyond just liking to annoy her. In fact, annoying her had been the farthest thing from his mind when he'd touched her lip.

A hard kick of desire assaulted him again and he swore internally. It didn't help that he was going back down to Carly's office today to drop off some more donations. When he'd volunteered to help organize the thing, he hadn't counted on having to deal with Carly on what was turning into a daily basis.

He was half hoping she wouldn't be around and he could just leave everything with the receptionist.

It was just his luck that the receptionist wasn't there, but Carly was.

She looked up and he noticed she didn't pucker. He could tell she was fighting the urge to, her mouth twitching at the corners, but she did manage to keep her expression neutral. "Good afternoon, Lucas. Get your hay baled?"

"I didn't bale any hay today."

"Ah, I see. What did you do?"

"Rode a few horses, made sure they were still in top condition."

"Ah, well, it's not helping establish a new art program,

but it sounds like damn hard work." There was actually a ghost of a smile on her lips. The sight made his gut tighten.

He chuckled. "You're a funny woman, Carly."

"What do you have for me?"

"More donations. They came in from John's."

"Great."

He put the bag on the desk and she unzipped it, taking the total slip out, a genuine smile spreading over her face. "This is just great. I think we're going to be able to come up with something really amazing. And I think we'll earn a lot of money for the hospital."

"You ought to quadruple the donations made, at least," he said.

She stood up from behind her desk and stretched. His eyes were drawn to the rounded shape of her breasts, pushing against the prim little jacket she was wearing. She was just so polished and neat. Pink, short-sleeved jacket, matching pencil skirt. Blond hair pulled into a loose bun, a little pink band with flowers on it adding that touch of hyperfemininity that Carly was never without.

"I'm getting excited about it," she said.

"Getting in the dunk tank?"

She narrowed her blue eyes. "No."

"Aw, why not, Councilwoman? Making an ass of yourself in public for charitable purposes is a time-honored tradition."

"Not one I partake in," she said, her tone crisp. "I think we should enlist you or one of the other cowboys to do it. We could have you do it shirtless and charge extra." She looked like she wanted to shove the words back in her mouth as soon as they escaped.

He arched an eyebrow. "You think my bare chest is worth extra?"

"I said you or one of the other cowboys. Generic bare cowboy chest is worth extra. You know, in the estimation of some women, not necessarily me."

"Not your type?"

Her eyes drifted to his chest and then back up. "Not so much."

"What is your type?"

She blinked a few times. "Uh . . . an accountant might be nice. I hate doing my own taxes."

"Wow. An accountant. You sure are living fast and loose there, Carly."

"I didn't ask for commentary, Miller."

"I mean, wouldn't you stay up late nights worrying about his safety? What if he has some kind of horrible paper tray accident while trying to make copies of annual earnings reports?"

Then she shocked him, completely, by laughing. A short, snorting sound, like she'd been trying to hold it in. "I'm a rebel," she deadpanned. "What can I say?"

"Obviously."

"I'm actually just headed out," she said.

For some reason, he was reluctant to let her go. He'd felt that way the past few times he'd seen her and, all things considered, it didn't make any sense.

"To?"

She blinked. "Lunch."

"How about I join you?" Again, he wasn't really sure why he felt like sitting down and sharing a meal with her, all things considered. He was just sure he wanted to stay with her a little bit longer.

She hesitated and he could tell she was weighing how much she cared about seeming "mean" versus how badly she wanted to get rid of him. "Yeah, okay," she said finally. "We can discuss some more about Ride for Hope."

He shrugged. "Whatever makes it palatable."

"I don't want to start rumors either." She reached to close the laptop that was sitting on her desk and unplugged it from the monitor, shoving it into a large, patent leather bag. "Working lunch will do."

"Whatever helps," he said, following her out of her office and onto the main street.

"What's that supposed to mean?"

"You're looking for ways to justify letting yourself spend time with me." Which he'd been doing just a minute ago, but he'd decided not to worry about it. He wanted to be with her, and he was going to choose to believe it had nothing to do with the way her top molded to her curves.

"I'm not . . . pfft. I'm not *letting* myself spend time with you. You're here, I'm here, we're people, we need to eat. And also, we have a working connection."

"You're doing it again."

"I'm not—" She shut her mouth, cutting herself off. "I usually work over lunch. Maybe that's what I'm justifying." Because there was no point in her pretending she wasn't justifying something. They both knew that.

"I don't think that's it."

"Oh, for heaven's sake, Lucas, do you practice being this obnoxious in the mirror?"

"Right after I finish practicing my pickup lines," he said. "How long have you known me now, Carly? More than a decade?"

"Eleven years," she said. Interesting how quickly she knew the answer to the question.

"Right. And still you have to come up with a million excuses for why having lunch with me is okay." He opened the door to the bistro and held it for her, the little bit of chivalry his mother had imparted on him before she'd left him and his dad.

Carly walked in past him and went straight through to a table in the front corner. "My spot," she said, taking a seat.

"A regular, are you?"

"Well, I don't go to the bar for lunch."

"Neither do I. I'd run the risk of running into my dad."

"Or mine," she said.

"True enough."

"My dad and a companion even," she said, her tone brittle.

"We have awesome parents, don't we?"

"If nothing else, we've all proven that you can have success regardless of where you start out in life."

"You sure have, Ms. City Councilwoman."

She toyed with the edge of the menu that was already sitting on the table. "You like my title, don't you?"

"I'm impressed with it," he said, the honest truth.

"Well, thank you."

"You got yourself into college, and through it. You got yourself elected, when your family's reputation was pretty damned abysmal. I'd say I'm very impressed with you and what you've done."

Her brow wrinkled. "Thank you."

"I've never seen anyone look so distressed over a compliment."

"I've never gotten a compliment quite like that from you."

"Well, I've never gotten a compliment from you," he said, badgering her because everything had been too sincere there for a second.

"Fine. I'm impressed with you too. You've done well for yourself. You did great in the rodeo, obviously, considering the size of your ranching operation, and you helped Mac too."

"Mac helped himself. He had a great idea, I just helped him start up. And I'm a better investor than I was a bronc buster. I'm practically an accountant, actually; you just wouldn't know it."

"Are you serious?"

He shrugged. "Turns out I'm better at investing than riding."

"I just thought . . ."

"That I was a dumbass who did a good job of holding on to a horse?"

"No. I never thought that."

"Yeah, you did."

"I have total respect for riders," she said. "It's a skill. I can't tell you the last time I was on a horse."

"I can't imagine you riding in one of your prissy little suits."

"It's just not really my thing."

"What's not?"

She shrugged. "The whole . . . physical thing. I'm not big on sweating."

A very clear, dirty picture flashed through his mind of just what it might take to make her sweat and like it. He blinked, trying to will it away. "You used to like it. I have a very clear image in my head of the first time I saw you. You had mud up to your elbows, and the skin on your face was peeling from a sunburn. You'd been out catching frogs, I believe."

Her cheeks turned a delicate shade of pink. "Well . . . I've changed."

"I've noticed."

"Hi, Carly," a smiling waitress said as she approached the table. "The usual?"

Carly smiled. "Yes, thank you."

"And, uh . . . for your friend?"

"Just a burger is fine," he said.

"I'll have it up in a second," she said, casting Carly a long, questioning look that Carly very purposefully ignored.

"Now the rumor mill will get going," she muttered.

"Why? Because we're having lunch together? Almost everyone knows who I am. They know we're family friends."

"Is that what we are?" she asked. "Family friends?"

"I suppose so. But 'friends' might be a strong word for it." He studied her face, the hard lines, the exhaustion. She tried so hard to be perfect, he was afraid one of these days it would break her. "It didn't used to be though."

"Things change, Lucas."

"What changed, Carly?"

She let out an exasperated breath. "Does it matter?"

"I think you're the only one who knows that."

"Just leave it." She pulled her computer out of her bag and opened it, typing for a moment and then looking back up at him, her composure so firmly in place, it was laughable. He had to wonder if she ever lost control. "All right, let's talk charity. I think we can do that without bickering."

And they managed, keeping the topic to the Ride for Hope events, until their food arrived.

"Grilled chicken salad with dressing on the side," the waitress said, putting a plate in front of Carly. "And a burger," she finished, setting Lucas's lunch in front of him. "Holler if you need anything."

"Thank you," Carly said. She dipped her fork into the dressing and started flicking it over the lettuce leaves. She was so meticulous in everything she did. Every movement a practiced routine. She was tied up so tightly inside that even eating a salad was a ritual. He'd never seen anything like it.

He picked his burger up, in defiance of her restraint, and took a bite. He noticed that while she ate her salad, she kept her eyes pinned to his french fries.

"Do you want one?" he asked. She looked at him like he'd just asked her to come to the Dark Side.

"I shouldn't."

"Do you ever do anything you shouldn't do?"

She frowned. "No." Her denial was followed by another bite of salad.

"Doesn't that get boring?"

"It's not boring. It's stable. I had all the unstable I could get growing up. There's a reason for restraint, you know. A reason for . . . behaving a certain way."

"So you always behave?" he asked.

"Yes. Always. I'm a representative of the people of Silver Creek. I can do nothing less."

"You're twenty-four years old, Carly. This much self-control can't be healthy."

"The lack of it certainly isn't healthy, I don't care what age you are," she said. "Look at our parents for your example."

"Granted"—he picked up one of his french fries—"but eating a little fried food is hardly equivalent to being an alcoholic."

"Slippery slope," she said, eyeing the offered treat.

"Come on, Carly," he said. "Eat a fry. Live dangerously."

"You're such a pain," she said, taking the french fry from him and making quick work of it.

"Do you regret it?" he asked.

"No," she said around a mouthful of potato.

"See? The world didn't even cave in. Living dangerously didn't hurt you at all."

"One french fry isn't going to entice me to change the way I live."

"That would be pretty ambitious for a french fry." She snort-laughed again, turning her focus back to her salad. "Is that why I bother you, Carly?"

Her head snapped up, blue eyes meeting his. "What?"

"That I don't play by the rules of what's safe to you?"

Her forehead crinkled, eyebrows drawing together. "You think I'm jealous of you, is that it?"

"Well, is it?"

"Am I jealous of you, Lucas Miller, who changes women like most people change their socks? I am in no way jealous of that kind of behavior."

"And where are you getting this impression of me?" Lucas had been celibate for eight damn months. Casual hookups had been fine for him a few years ago, but these days he liked to be in a relationship with a woman before he took things to the bedroom. Maturity or something like it, he assumed. The kind of behavior she was talking about was a thing so long in his past, he could hardly remember ever doing it, so he was hardly going to sit there and listen to Carly Denton call him a player.

"Where did I . . . Are you kidding me? Do you forget about them all too?"

"All who?"

"The brunette against the barn, who was getting a bit more than a kiss. The woman you were making out with at Christmas the same year. Then there was your little spring fling. Every time I saw you that year, it was someone new."

A rash of heat broke out over his skin. Embarrassment. He couldn't remember the last time he'd felt embarrassed, but he sure as hell did now. The thought of eighteen-year-old Carly catching him . . . Well, he knew exactly what she was talking about now. There had been a lot of someones, but not so many that he couldn't remember an encounter that was that specific.

Things had gotten a little hot and heavy in a public place, but it had ended at second base. Still, he wasn't thrilled that Carly had seen it. He couldn't even really explain why it bothered him so much.

"Carly . . . I'm sorry you saw that. That's . . . well"—the embarrassment was just starting to piss him off now—"look, it was on my property, I can do what I want on my own property. It wasn't intended for your . . . viewing pleasure."

Her lip curled. "It wasn't a pleasure, trust me. And I get that men have relationships, but there's a difference between relationships and constant flings. Men who get involved in that . . . It doesn't stop, Lucas, I know that for a fact."

There was something in her voice—anger, disgust, but that was easily identified. It was the other emotion, vibrating beneath her words, that's what was pulling him up.

Hurt. It had hurt her.

The realization hit him hard in the gut. "I'm sorry it hurt you."

Her mouth dropped open. "Hurt me?"

"Yeah."

"Oh, that's funny. Why would it hurt me?"

"I don't know."

"Well, then . . . why would you say that?"

"Why would you still be so bothered by it?"

"Why aren't you? I can't be the only person who thinks you're . . . you're a . . . a manwhore."

He shrugged. "Why would I care about that?"

"Because. Because it should matter what people think."

"News flash, Carly, I don't care what people think." Maybe that's why she was so mad. Because he didn't care. And she did. So much she was crippled by it. "You should try it sometime. Let your hair down. Get your back up against a barn wall."

She stood up quickly, slamming her laptop shut. "This has been lovely," she said. "But I'm going to go and do something more enjoyable. Like maybe stick barbed wire under my fingernails. I've got lunch." She stuck a twenty on the table and turned and walked out of the diner.

Lucas took the twenty and crumpled it in his hand. Then he pulled his wallet out and replaced her cash with his. He'd return hers to her later. Maybe by mail. Or he could always deliver it in person. Picturing the look on her face, the one of pure annoyance, that she would get if he did it, did a little something to reduce the knot in his gut.

But only a little.

Four

Carly settled into the couch, her legs tucked up underneath her. She tightened her hold on her cereal bowl and took a bite. It wasn't grown-up cereal. It was the sugary kind, with marshmallows.

They'd never had it growing up. Not because her mom liked to feed them healthy food, but because she often forgot to go grocery shopping. They'd always had eggs from the chickens though, so there had been breakfast.

But keeping a variety of cereals stocked was one of Carly's indulgences. One she'd started the minute she'd gotten her own place. And one of her other private indulgences was eating that cereal for dinner, which she was doing now.

And it had nothing to do with Lucas's parting shot at the restaurant. No, it did not.

Though she was starting to wonder if it was true. If part of her was so angry at him because he just didn't care. He was impervious to what people thought. And she . . . she was crippled by it. Because in school, everyone had known, always, what was going on in her home, because her parents had made their fights so ugly. So public. Because their parents would gossip about the fact that Dan and Holly Denton had been screaming at each other outside the bar again.

No one had ever let their kids come over. Not that she could blame them. But it had meant no sleepovers for her. Very few friends. The only outside presence in the house had been Lucas, and part of that was because he'd been just as much of a misfit.

He hadn't cared then. He didn't care now.

Why didn't he care? She did. So much, she felt frozen with it sometimes. She wanted to change the way people saw her. And it wasn't enough to just move away and start over, because people back in Silver Creek would still think the things they did.

But she'd gone to school, and she'd come back and proven that she'd succeeded. And then she'd gotten elected to the city council. She was the youngest person to serve on the council in the town's history.

She and Mac were making a new story for the Denton family and she was proud of that. She worked hard to protect that.

There was a knock on her door and she set her cereal bowl on the table, her hand going straight to the ponytail she'd done haphazardly after her shower. She was in her sweats, she didn't have makeup on, and she was a mess. So not the time for company.

"Who is it?" she called, heading to the door.

"Lucas."

She cursed fluidly under her breath and opened the door, pasting a smile to her face. She wasn't going to act bothered. No. He would like that too much. "Lucas," she said, far too brightly, blocking the doorway, "what brings you here?"

Her held his hand up, a twenty-dollar bill folded between his fingers. "You forgot this."

"I paid," she said.

"Nope. I did."

"Oh, of all the macho . . ." she started to say, then took the money. "Thank you. Thank you very much. I'll see you . . . later." Hopefully much later.

"I'm sorry," he said.

The words stopped her cold. "You're what?"

"Sorry. For what I said earlier."

"I . . . Thank you." She dropped her hand from the door frame and took a step back. "It's . . . it takes a lot to admit when you're wrong."

Lucas seemed to take her movement as an invitation to enter the house. He walked past her and into the living room. "Oh, I wasn't wrong. But I'm sorry I said what I said the way I said it."

She narrowed her eyes. "Excuse me?"

"You're wound up tight, sugar, no mistake. I wasn't wrong about that. But I shouldn't have picked a fight with you, not over something so sensitive, and not in public."

"I'm not . . . sensitive. And I didn't invite you in."

"Family friend, remember? I'm allowed to come in."

"Why are you so dead set on driving me crazy this week?"

He paused. "A good question. And I could ask you the same thing."

"What? I thought you were going out with my brother tonight anyway."

"Blew him off."

"Why? I thought you were going to go hook up, or whatever you guys call it."

"Not interested." His dark eyes clashed with hers and her stomach tightened. "At least, not with some random girl from the bar."

She swallowed hard, her stomach so tight it was painful. "I don't . . . I . . . And what do you mean you could ask me the same thing?"

"Why are you so dead set on driving me crazy this week?" he asked.

"I'm . . . I'm not. I haven't done anything to you. Everywhere I've been, work, my brother's house, my house"—she made a sweeping gesture with her arm—"you are. That's not me doing anything to you. That's all you."

He shook his head. "That's not what I mean."

"What do you mean then?"

"You don't know what's been going on in my head, sugar."

"No. No, I don't. And I probably want to keep it that way, so maybe you should . . ." He took a step toward her and brushed his thumb over her bottom lip. "You keep doing that," she said, his thumb still touching her skin.

"I know," he said, "and when I'm not doing it, I'm thinking about doing it. I don't think I ever should have touched you."

Her heart started pounding hard. "What do you . . ."

He raised his other hand and placed it on her cheek, shifting so that both palms were cradling her face, his dark eyes intent on hers. "This was also a bad idea," he said, his voice rough.

"What was?" she asked.

"Well, touching you more. That little bit was bad idea enough. This . . . this is even worse."

Carly couldn't remember the last time a man had looked at her like Lucas was looking at her now. Like he was starving and she was the answer to the hunger inside of him.

The reason she couldn't remember the last time she'd been looked at like that was because she never had been. And she was very aware of it in this moment. Aware that she was on the verge of something that was well outside her experience.

The strangest thing was that, right now, she wanted it. She knew, somewhere in the dim, hazy corners of her mind, that she might regret it later. No, that she would. But right now, for some reason, she didn't care. Not even a little bit.

Because all she could focus on was Lucas. His eyes, his lips. Lord, but he had beautiful lips for a man. It had been years since she'd let herself notice them. She had before though.

There had been a time when this moment, the possibility of it, had been her dearest fantasy. And it was something she didn't even let herself remember now. There had been a time when she'd dared to want.

His words from earlier rang in her ears.

Live dangerously.

Just a little. Just a taste. It wouldn't be so wrong. Not any worse than one french fry.

She leaned in, her lips brushing his. Her breath caught in her throat and held, electricity shooting through her veins, immobilizing her.

But Lucas wasn't immobile. Far from it. He dropped his hands from her face and wrapped his arms around her, pulling her tight against his hard, muscular body.

She whimpered and he deepened the kiss, his tongue sweeping the inside of her mouth. The wet friction stole every thought from her head, made it impossible for her to do anything but feel. She was lost, completely, in his touch. In a whole world of new desire and need.

She'd thought she'd known what attraction was. Had thought she'd known, intellectually, how she would handle it. But she'd never felt anything like this. She hadn't known. Not at all.

She pressed her hands to his chest, curling her fingers around his shirt fabric, clinging to him as he kissed her, long and deep.

"Kiss me back, Carly," he growled against her lips.

And she obeyed. She couldn't do anything else. She wanted him, so much she was drowning in it. She tasted him, her tongue tracing the seam of his lips, delving inside his mouth.

He was perfection. He tasted like temptation, like an invitation to a kind of wildness, a kind of freedom, she'd never even dared to imagine.

She wanted to drown in it. In him. She'd never felt restricted by her life. Never felt like she was missing anything.

But right now she felt like she was suffocating. Like she was being tied down, bound in the strictures of her life. Strictures she'd set out for herself.

She wanted to tear them off. And tear his clothes off with them. And her clothes. And she'd never, ever wanted anything like this ever. And it should scare her. But in that moment, it just didn't.

Because her senses were filled with Lucas and nothing else seemed quite as important.

A growl vibrated through Lucas's chest and he slid his hands down to her backside, cupping her, drawing her even more tightly against him, against the firm length of his erection.

And that, right there, jolted her back to reality in a very big way.

She pulled away from him, gasping for air, her head spinning. She felt like she'd just broken through the surface of the water. The haze and silence fading. Now everything seemed too clear, harsh, cold and loud. Their fractured breathing a very potent, and embarrassing, reminder of everything that had just passed between them.

What was wrong with her? What the *hell* was wrong with her?

"Oh . . ." She put her hands on her lips. They felt as hot and swollen to the touch as she feared they looked. "What just happened?"

"Something that's been on a slow burn for a while now just combusted," he said, his voice strangled.

"It has not been on a slow burn," she said. "There's no slow burn."

"Oh, darlin', there's a slow burn. Or there was."

"No, no there isn't."

"Why do you think we fight so much?"

"Uh . . . because we don't like each other?"

"Verbal foreplay."

"No."

"Remember what I said, Carly? Either you treat me like you do because you don't like me, or . . ." He let the thought trail off.

"I'm not doing playground politics with you, Lucas," she said, even as she questioned the truth of the statement. "I treat you like I do because I don't have the patience to put up with a guy who . . . who . . ."

"Who what?"

"Who makes me want so many things I can't have," she exploded, the words unexpected and not at all what she planned. "Who makes me wish that I could . . . do something more with myself. That I could find a way to just give the world the middle finger and go on with life, like you do. But I can't. I just can't, okay? I have to . . . to be this way. I have to keep it all locked up, because if I don't . . . what will happen? What will people think?"

"Who gives a damn what people think?" he bit out.

"I do," she yelled, fighting tears now. "I do. Because do you . . . do you see what happens when you don't? When you just quit caring?"

"Your mother," he said.

"And my dad. And your dad. They just didn't care anymore, and what they felt like doing, what they *feel* like doing, is more important than the right thing, or the thing that at least looks right, and our childhoods were . . . a disaster because of it. And I don't want my life to be a disaster anymore."

"What? So you push down all of your desires, blame me, and try to keep me out of your space so you aren't jealous? Because regardless of what you say, Carly, you are jealous."

"No."

"Change the way you do things if you aren't happy, Carly, but don't make it my problem."

"I'm not unhappy with how I do things when you aren't around."

He chuckled, a sound that held no humor. "You make choices, Carly, every day. No one is forcing you to behave this way, and the 'my childhood sucked' excuse only holds for so long. So figure out what you want, and do it. But don't turn your problems into mine."

"Get out, Lucas."

"You're dismissing me now?"

"Yes. You can't just come into my house and kiss me and then . . . yell at me. Now go away."

He nodded his head. "Fine. See you later."

He turned and walked out the front door, slamming it behind him. Carly uncurled her fist and saw that the twenty was all balled up in her hand.

She growled and threw it across the room, not caring that it was a stupid thing to do. Right now, she hated Lucas Miller. She hated his smug smile. She hated how he'd just . . . pulled her up against him and kissed her. Hated the way electricity was still sparking through her body.

Most of all, she hated just how right he was about her.

She was a coward. A damned, unhappy coward who was a prisoner in her own life. Who was afraid to take hold of anything she felt overly passionate about for fear she'd lose her grip on her tightly held control.

For fear people might see inside of her and find her lacking somehow. Find her weak. Her mother wore everything out in the open, all there for people to judge, and judge they did. Carly had never wanted that. Had never wanted to expose herself in that way.

She stalked back to the couch and picked up her bowl. She took another bite of her defiant breakfast-for-dinner. She grimaced. It was soggy.

And she really didn't feel all that triumphant either. She felt alone. And turned on. And fixated on Lucas Miller. And too scared to do anything about any of it.

CHAPTER

Five

Carly's head hurt from reading too many city ordinance amendment propositions. In all honesty, as much as she cared about Silver Creek, she couldn't care less whether or not the regulations on historic colors should extend to the interiors of homes and businesses with rooms visible to the street.

It was all a bunch of people trying to feel more important than they were, in her opinion. And she just sat there and smiled and nodded. She did well on the council, but when it came to opposing people who were serving their sixth term, she wasn't exactly super bold.

She was a pansy, is what she was. A big old yellow-bellied coward. She wanted to be perceived well more than she wanted to make a difference. She wanted people to think of her as something other than "that poor Denton girl."

Now she was withering up inside of herself. She didn't even know what she really wanted.

That was a lie. What she wanted, what she really wanted,

and had wanted since she was a teenager, was Lucas Miller. And yes, when she'd been a teenage girl, she'd woven stupid romantic fantasies about him. Fantasies that were about emotion and love and hearts and crap.

But she was a woman now, and her fantasies were a whole lot more physical. And physical, she knew he could do.

The simple fact was that she wanted Lucas Miller, no strings, no consequences. She wanted to flip the world off, discreetly, for a while and get rid of her inhibitions and her clothes with the one man she knew who seemed to just be who he was with total ease.

Oh, what would people say if they knew that staid, sensible Carly Denton wanted things like that? A physical affair, a night of passion and sex with a man who was from a family just as screwed up and gossip-worthy as her own.

She didn't care. Not right at the moment. She just didn't care.

She turned her car off the main road and started heading out of town, heading toward Lucas's ranch. She hadn't been out there since that day. That day she'd seen him with that other woman.

She was admitting it now, to herself at least, that that experience had crushed something in her. It wasn't Lucas's fault either—something else she was going to admit now, and also only to herself.

He didn't know she'd had a crush on him. They weren't attached, and he owed her nothing.

It had still hurt. It was still part of why she treated him badly.

She pulled off the paved two-lane road onto a winding, one-lane gravel road, fighting the urge to turn around and head back to town, toward her little subdivision. Toward safety and security and propriety.

The problem was, tonight, she just didn't want propriety. She wanted to know what it was like to be, figuratively, the woman up against the side of the barn, with her head thrown back, all of her focus going into what she felt, not what she thought, not what was right, but on her own needs, her own pleasure.

She pulled up to Lucas's house and killed the engine, taking a deep breath and trying to gather up the courage to get out and grab life, and Lucas Miller, with both hands.

She pushed open the driver's door and walked up to the steps. Her legs felt detached from her body, like they were acting without her permission. Because she felt like her brain wasn't fully committed to the decision yet. But her body was. Big time.

She took a breath and knocked on the door. And waited. For a lot longer than she'd anticipated waiting. She had a horrible thought. What if he was in there with some woman right now? Wouldn't that figure. She comes back to his ranch for the first time in six years and catches him banging—

The door swung open. It was Lucas, alone, wearing nothing more than a pair of jeans that rode low on his lean hips, showing off his flat stomach and well-muscled chest.

Her body did a victory dance. Just to let her know she'd made the absolute right decision in coming.

"Hi," she said, knowing she sounded brisk and a little bit breathless, but not caring too much.

"What a surprise. Are you here to tell me more about why the way I live my life is ruining yours?"

She shook her head. "Nope. Not that."

"What are you here for then?"

Sex. She was here for sex. Wild, hot, sweaty, against-the-barn sex. But of course, she couldn't say that. She'd never had it before; how could she say it?

Of course, if she couldn't say it, what business did she have experiencing it?

She took a breath. *Just say it.* "Sex," she said, the word pouring out and hanging between them. It had been too loud and too direct, and now she just wanted to crawl under the porch and curl up into a ball.

She'd said some pretty rude and strange things to Lucas Miller, but never once had she seen him make the face he was making now. Like he'd been struck in the chest with a two-by-four.

"What?"

"Do I really have to repeat myself?"

"Maybe," he said.

"Can I come inside?"

He stepped out of her way and she walked into the house. It had been a long time since she'd seen his house. He'd updated it since she'd last been there. The space was open, with high ceilings and large windows that gave a perfect view of the pastures and mountains. Everything was neat— spotless, really, which she put down to a good housekeeper.

It was good to know though. Clean house. Which was nice, since she figured she might get naked in it.

Oh, Lord . . .

"So are you speaking in code?" Lucas asked, crossing muscular arms over his chest.

"No. Why?"

"Because I'm trying to work out what the hell you mean by 'sex.'"

Heat flooded her face. "Come on, Lucas, I think we both know you know what sex is. I've seen you . . . doing it pretty much."

"That's not what I meant, and you know it," he said. He turned away from her for a moment, forking his fingers through his hair before turning back to face her.

Her eyes were drawn to his pecs, lightly dusted with dark hair, and down to his abs. They shifted in the most interesting way every time he breathed. Lucas had always been handsome, and she'd seen him without his shirt lots of times. But that had been years ago. He'd had muscle then, but he'd been slighter. He was a man now, broad and big and so sexy she thought she was going to melt right where she stood.

"All right. Then I guess I mean sex in the traditional, accepted sense of the word. You know . . . a bed and two people and . . ." Her throat closed in on itself.

"You don't make any sense, do you know that?" he asked. "You spend the past . . . forever, biting my head off every time we're in close proximity, and now you want to sleep with me?"

She blinked rapidly, trying to get ahold of her nerves. "There was a . . . slight transition period in there where we kissed, if you recall."

"Oh, I recall," he said. "I recall very well. It ended in you pushing me away and then telling me about how I ruin your happiness. So it wasn't the transition you might think. It was more of the same, but you put your tongue in my mouth before you decided to try and cut my skin from the bones with it."

"You were right," she said. "You were right about me, okay? Are you happy? I am scared. I'm scared of feeling too much, wanting too much, and I'm scared of losing control. And you don't care, you don't give a damn what anyone thinks, and I envy you. You were also right about the fact that the choices are mine to make. And if I'm not happy . . . I should change them."

"And this is how you want to do it?"

"I'm never going to not care what people think. I still want . . . I want to be who everyone sees now. I like that person. She's put together, and people respect her. No one feels sorry for her. But just . . . just for a little while, I need something for me. An indulgence."

"An indulgence? What the hell am I, a box of chocolates?"

She bit her lip. "Don't be like that."

"Like what?"

"Don't act like I've wounded you somehow. It's not like you don't have casual sex."

"I don't have casual sex with my best friend's younger sister."

"You made out with me yesterday."

"There's a lot of mileage between making out and sex, Carly."

"I know that," she said. "But do you really think of me just as Mac's little sister? I'm hardly a child. I'm an adult woman, and I have an identity outside of my relationship to my brother."

"Yes, well, I'll be sure to tell him that when he brands my ass with an iron after he finds out."

"Is that the only reason you don't want to?"

"What?"

"Mac. Is Mac the only reason you don't want to sleep with me? Or is it me?"

Lucas drew his hand over his face and shook his head. "You're right, I've had casual sex. But one thing I've never done is sleep with a woman who doesn't like me. That's a heavy deterrent at the moment."

"I'm not going to beg you for sex. This is already bordering on that, so just . . . fine. If you don't want me, then say it." Humiliation and shame tightened her chest. She wanted to vomit. She'd put herself out there for the first time . . . ever. Had gone for something she'd wanted on an emotional level, a physical level, rather than just a cerebral one, and she'd been turned away.

"You think I don't want you?"

"Well . . . yes."

"You think I don't want you?" he repeated. "I've been sleepless for the past week thinking about what it might take to get your puckered lips to soften under mine, and last night I found out. Hell, woman, it's been hell since then."

"You do want me?"

"Yes, dammit." He crossed to her and hauled her up against his body, his hold tight, his skin hot beneath her hands.

"Then wh-why . . . ?"

"The real problem is that we're both talking too much. Thinking too much. I don't want to do either anymore."

Okay, so talking to her, and thinking too much about what they were about to do, might put him off, and that wasn't the most flattering thing in the world, but it was Lucas, so she wasn't sure what she was expecting.

And since he didn't want to talk, it meant he didn't want to hear about the little potential complication she had forgotten to mention, which was just fine by her.

She didn't particularly want to tell him she'd never done this before. It was far too embarrassing. Because he would either think it was stupid, or he would start treating her like some innocent in need of his protection and honor. And she really didn't want to deal with either.

But she didn't have to, because he dipped his head and started kissing her again, hot and wet and everything she'd remembered and more.

A sharp sound of pleasure climbed her throat and she wrapped her arms around his neck, threading her fingers through his hair, holding him to her.

Lucas put his hands on her waist, his fingers gently drifting along her back, down to her hips, teasing her skin just beneath the waistband of her skirt. She arched against him, pressing her breasts to his chest, looking for some relief for the ache that was spreading through her now, beating a pulse at the apex of her thighs.

He angled his head and deepened the kiss, his tongue sliding against hers. She dug her nails into the back of his neck, trying to anchor herself to the ground, trying to keep her knees from folding beneath her. No wonder Lucas had so much success with women. If word got around, and she was sure in some circles it did, about what he could do with his tongue . . .

He would have to pry women off of him with a crowbar. Which he basically did, so clearly word had gotten out.

But tonight, tonight he was hers. All hers. It didn't matter how many other women there'd been, or even how many there would be after her, because all that mattered was now.

He abandoned her lips and blazed a trail of hot, open-mouthed kisses down her neck, across her collarbone and down the V-neck of her blouse, to the curve of her cleavage.

"You, Carly Denton," he rasped, "need to be unbuttoned, very badly."

He slipped the top button of her blouse through the hole. The fabric separated, and he bent his head, kissing the slice of newly revealed skin. Then he did the same with the next button, and the next, with a kiss for each new bit of her body he revealed.

He reached the button beneath her bra and dropped to his knees, kissing down her stomach until her shirt was completely open. Then he traced a line up her midsection with the tip of his tongue as he got to his feet again, pushing her blouse from her shoulders and letting it drop to the floor.

It was going to wrinkle. Badly. It would be a big pain in the butt to iron. She might even have to get it dry-cleaned. But as the thought ran quickly through her mind, she found she simply didn't care.

"You need to let your hair down," he said, his lips firm and warm on the side of her neck. He reached behind her head and pulled the clip from her hair, letting it fall loose around her shoulders. "Have a little fun."

"Oh, Lucas," she said, saying his name, a reminder of who she was with. A shiver of need shook her, tightening the coil of desire that was intensifying inside of her with every touch of his mouth and hands on her skin.

This was Lucas. Lucas Miller. And for the first time, she could acknowledge that he was the man she'd always wanted to be with like this.

Maybe that was why it had been easier to simply treat him like she had. Because anger was easier to deal with than longing, unrequited and so deep that, right now, she shook with it.

But now it would be answered. Right now, it was requited, and right now, it was being sated.

"You like this?" he asked, kissing her lips again, light, a tease. A perfect, torturous tease.

"Yes," she said, her voice trembling.

"More?" he asked.

"Yes."

He reached behind her and unclipped her bra, letting it fall loose. She took a step back and pushed the straps down her arms, letting it fall to the floor with her blouse.

She was too turned on to be embarrassed, too full of want to worry about the fact that she was half naked in front of a man for the first time. She just wanted to know what he'd do with this new part of herself she'd revealed.

He didn't disappoint. Lucas leaned in and ran the flat of his tongue over one tightened bud before sucking it deep into his mouth. A sharp, hot arrow of desire hit her straight in the stomach and radiated out, making her internal muscles pulse, making her conscious of a deep, empty ache inside of her. An ache, an emptiness, she knew could only be satisfied by Lucas.

She wasn't sure how she knew, only that she did.

He cupped her other breast with his hand, teasing her nipple with his thumb while he continued to lavish attention on the other with his mouth.

She felt like she was falling, weightless, the room, the world, the bonds that had felt so tight around her dropping away and leaving nothing more than this. Nothing more than Lucas, nothing more than Carly.

"How about we get comfortable?" Lucas asked.

She was expecting him to suggest they head upstairs, which made her a little bit nervous, a pang of angst cutting through the desire. "Okay," she said. Because she wasn't going to stop now. She couldn't.

Lucas lifted her with ease and took a few steps across the room before depositing her gently onto the couch. "This'll do," he said.

Now she felt a little embarrassed. Sitting topless on Lucas's couch like she'd come over for a drink and forgotten half of her outfit.

He was devouring her with his eyes, the heat in those dark depths sizzling across her skin. And that made it hard for her to hold on to embarrassment. Hard for her to hold on to anything but the need. The driving, hungry need that was making her body feel like it didn't belong to her anymore.

Lucas dropped to his knees in front of her, taking hold of her foot and lifting it, pressing a kiss to her ankle.

Oh, no, her body didn't belong to her. Not right now. Her body belonged to Lucas.

"I think I want your shoes on," he said, his voice rough. He put his hands on her thighs and pushed her skirt up, revealing more skin. "But I want these"—he moved his hand to the top of her legs, brushed his thumb along her hip bone, over the thin fabric of her panties—"off."

Before she could think say anything, or even process the rough words, he'd hooked his fingers into her underwear and started tugging them down her legs.

"Better," he said. "Much better."

When he leaned in, his shoulders forcing her legs apart, she felt a jolt of uncertainty.

She looked down at the top of his head, at those wide shoulders. This was Lucas. Lucas as she'd never experienced him before, but Lucas all the same.

There was comfort in that. Comfort and an illicit thrill. To have the man who she'd had so much longing for when she was younger, finally on his knees in front of her. Of course, what she'd wanted from him then had been a lot more innocent.

But this was a lot more fun.

The first pass of his tongue over her sensitized flesh shocked her, and she bucked beneath his mouth, the pleasure so sharp, so intense, she wasn't sure she could handle it.

His hands gripped her hips, blunt-tipped fingers digging into her skin as he held her still, forced her to submit to the sensual assault.

She covered her eyes with her arm, her hips moving in time with the strokes of his tongue. "Oh . . . Lucas. Oh . . ." She couldn't do anything but moan the words, over and over. She felt like she was going to burst, the tension, the need, so intense and tight inside of her, she didn't think she could take any more.

It was building, so fast, so big, filling her, taking over.

He released his hold on one of her hips and dropped his hand down between her legs, his fingers joining with his mouth. He teased the entrance to her body with his finger, just teasing, as he continued to taste her, to lavish attention on her clitoris.

Then he slid his finger deep inside, the sensation completely new, satisfying and exaggerating the ache that had built now to the point of pain. He added a second finger, stretching her, the slight bit of pain it caused easing the moment his tongue worked its way over the sensitive bundle of nerves again.

He worked his fingers in and out of her gently, establishing a rhythm with hands and tongue. When she thought she would break, shatter with the force of the pressure building inside of her, it released.

The wave of pleasure broke over her, leaving her powerless to do anything but simply let it direct her, control her, carrying her body along the current as pleasure surged and ebbed through her. She grabbed fistfuls of Lucas's hair, trying to anchor herself, trying to keep from floating away, lost in the endless flow of release.

When she came back to herself, she was aware, again, of the fact that she was sitting on Lucas's couch, mostly naked. The fabric was rough beneath her bottom, on her back. And he was kneeling in front of her, getting a very intimate view of her body, his fingers still deep inside of her.

There was no sound, not beyond their fractured breathing. It was the fact that he was breathing hard too that kept her from pulling away from him in embarrassment. The fact that his cheeks were flushed with desire, his chest rising and falling sharply, told her he'd enjoyed what had happened just as much as she had.

"Lucas, I—"

He leaned in and captured her lips with his, withdrawing slowly from her body as he did. "I hope you still want more," he said, his voice strangled. "Because now I don't think I could turn back if Mac was pounding on the door."

She grimaced. "We don't need to mention him."

Lucas shook his head. "No. We don't."

She wanted to say something more. Wanted to . . . thank him, maybe, for what he'd just done. She'd never experienced anything like it, had never, in her life, felt so weightless. So unbound. She'd had to surrender herself completely, but in that surrender, she'd been shocked to find freedom.

"Take me upstairs now."

He nodded, standing, then reaching down to take her hand in his, drawing her up against his chest and kissing her. Then he scooped her up again, as easily as before, and carried her up the stairs and down the hall to his bedroom.

He set her down next to the bed.

"A girl could get used to traveling that way," she said.

"You think?"

"Yes, it's kind of nice to let someone else do the work for a while."

"I plan on doing a lot more . . . work for you tonight."

She felt herself blush, and she marveled for a second that after what had passed between them, she still had the ability to blush. "I think I can handle that."

"Just a second." He turned and walked out of the room,

into the bathroom, appearing a moment later with a box of condoms. He tossed them on top of the nightstand. "Better than trying to remember later," he said.

She nodded, grateful, in that moment, for his experience, because her thoughts were shattered, and trying to get a clear picture of what should happen next was nearly impossible.

She looked down at the aggressive bulge in his jeans and she felt another little flutter of nerves. But everything so far had felt good. And even when it had hurt for a second, it hadn't taken long for the pleasure to eclipse it.

So this should be no different. Maybe.

"Kiss me?" she asked. Things seemed easier when he kissed her, the world a little softer, a little hazier. She'd never realized a kiss could have so much power until she'd kissed Lucas.

"Of course, sugar," he said, circling her waist with his arms and kissing her with a tenderness that stole her breath and started the empty ache in her again. Even though he'd just satisfied her, she felt all needy again.

"I want you, Lucas," she said, needing to say his name again.

"I want you too, Carly." She was stupidly pleased that he'd said her name. That he wanted her, and not just sex.

Because even though this would never be anything more than one night, she wanted him to want her. Because she wanted him. Because, as much as this was about wanting a new experience, wanting a few hours of uninhibited freedom, she knew it wasn't an experience she would crave if it wasn't with Lucas.

She put her palms flat against his chest, the hair rough beneath them, and slid them over his muscles, a little thrill running through her. Having all that masculine power beneath her fingertips was a turn-on she hadn't anticipated. Having access to a body like Lucas's was a thrill all on its own, even without his wicked tongue.

She stopped at the waistband of his jeans, running her fingertips along the edge.

"Tease," he said.

"Just trying to decide what to do next," she said, an admission that was maybe a little too honest, but she was too bare to be coy. Too naked to lie. Emotionally more than physically, since she was still wearing her skirt and shoes.

"I can help with that." He gripped the tab on her skirt zipper and tugged it down, letting her skirt fall around her feet. "And now you can lose the shoes," he said.

She complied, kicking her pumps off and kicking them, and the skirt, to the side. She was totally naked now, and he was still wearing those jeans.

"Sexy as these are," she said, not recognizing the husky voice as her own, "it's time for them to go."

"I agree, sugar." He undid the snap, then lowered the zipper, and her heart caught in her throat. He shucked his pants and underwear in one fluid movement, revealing the extent of his arousal to her.

She might have gone slack-jawed. She was pretty sure she did. "Oh . . ." She'd never been this close to a man before. Had never actually seen a man naked and aroused. She reached out and encircled his length with her hand. Because she wanted to. Because this was about doing what she wanted. "You're so hard." She felt awkward, stupid, the minute the words left her mouth.

His erection pulsed in her hand. "You know the right things to say," he said.

"I'm just . . . saying the first things that come to my mind," she said. "Maybe I shouldn't talk. You said you didn't want to talk."

"I don't," he said. "But I do like hearing you say things like that. That's different than having a conversation."

"I suppose so."

"Anyway, a conversation will be kind of difficult to carry on in a few minutes."

She nodded. She was sure he was right. She was having a hard time even thinking coherently at the moment.

He put his hand over hers and squeezed, his eyes closing and a sharp curse escaping his lips.

"Like this?" she asked, squeezing him hard, like he'd done.

"Yes."

She did it a couple more times, until she felt the muscles in his chest tense, quiver. She was satisfied by that, because she wanted to make him feel what he'd made her feel. Wanted him to lose his mind the same way she had.

"Bed," he said, short, clipped.

She nodded and sat on the bed. He leaned over her, one hand resting on the mattress behind her, and he kissed her. He hooked his arm around her waist and hauled her backward, bringing them both to the center of the bed.

Then he reached over and into the box of condoms, producing a plastic packet. "See, forward thinking. Good idea."

She nodded. "Yes, it was."

He tore it open and rolled it onto his length quickly, kissing her again as he settled over her. She parted her legs for him, the action instinctive. The blunt head of his erection pressed against the slick entrance to her body, and she knew a moment of serious anxiety. He was much bigger than she'd anticipated, and two of his fingers had hardly prepared her to take all of him.

He tested her, and she tried to relax, tried to focus on the fact that it was Lucas.

Lucas. Lucas. He would take care of her, at least in this way. She could be sure of that.

He pushed inside her in one fluid movement and she bit back a cry of pain as he stretched her all at once, burying himself to the hilt.

His dark eyes were wide, searching hers. "Are you okay?"

She nodded, the pain starting to fade. Now she felt . . . full. She'd felt so empty before, and she'd ached with it. And now, that part of her at least was satisfied. Though that need was starting again, that deep need that made her feel restless and reckless and desperate.

He moved slowly at first, his eyes never leaving hers. "Yes, Lucas," she breathed as his hips flexed, his pelvis hitting against her clitoris, sending a sharp, hot sweep of sensation through her.

"You like that?" he whispered, repeating the motion.

"Yes," she said, the word catching as another wave of pleasure hit.

"More?"

"Yes."

And then she was lost, completely. In the rhythm, in the slide of his skin on hers, his heat, his strength. She slid her hands over his back, over his muscles, felt the hard ridges move beneath her fingertips, the evidence of his strength arousing her further.

He moved his hand down to her thigh, hooked it over his hip and increased his movements. Harder. Faster.

"Lucas," she breathed, pleasure bursting through her, her core muscles tightening around him, her orgasm rolling over her in a slow wave, dragging her under.

Lucas lowered his head and thrust into her one last time, a harsh groan escaping his lips as his own release rocked him.

She clung to his shoulders, holding him to her, focusing on her body, on the buzzing, fuzzy feeling coursing through her veins like champagne. On his chest pressed against hers, his heart thundering so heavily, she could feel it. On their fractured breathing.

For the moment, she felt like she and Lucas were on the same page. Like they both felt the same things, like they'd both just walked through the same fire and come out the other side.

It wouldn't last. She knew that. There was no way this much harmony with Lucas could last for more than a few minutes. But it was nice.

"Dammit, Carly," he breathed, rolling to the side.

The loss of his body over hers made her feel cold. Exposed,

"What?" she asked, staring at the ceiling.

"I'll get back to you when I can form a more coherent thought."

"That's good though, right? Not having a coherent thought?"

"For you, right now, it's very good." He put both hands over his face and drew them down. "Why didn't you tell me?"

"That's a very open-ended question. Why didn't I tell you that Pluto isn't considered a planet anymore? Why didn't I tell you that I *can* believe it's not butter?"

"Why didn't you tell me you were a virgin?"

"Oh . . . that. I forgot."

"You forgot?"

"In my defense, your hymen doesn't really do much, so it's easy to kind of let it slip your mind."

"Carly . . ." he said, a warning note in his tone.

"Fine. I didn't think it would matter. Or, rather, I figured it would matter but I didn't want it to, so I thought I'd leave it out of the conversation."

"You should have saved that for someone special." The impact of his words hit hard.

"Why? I wasn't saving it for anyone, I was just being a stupid scaredy-cat who didn't want to get hurt. Who didn't want to run the risk of getting too wild for fear that if I lost too many inhibitions, I might . . ." She took a breath. "Anyway, I wasn't saving it for Mr. Right, okay, so don't look at me like that."

"Like what?"

"Like you're afraid I'm going to handcuff you to the bed."

His eyes widened. "I don't think you know exactly how not scary that is."

She growled. "You know what I mean. I'm not trying to rope you into commitment or anything. In fact, that's the very last thing I want. I wanted a night, a night to . . . let my hair down, which you did quite nicely, and thank you."

She slid out of the bed, clutching the covers to her chest, effectively pulling the covers from over his body, revealing all that he had to offer. She turned away sharply. "I'm just going to go," she said.

"So, wait a second, I was just your one-night good time?"

"Like it could ever be more, Lucas? We don't even . . . get along."

"We got along fine tonight," he said.

"That's different. We were . . . y'know. Not talking. And see, now we're talking again and it's turning into fighting, which seems to be the way it works between the two of us."

"Because I found out you were keeping an important piece of information from me."

"You wouldn't have slept with me if you'd known I was a virgin?"

"No," he said.

"Well . . . so you're saying you regret it?"

He rolled into a sitting position, and even though she was mad at him, her eyes were glued to his muscles. "No. Stay there." He walked into the bathroom and came back a moment later, having discarded the condom. "I don't regret it."

"You can't have it both ways," she said.

"Yes. Yes, I can. I wish I would have known. I would have turned you away. I would have told you not to make your first time happen with a guy you don't even like. And then I would have regretted my chivalry, but I still would have done it. I don't regret this. I can't, but I should. Your brother—"

"Has absolutely no place in a conversation we're having while completely naked."

He put his hands up. "Fine."

"I'm going now."

"Great," he growled, sitting on the bed and leaning back, his arms crossed over his chest. "See you around."

She huffed and started looking around.

"The rest of your clothes?" She nodded. "Downstairs."

"Grrr," she said, hoisting the covers up so she wouldn't trip and heading down the stairs.

Lucas let his head fall back against the headboard. He was pretty sure his body was seconds away from bursting into flame if he didn't get inside Carly again as soon as possible. But that was if his head didn't explode first from the sheer exasperation the woman made him feel.

A virgin. A damned virgin.

As if the whole thing could have been any less appropriate. She was Mac's younger sister, and he knew, knew for a fact, that his friend would castrate him with ranch equipment no matter her status, but that she'd never even had a lover before put him danger of being hog-tied and run over by a tractor.

Not that he would ever find out about any of it, but it was the principle. More than that, it was the fact that he felt like she deserved more. More than she was asking for. More than he could give.

And all he really wanted was to do it again.

She doesn't want you anyway. Not forever. She just wanted a good time.

That really shouldn't surprise him. She saw him as some kind of good-time guy. A way for her to scratch an itch without being in danger of getting in too deep. Which made sense, really. He wasn't the kind of man people formed lasting attachments to. That had been proven in his life time and again. Most notably with his mother, who, since she'd walked out the door just after he'd turned ten, had never been back.

Why should Carly be any different? Why would she be the one who suddenly wanted more from him?

Damn. He wanted more. More of her body at least. Another round.

He hit his head against the headboard a second time for good measure.

There would be no other round. There couldn't be.

"I think this is absolutely perfect," Carly said, turning to shake Dave Callahan's hand. The old rancher had graciously offered up his entire property, free of charge, to be the site of the rodeo and all of its events. "Thank you so much."

The ranch was much better than the arena they'd originally planned on using. Here they would have room for parking and for setting up games and prizes, the dunk tank, food carts and face painting.

She put her hands on her hips and surveyed her surroundings, taking in a deep breath of the warm, hay-sweetened air.

"Yeah, this should do just fine, but I'll need to see the arena."

Carly whipped around sharply just in time to see Lucas getting out of his pickup truck. "What are you doing here?" she asked, her heart in her throat.

He was so sexy, his hard, muscular body leaning against the side of the truck, lean hips and . . . other assets displayed by his tight, dark jeans.

"I'm here to make sure this venue will work for the riders.

We're talking lots of stock trailers and trucks, plus the arena needs to be workable for us to set up chutes."

"Professional consultation?"

"You could say that." He stepped forward and shook Dave's hand. "Which way do I go, Dave?" he asked.

"Just over that way. If you can find it yourself, I've got some admin work to finish up in the office." He tipped his hat. "Been a pleasure, Ms. Denton."

"Thank you, Mr. Callahan," she said. She sort of wished she could call the old cowboy back and make him stay because she really needed a buffer between her and Lucas right then.

"Take me to the arena," Lucas said.

He didn't seem different, which sort of made her feel . . . bad. She had thought maybe he'd act awkward. She felt awkward. It just didn't seem fair that he was walking around with the same ease he always had after he'd . . . after they'd . . . less than twenty-four hours earlier.

Her whole world was freaking rocked and he just seemed fine.

Lucas followed Carly, his eyes glued to her backside, swaying in that fitted pencil skirt of hers. She looked out of place on a ranch. All tailored and prim. Buttoned up. He'd just unbuttoned her the night before, but it hadn't seemed to take.

She was so damn sexy. And the worst, or maybe best, part of it was that he knew what that ass looked like bare, knew how soft her skin was. He gritted his teeth and waged a war on his hardening erection.

He wasn't some horny teenager. He knew how to keep his body under control. At least, he usually did, but Carly was testing him. And this was not the time or the place.

The condom burning a hole through his wallet mocked that thought. He never did that. Never stuck one in his wallet just in case, because he liked to plan things better than that. He didn't meet up with women just for sex. He always took them out at least once. And maybe that was a feeble attempt at making past behaviors seem acceptable, but it was what it was.

Still, the fact that he'd come packing today made a mockery of all those rules. But then so did sleeping with Carly in the first place.

An image flashed through his mind, her arching against him, bare breasts against his chest. He nearly groaned out loud.

"Okay, here it is," she said, indicating the large, covered arena. "We'll have to rent bleachers, but that shouldn't be a problem."

"Right." He was supposed to be focusing on the facility. On whether or not it would be a safe place for the cowboys to ride. But he was having a hard time focusing on anything other than the generous curve of Carly's breasts.

"Do you think it looks good?"

"So good."

"Oh . . . great."

Damn. He'd meant her body, not the arena. He hadn't looked closely enough at the arena. He walked away from her and paced a circle around the area.

"Yeah, everything's fine," he reiterated.

"Great, then I think this is the ideal place to have it, and the best part is, we get to use it free of charge. We'll have to make sure we're extra diligent with getting a cleanup crew out here, but I think it will be perfect."

She turned to face him, impish excitement glittering in her blue eyes, and for a moment, she looked like the Carly he used to know. "Did I tell you we get to use the barn for booths?"

"Which barn?"

"There's an old one he never uses. There are some tractors in it, but it will be easy to clear out for the Ride."

"Show me," he said, the command anything but innocent.

Carly seemed to miss the rough undertone in his voice.

Or if she heard it, she'd managed to become a better actress in the space of the past day.

"It's across the field, but we could take the access road and keep the mud off our shoes," she said.

"I don't mind a little mud on my shoes," he said.

Carly rolled her eyes and lifted her foot. "These have three-inch heels."

"Take them off."

"Lucas, I'm not going to take my shoes off and run barefoot through a field."

He shrugged. "Why? You used to do it all the time."

"But I'm an adult now."

He took a risk. "And up until last night there were quite a few things you hadn't done, but you changed that. Too afraid to change any more?"

Color flooded her cheeks, a cool blue flame igniting in her eyes. "Are you . . . daring me?"

"Yeah," he said, hooking his thumbs through his belt loops. "I'm daring you."

"What are we, twelve?"

"I think we recently proved we aren't. Did you use up all your bravery last night?"

She looked like she didn't know if she wanted to punch him or smile. Instead, she bent down and started taking off her shoes. She straightened, the high heels dangling from her fingertips. "Fine. Let's go."

She turned and started to cross the gravel parking area but stopped at the edge of the field, at the short wooden fence that probably didn't do a very good job of keeping anything in or out. "Remember how to climb a fence?"

"I still climb fences as part of my day job. It's not my fault I got to grow up to be a cowboy while you had to settle for turning into a grown-up."

He planted his boot on the bottom rung and swung his leg up over the top, planting it on the bottom board on the other side before dropping down into the field.

She followed him, her pace a bit slower, as she was negotiating climbing a fence in a pencil skirt, but she made it to the other side. "All right," she said, "let's go. And pray, Miller. Pray I do not step in a cow pie, or your head will be the new centerpiece for my office."

"Because you like looking at me so much."

"Oh, please." She looked around the field. It was empty, no cows, no horses. "Race?"

"I'm going to win."

She shrugged. "Not if I cheat." She then took off running, tugging her skirt up over her thighs as she went, trying to lengthen her strides. And he couldn't do anything for a full twenty seconds but stand there and watch her.

Something in his chest expanded, a strange tightness invading his gut. He didn't know what the hell Carly Denton was doing to him, but he kind of liked it.

He shook his head and took off after her, making sure he didn't pass her by. He liked the view far too much to do that.

When they reached the barn, they were both out of breath. Desire kicked him hard in the gut. It reminded him too much of last night. Of how if had felt to lose himself inside of her, how hot and tight she'd been . . .

He shook his head and tried to fight off the surging tide of lust that was threatening to overpower him.

"Come on," she said, pushing open the barn door and pausing for a moment to put her shoes back on. "I don't need any rusty nail incidents."

He stopped and looked at her, her cheeks flushed, her hair coming out of its bun, strands curling around her face. The run had even made her sweat a little bit, and he was sure he could see some of those freckles of hers showing through her makeup.

He could see Carly.

And he couldn't stop himself from touching her. He

leaned forward, skimming her cheekbone with his thumb. "You're beautiful, Carly, do you know that?"

Her eyes widened. "I don't think about it that much."

"What do you mean?"

"I mean . . . I make myself look as nice as I can, but I don't think that much about it."

"Well, I'm sorry no man ever told you then, because they should have. You're beautiful. Not just everyday beautiful, either. It's like . . . no matter how many times I look out my window in the morning and see the view, I have to stop and really take it in. You're like that."

It wasn't the most poetic speech, but he wasn't the kind of guy who was used to making speeches of any kind. Still, he wanted her to know. He wanted her to know there was more to life than being respected. There was grass between your toes, the sun on your back, soft skin beneath your hands. Oh, he wanted her soft skin beneath his hands again.

She swallowed. "Lucas, you don't have to say things like that."

"I know I don't have to, but it's true."

"So you decided to be nice today, huh? What changed?"

"What do you mean?"

"You were kind of a jackass last night, to be honest."

He shook his head. "I didn't handle that very well. I'm sorry." His brain had nearly short-circuited when he'd found out she'd never been with anyone else. He'd never considered himself the kind of man who would care about something like that.

Truth be told, he didn't think there was a virgin left in the pool of women he would be choosing from. He'd never encountered one before, so he didn't see any reason why he would now.

But it had mattered. Because, like it or not, he was her first. And you remembered your first. He remembered his first vividly, after more than ten years. And now he'd shared that with Carly, who he had no hope of leaving behind—not like his first lover, who he hadn't seen since high school.

Carly was part of his life, and when he'd discovered she was a virgin, it had really driven home what he'd already known: This wasn't something she normally did. And it was going to change things.

That had brought some hefty guilt along with it.

Still, he was here, in the barn with her, and he wasn't even going to pretend his intentions were anything close to chaste or honorable.

The condom in his wallet was proof.

"I'm going to kiss you now," he said.

She blinked. "Why?"

"Because you need to be kissed."

"I do?"

"Hell if I know. Fine, I need to be kissed. I need you to kiss me because I haven't thought of anything but you since last night. Probably since before then."

Her breathing quickened, her breasts rising and falling sharply. "Well, if you need a kiss, I suppose I could help you out."

She leaned in, her lips cool from the run through the field, pressing against his, her tongue tracing the outline of his mouth. And he let her in.

He wrapped his arms around her and pulled her tight against him, loving the feel of all those lush curves, of the softness of her lips, the little sounds of pleasure she made in the back of her throat when his tongue stroked hers.

If there was a woman alive sexier than Carly Denton, he couldn't think of her. And he didn't want to. He just wanted Carly. Only Carly.

He couldn't remember a woman ever mattering so much. He slid his hands down her back, over her ass, bunching up the fabric of her skirt.

"What are you doing?" she whispered against his lips.

"I want you," he said. He hardly recognized his own voice. "Here. Now."

"Here?"

"Live dangerously, sugar." He leaned in and kissed her neck, nipping her earlobe. She shivered beneath his touch and he knew that she was going to say yes. Because she couldn't say no. He knew that because he couldn't. Because he was utterly powerless to do anything but give in to the surge of heat that was pouring through him.

His cock ached, pressing hard against the seam of his jeans. He needed her. Needed this. But he would wait for her response. Would wait for her to say yes.

"After this we're going out for french fries," she said, kissing him again, deeper, harder.

"Sounds like a plan," he said. He gripped her thighs and hoisted her legs up around his waist, walking her deeper into the barn. "Panties off," he said, setting her down, waiting for her to find her balance on her heels before he released his hold on her and started undoing his belt.

She nodded, her eyes never leaving his. She drew her panties down her legs and held them, unwilling, he could tell, to leave them on the floor of the barn.

He held his hand out. "I'll take those."

Color suffused her cheeks and he almost laughed. Instead, he took the delicate silk scrap from her hand and shoved it deep into his pocket. "A little safer," he said.

"You read my mind. I want to live dangerously, but not in underwear that's been on the floor of a barn."

"Fair enough."

She took a step back and leaned up against the wall. "I saw this somewhere once."

Shame pricked the back of his neck. "Carly . . ."

"No, don't . . . don't feel bad, it's . . . I've never been able to say this before so you're going to have to let me say it without interrupting." She took a breath. "I've thought about this. Wondered how it felt. What it would be like to be the woman, the person, who was brave enough to just take what I wanted in the moment and not worry about . . . anything. Not worry about anything but what I wanted. I want to be that woman now, with you."

She started to unbutton her shirt and he watched, his heart pounding hard, his cock so hard he was afraid he might end up with permanent damage.

"You might want to leave the shirt on," he said. "Splinters."

"Right."

He took a step toward her and cupped her cheek, kissing her deeply. He moved his fingers up her inner thigh, sliding them over her wet heat, drawing moisture from inside of her and rubbing it over her clit.

She arched into him, breasts pressing against his chest. "You're good at that."

He chuckled, parting the edges of her shirt, leaning in and sucking her nipple through her bra while he continued to stroke her. "Nice to know it's working for you."

"Oh, yeah."

He pushed a finger inside of her and her hands flew to his shoulders, nails digging into his back. "I have to make sure you're ready."

"I'm ready," she said, panting.

"I'm not convinced." He added a second finger, still teasing her clit with his thumb.

"Lucas."

"Just a little more. You like it, just enjoy."

"So . . . arrogant."

"Yep. But you like that too."

He kept his eyes on hers, watched the color deepen in her cheeks. "Tell me you like it," he said. He stilled his hand. Waited.

She dug her nails into his shoulders. "Lucas," she gasped.

"Tell me you like that I'm an arrogant son of a bitch."

"No."

"Tell me, or you don't get to play anymore."

He wasn't sure why it was important that he won this battle. Except maybe he just wanted to hear that she liked him. Maybe she was right. Maybe there was a playground element to their relationship. Though, right now, her body was more fun than any playground he could ever remember.

"Touch me," she said, a distinct, pleading note in her voice now.

"Not until you say it, sugar."

"I like it."

"You like what?" he asked, tantalizing her with another sweep of his thumb.

"I like it that you're an arrogant son of a bitch. I like you. Now keep touching me."

He chuckled, relishing the victory and making good on his promise as he worked his fingers in and out of her body until she stiffened against him, internal muscles pulsing around him.

The force of her orgasm, the evidence of it on his hands, nearly made him come then and there. But not yet. He needed more. He reached into his back pocket and pulled out his wallet, taking out the condom packet and holding it up between his thumb and forefinger.

"I want you to know," he said, "I put this in there this morning, and it was with you in mind. So you can be mad about this being somewhat premeditated, but I don't want you thinking I just carry these around with the aim of hooking up, that I intended to use this with just anyone. It's for you. For this. I've actually never done this in a barn. What you saw didn't make it as far as we're going to."

She nodded, biting her bottom lip.

He reached down and undid the snap on his jeans, lowering his fly carefully, and tugging his erection free. He rolled the condom on and pressed his body against Carly's, kissing her deep and long before hooking her leg over his hip and testing the entrance of her body with the head of his cock.

She was so hot, so wet, and the tip of his shaft slid in easily.

He gritted his teeth, trying to take it slow, trying to be gentle because of her inexperience. But she was panting in his ear, her hands moving over his back. Then she kissed his neck, flicking his skin with the tip of her tongue.

"Careful, Carly."

"This isn't the time for careful. This is dangerous, remember?"

She slid her hands down his back and below the waistband of his pants, planting her hands on his ass and gripping him tight, urging him on. And he obliged, taking every last ounce of his control not to explode the minute he was buried inside of her.

"Oh . . . damn, baby."

"I was going to say the same thing," she said.

And then neither of them said anything. He got lost, in everything. In her scent, in the feel of being deep inside of her, in the hot, hard rhythm of thrusting into her, of her arching against him, countering his every move, the flex of her hips making her tighten around his cock. Driving him closer to the edge.

Not yet. He had to make her come one more time. And then, then he could lose it. But not before that.

Her movements quickened with his, nails digging into his skin, hard. And then there was no thought of hanging on to control anymore, there was no more thought, just his blood roaring in his ears, a flash-fire of pleasure that poured through his veins, burning through him, raging. Dimly, he heard himself groan, heard her sharp cry, felt her pulse hard around him, and then he put his hand flat on the barn wall and tried to use it to brace himself. To keep his knees from buckling.

Then he heard the sounds of the birds outside. Felt the breeze coming through the half-open door.

"Damn," he said. "We have to get dressed."

He eased away from her and started straightening his pants. "Shit," he said.

"What?"

He tugged off the condom. "I didn't think this part through. And I'm not leaving it for someone else to deal with."

She screwed up her face. "Oh no." Her eyes brightened. "Oh! Wait." She reached down and lifted her purse from the barn floor. "I have a little first aid kit for emergencies. In a plastic baggie." She fished around and produced a sandwich bag filled with Band-Aids, a couple of pill bottles and some topical medicine, then she dumped the contents into her purse. "Here. I'll trade you for my panties."

He took the bag from her hands. "Nope, I'm keeping those." He turned away from her and took care of the condom, then tucked the bag into his other pocket.

"I need them, Lucas," she said.

"Why?" he asked.

"Because I can't . . . go without."

"Why?"

"I have work to do."

"So work. Without them. And remember why you don't have them."

Her cheeks flushed. "I'm hardly going to forget."

"Live dangerously."

She crossed her arms under her breasts. "All right. Fine. No panties. I can do that. No one will know."

He turned away from her, headed back toward the entrance of the barn, then he paused. He looked back, winking at her. "I'll know."

And he would think of it for the rest of the day. Until tonight, and dammit, there would be a tonight. He wasn't letting her get away that easily.

Seven

Carly's body was still burning hours after her encounter with Lucas. She couldn't believe what she'd let him do. No, what she'd begged him to do, in a public place. While she was on the job.

She tore up pieces of lettuce with more aggression than was warranted and threw them into the wooden serving bowl that was sitting on the counter. She had deducted the time spent with Lucas from her workday. She was not allowing herself to get paid for that steamy half hour in the barn. That was just taking it all into a territory that was best avoided.

And she'd spent the rest of the day without panties. And damn if it hadn't turned her on. It had done just what he'd hoped it would do. Had put her mind right back there in the barn with him.

Of course, before she'd come to Mac's house, she'd stopped by her house and put a pair on. There were limits to her debauchery.

She was completely weak where Lucas was concerned. So why didn't she feel weak? Why didn't she feel like she was on the edge of losing the essence of herself? Because that was truly what she'd always imagined an intense, passionate relationship would do to her.

She'd always been afraid she'd turn into her mother.

She picked the bowl up and walked it over to the dining table. Mac had invited her over for dinner again, which really meant he was hungry and wanted her to cook for him. Well, she was sure he wanted to see her too; she just knew his appetite had been a factor.

Mac walked in, right on time. "You need a new housekeeper," she said. "I'm not cooking for you for all eternity. And I'm definitely not doing your laundry again. You're a grown-up, you know."

"I know." He sat down at the table. "Lucas is on his way. Play nice."

Heat flashed across her skin, creeping up her neck. "Lucas is coming?"

"Yes. I invited him."

So, Lucas hadn't invited himself. But he'd been planning on coming over tonight, later. Or having her over. Not that she'd agreed. Diving headfirst into an affair with him hadn't really been her plan. But then, the one-night-stand thing clearly hadn't worked out either, so she really had no idea what in the hell they were doing.

"Okay." She turned to the cupboard and got down an extra plate. "Tell me next time so I make enough food."

"You made enough for a small army. It was like you were expecting him."

She paused. Yes, she had. Interesting that she sort of naturally made room for him. Or not that interesting. He'd always been there when they were kids. There had been a time when cooking for Lucas and Mac was normal.

"How's everything going with Ride for Hope? Lucas mentioned you two were working together on some things."

She nearly choked. "Uh . . . yeah. Everything's going good."

"You two at each other's throats?"

An image of earlier today, of licking Lucas's throat, passed through her mind. "No."

"That's good. He's not a bad guy, Carly. I don't know why you don't like him."

And another little flash, of her telling Lucas just how much she liked the way he stroked her . . . "I like him," she said.

"You don't act like it."

More flashes, his hands on her skin, his mouth hungry on hers.

"Oh, I do sometimes," she said.

There was a knock at the door. Lucas was knocking. Giving her a warning maybe, which was unexpectedly considerate of him. Or maybe it wasn't all that unexpected.

"I'll get it." She dashed across the room and to the door, tugging it open. "Hi, Lucas," she said, bright, casual. Probably too bright and too casual.

"Carly," he said, inclining his head, taking off his hat as he crossed the threshold. "I thought you might be here."

"And I didn't think you would be here."

"Is it okay if I stay?"

"Why would you ask that?" she asked, still smiling. "You never ask that." He wasn't acting natural. He was being too nice.

"My mistake. I was testing out this thing they call manners. You may have heard of them."

A rush of relief went through her. "Yes. I'm just surprised you have."

"Behave, you two," Mac said.

She and Lucas exchanged guilty looks. "Promise," she said.

Lucas's eyes never left hers. "I'll behave. For now."

She shivered, the heat of his words flowing over her skin. "Lucas," she muttered. It sounded sexual to her, and while she knew it probably wouldn't to anyone not in her head, it made her feel very awkward.

Not that much could make the evening more awkward.

"Okay, dinner's ready, have a seat."

She ushered Lucas to the table and took the seat across from him. She let him and Mac fill the silence with conversation. And she found her gaze continually wandering to Lucas. To the way his Adam's apple moved when he talked. To the square cut of his jaw. The long dark lashes that framed his eyes. How had she missed those? How had she not realized just how perfect he was?

She blinked rapidly, that thought pulling her back to reality. She turned her focus back to her dinner.

"Do you have a venue for the Ride yet?" Mac asked.

Her focus flew back up, her eyes clashing with Lucas's. "Yes. We do. I mean, the council does. Not . . . we. It's not like it's just the two of us working on this or anything . . . anything like that." She couldn't have sounded more suspicious if she'd tried.

"Okay," Mac said, looking between the two of them.

"Well," she said, standing suddenly, "I have an early morning, so I should get going."

Lucas stood too, his plate in hand. "So do I. On the ranch."

"You always have an early morning," Mac said, keeping his seat.

"It's earlier tomorrow," Lucas said. "I have calves to . . . castrate."

"Not by yourself," Mac said.

"Oh, no, I have help."

"You should have asked me," Mac said.

"As much as I know you like the process, I figured I'd pay some guys to do it," Lucas said, the lie growing. "You know, since you have your own operation to run and all."

Mac grunted. "Suit yourself."

Carly scurried to the counter and set her plate down before returning to the table, bending down and dropping a kiss on Mac's cheek. Guilt ate at her. But there was no point in Mac finding out about her and Lucas because, really, there was no her and Lucas. There was . . . whatever this attraction was between them. An attraction that was currently burning out of control.

The honest truth was, she didn't think she could keep sitting in the same room as Lucas without mentally undressing him, and without it being very obvious to anyone looking at her.

And it was just too damned awkward to sit across from her brother while she was in the throes of deep sexual longing for the man sitting next to him.

"Right, well, good night, Mac. Good night, Lucas."

She turned and walked out of the dining area, and out the front door, letting out a breath she hadn't realized she'd been holding the minute she hit the cool night air.

She was unlocking her car when she heard the front door close behind her.

"I'm curious, sugar."

She turned and looked at Lucas, her heart in her throat. She should tell him no. She should tell him it wasn't happening again. She should end it before it got more complicated. Before she got hurt.

"What about?"

"Did you spend the day without panties?"

"Lucas," she hissed. "Mac is right inside."

"And he can't hear us." Lucas walked over to her car, his gaze hot, intense on hers. "Did you spend the day bare under your skirt?"

Heat rolled through her. "Yes."

"What about now?"

"Well, I went and put some on before I came here."

"That's a shame. But I don't mind taking them off of you again."

Her throat tightened. "Is that so?"

"Your place or mine?"

She should tell him no. She should tell him he should go to his place, and she could go to hers. "I have a full-size bed. Your feet would hang off the end."

"Mine then," he said.

She nodded and got in her car, her hands shaking as she started the engine. She was going. There was no use pretending she wasn't. Logic wasn't winning. Not tonight.

The moment they were both in the driveway and out of their vehicles, Lucas scooped Carly up into his arms and charged into the house and up the stairs.

"I'm impatient," he said, setting her down on the edge of the bed, tugging his T-shirt up over his head. Carly could only stare open-mouthed for a moment. All those gorgeous muscles. And they were all hers. Only hers.

For a while at least. Until he got bored. Or tired of her.

She pushed that thought to the side and focused on his body again. On how she felt when she looked at him. On how she felt when she was with him. Like she'd been let out of a cage. One she'd shut her own self in.

"The rest," she said, pushing herself back into the center of the mattress.

He arched one dark brow. "The rest of my clothes?"

"Yes. I want a show."

"Two days and you've gotten completely corrupted," he said, his hands going to his belt. She couldn't help but notice the very clear outline of his erection beneath the denim.

"I blame you."

He shook his head, tugging his belt through the loops, his hands strong, his fingers . . . those were talented fingers. Fascinating. He had the sexiest hands. Sexier now that she knew just what he could do with them. "I blame me too."

"I didn't mean it in a bad way."

"Well, that's good to know." He unsnapped his jeans and shoved them down his thighs, along with his underwear, kicking them aside.

She surveyed the sights, fire scorching along her veins.

"Commentary?" he asked.

"Damn, you're hot," she said, letting the words escape in a rush.

His eyes darkened. "I like it when you say things like that."

"Totally stupid things like that?"

"Honest things. What you're feeling, what you're thinking. I like that much better than the snark you used to dish out."

"The snark was honest," she said.

"I don't believe you."

"You've always made me feel . . . tight. Like my skin didn't fit. And that made me act like I did. Well, it was part of it. And now . . . I have another way to release it. I recognize what the feeling is a little bit better."

"And what is it?"

"Lust," she said, embracing it fully now.

"I see. What do you want?"

She looked away. "You."

"No. Tell me, specifically, what you want."

She looked back up, met his eyes. She'd taken his challenge on earlier, and it had ended in ecstasy. She wanted to do it again. Wanted to stop hiding behind layers of civility that she'd put into place to make everyone else feel comfortable but had nothing to do with who she actually was. Had nothing to do with what she wanted—just with what she wanted people to see.

"I want to . . . to taste you," she said.

"Where?" he asked, his voice rough.

"Your . . ." She knew some dirty words but she'd never said them out loud. She supposed now was the time. "Your cock."

Heat flared in his dark eyes. "Then what?" he asked, his voice rough, hoarse.

"I want you . . . inside of me."

"Is that all?"

"I want you to make me come," she said, keeping her eyes on his, ignoring the burning in her cheeks.

He moved to the edge of the bed and she scooted forward on her knees, looking up at him, and she lowered her head and ran her tongue along the head of his erection. His hands went to her hair, his fingers tightening, pulling. It hurt a little, and she found she didn't dislike it. Not at all.

She took more of him into her mouth, her hands curled around his hips, fingernails digging into his buttocks. She could feel his muscles trembling beneath her palms as she continued to lavish pleasure on him, as she continued to explore him.

He was hers. Hers. And she would do with him what she wanted. Touch him, taste him. All of him.

She ran her tongue along the length of him, relishing the tremor that racked his body, the tightening of his fingers in her hair. He was close to the edge, close to losing it, because of her. She was close to bringing Lucas Miller to his knees.

She wrapped her fingers around his shaft and squeezed him tight as she circled him with her tongue.

He let out a sharp curse. "Okay, if you want to get to the rest of your fantasy, you're going to have to let me go now."

"Mmmm," she said, lifting her head. "I don't want to."

"Well, if you want to come too, you're going to have to."

A second later she was flat on her back, Lucas, hot and naked, over her, kissing her long and deep. She arched into him, lacing her fingers through his hair as he worked at the buttons on her top, his hands clumsy now, where before they'd been smooth.

It took him only a few seconds to get her completely naked, to pull her against him, skin to skin. It felt so good.

He felt so good. Better, more intimate than she'd ever imagined sex could be.

He reached over to his bedside table, where the condoms still sat, and took care of precautions before sliding deep inside of her.

He kissed her, driving them both to the height of pleasure with an ease that startled her. Her orgasm washed over her, pushing every thought from her mind, leaving her filled with the deepest, most powerful emotion she'd ever felt. Leaving her weak and shaking.

And she watched Lucas's face when he reached the peak, held him while he shuddered out his own orgasm, his mouth hot on her neck, her name on his lips.

And afterward, he just held her, stroked her hair, told her how beautiful she was.

After Lucas took care of practicalities, he slid back into bed beside her, tugging her up against him. She rested her head on his chest, felt his heart pounding hard beneath her cheek.

She felt like a dam had burst inside of her. There were so many things flooding through her, a sense of freedom, pleasure, emotion, like she'd never known before.

When she'd said those things to him, told him what she'd wanted . . . never in her life, not even forty-eight hours ago, had she imagined she would ever say anything like that to another person. That she would ever expose those intimate thoughts and desires to someone else.

It had turned her on to talk to him like that, and exposing that piece of herself, the part that wanted to make demands in bed, and submit to her partner's, took a measure of trust that went way beyond lust.

Because these were desires she'd barely let herself acknowledge she had. And now she'd exposed them to Lucas.

But it didn't scare her. It should, and she knew it, but it still didn't.

"Tell me something, Lucas," she said, suddenly desperate

to try and even the score between them. To know something about him that no one else knew.

"What do you want to know, sugar?"

"I don't know. Something. Those nights you came to our house for dinner . . . what was happening at your house?"

"You know what was happening."

"I know. I mean . . . I know that your father was drinking. But . . ."

"But you want details?"

It felt intrusive, but she wanted to understand him. To have a piece of him. "Kind of."

"He wasn't violent when he drank, Carly. He never has been. He's still not. He gets maudlin. He cries sometimes. He mainly sits in front of the TV until he passes out. Oh, I hated finding him passed out. I found him more than once out stone-cold on the bathroom floor, his head in a puddle of his own vomit. It's ugly, Carly, and I didn't want to see it. I didn't want to see how weak he was."

Her chest tightened. "Oh . . . Lucas, I'm sorry. You don't have to—"

"No. That's not really the sad thing. The sad thing is that my mother did that to him. To us. He was actually all right before she left. I think people thought he was drinking beforehand, that he drove her away. You know how people talk."

"Oh boy. I do."

"She just left us. I've always wondered what was wrong with him. What was wrong with me. What mother leaves her child?"

Carly's stomach ached, her entire body hurting for him. For the boy he'd been. For the man he was. She dropped a kiss onto his chest. "Not a good mother. It wasn't you, Lucas, you have to know that."

"I do. But . . . not always. You know how it is."

She swallowed hard. "In my experience, people who don't deserve it get left. People who deserve to get left don't.

The fault lies with the one who left, or in the case of my family, didn't."

"Your dad's a bastard."

"I know. He is. But why does she stay?"

He put his hand on her shoulder, his fingers tracing a path over her skin. "I don't know."

"She lets him make an idiot out of her. She doesn't even threaten to leave anymore. She just lets him do what he wants, and then she wails about how much he hurts her. About how sad her life is. And she does it in public so the whole world can see. She wears her total and utter devotion, her crazy version of love for this man, on her sleeve and he doesn't deserve it. Any more than you deserved to have your mom leave. People just do things. Stupid things."

"And that's why you've avoided men?" he asked.

She took a deep breath. "Yeah. Essentially. What if she was like me before she met him? What if she was strong and independent? And had goals and plans and then . . . and then she just let him steal it all? Let her obsession with him make a fool of her, turn her into a shell of the woman she could have been."

"I suppose my dad's let love do the same thing to him," he said.

"Is that why you avoid relationships?"

"I don't really avoid them. I've just had temporary relationships because I haven't found anyone I want to keep yet. Or anyone who wants to keep me."

"Hmm."

"What?"

"Nothing." She rested her head on his chest again, trying to ignore the small tearing feeling in her chest. Lucas hadn't settled down because he just wasn't the kind of man who would easily consider it. Sometimes she wondered if any man settled down, or if some of them were just better at hiding their infidelity than others.

But Lucas . . . she couldn't really imagine Lucas betraying anyone. Lucas was so much more than she'd given him credit for. She'd imagined him as some kind of pleasure seeker, the kind who got his kicks from the number of notches he got to carve into his bedpost.

But she didn't think so now. Not now that she was really seeing him.

Her chest burned. How in the world had Lucas Miller gotten himself so tangled up in her heart?

And then she knew the truth. He'd never been untangled from it.

Okay, so he was a liar. He'd lied to his best friend in order to get the man's little sister into his bed. And he couldn't muster up any guilt about it. Not when he felt like he did. Sated and hot for her at the same time, his body buzzing with the lingering aftereffects of a whole night of pleasure.

He felt happy. The kind of happy he couldn't remember ever feeling before. The kind that went deep, made him feel a sense of peace. Contentment. And it was all because of Carly.

The early morning he'd told Mac about was basically a late night, since he and Carly had hardly gotten any sleep. Short naps in between jumping each other were about the extent of it.

And right now, he was getting ready to make Carly pancakes. She was still sleeping, soft and naked and beautiful in his bed.

He was starting to think he wanted to keep her there for as long as he could. Forever would be nice. He'd never wanted forever from anyone before, but from Carly it seemed like a necessity. The other alternative was not having her, and that just wasn't an option in his mind.

Of course, he might want forever, but actually being able to have it—that was another thing entirely.

He didn't know where the thought had come from. Or why he'd thought, even for a moment, it might be possible. Carly was . . . well, she was much too good for him. In terms of playing for keeps anyway.

His own mother hadn't wanted to stick with him. There was no reason on earth that a woman like Carly, a woman with a business degree and perfectly tailored suits, a woman who didn't like dirt and didn't like to sweat, would want to stay with a man like him.

A slight smile curved up the corners of his lips. He'd made Carly sweat last night and she hadn't seemed to mind. So maybe there were some things about him that would make the negatives seem worth it.

There was a sharp knock on the door, and Lucas headed that direction without giving it too much thought. It was early, but a lot of his hired hands got early starts.

He swung the door open and froze when he saw Mac standing there. Hell. How had he found out? He could see Mac's truck, could see the rifle up in the rack in the back window. If he went for it, Lucas would have time to haul ass if needed.

Not that he really thought his friend would use it. Not really.

Then his eyes fell to what his friend was holding in his hand, and that put the fear of God in him. The gun wasn't a worry, but the Burdizzo, a handy castration implement currently in Mac's possession, was a damn big one.

He swallowed. "What's up, Mac?"

"I came to help with the calves."

That answer sent a wave of relief through him. Relief that only lasted for a second, since it dawned on him that there would be no calf castration today, and that meant his friend was here for no reason. With a tool that could easily separate his balls from his body. While Mac's little sister slept upstairs. Naked. Recently tumbled. In his bed.

Shit.

"I rescheduled," he said, crossing his arms over his bare chest, blocking his friend's entry into the house.

"You rescheduled? That doesn't make any sense."

"Well, I told you I didn't need your help."

"Which also didn't make sense. We help each other out with this stuff."

He cleared his throat. "Well, I don't have anything going on that needs . . . help."

He heard the padding of bare feet on the stairs behind him and his heart stopped. He didn't look. He didn't want to draw Mac's attention. He stepped slightly to the right and tried to block the view with his body, but Mac was already trying to look around him.

And then the footsteps stopped, and he knew exactly what Mac was seeing over his left shoulder. Carly, wearing some piece of clothing or another, frozen, staring open-mouthed.

The shift in expressions on Mac's face would have been funny if Lucas's demise wasn't imminent. The expression went from confused, to more greatly confused, to a kind of cold fury that seemed to radiate from him.

He pushed past Lucas. "What the hell are you doing here?" he asked.

Lucas turned and saw his theory confirmed. Carly, in his T-shirt, which just touched the top of her thighs, her hair a tumbled mess, standing at the base of the stairs, looking utterly horrified.

"I was . . . going to help with the cows?" she said, her voice pitched much higher than it normally was.

"Right," Mac said, crossing his arms over his chest, the Burdizzo still in his hand. "Start talking."

"Why?" she asked, pushing her blond hair off of her

forehead. "I'm a grown woman, Mac, I don't have to explain my actions to you."

"When your actions appear to be bunking with my best friend, you damn well do."

"Mac, leave her alone," Lucas said. He was fine catching heat from Mac—he deserved it, in fact—but he wasn't going to let him yell at Carly about it.

"Fine." Mac rounded on him. "Then you start talking. Explain why the hell my little sister is at your house wearing your shirt and nothing else." Lucas had only ever seen Mac angry a few times. And every one of those times, the anger had been directed at Mac and Carly's father for his continued horrible treatment of their mother.

But right now, for the first time, it was directed at him. And he wasn't sure he was going to escape it without having some punches thrown at him.

And he deserved it. Not for sleeping with Carly, because Carly had wanted him, and what she wanted mattered, not what Mac wanted.

But for lying. Yeah, for that he deserved a punch in the face.

All right, and a little for sleeping with Carly, but only because if he'd had a sister, he would have done the same.

He shook his head. "I'm sorry, Mac. But this was just between Carly and me, and I really didn't see the point of bringing you into it."

"You shouldn't be in it at all. She's my sister, you asshole."

Lucas scrubbed his hand over his hair. "I know."

"And I trusted you. And you're a lying bastard who slept with my sister. And we both know you aren't going to marry her or anything."

Now it was Lucas's turn to want to hit something. "Are you accusing me of using her? That's one too far, Mac."

"What? You're telling me you aren't? All you do is use women. I know, I've been doing it with you for the better part of my adult life."

"So you assume I'd do that to Carly? Because I was as much of a jackass as you were when we were younger, that's all you think I am now?"

"You don't even like Carly! She doesn't like you. You're at each other's throats constantly. You can't pretend you suddenly have feelings for her."

He did, though. And he understood just how strong they were the moment Mac accused him of not having any. The realization was enough to bring him to his knees. But there was no way he could say anything about it. Not yet. Not when he was just realizing that they existed. Not when he had a very angry audience looking on either.

"Get out, Mac."

His friend crossed his very large arms over his chest. "You can't tell me to get out."

Lucas looked around the living room. "Uh . . . yes, I can. This is my house."

"And that's my sister."

"Who has free will, I believe."

"Who is standing right here," Carly said. "Mac, shut the hell up. Seriously. Stop acting like I'm not in the room. Stop acting like I can't make my own decisions, or like I'm some damsel in distress when I am damn well not." She turned on Lucas. "And you, you stop it too."

Lucas threw his arms out wide. "What did I do?"

"The same thing he did. Speaking for me."

"Well, you weren't speaking."

She turned pink to the roots of her hair. "I'm standing here half naked, and I'm embarrassed, and actually"—she directed her focus to her brother—"Mac, get out."

"I'm not leaving."

"Why? Do you think Lucas dragged me to his bed by the hair? I hopped into it," she said, her voice trembling now. "I made the choice, okay? So it's not really any of your business. I'm sorry it makes you mad. No, no, I'm not sorry it makes you mad. You have no right to let it make you mad.

I'm not yours. I'm not . . . anyone's. I'm mine, and I can make my own damn mistakes."

"So, now I'm a mistake?" Lucas asked, anger burning through him.

She held up her hand. "Not the time, Lucas."

"You just called me a mistake."

"You will be," she said, her voice rising. "We both know that."

"Why, because Mac says it will be? Because Mac says he doesn't think I want anything from you but sex?"

"Watch it," Mac said, teeth gritted.

"Out," Lucas said.

Mac looked from Carly to Lucas, and for some reason, he decided to comply. Then Lucas looked back at Carly and understood why. Carly's face was red, her hands shaking, her eyes glistening.

"You're not off the hook, Miller," Mac said. "And neither are you." He directed the last line at Carly, before walking out of the house and slamming the front door behind him.

A tear slid down Carly's cheek and she wiped it away. "That was awful," she said. "Awful. All that was missing was a bar of crowded people looking on and taking bets on whether or not there would be bloodshed."

Lucas shook his head. "You're not your mom, Carly. That wasn't what this was. I lied to Mac, which is half of why he's pissed."

"But look what happens! Look what happens when there's all this . . . passion. It makes everything so uncontrolled. So crazy. And I just . . . I don't want this." She sounded frantic, panicked almost. Being with him, the thought of it, made her panic. Well, hell.

"You don't want this?" he echoed. And just like that, the visions of forever dissolved around him.

"No."

"How can you say you don't want this, Carly? We had sex all night. I had you begging for me to take you. Over and over again. How the hell can you stand there and tell me you don't want this?"

"I don't."

"You're a liar."

"Wanting sex and wanting this," she said, waving her hand around, "are two very different things. And I don't want this kind of drama, which means I can learn to live without the sex."

"Because that's all it was to you?"

"It's all it was to you."

"And you know that because you know I had some casual sex more than half a decade ago. You honestly think I would sleep with you just for kicks, use you, like Mac said, is that it?"

"What else could it be, Lucas?"

"Did it ever occur to you that I might care for you?"

She shook her head. "No. When was I supposed to pick up on that? In between our constant bickering?"

"That was you, sugar, that wasn't me."

"You were always putting the bait out."

"To see you get riled up. Because I love the way your cheeks flush when you're angry. Because I love to spar with you. Because I live for that next witty one-liner I know will come out of your mouth. And because I love the moment when I've gotten you so good, you don't have one, and you're just speechless. That's only happened once or twice. And now that things have changed between us, I love the way you look when you're just about to come, I love the sound of my name on your lips. Most of all, I discovered that I love you."

She took a step back, like he'd landed a physical blow. She shook her head, her mouth hanging open. "No."

The look on her face, the horror, should have been enough to get him to stop talking. But it wasn't. Now that he knew it, he had to say it, no matter the cost. "I love you, Carly."

"You don't. You're just saying that."

"I'm not. Why in the world would I just say that? Why the hell would I tear myself open for you if I didn't mean it? I've never said that to anyone in my life, and that includes family. I've never felt it before."

Tears pooled in Carly's blue eyes and she blinked hard, looking away from him. "So then . . . how do you know what it is?"

"I knew what it wasn't. It wasn't my mom walking out on me, or my dad drowning his own sorrows, too wrapped up in his own crap to care about me. It wasn't that woman you saw me with six years ago. And this . . . this is different from any of that. I feel it. I feel it here," he said, pressing his hand to his chest. "It hurts like hell but I like it."

She shook her head slowly, backing away from him. Withdrawing. And he felt her withdraw emotionally too. Felt her cutting the connection between them. "I can't do this."

"You can't do what?" he asked, his voice hoarse.

"I don't want this," she said. "I don't want to spend my life wondering when the other shoe is going to drop, Lucas. I can't do it. I can't wonder when you're going to start looking at other women. When you're going to start sleeping with other women."

"There's this thing called marriage vows, Carly, and there's a line in there about that kind of thing. If I made vows, I would damn well keep them."

"But people don't. You and I both know that, they just don't keep them. And I'm sure that both of our parents made vows imagining they would keep them, that love or whatever they thought they had would be enough. But I've never seen it be enough."

"You really think that of me? That I would do that to you? To anyone?" He made a move toward her, and she took another step away. Expanding the distance in every way.

She wiped a tear away from her cheek, and all he could think of was that he should be the one to erase her tears. But she wouldn't let him.

"I would make an idiot out of myself over you," she whispered. "I can't let myself do that." She turned and started walking up the stairs, and his heart cracked in two.

"That's fine, Carly. Because I can't live my whole life with a woman who doesn't trust me."

"That's not it. That's not fair."

"It's exactly it." He let anger fuel him now. At her, at himself. At the screwed-up lives they'd both led that had brought them to this point, too broken to make things work together. "You're so bound up in your own hurt that you don't see it. You wanted to sleep with me, and get what you wanted, and not have to give anything back. You don't really want freedom. You want to hang on to the past and hold it up in front of you like a shield. That's what you want. To spend your life hiding behind your tailored suits and perfect hair, so that no one will see what a disaster you are inside."

"Stop it, Lucas."

"Why? It's true. You want to pretend that because I had some girlfriends a few years ago, I'm somehow never going to settle down, because that suits you. Because then, it makes me off-limits to you. You wanted to take from me and not give anything back. Not emotion or trust. You're so afraid that someone might get close to you that you have to push me away now. Because I've seen it. I've seen that under that composure of yours, under your makeup mask, you're still just a scared little girl."

"I didn't ask you to psychoanalyze me!" she spat. "You think you get relationships? What the hell would you know about a healthy relationship? How did you think the two of us would go about having one?"

"I thought it would involve letting go of the past and embracing the future. But it's clear to me that you can't do that."

"Because this isn't what I wanted. It's—"

"Scary," he said, his voice thin, tight. "And you want to be safe. You want everyone to look at you and see your control, and your poise, and pat you on the back for what? For feeling nothing?"

Carly balled her hands into fists at her sides. "I'm not going to be like my mother. I'm not doing that. I'm not making a public spectacle of myself. And this morning came way too close to that."

"So what other people feel matters more than what you feel?"

"Yes," she said, exploding. "Yes. Because how else will I know if I'm doing it right? You can't trust your own heart, Lucas, it makes you do stupid things."

"Your fear is making you act a hell of a lot stupider than your heart would. Maybe the problem isn't that you don't trust me. It's that you don't trust yourself."

Or that he just wasn't worth the risk. The thought sent an arrow of pure agony straight to his heart. He'd been stupid to think this could end any other way. Stupid to imagine that he was the one who would make Carly Denton want to take a chance.

"I'm going to get dressed now," she said. "And then I'm going to go."

"Great."

He watched her walk up the stairs and tried to ignore the stabbing pain in his chest. He wanted to beg, but he wasn't going to do that. He'd lost enough of his pride already.

In the end, it shouldn't surprise him. His own mother hadn't stayed with him. Why the hell should Carly stay?

He gritted his teeth, tried to take a breath. Tried to keep the hot, burning emotion that was searing his heart from bringing him to his knees. This was a good thing. Good it had happened like this. Good it had happened now. It was the reminder he needed. Why he didn't do love. Why he never had.

It was too much work to love people who would simply never love you back.

CHAPTER

Nine

Life was annoying. It kept just . . . going on while Carly was trying to wallow in misery. She wanted to curl up into a little ball and wail for a week straight, but she couldn't. She had to finalize all the details for Ride for Hope and see to a million other civic duties.

She had to be on show, which she'd never minded before, because she'd never fully grasped just how "on show" she was. Had never truly understood everything she was hiding so she could put on a public face that would seem acceptable, and wouldn't make waves or any controversy.

Now she saw it. Now she felt the chains tightening around her wrists.

Lucas had made her feel free. Had helped her find bits of herself she'd never known had existed.

And the first moment those parts of herself had been exposed to someone else, she'd curled back in on herself. Buttoned back up. Stepped into her cell.

She'd been back in it for over a week now. And she felt it.

She rested her elbows on her desk and put her face in her

hands. She missed Lucas so much, it was an ache that went through her entire body. A physical pain. She'd known that passion could make you crazy, but she hadn't known it would hurt like this.

It wasn't just passion. She knew that.

I love you.

He'd said that he loved her and she'd thrown it back at him. Because it had terrified her how much she'd wanted to believe it. How badly she'd wanted to latch on to those words and hold them close forever. To keep Lucas forever.

But she couldn't. And she knew, absolutely and beyond a shadow of a doubt now, the real reason she'd been so angry at him for the event six years ago. Why she'd let that sight of him with another woman turn him from childhood crush to mustache-twirling sex villain.

She'd needed him to be the villain so that she could protect herself. So that she wouldn't fall for him. Because even then, she'd known that she could. Some part of her had recognized that if she didn't do something about her feelings for Lucas, they were going to grow.

So she'd taken the coward's way out. And she'd done it again last week.

Trust. He was asking for trust. And that was the one thing she wasn't sure she could give. And he was right. He deserved a woman who trusted him. A woman who wasn't so afraid.

She closed her eyes and thought of Lucas, of his smile, of the way he touched her, the way he looked at her like she was the only thing he could see.

She thought of how he'd treated her. The care he'd taken. Pushing when she needed to be pushed. Holding back when she needed time.

How could she have ever said those things to him? How could she have stood there, after he'd confessed his love, and told him he was going to cheat on her someday?

"You're such a bitch, Carly," she said out loud to her empty office.

And she was. There was no denying it. A scared one. One who had pushed hard at Lucas because he had reached her heart. Because he had challenged her when she wasn't ready to be challenged.

She'd acted like it was Lucas who was wrong, but the truth was, it was her.

She was pretty sure she didn't deserve Lucas, not after that. Not now.

Carly slapped her palms on the desk and stood up. Maybe she didn't deserve Lucas. But she was going to try to get him back anyway.

"What the hell are you doing here, Mac?" Lucas asked, growling at his friend, the friend he hadn't spoken to in over a week.

Mac walked the rest of the way into the barn, like he had every right to be there. Which usually he did, but not now, because Lucas was still pissed at him.

"I don't know," Mac said.

"Maybe you should have thought of a good reason before you drove over here." Lucas bent down and picked a shovel up from the barn floor, standing it up.

"All right, I do know why I'm here."

"Enlighten me then."

"I'm here to apologize."

Lucas froze. "Why exactly?"

"For cheating off of your math test when we were twelve. Why the hell do you think?"

"I should apologize to you."

"Well, you should, but you can do it after I'm done. I'm being the bigger man here."

Lucas leaned back against the barn wall and crossed his arms over his chest. "Go ahead then."

"I think it's pretty obvious I caused some problems between you and Carly. I also embarrassed Carly, which wasn't my intent."

"And you called my character into question, accused me of using your sister for sex."

"Yes," Mac said, teeth gritted. "I did that too."

"And?"

"And I'm sorry."

"Great. I'm sorry I lied to you."

Mac stood there, his expression expectant. "Is that all?"

"Yes. That's all. I'm not sorry about my relationship with Carly, even though, yes, you did screw things up and now she's not speaking to me."

Mac cursed and tugged his hat off, rubbing his hand over his hair. "I'm sorry. I didn't think you were serious about her."

"Honestly? I didn't either. Not at first."

"But you are?"

"I love her."

"Then what's the problem?"

"She doesn't love me back. Or maybe she does, but not enough to stay. To try and learn to trust me."

"The thing with our parents . . . it's been really hard on her. Embarrassing, because she cares what other people think. More than that though, even if she doesn't know it. She's always acted like she was afraid of dating."

"I don't blame her."

"But you want her to change."

"Yeah, I do. But I don't think she will. Not for me. Not right now. Someday, but it's . . . it's not me. I wish it was. But I'm not going to force myself on her."

"If you did that, I would have to kill you."

"I know it." Lucas let out a long breath. "She deserves to be happy. And this relationship scares her."

"So you're just going to let her walk away?"

"That's the thing, Mac. I respect her enough to let her.

Not because I want her to, but because I won't hold her to me. Losing my mother destroyed my dad, but he let her go."

"And our dad won't let our mom go," Mac said.

Lucas shook his head. "I wouldn't cheat on her, ever. But I won't hold her to me when she'd be better off free."

"And that right there makes me think you're the right man for her," Mac said, putting his hat back on and turning away, walking out of the barn.

Lucas pushed the shovel back onto the ground. If only that were true. But she would have to love him to stay, to work at getting over the kind of pain and distrust that had been burned into her over a lifetime.

And he wasn't sure he was the kind of man who inspired that in people.

One thing was sure—people felt empowered to leave him.

But he would give anything for Carly to stay. Anything except her happiness. It was the one cost that was too high, even if it meant he spent the rest of his life being completely miserable.

That, apparently, was love.

Love sucked.

Lucas surveyed the setup of Ride for Hope. Everything was going off perfectly so far. The entire town seemed to be in attendance, and a good percentage of the population from the neighboring towns was there too.

It should have felt good to see so many people turn out for such a good cause. It should have felt good to be a part of it. To have gotten his old rodeo buddies involved.

But nothing felt good at the moment.

Nothing had since his final argument with Carly. Not even making up with Mac, which should have helped a little bit.

The rodeo events hadn't started yet, but people were milling around, eating and playing the different games that had been set up.

A band was playing on the stage, lively country music that made Lucas want to drill a hole in his skull so it could pass through. He didn't want anything lively. He wanted to get drunk and wallow in his problems.

But he wasn't going to. He'd seen what happened when

a man did that. Which meant the only option left was to bear
the full brunt of the pain.

The band stopped playing, a mercy to his ears, and the
lead singer started talking. Thanking everyone for coming,
blah blah blah.

Then he said something that made Lucas's ears perk up.

"Councilwoman Carly Denton is in the dunk tank, and
the price on her head is high. If you want the chance to dunk
Silver Creek's finest lady, you can purchase tickets over at
the concession booth."

Lucas looked over and saw Carly perched on the dunk
tank bench in shorts and a T-shirt, her hair loose around her
shoulders. And if he wasn't mistaken, he could see some
freckles.

His heart stopped for a second, and all he could do was
stare. Then he started walking toward her.

He opened his wallet and pulled out a hundred-dollar
bill, pausing at the concession stand to pick up a ticket and
giving the very shocked woman behind the counter the bill.
"Keep the change," he said.

He didn't take his eyes off Carly as he walked across the
graveled area. Everything in him felt tense, tied up in knots.
And none of it mattered anymore. Their confrontation, all
the things she'd said. It just sort of evaporated. And it left
her. Just her. And she was the only important thing.

He presented the man in front of the tank with his ticket
and collected his ball. He looked at it, at the target, and then
back to Carly. "What are you doing, Carly?" he asked.

There were hundreds of eyes on her, on them. It was a
spectacle, no mistake.

"I thought it was time I put myself out there a little bit.
It's for a good cause and all." She smiled at him, a real smile.
No reserve. No snark.

"You'll mess up your pretty hair."

"It doesn't matter. It's just image, after all."

"It doesn't matter at all," he said, his throat so tight now, he could barely speak. He looked down at the ball in his hands again.

"Oh, but wait just a second before you dunk me." Carly put her palms flat on the bench and pushed herself up into a standing position. "While I have everyone's attention, I wanted to do something."

"What are you doing?" he asked.

"Making an idiot out of myself," she said, her voice low enough for only him to hear, her blue eyes glittering with tears. More public emotion. All for him. Then she straightened and went back to making her announcement. "I just wanted everyone to know that I am in love with Lucas Miller."

There were some cheers, and a lot of laughter. Carly waited for the roar to calm down, and then continued.

"I've spent the past . . . decade really, caring more about what everyone else thought of me than what I thought of myself. And then Lucas . . . helped me find me. And in the process, helped me stop being so afraid. He taught me that love is worth it. And that laughing, having fun, being comfortable in your own skin is more important than being respectable. And that's all." She sat back down. "Dunk me, Miller."

He dropped the ball at his feet. "No way."

"Yes. I'm making a big gesture. Don't steal my gesture. And it's for charity."

"I bought my ticket already." He rounded the back of the dunk tank and climbed the ladder and up onto the bench. "I love you too, Carly."

"Even after what I said?"

"What about what I said?" he asked.

Carly put her hand on his cheek, her thumb sliding over his skin. "You were right, though. I was scared. So I ran. I ran just like I did six years ago. I put walls up between us because I've always known, Lucas. I've always known that you could be the man who meant the world to me. And it terrified me. To know that someone could own that much of me. To know that one person could be everything."

He looked at her face, at the pure, unveiled emotion shining from her. "But the thing is, Carly, you're the woman who means the world to me. And I'll never take you for granted, I'll never betray your trust. I understand what it costs you and I would never, ever do anything to violate that."

Carly smiled, a tear sliding down her cheek. A happy tear this time. And now he knew she would let him wipe it away. He moved his thumb over her damp skin, erasing the trail the drop had left behind. "I believe you."

"My life hasn't had a lot of happy moments," he said. "But this one is so close to perfect, the rest don't seem to matter as much."

"I feel the same way."

He wrapped his arms around her and pulled her in for a kiss, which brought a roar of cheers from their spectators. Everything fit. For once in his life, everything just fit.

"Ready to take a chance with me, Carly Denton?" he asked, kissing her cheek, her forehead.

"More than ready," she said.

And then he held her tight against him and pushed off from the bench, submerging them both in the cold water below.

When they came back up to the surface, she was laughing. "What was that for?"

"I didn't want to spoil your grand gesture, but I didn't want you to make it alone either. We're in this together. We can look like idiots together, and laugh at the whole world."

She kissed him, her lips slippery, cold over his. "I guess you could say we've made a pretty public spectacle now," she said, resting her forehead on his.

"Yeah . . . we did. Are you okay?"

"I've never felt better in my life."

"Great. Now let's get out of this water. I'm experiencing shrinkage."

She slapped his shoulder. "You're such a man."

"Yeah, but you like it."

"I do."

He lifted her into his arms and she clung to his shoulders while he got them both out of the tank. He deposited her slowly back onto the ground. "You need shoes," he said.

She shook her head. "I can be barefoot for a bit."

"Well, Carly Denton, there you are," he said, brushing his thumb over her freckled cheek. "You've been hiding for a long time."

Carly's heart felt like it was going to burst. Looking at Lucas, at the love in his eyes, made her feel strong. It made her feel brave. It made her feel like she didn't have to hide.

"Freckles and all," she said. "But that doesn't mean I won't still put on makeup and nice clothes and high heels."

"I have no issue with that. I think you're beautiful no matter what you wear, or don't wear."

She pulled his hat off of his head and put it on her own before putting her hands on his cheeks and pulling him down for a kiss. "Same goes. You're a man worth making a fool of myself for. You're a man worth the risk. A man worth staying with. Always. I mean, if you want to deal with a woman with a supersized amount of neuroses and a shoe collection that may someday take over the tristate area."

He grinned, that Lucas Miller grin that always made her toes curl. "You know, I think I'm up for it."

Lucas put his arm around her and they walked away from the crowd, out toward the parking area. "Where are you taking me?"

"Somewhere private. Because as thrilled as I am that you're all right sharing our relationship with the public, I'd like to be alone with you too."

"Sounds promising."

"Not just for that," he said, his smile wicked. "I'm going to ask you a question."

Carly's heart fluttered. "Oh, really?"

"Something to do with you letting me love you. With you loving me. With us facing this head-on instead of running away from it."

"You know what?" she asked, her throat tight, tears spilling down her cheeks. "I bet you I'll say yes."

"I'm glad to hear it."

"Lucas," she said. "It's the strangest thing. I always imagined that if I fell in love, it would take something from me. Make me weaker, because it's what I saw in my mother. I don't feel weaker. I feel stronger. I feel more myself than I ever have."

"Well, that's good, Carly, because I love who you are, and I would never want you to be anything or anyone else."

"You make it so I'm not afraid to be myself."

"Do you know what you make me feel like, Carly?"

"What?"

"You make me feel like being myself is enough. I've always questioned it. I wasn't enough for my mother, I wasn't enough for my father, but you make me feel . . . good enough."

"You're so much more than good enough, Lucas Miller." She put her hand on his cheek, her heart overflowing. "You're perfect."

Epilogue

Lucas sometimes wondered if Carly Denton reserved that facial expression particularly for him. He'd never seen her make it at another person. When she smiled at him, it made her eyes glitter with mischief, her cheeks flushed as if she'd just run barefoot through a field.

She smiled at other people, but not like this, never like this. And no one else could make him feel like she did with just one look.

Right now, he thought he was going to burst with that feeling, watching Carly, smiling, floating down the aisle in a white dress, pink flowers in her hands.

"What are you doing here, Lucas?" she asked, an impish smile on her face.

"I'm here to marry you," he said.

"Oh, good, because that's what I got dressed up for."

"This is a pretty public display," he said, taking her hands and pulling her to him.

"Good." She put a hand on his cheek and kissed him. "Let's give them something to talk about."

"You weren't supposed to kiss me yet," he said, looking over at the pastor, who was waiting for them to get down to the business of vows.

"Yeah, but I live dangerously."

"Do you?"

"Yeah. After this, I say we go get some french fries."

"You live on the edge."

"I know," she said. "I know. See if you can keep up."

"I'd love to."

One

Lucy stopped breathing when the front door opened. Oh, Lord. It was Mac Denton. As if her humiliation couldn't be any more acute. As if life had thought all of the sewage it had already rained down on her needed a cherry on top.

Mac Denton was the cherry. And not in a good way.

Well, maybe someday you'll be cleaning my floors.

Echoes from that long-ago yelling match in the halls at Silver Creek High School sounded in her head.

Well, damn. At this point, she hoped she *would* be cleaning his floors, because she needed the money and the place to stay, and she did not have the luxury of being picky.

It was her fault for coming back to Silver Creek. She should have stayed back east. She could have. But she'd kept feeling the pull to home. To a chance to start back at square one and figure out what had gone wrong. To take different steps this time.

Of course, she'd also imagined her parents would be happy to see her, but nothing could have been farther from the truth.

"Hello," she said, straightening her shoulders and trying her hardest to give Mac her cocktail-party smile. The one she'd perfected for her husband's satisfaction during their eight years of marriage. "I'm here about the job. I don't think you and I spoke on the phone. It was someone else."

"My sister." Mac frowned and leaned against the door, his arm over his head, resting on the frame. She couldn't help but notice that he had matured a little bit since high school. And by "matured," she meant he'd gotten an impossibly broad, well-muscled chest and well-defined biceps. Not that she cared about things like that.

"Great. Great," she said. "Nice of her to facilitate this for you."

"Isn't it? Why don't you come in."

He was looking at her funny. Like he hadn't recognized her yet, but like he was sure he was supposed to. She was hoping that he wouldn't get a sudden realization anytime soon, or he'd show her right back out to the front steps and slam the door in her face. And she would deserve it a little bit. But she was hoping in this instance she wouldn't get what she deserved. She needed something a whole lot better than what she'd earned from Mac Denton, and she hoped he was in the mood to give it.

Lucy stepped inside. It was an incredible house, as far as the structure went. Nothing like the homes she'd gone to with her husband during visits to the Hamptons. Nothing even like the homes of her parents' friends. This was the home of someone who worked for a living. A man, obviously, since there was nothing superfluous or soft. The only decor had antlers. There were no curtains. No framed art. No rugs.

Just a large, open living area with exposed beams that flowed into a kitchen with slate-gray flooring and gray marble countertops. The view was the only thing that could be called beautiful. Mountains still capped with snow, marbled blue and white in the distance, and acres of green fields partitioned by fences were all she could see.

No buildings. No streetlights. And the quiet—quiet that was impossible to find in Manhattan.

Yes, there were things about Silver Creek she'd missed. Ironically, the very things she'd often hated when she'd been growing up here.

"Mac Denton." He turned and held out his hand to her, and she held back the *I know* that was hovering on her lips.

"Lucy Carter." It was her married name, and it might just keep him from figuring her out for another few moments. Maybe those few moments would be enough to buy her a little sympathy.

He frowned. "Lucy Carter?"

"Yes."

He gave a slight shrug and then gestured to the couch. "Have a seat." She complied, straightening her skirt as best she could and folding her hands in her lap. "Tell me about your previous work experience."

"I . . . I don't have any."

"You don't have any?" He paused and ran his hand over his hair, his eyes narrowed, his jaw tight. And then he leaned back, a strange half smile curving his lips.

So much for sympathy and anonymity.

"Lucy Ryan. You're Lucy Ryan."

Mac looked down at the woman sitting on his couch. She looked far too expensive to be applying for a position as his housekeeper. It had been his first thought when he'd seen her. Well, his second thought, after he'd done a little appreciating of her figure and just how the black jacket she was wearing conformed to it.

Right after that was when he'd noticed that it really was an expensive jacket. And that it was odd that a woman coming to him for this kind of work would be wearing an outfit that probably cost more than his entire collection of Carhartts combined.

This knowledge of clothing had been brought to him by an array of ex-girlfriends he'd taken on shopping trips out of town. Shopping trips he'd bankrolled, and happily. Being in the position to do that was his greatest achievement in life so far. He'd come from nothing. And funnily enough, the person who'd spent all of high school telling him how nothing he was, was currently sitting on his couch asking for a job.

Interesting.

Lucy Ryan. It all made sense now. He hadn't recognized her. For one thing, she'd given up lightening her hair. It was all dark now, pulled back into a bun, rather than loose around her shoulders. Her makeup was restrained, perfect, designed to make her look elegant and sophisticated. She looked like a woman now, rather than a girl let loose with Daddy's credit card.

"What exactly brings you here to apply for this job? Did you lose a bet?" Maybe against someone who had a long memory of just what a bitch she'd been in high school. To him in particular.

Your mother cleans my floors, you know.

He'd hated her. And all of her friends. Because he really hadn't wanted to care that he and his family were on the bottom rung in terms of respectability, and most days he didn't. But the days he did, the days he went home with his skin crawling with humiliation, usually involved Lucy Ryan and her acerbic tongue.

She lifted her chin, straightened her shoulders. "No. Strange as it may seem, I'm here to apply for a job because I need a job."

"Why do you need a job?"

"I've grown accustomed to sleeping with a roof over my head. I'm also quite fond of eating, so I thought I would take steps to assure it continued."

This Lucy was a very different Lucy. She was brittle. Like a thin sheet of ice. Cold, hard and very delicate. He had the feeling that if he pushed too hard, she might break. Ten years ago he would have liked to watch her break. Would have relished the revenge. It felt different now.

Not as sporting, since it seemed like life might have taken enough potshots at her already.

He wasn't really sure he wanted her in his house. Wasn't sure he owed her anything. In fact, in a lot of ways, it would be a kindness if he sent her somewhere else. So that there wouldn't be any temptation to enjoy the reversal of fortunes.

He should tell her to go. And he opened his mouth to do just that, but different words came out instead.

"That I can help you with. If I decide to give you the job, I'll pay you well. You get a place to stay, and since you'll be cooking for me, there will be food for you as well."

"I get to . . . eat with you?"

"You get to eat my food," he said. He wasn't quite prepared to sit down at a table with her, but then, what was he going to do? Send her to eat outside? That was just a dick move. "With me, of course."

"That's really generous," she said, subdued.

"Not exactly. It seems like it would be a waste to do anything different. You're already cooking."

Lucy grimaced internally. Oh, yes, cooking. She would be cooking. Which she had only a remedial knowledge of, and even less firsthand experience with. Unless building a menu for a caterer counted.

"Of course," she said. She was determined to fake her way through this. She wasn't stupid, and she could work darn hard if she had to. She was sure she could. But when she'd seen the ad in the paper for a housekeeper at a ranch, with room and board in addition to pay, she'd known she wouldn't find anything better.

Not with her limited skill set. She'd quit college when she'd met Daniel, four years her senior and ready to marry her and get on with making a place in society.

"I have to ask what brings you back here."

Of course he did. "Go ahead," she said.

"What brings you back here?"

"I was tired of the urban lifestyle. New York is a little crazy for me."

"And your husband is . . . ?"

"In New York. And he is my ex-husband," she said. It was such a relief to say that. Such a relief to have it be true. She'd met Daniel and fallen for him in almost the same moment. Their entire courtship had been a blur. Unfortunately, their marriage hadn't been quite so blurry.

She'd felt every day of it. All two thousand nine hundred and twenty days of it. Eight years of wedded non-bliss.

No, she supposed that wasn't fair. She'd been happy for a while. Happy until she'd really started to understand that the reason she was starting to feel so inept, so stupid, so ugly, was that every day her husband chipped away at more and more of her self-esteem. His words eating at who she was like acid.

By the time she'd realized it, he had completely changed the way she'd seen herself. She'd been so far down, so far removed from the woman she'd been when she'd met him that she feared his words had turned her into that new woman forever. The woman who would never be anything without him.

Well, she was going to prove him wrong. Or herself, since, in the end, she'd really started to believe that what Daniel said was true.

"Sorry to hear that," he said.

She sniffed and looked down at her nails. "Well, it was for the best. We grew apart." An innocuous and somewhat untrue statement. There was so much more to it than that. But there always was. And she wasn't dragging her skeletons out of the closet for Mac Denton's amusement.

She would be enduring humiliation enough here; she hardly needed to add to it.

"Is that so? Too bad they don't cover 'unless we grow apart' in marriage vows."

She tried not to wince visibly. It was, she found, very easy for other people to pass judgment. She tried to think of all the times she'd been guilty of doing the same. "It's not a popular one at ceremonies," she said. "Tends to dampen the mood."

"I imagine." He looked at her, his blue eyes assessing. "Lucy, you don't have any job experience at all, do you?"

"Well, not as such. But I did organize a great many events at my husband's family estate. Big events for hundreds of people. That required exceptional organization skills and the ability to work well with an array of different people."

"I'm not a big one for organization, and I don't really have an array of people at my ranch, so I'm not sure if this is the place for you."

"Mac," she said, her voice trembling a little bit, to her utter horror. "Please. I need this job, and I haven't got a hope in hell of getting hired anywhere else. You know that." If she'd had any pride left at all, it would be in pieces on the floor right now. But she didn't think there was any room for pride in this situation. She was desperate. Simple as that.

"You haven't got a hope in hell of getting hired here, sweetheart. Given our history, it took some pretty serious cojones for you to come up here asking at all."

"I didn't know this was your ranch."

"No, I imagine you didn't. Bet you thought us Dentons would never crawl our way out of the gutter." Again, she fought hard to keep her expression composed. Every inter-action she'd ever had with him before had been negative. And it had been because of her. Hearing her own words turned around like this . . . it was humbling. And she hadn't thought it was possible to be more humbled than she was. "Well, my parents haven't. Oh, they're kept comfortable by Carly and me. Physically. We can't do anything about their emotional well-being. They're still putting on Silver Creek's favorite soap opera. But as far as Carly goes, as far as I go, we've moved up in life a little."

"As you can see," she said, nearly gagging on the words, "I've moved down a bit."

"Go on, Lucy, why don't you go ask Mommy and Daddy for a bailout?"

"You don't think I tried that first?"

That stopped Mac short. "They wouldn't help you?"

"No. They figure if they refuse to help me, I'll have no choice but to go back to my husband. Where I belong. They think I won't be able to make it by myself. And so does he."

"I don't know a whole lot about the guy you ended up married to, but isn't he loaded?"

"Big-time loaded," she said. It felt good to say something like that. To say something that felt more genuine, and not so stiff and formal.

"And why isn't he now half as loaded as he was before? Shouldn't you have walked away with something?"

"I signed a prenup. Which I thought was silly, because— we were getting married for life. But it was for our protection, you see. Mine too." She bit the inside of her cheek and tried to keep back the tears of frustration that were building. "Because I instigated the divorce, I didn't get anything."

"But you did it anyway?"

"My sanity was worth more than money."

"And you thought your parents would help you land on your feet."

"Well, yes. I did. More fool me."

"And now you think I'm going to help you land on your feet?"

She tilted her chin up, every cruel and hideous thing she'd ever said to him ringing in her ears. "I don't expect you to give me anything, Mac Denton. I just want to work."

"You happy to scrub my floor, princess? If I recall, just

being the son of the woman who cleaned your kitchen was enough to make me dirt beneath your pretty heels."

"I'll do whatever I have to." She tried to ignore the shame that was slowly creeping over her.

"Now that's a real interesting thought, darlin'." His voice was deep, and if she wasn't imagining things, and she was sure she wasn't, laced with innuendo.

It should have made her angry. Should have shocked her. Upset her.

It didn't. Instead, it sent a little shiver of deep, unending longing through her. She recognized it, because longing for things out of her reach, things she couldn't have and shouldn't have, was something she did all the time these days.

She looked up at him. "I'll do whatever you want."

Well, hell. This entire encounter was starting to sound like a porno. He had a gorgeous woman in high heels applying to work for him and promising to do whatever he wanted. Now all that was left was for her to show him her *qualifications.*

Rather than turning him on, that thought only made him feel dirty. He wasn't into taking advantage of women; not in the least.

And while his body wasn't immune to Lucy Carter née Ryan, the thought of taking that *anything you want* offer and twisting it to suit his physical needs made him feel sick inside.

He just wasn't that particular brand of bastard.

Now he *was* the brand of bastard who enjoyed the thought of Lucy scrubbing his floors. To enjoy watching her slum it for a while. Yeah, he was that much of a bastard, and he was self-aware enough to admit it.

And then when she was done playing at being a big strong independent woman and went back to her husband, fine. But in the meantime, he would enjoy watching the princess of Silver Creek get her hands a little dirty.

And just like that, his decision was made.

"All right, Lucy, when can you start?"

"Now?" she asked, her eyes wide, as though he'd shocked her completely with the question.

"Now?" he echoed.

"Well, I'm basically homeless until I start this job."

Well, now, that did make him feel a little like an ass. "Not anymore. Come on out back with me." She sat, clutching her handbag in front of her. He looked down at those long, shapely legs, and farther still to her shoes. "I don't know how those are going to survive the mud."

"I'll be fine," she said.

"All right then, this way." He started to head out of the living area and toward the kitchen, but he noticed Lucy was still sitting on the couch, dark eyes wide. "Are you going to follow me?"

"Did you just give me the job?"

"Yes. Unless, of course, you intend to do it from the couch, in which case I may have to rethink the offer."

"No"—she scrambled to her feet—"no, I'm ready to go. Just show me the . . . stuff."

"Kitchen," he said, indicating the big open space. "I eat lunch with the hands, and I have a guy who cooks in the big kitchen out by the barns for everyone, so you're off the hook for that. But I take breakfast in here, and dinner. And I'll need you to take care of that. Otherwise, during the day, just regular housecleaning stuff. I have a full laundry room, there's a vacuum somewhere. I'm only one guy, so it shouldn't be too hard."

Truthfully, he didn't really know what all went into taking good care of a household. His mother had done it as a job for other people, and she'd been too tired at the end of the day to do much of it for them.

And, of course, he didn't do a very great job of it himself. He was way too tired at the end of the day to do anything but put a frozen pizza in the oven. Carly had been coming over and making sure he didn't starve, either by giving him the leftovers of her and Lucas's dinner or by coming over and cooking for him.

She'd drawn the line at laundry, though, and he'd been managing to get the clothes clean and dry, but he hadn't managed to get them in the closet.

He'd been fishing his clothes out of a laundry basket every day for the past few months, ever since the loss of his previous housekeeper.

Still, though, with full-time hours to devote to the job, it couldn't possibly be too hard.

"Otherwise, the cottage is back this way."

"Cottage?"

"Yeah, that's the 'room' part of the room and board that was in the ad," he said.

"I wasn't expecting a cottage. I was thinking . . . a room."

The idea of sharing a room in his house with Lucy sent a shot of heat through his veins that burned like whiskey. He wasn't sure why he was reacting so strongly to her. Why the room he'd thought of had been his own bedroom. His own bed.

Lucy was beautiful; she always had been. But a sweet face didn't atone for a personality as sour as hers. Not that she seemed overly sour now—but she'd come to apply for a job. And even in those circumstances, there was a little bit of tartness to her.

He shifted his weight and tried to ignore the heat pouring through him. Assigning her a flavor, even a borderline unpleasant one, wasn't helping with his issues. Because now he was wondering if she tasted as sour as she seemed, like a green apple, or if she was sweet like she looked. Like a peach.

Oh, dammit.

He shifted again and tried to redirect his blood flow back to where it belonged.

He opened the back door and held it for her, waiting for her to walk outside before he closed it. She brushed past him, and the wind kicked up, blowing her scent back in his direction. Honeysuckle.

She smelled sweet. Which made him think she very likely tasted—

No. Not going there.

He led the way down a trail that was worn through the grass. It was only wide enough to walk single file, and Lucy stayed resolutely behind him.

"This was one of the original structures on the property. It's pretty old, and it's not fancy, but . . . it ought to do." For the first time he wondered if it would do for Lucy. He knew what kind of house she'd been raised in. A house on the waterfront in Silver Creek's premier gated community. Not a ranch house. Not even a ranch.

And then there was that husband of hers. Everyone in town knew about Daniel Carter, how well Lucy had done for herself marrying him. Her mother had made sure of it. He was part of the elite social set over in New York, an old money family that still had money. And manor houses. Anyone who talked to Mrs. Ryan for longer than a few moments heard about the family's impressive collection of manor houses.

The cottage came into view, and Mac couldn't help but feel a small bit of amusement over the situation. This was no manor house. Just a small, faded blue structure with a slab foundation and poured concrete steps leading up to a screen door that squeaked when it swung open.

"It's clean," he said. "At least it should be. Carly said she hired a one-time cleaning service to come in and make sure it was nice for you."

Lucy was looking at the cottage, her expression bleak. "So, you and Carly are still close?"

He nodded slowly. "Yeah." He couldn't imagine not seeing his sister a few times a week. She'd been a huge part of his sanity and stability while they were growing up. "Especially now that she's marrying Lucas."

Lucy blinked a few times. "Lucas . . . Lucas from school?"

"Yep." He wasn't surprised that Lucy couldn't remember Lucas's last name. Neither of them had rated on her social radar.

"That's nice."

Her tone was so even, so carefully modulated. He could tell she was hiding a whole lot of emotion— he wasn't sure what she was hiding, but he was sure there was something. What he didn't get was why he wondered, even for a second, what it was. It didn't matter. He wasn't going to try to get to know her, or get her to talk about her feelings. He was hiring her to clean his house.

"I'll let you go in and get settled," he said.

Mac nodded once, then turned and walked away, leaving Lucy standing there in front of a house she was afraid might fall down around her ears.

This wasn't what she'd expected. Not at all. She should go inside and see where she was living now. See just how far she'd fallen.

She opted, instead, to watch Mac Denton walk away for just a little while longer. It wasn't often, if ever, that she allowed herself the illicit thrill of checking a man out. And with Mac, there was a lot of good there to check out.

She could have laughed at the absurdity of it if she thought she could possibly show that much emotion without crying.

Here she was, newly divorced, disowned by her parents, about to move into a place the size of one of the walk-in closets she'd had in her ex's house, and she was looking at the way the denim of Mac's jeans hugged his butt.

Well, there had to be *some* perks to her position.

She blew out a breath and walked up the concrete steps

that led into her new house. They were bowed up and cracked on the edges. The screen door pushed open easily, and she wondered if it latched at all. It also squeaked like a son-of-a-gun.

The kitchen was tiny. Faded yellow cabinets lined the wall, and peeling linoleum was spread over the floor. She'd never been in a place this run-down. Unless you counted structures that bore the title "barn" and not "house."

The floor creaked beneath her feet as she walked past an old living room with a chair and little else, down the hall and to the single bedroom. There was one window, lace curtains and a bed with a patchwork quilt.

She moved to the bed and sat on the edge, the springs groaning beneath her.

"What did I get myself into?" she asked. No one answered, of course.

She had to wonder, for the very first time, if leaving Daniel had been a mistake. She'd been unhappy with him, but she didn't feel particularly happy now.

She thought back. Could see his face—distant, haughty, angry, disdainful. Could hear his words. So cold, designed to cut away what remained of her self-confidence. What remained of the way she saw herself. He was intent on removing vital bits of her, leaving her unable to function without him.

And finally, just as he'd been about to succeed, she'd looked in the mirror and seen how much she'd changed. Had seen that she was too thin. Her dark eyes flat, cold. The light behind them snuffed out.

He never hit you, did he, darling?

No. The answer to her mother's question had been no. Daniel Carter would never do anything so common as to use his fists to control a woman. And he didn't have to. His words were even more effective.

Everyone has bad days. He has stresses at work, surely. He can't spend all of his time propping up your self-esteem.

Her mother's response to her denial of physical abuse had nearly broken her. Because it had taken Lucy so long to realize that the things Daniel said to her were wrong. To realize that his words were a form of abuse, and that she didn't have to take it.

Only to have that realization undermined when she'd arrived home.

"I didn't deserve that," she said. "I didn't."

She only wished her own parents didn't think she did. Or maybe that was the wrong way to look at it—but it felt like they thought she must have deserved it. Like the vows she'd taken to the smiling man on her wedding day should have, logically, extended to the monster he'd revealed himself to be.

And she just couldn't believe it. Not anymore.

Which meant that regardless of the shabby state of her new home, it was *her* new home. And she wouldn't doubt her decision again.

Because no matter how run-down it was, there was no one here to insult her. No one here to berate and belittle her.

Just then, the little house seemed more beautiful than any manor home ever had.

Three

How hard can it be?

Lucy asked herself that question while she rummaged through the pantry. Mac had food. Plenty of it. There had to be some way to combine some ingredients to make an edible meal.

She felt a little shot of panic when she looked at the schedule that was posted on the fridge. She imagined the schedule—useful, neat and organized—had not been made by Mac.

Another helpful tidbit from Carly, she imagined. But it wasn't helping her now. She only had an hour to make dinner, and she was pretty sure she'd never cooked in her life. Unless pouring cereal counted. And she was pretty sure it didn't.

Lucy did some more digging and found a cookbook in one of the cupboards. There was a recipe for tacos, which seemed straightforward enough. Especially if she opened the jar of salsa and the can of refried beans, rather than making her own from scratch. And Mac had both of those things ready to go.

A couple of thawed-out chicken breasts would boil quickly, and she put them in a pot of water and put the burner on high heat.

Then she found an apron stashed in the pantry and tied it around her waist, hoping to shield her nice outfit from any potential oil splatter as she prepared to make the taco shells.

The instructions were clear, but after mangling a couple of tortillas, she opted against folding them, and just laid them flat in the pan and let them fry. Tostadas would be good too. They were basically the same thing anyway.

An hour later, she had a spread that looked more than vaguely edible and a sense of pride that was so unexpected, so foreign, she was hardly able to identify it at first.

Along with that came a significant hunger pang. She was more than ready to eat, and Mac had invited her to eat with him, but the idea of that seemed . . . wrong, somehow. Strange.

If they were strangers, it might have been easier. But they weren't. They had a pesky history that made her blush just thinking about it. She'd been so full of it back then. So sure that life couldn't touch her because she was a Ryan. She was set for life. College paid for. A ticket out of Silver Creek and into society anywhere else if she wanted it, and she had wanted it. And she'd taken it.

And now she was back. With none of the certainty. With none of that feeling of inborn sparkle that she'd thought made her better than other people.

She jumped when the front door slammed shut.

"Smells good."

She looked up and saw Mac walking toward her. "Great. I'm glad. Everything is . . . set out. So if you want to go ahead and sit, I'll just leave you to it."

"I thought I told you that you could eat with me."

"You did. But . . . it just feels awkward. I mean . . . did your last housekeeper eat with you?"

"Yes."

Lucy felt a brief burst of annoyance at the thought of another woman sitting down to dinner with him, and she wasn't sure why. Just because it was another reminder that she was in no way unique, maybe.

Get over yourself.

Yeah, she had to get over herself. And over all the junk that Daniel's words had buried inside of her, beneath her skin.

Probably not today, though.

"So you were . . . friendly with her, then? Why did she quit?"

"She retired. To spend more time with her grandchildren. They live out of state, and she moved closer."

"Oh." The fact that the other woman was a grandmother made her feel better. It shouldn't have, because she shouldn't have felt bothered to begin with.

"Yeah. Have a seat."

She complied. She was hungry, after all, and this was, apparently, normal to him.

Mac put two of the tortillas on his plate and loaded them up with all of the fixings she'd provided. Then he got up and went to the fridge, and her stomach sank a little bit.

"What did I forget?" she asked.

"Beer. Want one?"

She almost said no. She didn't drink beer. Never had. Wine and wine coolers, yes. Some nice mixed drinks at a party, yes. But nothing so common as beer.

"Yes," she said.

He nodded and pulled two bottles out of the fridge, pausing to pop the tops before returning to the table and setting one down in front of her.

"Sorry, I'll remember next time," she said, curling her hand around the cold glass.

"It's no big deal. First day and all."

"Still . . . thanks."

He raised his bottle. "To new beginnings?"

She raised hers too. "Why not?" She tipped it back and took a sip. It was kind of disgusting, but she relished the choice. If Daniel could see her now, drinking beer from a bottle across the table from a cowboy with muddy boots, he would think she'd gone crazy. Maybe she had. But why not? Her entire life was tilted sideways. She might as well enjoy it. With a little alcohol and a little eye candy.

She took another sip of the beer and grimaced. Okay, "enjoy" was too strong a word where that was concerned.

"What do you like for breakfast?" she asked.

"Eggs. Bacon. Whatever. Normal stuff."

Not cereal then. Damn. That would have been easy.

"Great." She looked down at her plate. "I bet you're used to a slightly larger spread than this too."

"Usually, but this is fine."

"You don't have to go easy on me."

"Trust me," he said. "I'm not."

"You don't just feel sorry for me?"

"Not in the least."

She frowned. *She* felt sorry for her. "All right. What do you feel?"

"Amused, mainly, that my little jab about you cleaning my floors has come to pass."

She set her fork down. "Low blow, Denton."

He shrugged. "Maybe, but no one's perfect, and I haven't forgotten our last big conversation."

Neither had she. It was weird, because she didn't know what had started it. Not really. She'd said something terrible; she had no doubt about that. She couldn't remember what— only that this time Mac's ears hadn't turned red, and he hadn't looked down and walked away. This time, he'd turned around, hands clenched into fists, and he'd hit her back verbally. Called her on what a bitch she was. He was the first person to ever do that.

And then he'd told her to watch what she said, because someday, she might be cleaning his floors.

Karma was, in fact, a bigger bitch than *she* was.

"Can you call a screaming match a conversation?" she asked, feeling subdued.

"I don't know. Maybe confrontation?"

"Maybe."

"Do you remember it?" he asked.

"Of course I do. It wasn't every day I went toe-to-toe with a guy twice my size with half the school looking on."

"No. Because most people never stood up to you."

She shook her head. "No. They didn't. So what made you do it?" she asked. It was suddenly imperative to know what made someone change the way things worked. What the last straw was.

Weird that she was asking with herself cast as the bully. But she wanted to know. Because she'd hit a wall a year ago with her husband. The enough-is-enough point. She wanted to know what had made Mac reach that point with her.

"I had a whole lot of opportunity to feel like I was beneath the people around me. I was reminded of it whenever people invited friends over and I wasn't included. Or when I was and I couldn't reciprocate because there was no way I could have anyone over to my house. Only Lucas ever came, and that's just because he was worse off than I was. My whole life was a reminder of how far beneath you I was, and I wasn't going to listen to you tell me about what I already knew."

She felt like she'd been punched in the stomach. "I'm sorry I did that," she said. "To everyone, not just you."

"You live and learn."

"Yeah. You do." She looked down at her food. "So, is that why you hired me? A little revenge to go with your dinner?"

"There's a lame joke in there somewhere about what dishes are best served cold, but I'm going to skip it. And yeah, a little bit, I'm not going to lie."

"Fair enough."

"But I'm still going to pay you. I'm still going to let you stay here. Until you decide you've had enough."

"Of what?"

"Of slumming it with the peasants. I'm not trying to be cruel here, Lucy, but work is hard. Most people wouldn't do it if they had the choice, and you've proven that by *not* doing it when you had the choice. I can't imagine, with other options open, you'd choose to stay here."

"Okay, and how do you think I'll go back to not needing work? How is it you think I'll magically slide back into my old tax bracket?"

He just looked at her, blue eyes locked with hers. "You'll go back to your husband."

"You think so?"

"I do. Because in the end, whatever was going on between you two, I doubt it's worth giving up all that to come and clean all this," he said, sweeping his hand over his surroundings.

She put her hands flat on the table. "Yeah, of course. Money is awesome, right?" she said, feeling a little bubble of hysteria forming in her chest. "I mean . . . why would you ever leave money? What the hell could be more important than the money? Why would you need to be treated like a human being with thoughts and emotions when you could have all the money? Screw love and affection. Who needs it when you have Prada?" She picked up her fork and pushed on the tines with her forefinger. "Yeah, you're right. I'll probably go back. Because it was so great to live with a man who was always telling me what an empty-headed bimbo I was. I mean, it wasn't ideal, sure, but we had money. And money wins in the end, right? Not strength. Not anything else."

"Lucy . . ."

She stood up. "I would like nothing more than to quit. And to storm out of here with my dignity and my scruples and to not give you the satisfaction of ever, ever seeing me scrub your damned floors. But I can't. We both know it. At least, I hope now we both know it. This isn't a game, Mac. I'm not playing at self-respect and independence. I *need* it. I can't go back to not having it."

She pushed her chair back and walked out of the room, her hands shaking, her breath coming in short, harsh gasps. She'd never yelled at Daniel like that. Not once. Even when she'd told him she wanted a divorce, she hadn't said that much. She'd learned not to give him any of her emotions. She'd been tired of having them used against her. Tired of having all of her vulnerable spots exposed and wounded.

But she hadn't been able to hold it back with Mac. Because she couldn't stand the thought of him believing what everyone else did.

You'll have to go back to him, her mother had said, wringing her hands.

You'll come back on your hands and knees. A promise from Daniel.

No. She wouldn't. She was better than that. Stronger than that. No one else thought so. Hell, she wasn't even sure if it was true. But she had to keep going. No matter what.

She couldn't go back to being Lucy Ryan, queen bitch of Silver Creek High, and she didn't want to go back to that anyway. She couldn't go back to being Lucy Carter, Daniel Carter's wife. His trophy in public, his verbal punching bag in private.

That meant she had to find something else to be. And since she wasn't getting help from anyone, she would have to do it herself.

Days later and Mac still felt like a total ass. Which he was. He hadn't been able to resist taking a dig at her, and when he'd done it, he'd unearthed a whole bunch of stuff he was sure they both would have rather had stayed buried.

Yeah, he admitted, he'd assumed that the deal with her

husband had been something petty, like him slashing her shoe allowance, but that was only because he'd envisioned adult Lucy being the same as seventeen-year-old Lucy.

But he'd miscalculated. She was different. She was older. Sadder. Tougher. Not in that way she'd been as a teenager. Not tough like she'd pretended to be, walking down the halls of the high school, insulated by family money and reputation. This was something deep. Something solid.

A stone wall that she'd put up inside of herself, shoring up her defenses so she couldn't be hurt.

He knew all about that.

He didn't want to relate to her. Didn't want to find common ground with the society princess. But there it was. Common ground, whether he liked it or not.

Of course, they wouldn't have a chance to explore that common ground, not with the way she was avoiding him. She was serving up dinners—simple dinners at that—and ducking out to do the laundry or some other chore, then cleaning up and taking her own meal back to her room.

Which was fine. Her prerogative. He was hardly going to force someone who worked for him to join him for dinner. That would just be sad.

But still, he sort of wished she would. And it had everything to do with the fact that he was a little lonely for human companionship since Lucas and Carly were engaged and involved in their own life together now, and not so much in his. And it had nothing to do with the fact that Lucy Carter smelled like honeysuckle and had a bite like a tart apple.

No. It had nothing to do with that.

Lucy's little blue car pulled into the driveway and up to the house, and Mac watched her park. Watched her movements a little more closely than a non-creepy person who signed a woman's paychecks should, he realized.

But the realization didn't stop him from watching.

She got out and went to the trunk, pulling a couple of

paper bags out and shutting it before heading up toward the house.

"Can I get those for you?"

She stopped. "These?" She looked down at the two bags. "I kind of have them already." She turned away from him again and started up the steps to the front porch. He followed at a quick pace and beat her to the door, pushing it open for her.

"What's for dinner?" he asked.

"I'm trying a roast. I went and bought vegetables. I assume one could easily find beef around here."

"Yeah. One might," he said dryly. He had some of the most highly sought-after beef in the country. And that wasn't a euphemism.

"Anyway, I thought I might make an apple pie too. I have a cookbook—how hard could it be?"

"Hard," he said. "Had you ever cooked before last week?"

"Not once."

That explained the hit-or-miss nature of the food that had ended up on his plate. She'd more or less done a decent job, but his previous housekeeper had kept the house up and provided him with fresh-baked bread for every meal, home-made pies and cakes, real mashed potatoes with an ungodly amount of butter and meat roasted to perfection.

Americanized tostadas, spaghetti with sauce from a jar and hot dogs weren't quite in the same league, though he'd said nothing. Not even when he'd crunched his way through that pasta.

He wasn't sure why he was preserving her ego. Why he felt the importance of letting her have this. He really wasn't sure at all. It would be more fun to simply ignore the fact that she was hurting, that she was human, and take a certain amount of petty glee in her circumstances.

But he found he wasn't as big of a bastard as he'd previously believed.

"Well, you're doing all right," he said, crossing the living room and following her into the kitchen.

"Effusive praise coming from one such as yourself," she said, her tone stiff.

"Effusive praise?"

She set the bags on the counter. "Yeah. I feel honored that I did 'all right' for you."

"Fine, your cooking is the best I've ever had," he said. "I can't remember any of the dinners I ate before yours. All that other spaghetti meant nothing to me, baby."

She rolled her eyes. "Please tell me you don't actually say that to women."

"Why? Something your ex might say?"

He didn't know what in the hell had possessed him to ask that. He was perfectly content to let her have her secrets. More than. He didn't care what had happened to her, didn't care what would happen to her. He was doing his slightly self-indulgent good deed by letting her stay here and work for him.

She laughed, but it wasn't a fun, light sound. It was brittle. Bitter. "Oh, no. Not even . . . no. That would require actually caring what I thought about him. It would require him having some idea of what I felt. Or at least wanting to preserve my feelings. He didn't want to do that."

"He didn't?" He was still asking. Why was he still asking?

"No. It's impossible to control a woman who thinks she's important. You have to remind her that she isn't, any way you can. And then she starts to believe that . . . that without you, she won't last. She won't have anything. So that, no matter what you do, she won't leave. And those men never have to explain it when they eat other . . . spaghetti."

He felt like someone had reached into his chest and clenched their fist tight around whatever organs they could grab. "That's not . . . that's not what real men do, Lucy."

"It's what plenty of them do, though. And not just men—women too. My mother is exhibit A. She told me to leave and not to come back without my wedding ring on. Like without Daniel I'm not even a whole person." She looked down, then back up, the pain in her eyes raw, too real. Too hard to ignore. "I worry that they're right sometimes. I was with him for so long, and I don't really know what I'm doing on my own."

He looked at Lucy, really looked at her. At the lines that bracketed her mouth, the shadows under her eyes, the sadness in them that made the deep brown color look flat. Haunted.

How had he missed it before? How had he missed just how much she'd changed?

"You're doing just fine," he said. "I'll be back in for dinner."

She nodded. "Okay."

"Okay." He turned around and walked away. And he still couldn't breathe.

Four

Lucy didn't remember ever having to saw through a pie before. But that was essentially what she was doing with her pie. She was trying so hard. It wasn't fair. She'd even accosted Sarah Larsen in the produce aisle, someone she'd vaguely remembered from high school as being wholesome and the kind of girl who probably watched Martha Stewart after school, and asked her for tips.

She made it through the final crust layer and used the pie server to get it onto Mac's plate. The filling oozed out, and it looked good at least. Well, the crust looked good too; it was just more like a piece of wood in texture than it was a flaky pastry.

The plan was to scurry back to her own house and not join him for any portion of the meal, as she'd been doing for the past week. It was just more comfortable that way. There was something about him, a sexy something about him, and she really didn't like that she noticed it.

Not to mention the fact that she had told him too much about her relationship with Daniel. And also Mac was most definitely in a position where he might enjoy hearing about all the junk that had happened to her since she'd left Silver Creek, and that was really quite off-putting.

Mainly, though, it was the sexy thing.

She walked over to the dining table and set the dessert in front of him. "Enjoy," she said, handing him a fork, a false smile firmly plastered on her face.

"Thanks," he said. "Aren't you going to join me?"

"Uh . . . no. I haven't even had dinner yet, so I'll probably just take my plate of pot roast out to the house."

"Why don't you sit and have pie?"

"I just said."

"Did you?"

She nodded slowly. "Yes. I didn't have dinner."

"So what? It's the perk of being an adult. Of being your own person. Eat the pie first."

"It's not how you're supposed to do it."

"So. What. Lucy Ryan . . . Carter. Whichever. You need to eat dessert first."

She looked at Mac, at the slight quirk in his lips, the sparkle in his eyes, and a shiver ran through her, whispering along her veins like electricity over a wire. There was something irresistible about that look he was giving her. Something intense. That there was anything in his eyes at all, beyond boredom, or amusement, or disdain, made it all feel new. As if a man had never looked at her before.

And for a moment, she could almost believe it was true. Could almost feel the last eight years fall away. Could feel something warm and hopeful building in her chest.

"All right." She turned on her heel and walked back into the kitchen, sawing herself another piece of pie and plopping it onto a plate. She was extremely skeptical of the pie's viability, but she wasn't going to show him that she was aware of her vulnerability. She wouldn't be able to hide its existence, not once he took a bite, but looking scared of her own food just wouldn't do.

She returned to the table and took a position in the chair at the very end corner of the table, as far from him as possible without sitting directly across from him. She'd been at the foot of someone's table for too long. She wasn't going there again.

Mac was the first one to take a bit of the pie. His fork clunked against the ceramic plate when it finally broke through the crust, proving just how much force it had taken.

She winced, but watched him lift the bite to his lips. He put it in his mouth and chewed for a lot longer than anyone should have to chew a bit of pie.

He swallowed, and the motion looked labored. "See? Dessert first is good for you."

"You aren't having dessert first, you already had dinner. And you don't sound very convincing."

"I've never had piecrust done in quite this style," he said, poking at the dessert on his plate with his fork.

"I'm sure it's not that different," she said, pushing her own fork through the crust and quickly shoveling a small bite into her mouth.

Oh, Lord, it was chewy. So chewy she was having a hard time getting through it.

She swallowed. "Okay, yeah, that's pretty bad. But the filling isn't. Is fifty percent a passing grade?"

"Not so much."

She peeled the top crust back from her piece and selected a cinnamon-and-sugar-covered apple from the center. She took a bite and smiled. "Actually, it's really good without that rubber crust."

Mac stood up and went to the counter, taking the pie plate and bringing it back to the table. He took his fork and pried off the entire top of it, leaving only the filling exposed and digging a forkful of apple from the center.

"You can't do that!" she said.

"Yes, I can. I can eat the part I want, and you can eat dessert first. Pull your chair this way."

"You're lawless, Mac Denton."

"Happily."

She stood up and moved down to the chair that was just next to his and followed his lead, taking an apple-only bite. "Okay, this is better."

"There are perks to being a little bit lawless."

"Fine. Fine, there are perks."

"Like not having to take the good with the bad. You just remove the bad."

"Too bad life doesn't actually work that way."

"Are you getting philosophical over pie?"

She shrugged and took another bite. "Over pie filling anyway."

"You seem like you might be a little lawless yourself."

She froze mid-chew. "Do I?"

"You left your husband, even though the decision was unpopular."

She swallowed and looked back down at her plate. "Uh, yeah, unpopular to say the least. But that was a little bigger than just dealing with inedible piecrust. He was . . . Daniel Carter is a competent businessman, a respected boss and a beloved friend to many in our little circle. But the thing about Daniel is that he likes to be in control. He can hide that okay in other areas of his life, or apply it and use it to his advantage. In terms of being married to someone like that though . . . I just couldn't take it anymore."

"Did he hurt you?"

"Not the way you mean. But that's half of the problem. I didn't show up at my parents' house with a black eye and horror stories about Daniel's temper. That, I think, would have made me justified in my parents' eyes. But . . . it was a lot more difficult to try and explain the way he was. The subtle ways he made me feel like I was beneath him. Like I wasn't smart enough to do anything. To get anything right."

Mac frowned. "What did he do?"

"It's . . . it's hard to sum up eight years of that kind of

thing. It's like waves on a rock, you know? It just wears you down over time. The best example I have is that I spent weeks working on organizing this dinner party for him and his colleagues. Everything seemed to go fine and I was so happy because he seemed happy with it. So when everyone left, I was shocked when he . . . he just turned around and asked me how I could be so careless with everything. He said it's not like I had to do any actual work for it. I didn't have to cook or clean, so why was everything done so poorly? The menu I picked was haphazard, the decorations were awful. And worst of all, I looked like I'd just rolled out of bed. He was always telling me I'd let myself go. That I was looking my age. Asking if I had put on a few pounds. That last time, that last dinner party, was my breaking point, and I don't think you can possibly understand it unless you realize that it was like that all the time."

She looked back up at Mac, who was silent, his eyes trained on her. Emotion, nerves, knotted together in a tight ball in her chest. She'd never told anyone. She'd never spoken the whole story out loud. Never acknowledged how bad it had made her feel. She looked for judgment there, for blame, and she didn't see it. She took a breath and continued.

"I didn't realize that was what he was doing, of course. I like to think if I had, I wouldn't have stayed for so long. But that night, the night of the dinner party, when I was standing there feeling like the biggest failure in the world because my husband thought that my choice of shrimp cocktail was cliché, I realized what he'd turned me into. I was a bitch in high school, but at least I liked myself. At least I was excited to get up in the morning and be me. By that point in my marriage I was struggling every day to be the woman he expected me to be. Not the woman I was. I didn't even know who I was, because I went from being an immature teenager to being Daniel Carter's trophy wife, and there was no transition period. No in-between."

"And you left."

"I waited to do that until I had seen a lawyer and gotten together all the legal papers that needed to be gathered. Then I had someone serve him at work when I was safely at a hotel."

"Did you really think he might hurt you?"

She shook her head. "Not physically. But I was afraid that I might not be strong enough if he got a chance to talk to me. A chance to dig his hooks back in. I got this amazing gift, this moment of clarity, and I didn't want to go back to how I'd been thinking before. To this simpering, ridiculous woman who did whatever Daniel wanted because I was trying to be his version of perfect."

"And the divorce is final now?"

"Yes. It went quickly because the prenup was so straightforward."

"And you knew that by being the one to serve papers, you wouldn't get a penny."

"I didn't care."

"What about now?" he asked.

"What? Now that I have to clean your house for a living? Okay, I care a little more, but I'd still rather be here and not have to deal with all that. I know for a fact that money doesn't matter all that much when you feel like absolute garbage all the time."

Mac shook his head. "If I ever meet that guy in a dark alley . . . Hell, if I meet him in a brightly lit street, I'm going to cave his face in."

A promise of violence shouldn't have made her feel quite so warm and fuzzy inside, but it did. Maybe because no one had ever stood up for her with such vehemence. Or at all. Her parents had been of the opinion that she should simply accept the dynamic of her marriage and not be so sensitive. Even her lawyer had seemed to quietly find her stupid, throwing away all that money over a few insults every now and again.

No one had seemed to think she was worth more. No one

had told her to take a stand, to take back her self-esteem. No one seemed to find her self-esteem all that important.

Except Mac, who really shouldn't have any reason to want to see her happy. Mac, who she'd insulted and belittled in high school. Mac, who knew what it was like to face real hardship in life.

He was the one who seemed to think she was worth more than a place on Daniel Carter's trophy shelf.

"You have no idea how much I appreciate that," she said, blinking back sudden and unexpected tears. She didn't know why she was feeling so emotional. She'd learned years ago to keep her emotions trapped beneath the surface. To let things look like they'd rolled right off even when they'd sunk down deep.

"You're an easy woman to please."

"Maybe I am," she said. "No one's ever really tried to please me, so the theory has rarely been tested."

"Then the people in your life really are idiots."

Something changed in his eyes, a heat sparking in the depths, and she felt an answering spark in her stomach, warming her, making her feel restless and needy and bringing up feelings she hadn't had in a very long time.

She and her husband had never had the most intensely passionate relationship, but in the beginning, she'd wanted him. She'd enjoyed sex with him. Not so much as time had gone on.

Desire, when one's husband was an ass, was hard to come by. There was resentment. There was a lot of lying back and taking one for the marital team. But there wasn't a lot of take-me-now happening; that was for sure.

But she felt a little of that now. With Mac.

She stood up, reaching across the table and grabbing her plate, then taking his. "Are you done with the . . . uh . . . pie . . . filling?"

"Sure," he said, putting his fork in the baking dish.

"Great, I'll just uh . . . wash up and then I'll head back to my room for that dinner that I saved for last."

"Are you okay?"

"Me?" The word came out overly shrill. "Pfft. I'm fine." She dumped the dishes into the sink and rinsed them quickly, then opened the dishwasher and started loading it.

"You don't seem fine."

"I'm just hungry. I want dinner."

"You can eat dinner here. You don't have to do the dishes first."

"No. I'll eat back in my . . . in my house." After talking about Daniel, she was just feeling stripped emotionally, which was likely where the heat was coming from. From a place of neediness and vulnerability that she didn't normally let herself feel.

She'd taken care to shore herself up in preparation for the divorce, and somehow, Mac and her sudden willingness—need, even—to confide in him, was breaking down all kinds of barriers that she relied on.

Mac stood and made his way from the dining area into the kitchen. He never took his eyes off of hers, his focus intense. "I know what I said about enjoying your situation, and that it's a huge part of why you've been avoiding me."

Not as huge as he might think.

"But I didn't understand what you'd been through. Honestly, that high school stuff doesn't matter anymore. Clearly we're different people now."

"Yeah." Her mouth was dry. She blamed Mac, Mac and all his untamed masculinity and muscles and things she'd been completely immune to for far too long.

Oh, geez. Why was she having a sudden sexual reawakening? She did not need this. Not now, not with the man who was currently paying her to work for him.

And he thought it was because he'd insulted her by saying he was enjoying her fall from grace a little bit. Oddly, she wasn't that insulted by that. Because she'd been a bitch in high school, and it wasn't like he'd had a front-row seat to everything she'd been through in the past few years.

Even with reason to be, he'd never been as awful to her as her ex-husband had been.

But it was fine with her if he wanted to think that was all her discomfort was about. Way less awkward than "I'm fixated on how your butt looks in those jeans."

Mac stopped in front of her, close enough that she could smell his aftershave. Nothing like the kind of cologne her husband and his associates had worn. None of that pretentious musk that was probably supposed to mimic male hormones or something.

Mac clearly didn't need to manufacture testosterone. He exuded it, and she responded. He smelled like leather and spice. And just Mac, which was sexier than any of the other things.

He paused, his eyes dropping to her lips, and her stomach went on a free fall down to her toes.

He leaned in, and she almost choked on her breath. He extended his hand, his thumb brushing the corner of her mouth and sliding beneath her lower lip.

"You had a little apple," he said, drawing his hand back and dropping it back down to his side.

"Oh," she said, feeling a rush of stupid, inexplicable disappointment. "Thanks."

"You sure you don't want to wait to do the dishes?"

"No," she said. "No, I'm fine."

He nodded. "Great. I'm tired, I'm going to head upstairs. Pancakes for breakfast?"

"Sure," she said.

"Great. See you in the morning."

"Yeah," she said, her voice hollow in her ears. "See you in the morning."

She watched him walk away and heard his footfalls on the stairs. When she was sure he was gone, she turned around and pressed her overheated forehead to the cool granite countertop.

"Stupid, Lucy," she muttered. "Really stupid."

Because for a second there, she'd really thought Mac might kiss her. And for a second, she'd really wanted him to.

She straightened, pushed the start button on the dishwasher, then picked up her plate of tepid pot roast. She would eat it back in her little house. If that wouldn't remind her of her place in life, of what she really didn't need to crave, of the fact that Mac was essentially her boss, nothing would.

And all of that should remind her that she didn't want Mac Denton to kiss her.

Lucy made the pancakes and vacated as quickly as possible, using another trip to the grocery store as an excuse.

She really wasn't in the mood to deal with Mac and his effect on her hormones again. Not so soon. Not after she'd very nearly terminally embarrassed herself the night before. What if she'd leaned in? Oh, it didn't even bear thinking about.

She could picture herself letting her eyes flutter closed, parting her lips so she looked a little like a goldfish sucking water and then tilting her head and . . . ugh!

She could also nicely picture Mac's eyes going wide with horror as he backed away as quickly as possible.

Mentally calling herself a myriad of foul names, Lucy put the car in park and got out, heading into the grocery store for the second time in a week. She'd spent more time in the grocery store recently than she had in her entire life before coming to work for Mac. She minded it less than she'd thought she might.

Before walking in, she spotted Sarah Larsen walking

down the sidewalk, a reusable shopping bag slung over her arm. Sarah still looked very much like she had in high school: hair parted down the middle with barrettes keeping the front off of her face, a sweater with buttons done all the way up to her throat and a skirt that went at least to mid-calf.

"Sarah!" Lucy called out to her and started to walk in her direction. Sarah stopped and held her bag up against her chest. Sarah always had a way of looking like a frightened rabbit. Or maybe that look was reserved for Lucy. She couldn't really remember, but she imagined that she hadn't been all that wonderful to Sarah back in high school.

"Hi, Lucy," Sarah said. "Did you . . . did you have any luck with the pie?"

"Not the crust. I followed the recipe but it was really chewy. I was wondering if you had any tips for that?"

Sarah blinked her wide brown eyes. "Uh . . . yeah. You need to make sure you use cold water. Refrigerate it if you need to. And don't touch it too much. It's not like making bread. You need it sort of barely pressed together."

Lucy grimaced. "Oh, geez. I kneaded it. A lot. I really was thinking bread."

"That's your problem then."

"I'm sort of relieved to hear it. That's at least an identifiable problem." Lucy blew out a breath. "What other desserts do you like to make? Is there anything easy? I'm feeling in over my head here."

"You basically can't mess up a simple chocolate cake. Especially if you just do it in a square pan and don't bother with layers."

"Great! What do you I need for that?" Sarah's expression was getting increasingly confused. "Sorry. You're probably busy."

Sarah shook her head. "Not really. I was just going in to pick up a few things for my dinner tonight."

"Am I bothering you?"

"No. Why?"

"You look . . . scared."

"I'm surprised you're talking to me. Not just because you're Lucy Ryan, but because not very many people just make conversation with me."

"Oh, well, if you don't mind, I'd like to make some conversation with you while we shop," Lucy said. She was suddenly very conscious of the fact that Mac was the only person she had to talk to. And most especially with how she felt at the moment, that just wouldn't do. "I'm sort of new in town, Sarah."

"You grew up here," Sarah said.

"A version of me did. But now I'm different. And the new me is new here. I need a friend."

Sarah smiled—sort of timidly, like most of her other actions, but it was genuine. "I can always use another friend."

Lucy had premade his pancakes. Clever girl. She was avoiding him very smoothly today, and he was pretty sure he knew why. That little moment of tension between them in the kitchen had sizzled. There was no way she hadn't felt it.

And he, idiot that he was, rather than just telling her she'd had apple pie filling on her face, had wiped it away with his thumb. As an excuse to touch her. To find out if she was as warm and soft as he thought she might be.

She was, dammit. And he'd had to fight the urge not to lick the apple off of his finger just to see if he could get a hint of her flavor beneath it.

And then he'd really had to fight the urge to lean in and kiss her. She was vulnerable. She was working for him. Her ex-husband was an asshole. And he wasn't going to follow suit and take advantage of her when he had a weird amount of control in her life.

The fact was, Lucy needed the job he paid her for. Very few other people would hire an unskilled housekeeper and give her room and board. He was doing it, though. And it wasn't really out of pity, because that made it sound like Lucy was incompetent, and she wasn't. For someone who'd never cooked before, she was actually pretty good. And the thing was, he was certain that whatever Lucy tried to do, she could get good at.

But she didn't know that. He could see it. And it ate at him. It was all her ex-husband's fault. That guy deserved a sharp uppercut to the jaw.

And then some.

Mac sighed and pulled his cap off when he walked into the house. His kitchen smelled good, which meant Lucy was already working on dinner. On what would be a successful dinner, if the smell was anything to go by.

He followed the smell and paused in the doorway of the kitchen. Lucy was bending down in front of the oven, pulling something out. He couldn't help but stand there and watch for a second. All of Lucy's clothes were too nice for her to do this sort of work in. They made her seem like his personal June Cleaver. Vacuuming in pearls and heels. Pulling a cake out of the oven in a pencil skirt that hugged her perfect, rounded butt.

His mouth dried. She was so sexy. She had always been beautiful, but the years had only improved her. She was a woman now, and it very much appealed to the man in him. That her husband had dared to say she looked old or heavy gave him fantasies of a different kind. Violent fantasies.

Any real man would recognize that Lucy had the kind of curves some women paid to get. And that age had only refined the beauty in her face, given more definition to her features. High, exquisite cheekbones that made her look even more sophisticated.

But right now all that mattered was her ass, since it was directly in his line of sight and he was enjoying it so damn much.

"What exactly is that?" he asked.

Lucy shrieked and straightened, setting a cake on the counter and tugging off her oven mitts. "Don't sneak up on me like that when I'm pulling hot things out of the oven! Better yet, don't sneak up on me like that ever."

"Sorry, not my intention. What kind of cake?"

"Chocolate," she said. "And I'm going to make chocolate frosting next."

"And you know how?"

"Sarah Larsen told me. And she assured me that I couldn't screw it up."

"Sarah Larsen? The Sarah Larsen from school who now teaches kindergarten?"

"Yes, that one."

"I didn't know you knew her."

"I didn't. Not really. Not before. But I saw her in the grocery store yesterday, and again today, and we hit it off."

"Really?"

"Yes. Really. When she stopped being afraid of me."

He laughed and walked to the opposite side of the counter to Lucy, resting his forearms on it and leaning in. "Well, you were a bit scary in high school."

"I know," she said. "I'm not really proud of that. But who loves who they were in high school?"

"Not me. I was a douche."

Lucy laughed, light and happy. It made something in his chest expand. "Were you? I didn't know, I didn't hang out with you."

"Oh, you know, nothing major. Mainly that I was sure I was God's gift to women. I couldn't afford to buy them anything, but I made up for it in . . . other ways. Lucas and I weren't good for each other that way."

"I never heard any stories about you going around the school."

"Oh, you wouldn't have. We didn't seduce high school girls."

"You seduced who, then?"

"Women we met in bars."

"Bars?"

He shrugged. "We had fake IDs."

"Fake IDs? Shameless, Mac Denton. That's what you are."

He arched a brow. "And lawless, remember?"

"Clearly."

She was smiling. Really smiling. And it meant more to him than it should.

She stuck a toothpick in the top of the cake and her smile widened when it came out clean. "I wasn't seducing anyone in high school. That was not where my head was at."

"You were seducing guys without even realizing it."

"I doubt it."

"Don't. You had my attention." It was the truth, one that had stung at the time. The fact was that the reason Lucy had gotten to him so much was because he'd had a bit of a crush on her. That he'd thought she was the most beautiful girl in the school.

Even knowing he never had a chance with her. It actually made her even hotter.

Until she'd given him a major setdown just for speaking to her in the hallowed halls of her high school kingdom. That had been a reality check.

"I did?"

"Are you kidding? You were a hottie back then."

"Back then, huh?"

"Not excluding now, but back then . . . that was what we called you."

"I bet that's not all you called me."

He grimaced. "No, there were other names."

"I deserved them."

"No, you didn't. We were all just stupid kids, and none of us really understood what any of us were going through. So we were mean."

"You weren't mean. The one time you were mean to me, I deserved it. Totally."

"You did."

"Ha! I thought you might argue a little bit."

"No. Not about that."

"Maybe if I had seduced a few guys in high school, Daniel wouldn't have seemed so incredible."

"Do you think?"

"First boyfriend. First . . . you know. I had first-love syndrome with him."

"First love or fifth love, honey, it doesn't matter. It still ties you in knots and turns your world upside down. Still makes you think the risk is worth it. That you should give up everything to have that other person."

"You've been in love like that?"

"Nope. But I've watched my parents. My dad falls in love often, with everything in a skirt. My mom only loves him. She sacrifices her happiness, her dignity, her self-respect for that love. And my dad lets her because of his . . . many loves. They would all call it love. I call it bull. And it doesn't matter how many years pass, or how many people you find it with. People are still jackasses for love."

"But not you?"

"Nope. Not me."

"So what do you do instead?"

"Excuse me?"

Lucy looked down and traced a curved line over the counter with the tip of her finger. "What do you do instead of falling in love? Instead of having real relationships?"

Mac looked at her, at her face, so flawless and lovely, and tried to ignore the sudden tightening in his gut. The rush of desire in his veins.

He was tempted to show her what he did instead. Thankfully, the counter was between them, so hauling her into his arms wouldn't exactly be a simple matter. But he wanted to do it anyway.

He should walk away. He should not say what he was thinking. But he did.

"I have sex," he said, the words coming out raw and harsh. Just the way the kiss he was fantasizing about would be. "Sweaty, hot, unattached sex."

Lucy blinked, her dark eyes owlish. "Oh."

He shrugged. "I'm a man. I'm not exactly going to live a celibate existence just because I don't want a relationship."

She frowned. "What does you being a man have to do with anything?"

"Men have needs."

She crossed her arms beneath her breasts. "Women do too."

"It's not the same."

"Like hell it's not. How long is the longest you've ever been celibate since your first time?"

The question caught him off guard. And made him feel a little dirty. "Maybe four months." Maybe.

"I'm running on ten. Ten. And before that it was months, if not years, of boring, lights-off, missionary-position sex between two married people who resented each other a whole lot more than they wanted each other. So I think I can tell you that women most definitely have needs. I can tell you because mine haven't been met in a real way in far too long and it . . . it sucks, quite frankly."

"So . . . what does that mean? You think you want to just have . . . sex? Meet needs?"

She bit her lip and started pacing around the counter, her focus on the air in front of her. "Yeah, I think some of that sweaty, hot sex wouldn't be so bad. No. It really wouldn't."

She stopped in front of him, her eyes trained on his chest. She was breathing hard now, her face flushed. The sight was making his heart beat faster, was making him feel sweaty and a tiny bit nervous, and he really couldn't figure out why.

He couldn't remember a woman ever making him nervous in his life.

Then she put her palm flat on his chest and flexed delicate fingers, the fabric of his shirt sliding over his skin, sending a spark of heat through him.

"Yeah, a little hot sex might be just what I need," She went up on her tiptoes and pressed her lips to his cheek. His knees nearly buckled.

Then she angled her head, and her soft, perfect mouth met his. Instinct took over everything else. He wrapped his arm around her waist and pulled her tight against him, her full breasts flush against his chest. Then he tilted his head and deepened the kiss, teasing the seam of her lips with his tongue. She opened to him and he took a long taste. One that seemed to meet with her approval.

She moaned, the sound vibrating through her petite frame as she arched into him, demanding more. Demanding hot, sweaty sex. And he really, really wanted to deliver.

But it was a bad idea. He couldn't exactly remember why it was a bad idea right now. Not when she was arching into him and all but purring, stroking her tongue against his. Harder still with the throaty little sounds she made every time he moved his hands over her back.

He didn't want logic, or thought. He wanted to pull her expensive skirt up around her hips, leave the designer shoes on, and bend her over the counter and show her all about hot and sweaty and definitely not missionary position with the light off.

But the warning, the one that was telling him *Bad idea*, was only getting louder and more insistent.

She works for you, you dumbass.

Oh. Yes. That.

And he was the asshole kissing his housekeeper. While she was making him a cake. A cake he was paying her to bake. And he was kissing her like a sex-starved teenage boy, and he couldn't seem to stop.

Stop. You have to stop.

And he did. Somehow. He put his hands on her hips and pushed her firmly back while he pulled away.

"Lucy. No. This is a bad . . . this is a bad, bad idea." His rock-hard cock begged to differ.

"Why?" she asked, her eyes huge, glittery.

"Because you work for me. You're my housekeeper. You cook my food, you . . . you . . ."

"I scrub your floors," she said, sounding dazed.

"I can't do this."

She drew back as though he'd slapped her. "I see. So . . . I'm beneath you now. Because I'm the housekeeper. Wow. That must have felt good, Mac. That must have felt pretty damn good."

"Lucy, that's not . . ."

"What? You're just not that into me? It's not me, it's you? You should just stop before it gets awkward. Oh, wait, that ship has sailed. Why don't you stop before I'm tempted to commit violence then?"

"Lucy . . ."

"Save it. I have frosting to make. And since it's the only dessert you're going to have today, you may want to make sure I don't screw it up."

"Women are fucking inscrutable."

"It's not even five, and you're at least one beer over your limit."

"I am not, Lucas," Mac said, knowing he sounded like the drunk ass he was.

"You used 'fucking' and 'inscrutable' in the same sentence. Yes, my friend, you are a bit drunk for a Monday afternoon."

Mac scowled into his bottle. He was still on fire from that kiss with Lucy. He wanted very badly for chocolate cake to be a pre-dessert to what would be his real dessert, which would involve Lucy and her naked body. In bed, against the wall, whatever, he wasn't particular.

"Women really aren't all that hard to figure out, Mac," Lucas said. "She wanted you. You said no. You damaged her pride. Simple."

"I was being a gentleman," he said. "Probably for the first time ever. And I get no thanks. None at all."

"No. You're a gentleman a lot more than you think. But go on."

"I was being a gentleman. Not pressuring the woman who works for me into having sex with me. A woman dependent on the paycheck she gets from me. Dependent on me for the roof over her head. Morally that ranks up there with stealing money out of your grandma's purse."

"It doesn't matter. She wanted you; you turned her down. When I was first with Carly—"

"I don't want to hear about you and my little sister. I don't care how relevant it is. I don't care if the story contains clues as to how to solve world hunger, I don't ever want to hear anything about how you hooked up with Carly."

"Fine. It might have helped you."

"It won't. I'm not in love with Lucy. I want to do it with her."

"You're classy when you're drunk."

"I don't want to marry her. She doesn't want to marry me. She just spent nearly a decade married to the biggest douchebag on the planet," Mac said.

"It sounds like you both want the same thing."

"Except I'm in a position of power."

"You don't seem real powerful to me, man. You seem like some woman has you by the balls."

"I wish she did."

"You have got to stop drinking."

Mac stood up and his head spun in a circle. Or maybe it just felt like it did. Either way, it sucked. "Yeah, okay. I need to stop drinking."

"What would Carly say if she could see us, sitting in a bar in the middle of the day? We're maligning the reputation the good councilwoman has worked so hard to build up."

"She's your problem. Not mine."

Lucas smiled and slapped him on the back. "I know. Aren't I a lucky bastard?"

"You're a bastard anyway."

"Great. Now I'm going to drive you home."

"My truck is parked out front. If it ends up here for hours on end, it's going to look bad."

"Great. Let people talk."

"Honestly, you know Carly hates that."

Lucas smiled, that smug getting-laid-all-the-time smile. "She doesn't hate it so much anymore."

"Your influence?"

"Yeah. I'm a baaaad influence on your sister, Mac."

Mac showed Lucas a choice finger and walked out of the bar ahead of him. The sun did a good job of stabbing its way into his skull and through his buzz.

He stopped by Lucas's truck and blew out a breath. "I don't know how much longer I can play gentleman, to be honest. I think maybe I should let her go."

"So, you'll fire her because you want to sleep with her, so that you don't sleep with her while she works for you and feel like you've taken advantage of her? One of those options is stupid."

"Oh really, which one?"

"Well, in one of them, neither of you has an orgasm and she's out of a job."

Mac looked at the ground. "Huh."

"And in one of them she still has a job and you both get some."

"I like the sound of that."

"I thought you might."

"You make it sound easy."

Lucas shrugged. "Stop trying to be her hero and let the woman make her own damn decisions."

"He turned me down."

"What?"

Lucy shifted the phone to her other ear and clamped it down with her shoulder so that she could open the oven and check her roast chicken. "He turned me down. Mac did. I kissed him and he told me to stop."

"This doesn't sound like a baking question." Sarah had the bad luck of being the only woman in Lucy's life who was speaking to her, and that meant she had to field all questions pertaining to issues of cooking and men.

"It's not. It's not even a question. It's more of a general whine. But I haven't made a move on a guy since my divorce. Scratch that, I've never made a move on a man in my life, and I'm only slightly bruised over the fact that I offered him sex. Sweaty, hot sex, no less, and he said no. Why would he do that?"

Sarah cleared her throat. "I'm, um . . . not sure I'm the person you should be asking for advice from on this . . . particular . . . subject."

"Seriously. Is there something wrong with me?"

"No!" Sarah answered quickly.

"I didn't think so. I've spent the past few months getting increasingly sure that there wasn't anything wrong with me, in spite of what my ex said. And stupidly, today made me feel like there was something wrong again. I'm tired of that feeling."

"It *is* tiresome," Sarah said on a sigh.

"What's wrong with a couple of adults with mutual needs taking care of those needs in a horizontal fashion?"

"Uh . . ."

"And what's wrong with a woman taking charge of what she wants? Of grabbing the bull by the horns, so to speak, and riding a man like a cowgirl? Huh? What?"

"N-nothing . . ." Sarah said it as if it was a slow revelation. "Nothing at all."

"Exactly. So why is he being such a prude?"

"Maybe you should ask him."

"No." Lucy rested her hand on the counter and drummed her fingers. "I don't want to do that. I'll sound desperate."

"You sound desperate to me."

"Because I am! For sex. Not a relationship. I've had

enough of relationships to last me my whole life. I just want sex. Nothing but meaningless, hot—"

She heard a noise behind her and turned around to see Mac standing in the doorway, looking like he'd just put his head in a horse trough.

"I gotta go." She hung up the phone. "What happened to you?"

"Don't change the subject," he said, his tone surly.

"From what? Why are you dripping all over the kitchen floor?"

"Lucas took it upon himself to sober me up. Frankly, I wasn't drunk enough to merit the punishment. You were talking about sex."

"And you were eavesdropping on my private conversation."

"That you were having on my phone. During your work hours."

"I called about a . . . cooking question."

"What question?"

"Something about chicken?"

"Lucy . . ."

"I'm not talking about this. A girl's ego can only take so many beatings. I'm not going to stand here and let you willingly punch it."

"I didn't punch your ego on purpose. Listen to me. You're working for me. You live here as part of your pay. If I take you up on your sweaty sex offer, I will always feel like I might have manipulated you into it in some way. And even if I don't feel that way, people will definitely question it if they find out. I pay you to work here, and I don't want people wondering if I'm paying you to share my bed."

"You're overthinking it, Mac. I didn't ask for anything other than one night."

"It would take a lot more than one night to burn all this out."

"You think?" she asked.

"I know."

"High opinion of yourself there."

"So? I know that I'm good in bed."

She couldn't help herself—she laughed. "Oh, really? And what guy knows he sucks in bed?"

"Trying to goad me into a demonstration?"

"Nope. Just asking. I'm sure my ex thinks he's a racehorse in bed, but he's more like those little Shetland ponies that get walked around on a lead rope at petting zoos."

"Then trust me, I know a lot more about what I'm talking about than you do."

"Oh, really?"

"Yes. I've had some really good sex, Lucy." His eyes met hers, the fire in them intense. "And you should try it sometime."

"Men always think sex is good. You can just have finished a bitter fight where they called you fat and ugly and they still get off. Let me tell you a secret: The woman doesn't. Unless she's into something freaky. And I'm not."

"Oh, baby, you've been missing out."

"All talk, Denton. You're all talk. You're too busy defending my honor to give me any sort of demonstration."

"Because someone should defend your honor!"

"Bullshit!" Anger rolled through her on a boil, her fingertips tingling, her face hot. "That's what everyone says they're doing! Defending my honor. Trying to get me to do the right thing. Stupid Daniel was just trying to help me be better. My parents just want me to be responsible. I don't want to do the right thing. Or the responsible thing. I want to do what I damn well please!"

She stopped, her breath coming in sharp gasps, her hands clenched so tightly into fists that her nails were cutting halfmoons into her palms.

Mac just looked at her, his eyes locked on to hers. Then, suddenly, she was in his arms, and he was kissing her like she'd never been kissed before.

Seven

Mac's lips were hot and hard on hers, and she was sure she would never get enough. He smelled like beer. And hose water. And he was still sexy.

She wrapped her arms around his neck and threaded her fingers through his damp hair, holding him tightly to her. She never wanted him to stop. Never wanted this to stop. She needed more, needed him, like air. Needed something to fill up that emptiness inside of her, to answer the unbearable ache that was building at the apex of her thighs.

She arched into him, trying to get some friction, trying to find a little satisfaction. The kind that had been denied her for way too long. And she wasn't just talking orgasms. Just having what she wanted. Something for her.

Rough, hot hands slid beneath the hem of her top and she couldn't hold back the groan that escaped her lips. She didn't want to anyway. She didn't care about being proper, or demure, or anything right now. Because this was about her. Her and no one else.

Mac's body was a carnival. And she so badly wanted to ride.

She moved her hands down his chest—his very muscular, sexy chest—and pushed her hands beneath his T-shirt. The fabric was wet and peeled slowly up from his skin. It almost made it better.

She broke their kiss for a moment so she could watch the dark fabric pull away and reveal washboard-flat abs and tan skin covered in just the right amount of golden hair. It was like he wasn't even real. Just a mishmash of her deepest fantasies brought to life in front of her.

She tugged his shirt over his head, and he helped. She sucked in a sharp breath and put her hand on his stomach. He was the sexiest sight she'd ever seen: shirtless, in a pair of low, tight jeans, with a belt that had a buckle at the center that was surely designed to point her gaze to the main attraction.

There was no hiding his arousal. No concealing the fact that he was a seriously impressive man.

She kissed the line of his jaw, his neck, her fingers sliding down to cup his denim-covered erection. He was heavy and perfect in her hand. Everything she wanted and more.

"If you don't want this," she said, her voice broken by short, sharp breaths, "then say so. I don't want you protecting me, but I'm also not letting you do this because you pity me."

He put his hand over hers and pushed it down harder on his cock. "Does this feel like I'm pitying you?"

"Nope." She squeezed him again, running her palm over the length of him. "But I need to be sure. I needed to give you the out."

"I don't want an out," he growled. "I should. But I don't. What I want is to tear off that prissy little outfit and have my way with you."

"I'm absolutely in favor of that."

"Glad we're on the same page." He tugged at the front of her blouse, popping a button off and sending it rolling across the stone floor. "Sorry," he said, his mouth quirked into a half smile.

"No, you aren't."

"Not in the least." He tightened his hold on her and pressed a kiss to her lips, walking her backward as he did, till her back made contact with the living room wall. He reached around her back and unhooked her bra in one swift motion that would have made her ex green with envy. No struggling over hooks and eyes for Mac, that was for sure.

He pushed her blouse off of her shoulders, and it and her bra fell to the floor. "So sexy," he said, his words sounding choked, labored. She liked it.

"You too," she said, hands on his belt buckle, making quick work of it and the snap and fly on his jeans. He shrugged them off and she did the same with her skirt and panties. She started to toe off her high heels but he stopped her.

"Leave them on."

"Really?"

"Fantasy. Needs fulfilling."

"Sounds fair."

And then he kissed her again, and she couldn't think, let alone speak. He raised his hands up to cup her breasts, his thumbs teasing her nipples, tightening them, tightening a coil low in her belly. She'd never been pushed so close to the edge so fast. She wanted him, all of him—forget gentle. Forget foreplay. Forget anything but just having him, hot, hard and perfect inside of her.

He parted from her for a moment, bending down and grabbing his jeans, fishing around in the back pocket for his wallet. He flipped it open and pulled a condom out, throwing the wallet carelessly back to the floor and rolling the protection down his length.

Then he was back, hot and insistent against her, kissing

her with all the passion of a man who had been wandering in the desert and found an oasis.

"Now," she said against his mouth. "Please, Mac. We'll do this other stuff later, and it will be great, but right now, I just want you."

"No argument from me." He grasped on to her thigh and hooked it up over his hip, the blunt head of his erection testing her, moving in slowly at first. Then he flexed forward and thrust hard inside of her.

She gasped and let her head fall back, nails digging into his shoulders, a white-hot streak of pleasure that was so bright it nearly blinded her moving through her body.

Nothing had ever felt so good. It had never been like this. She'd never simply enjoyed the act like this. Had never just reveled in being filled by her partner.

As he rocked against her, searing heat roared through her, his pelvis coming up against her clit with each movement, each thrust into her body. He lowered his head and took one of her nipples between his lips, sucking, teasing.

She forked her fingers into his hair and held on. She was probably pulling. And it probably hurt. But he didn't complain.

He gripped her thigh harder, blunt fingertips digging into her flesh, the rhythm and force of his movements increasing. She was lost in it. Surrounded by him. His heat, his smell, his body.

She moved her hands down his back, could feel his muscles shivering beneath her palms. Could sense the edges of his control fraying to the point of breaking. The evidence of her effect on him, of his need for her, was enough to push her over the edge.

Pleasure rolled through her like a thundercloud, dark, frightening, pouring release down on her, through her, sending flashes of light behind her eyes.

And then Mac followed her over, a harsh groan signaling

his orgasm, his body going stiff against hers as he lost himself in her. He buried his face in her neck, dropping a kiss to her sensitive skin.

Neither of them spoke. Neither of them moved. There was no sound in the room other than their labored breathing. Other than her heart pounding in her ears.

Then he withdrew from her, stepped away. He pushed his hand back through his hair and surveyed the clothes on the floor.

He took a breath and looked at her like he meant to say something, then let the air out of his lungs, put his hands on his lean hips and looked back down at the floor. He bent at the waist, muscles shifting beneath smooth golden skin, and started collecting their clothes.

"Yours, I think," he said, handing her the black lace bra.

"Unless you have a little secret you haven't shared with me."

"Not that kind of secret."

"I can handle a little kink," she said, hoping to use humor to diffuse the knot of emotion that was tightening in her chest, binding up her heart and lungs, making it difficult to breathe.

"Oh, can you?"

"I think so."

"You think so?"

"To date, the kinkiest thing I've ever done is have sex with you in broad daylight against a wall."

"We may have to work on that, Lucy."

"You're assuming I want a repeat performance." She did.

"Yeah, I'm cocky like that." He was. "But when a woman screams in my ear the way you just did . . ."

"I did not." She totally had.

"We can use the scratch marks on my back as exhibit A."

"I'm sure I didn't leave any . . ." He turned around. And it turned out she had.

There were raised pink lines going from the tops of his

shoulders down to the middle of his back. Five on each side and spaced just right so that if she put her hands against them in the shape of a claw, they matched right up.

Dear Lord, what had he done to her?

The kitchen timer buzzed. "That'd be the chicken," she said. For some reason that made her feel embarrassed, when nothing else had. Not the revelation of her marks on his skin, not standing naked in front of him save a pair of high heels. No, the fact that she was currently roasting the man a chicken, and had taken time out to do him against a wall—now that was embarrassing.

Mac walked out of the room and returned a few moments later, condom neatly disposed of.

"I'm sure we just violated some health codes in a major way," he said, tugging his jeans on.

"I'm sure."

She bent down and collected her clothes, dressing as quickly as she could, not looking at Mac once.

"Want to stay for dinner? It's the least I could do," he said, still buttoning his shirt.

She walked into the kitchen and took a pair of oven mitts off of the counter and slipped them on. "I don't know."

"After that? I owe you a meal."

"I thought you wanted to stay away from that whole sex-for-payment thing."

"But sex being . . . rewarded . . . with dinner is a tradition as old as time. I think."

She frowned, her body buzzing, her shirt gaping at the neck where Mac had permanently removed a button. "I don't think I want a reward, actually."

"Fine, bad choice of words. Eat with me because I want you to. I would like to have your company. How about that?"

"That's a little better." She took the chicken pan out of the oven and set it on the counter, and when she turned, Mac was right in front of her. "I think I need some time alone," she said.

He reached out and took ahold of her arms, just below her black, bulky oven mitts, and tugged her forward, pressing a deep, sensual kiss to her lips.

She put her hands on his cheeks, then realized she was still wearing her oven mitts. She lifted her hands and shook them off onto the floor behind them, and put her hands back on his face, returning the kiss with all the passion that was, surprisingly, still burning as hotly inside of her as it had been pre-orgasm.

He pulled away from her and took a step back, sweeping her up and down with a quick, very male look that lingered at her breasts and slowly, slowly returned to her eyes. "Yeah, it'll happen again. And you'll have dinner with me."

She didn't even have a good setdown for that. Nothing. Any biting remark she might have come up with was lost deep in the ether of arousal that was currently fogging her brain.

"Fine," she said. "But only because I don't want to eat the chicken cold."

"It's as good a reason as any. Hungry?"

"Starving." She hoped that didn't sound as euphemistic to him as it did to her. Her face felt flushed, and just that one kiss had her on the edge of release again. She leaned against the counter and pressed her knees together, trying to get a grip on the wild, animal, decidedly not-normal lust that was currently coursing through her.

"Great." He started setting the table and she just sort of stopped and watched, stunned by how bizarre the whole thing felt. And how comfortable it felt at the same time.

She didn't know what kind of reaction she should be having, but the one she was having didn't seem like it could possibly be right.

He looked at her again, the expression in his eyes positively X-rated. It wasn't hard to tell what he was thinking. More of what had already happened. Maybe on the table this time. An appetizer?

She needed her head checked. But she didn't care. She

started to walk into the dining room, her eyes locked with his, her heart pounding hard.

The front door opened wide, and Lucas Miller walked in with Mac's sister, Carly. She froze in place, realizing that the front door had been unlocked the whole time. And that they could so easily have been walked in on—which had been just seconds away from happening. Given ten more seconds she was reasonably sure that Mac could have had her topless and on her back.

"Hey, smells good in here," Lucas said, flashing her a smile.

Carly smiled and waved. "Hello. We were in the neighborhood. Thought we'd stop by and see if there was dinner. Do you have room for some additions, Mac?"

She and Mac were still frozen, staring at each other, with the dining table separating them. It took half a second, but Mac suddenly kicked into gear again.

"Of course," he said. "Let me get a couple more plates. Lucy was going to join me. She has been lately."

"That's nice," Carly said.

She and Lucas crossed the room, holding hands. The easy nature of their relationship hit Lucy hard. She'd never felt at ease with a partner before. Not with Daniel, certainly. She'd felt on edge all the time. And—not that Mac was her partner—but with him she felt on edge in a whole different way.

"Yes," Lucas added, giving Mac a meaningful look. "Nice." There was something about the way he said the word that made her feel like he knew just a little bit too much.

Lucy wanted to melt into the floor. "Mac is just beyond generous," she said, missing the potential double entendre until it was too late.

Mac snorted, and she wanted to kill him. "I am that," he said. "A candidate for sainthood, even."

"Right," Carly said, taking a seat at the table. "Ugh." She leaned forward and put her head in her hands.

"Rough day at the office?" Mac asked.

"Yeah, you know how everyone on the council is," Lucas said. "Older than dirt and traditional as hell. Carly was put in charge of organizing a banquet for the school."

"Which they want to be black-tie. Which . . . great, fine. They do that every year. But the thing is, it excludes every citizen that isn't part of the elite, no offense, Lucy."

"I'm hardly part of the elite now," Lucy muttered, grabbing two extra place settings and putting them on the table.

"You know what I mean," Carly said. "Anyway, I think that's a surefire way to alienate a good portion of the donations we could be getting. Every donation matters. We don't need to do twenty plates at two hundred a plate when we could do a barbecue for ten dollars and include the whole town. Plus we could do an auction. The Ride for Hope I put on a couple months back was a huge success. A little fall barbecue before it gets too cold . . . I think it would be great. And I think I've proven that this town responds well to a less formal event. Something that really celebrates the community."

Lucy brought the chicken to the table, and the green salad and broccoli, while everyone talked it over.

"There has to be a middle ground," she said without thinking.

"You think?"

"Yes. I mean, mostly back east we did formal get-togethers, but when we went to the Cape, we would usually do a traditional lobster bake type of thing. But of course, those sorts of people aren't going to sit in the wind and sand. So we just made sure to organize a seating area and chairs. We used real plates. But we would still have it at the beach and still have that nice basic food."

"So . . . you think we could do a formal barbecue?" Carly asked.

"I know, it sounds stupid, but—"

"No. I actually think you're on the right track. Something

that feels more elevated to the stuffed shirts, but still makes it open to other people looking to give back to the school district."

"It wouldn't be that difficult. I used to do this all the time for my hu—for my ex-husband."

Carly brightened. "Do you want to organize it, Lucy?"

"What?"

"I mean, if Mac can spare you for a while, I have plenty of money budgeted to hire a coordinator. Is that something you think you'd like to do?"

She did. She'd thought for a long time she had a gift for putting events together, but somehow, Daniel had always made her feel like she'd fallen short. She didn't feel as confident in it now as she had at first.

But she was a different woman now. She was the woman who had taken what she wanted. Who had walked away from a husband who was emotionally abusing her. The woman who had just done it against a living room wall with a man who lit her on fire like no other man ever had.

"I'd love to." She turned to Mac. "I won't let it make you go hungry, I promise."

"Hey, I'm not in charge of all your time, Lucy. If you want to take on another job, you're welcome to it."

"Thank you," she said, directing it at both Carly and Mac. "Thank you so much. I think . . . I know I can do this." It was a step in the right direction. A step toward the kind of job she could actually see herself doing and being happy with.

A step further in proving herself. In proving she could do things right. That she wasn't inept.

"Great. I'll send over all the details—numbers to expect, budget, et cetera—sometime tomorrow, and if you can turn a plan around to me that I can present to the council by the end of the week, we might just be in business."

"I . . . Great."

She looked over at Mac and he smiled. It made her feel

all warm and fuzzy inside. She didn't like it. She didn't want it. She needed to focus on her, and how she made herself feel. Not on Mac's smile, or the fact that he seemed to believe in her, or that he was as great at sex as he claimed to be.

They finished the rest of the meal making companionable conversation. Awkwardness was forgotten. The fact that Lucy was staff was forgotten. For the first time in recent memory, Lucy felt like she was home.

Eight

After Lucas and Carly left, the tension settled back into the room, thick and tight between them. Mac could hardly breathe just looking at her.

He wasn't sure what had happened today. Obviously, sex had happened, and it had been great. But it was the feeling that stayed behind, heavy and unbearably present, a feeling he just couldn't shake, that confused him.

He just wanted her again. It had to be intense physical desire. It had to be. Strictly physical. That was all he was after. All he'd ever been after. Love was way too psychotic. After watching his father use it as an excuse to continually and publicly screw around on their mother, and after watching their mom take their dad back after every indiscretion, there was very little that could entice him to view the emotion differently.

"You can save the dishes if you want."

"No," she said. "It's my job. I'm going to do them."

"Look, you don't need to."

"Yes, Mac, I do. I'm not going to not do my job because

of what happened earlier," she said, taking a stack of plates from the table and carrying them into the kitchen. "That's not how this works."

"What if I want you available for something else right now?" he asked.

"You're my boss when it comes to housekeeping matters, but you are not my boss when it comes to the demands of your libido, okay?"

"That's not what I was—"

"Yes. Yes, it was. If you think you can just order me around now, like all, 'Yes, please, I'd like you to go down on me and then bake me a cake,' you are flat out of luck, buddy."

"That isn't what I said."

"Go upstairs," she said, picking up a dish towel and flinging it over her shoulder.

"Excuse me?"

"You heard me. You always go upstairs about now and have a shower. So go do that now and leave me to do my job."

"Then what?" he asked.

"We'll see what time I get off."

"That's what I'm wondering," he said. "If either of us will get off."

Pale cheeks turned a deep rose. "Well . . . that . . ." She choked. Or it might have even been a laugh. "That's sexual harassment is what that is."

"You were the one who told me to stop protecting you, sweetheart. So I've stopped. But you can't have it both ways. Either you want to try and deal with me, with this, or I can go back to being a gentleman. Hands off. No dirty comments. No lingering looks. No nothing. But that's up to you. So you tell me, what do you want?"

She pushed her sleeves up and went over to the sink. "I can handle you," she said.

"You think so?"

"I know so. But understand this, Mac. It will be on my own terms. Now go upstairs."

"Are you going to join me?"

"I have work to do now. An extra job. I won't have a lot of time for extracurricular activities."

The underlying meaning in her words had him hard and aching in seconds. What was it about her? He shouldn't be on this light a trigger. It had only been a couple of hours since they'd had sex. He couldn't remember being this perpetually ready since he was a teenager. And maybe that didn't even count, because while he was ready, he wasn't getting all *that* much action as a scowly high schooler who came from the wrong side of the tracks.

He headed up the stairs, because in his mind, her words were a challenge. Lingering would make him seem desperate. And while he felt a little bit desperate, he wasn't going to hang around and show his hand.

Nope.

He went into his room and left the door open, stripping his shirt off and heading into the bathroom, taking his jeans down when he turned the shower on. He hadn't changed since his little incident with Lucas and the horse trough, and he was more than ready to wash off whatever was in that water.

Logic dictated he should take a cold shower and try to calm himself down. But logic wasn't in charge tonight.

He wanted Lucy again, and he didn't see why he should bother to cool himself off. Instead, he stepped under the hot spray, closed the frosted glass door and took his cock in hand.

If Lucy wasn't going to indulge him tonight, he'd damn well indulge himself.

Lucy waffled for a full minute and a half over what she was going to do before she started climbing the stairs and heading toward Mac's bedroom.

She was probably being an idiot. She should probably do what she'd said she was going to do and just go back to her little house and start thinking of some ideas for Carly's fundraiser.

Instead, she was following her hormones. And they were leading her into the lion's den. She was making bad decisions today.

Or maybe not. Maybe she was just finally making some decisions that she wanted. And maybe they would be disastrous, but she would have fun on the road to ruin.

She found some comfort in that. Cold comfort, but it was better than nothing.

The door to his bedroom was open, which made things that much easier. It was one more step taken out of the equation. Easy to just walk in. And she could hear the water in the shower running, steam flowing from the bathroom, which also had an open door, into the bedroom.

She took a breath and started taking her clothes off, dropping her top where Mac had left his shirt, dropping her skirt, shoes and underwear where he'd left his jeans.

She could see his silhouette through the frosted glass. And even though there were no details on display, her mind was doing a pretty good job of filling them all in.

She opened the door, and it took a moment for the image in front of her, one that altered the second she opened the door, to burn its way into her brain and process correctly.

Mac. His body all naked and wet, water drops tracking over muscles. And his hand wrapped tightly around his very large, very hard—she knew from experience—erection.

He dropped his hand to his side, his eyes wide, his expression almost comically shocked.

She'd never caught a man doing that before, and she found that it was rather intriguing. Oh, yeah, a little more than intriguing. It was hot. Of course, Mac had gotten her hot when he'd come in half drunk and dressed in wet clothes, so it wasn't like he had to work that hard to turn her on.

She crossed her arms beneath her breasts, and his eyes dropped down, shamelessly ogling, which was fine with her.

"Selfish," she said.

"What?" he asked, his focus snapping back up.

"I thought you were going to save that for me." She looked at him unashamedly. Because she wanted to. The thought made a little smile curve her lips.

"I didn't know you were offering," he said. "I thought it was up to me to do something about this."

"No." She got inside the shower and wiggled a little when the hot spray made contact with her skin. "I decided I would."

"You think you can play games with me like that?" he asked.

She put her hand on his stomach and sucked in a breath, trailing her fingers over wet skin, down to his shaft. She curled her fingers around him and squeezed. "I think I can."

"Careful, sweetheart."

"That close?"

She squeezed him again, and a harsh breath hissed through his teeth. "Yes."

"Good. I like having you on the edge." She leaned in and licked a stream of water that was running down his chest. "And I didn't play with you on purpose. I was confused."

"Were you?"

"I've never had sex that good. But I've also never had sex when I wasn't married to the man I was having it with. So I'm used to there being, if not feelings, a commitment. It's always been really important to me. So this whole just-go-with-your-baser-instincts thing is all new to me."

"You seem to be doing a pretty good job of it."

"Thanks." She pressed her palm flat against him.

"Geez." His hand shot up, fingers forking through her hair, tugging hard. "You're going to kill me."

"Nope. That's not the plan." She dropped down slowly onto her knees, her thigh muscles shaking a bit. "This is." She leaned in and flicked her tongue over the head of his shaft. She used the water sluicing over his skin to make her movements smooth as she worked her hand up and down his length, along with her lips and tongue.

She'd never really enjoyed doing this. Had never really wanted to. In fact, before, she'd always actively avoided it. But she wanted to do it with Mac. Wanted to explore every inch of him. To find a way to make him feel the same sort of explosion of release that she'd felt earlier. Because surely what she'd felt wasn't normal. Surely it was nearly impossible to match. But she wanted to try. Because he'd shown her something she hadn't even realized she'd been missing.

She lost herself in him, in the way his muscles shook beneath her hands, in the way he tightened his fingers in her hair when he got too close to the edge and had to anchor himself in some way.

She knew what he was feeling, because he'd already made her feel it.

"Okay, done now," he said, reaching down and gripping her arms and guiding her back into a standing position. "That was going to end way too fast."

"Well, we don't want that," she said.

"No, we don't. I'd like this to make it to a soft surface. The wall was nice but I'd like to go a little slower this time." He shut the water off and took her hand, pushing the door open and tugging her back out into the bathroom.

He took a towel off of the rack and draped it over her shoulders. He rubbed the terry cloth over her skin, down her back, her butt, her thighs. There was something so intimate about the simple action. Something that, for a moment, transcended sex.

And then he turned her around and pressed her body against his, kissing her deeply, walking her back into the bedroom, and just like that, she was rescued from the strange tenderness in her chest.

She managed to escape his hold and saunter to the bed, climbing on and lying back against the pillows. She didn't feel shy around him. Or like she needed low light, or to suck in her stomach and find a flattering angle. Because he didn't look at her with a critical eye. He didn't look like he was searching for a flaw, a weakness to exploit.

He looked at her, and all she could see was need.

He joined her on the bed, covering her body with his, every inch of him pressed against every inch of her. He reached to the bedside table and took a condom from the drawer, deftly rolling it on before positioning himself between her thighs.

"Wait," he said. "One thing first."

He lowered his head and drew her nipple into his mouth, sucking hard, an arrow of pleasure piercing her low in her pelvis. He moved down her body, tracing a trail over her skin with the tip of his tongue.

He sat up, then he gripped her hips and tugged her toward him, lowering his head to her core and tasting her slowly, leisurely.

She grabbed hold of his shoulders, and she was pretty sure she was adding to the marks she'd already left. And she really didn't care. She squirmed beneath him, heat roaring through her, a living, burning flame that threatened to consume everything in its path.

He shifted and penetrated her with a finger while he continued the sensual assault with his mouth. Stars burst behind her eyelids and she felt like she was falling. She held on to him hard, a sharp cry escaping her lips. And he didn't stop. Instead, he pushed her farther, faster. Another orgasm came on the heels of the first, leaving her spent and breathless. And sweaty.

"Oh," she said, her breath coming in harsh pants. She put her hand on her forehead and brushed damp hair back from her skin. "That was hot, sweaty sex," she said.

"Yes," he said, nearly as out of breath as she was. "And we aren't done."

She looked back down at his still fully erect body. "Oh. No. We aren't."

She didn't see how it was possible, but desire coiled low inside of her again, promise of another release.

He positioned himself at her entrance and pushed in with ease, kissing her mouth while he did. He moved slow and steady at first, each thrust measured, maddeningly controlled.

"Come on," she said, trying to push him on. Trying to get him to lose it. Because she had. She'd completely come undone for him and now she wanted the same. "Harder, Mac."

He complied, the next thrust rougher, a harsh sound on his lips when he was buried to the hilt inside of her.

She arched against him, her breasts rubbing against his chest. He moved his hand down and gripped her thigh, tugging it up over his back, his movements less contained now. She could see him losing his grip, could see him succumbing to his own need, to his own desire.

"More?" he asked.

"Yes," she whispered. "Don't hold back. Let go."

He pressed his lips against her throat, his head lowered, his skin slick with sweat beneath her hands. And when he let go, when all of his tension released and he let out a harsh growl of completion, she went with him.

They lay together in the aftermath, totally spent, completely unable to move. She'd never experienced anything like that before. Not even close. Eight years of sex with Daniel didn't add up to anything nearly so big, so powerful, as these moments in Mac's arms.

Emotion, big, scary, expanded inside of her. She wanted to run, but she was too tired to move. And Mac's arms felt so safe. His bed so soft. His body so strong and hot next to hers. She just wanted to give in to the emotion. She didn't want to fight it.

But she needed to fight it. She knew she did. Knew there was nothing but disappointment and pain down that road.

In that moment, the knowledge didn't make her want it any less.

So just for a little while, she would turn and snuggle into Mac's embrace, and there would be nothing more than them. Nothing more than this. The bed, Mac and Lucy.

"Feel like you had your needs met?" he asked, his voice thick, sleepy.

"Yes," she said, closing her eyes and trying to ignore the tears pooling behind her lids.

She was lying. All it had done was open up a whole new well of need. Exposed a chasm that she'd been doing such a good job of ignoring.

She tried to pull up images of Daniel. Words he'd said. Things that had hurt her and diminished her. Something to remind her of why she needed to keep the feelings out of it. Something to hold them at bay.

But she couldn't. Because with Mac, she was too far removed from that woman. She couldn't, for one moment, believe any of her ex's insults anymore, and it stole all of their power and vitality away from them.

She wasn't afraid of the memories. And they didn't hurt, not like they'd hurt at the time. Not even like it had hurt to remember them a few weeks ago.

It turned out that hot, sweaty sex could effectively knock off some pretty heavy chains.

It was hard to find boundaries when your current lover was a live-in housekeeper.

Mac didn't particularly want to send Lucy back to her little house every night. He wanted her to stay in his bed. But that would get tricky. Seeing as it was her job to get up early and make breakfast, pack his lunch and otherwise do a lot of things that a woman he was in a serious relationship with might do.

Or what he assumed they might do.

He'd never had a real, serious relationship. Some long-term casual dating of the same woman, yes. But he didn't have women come into his house and cook for him. Do his laundry. For heaven's sake, the woman he was sleeping with was handling his dirty socks.

There was a whole level of intimacy there that he'd never arrived at with another woman, and it had happened with Lucy by default.

Which meant that her going back to her house at some point in the night was necessary. It was on the same property, yes, but it added some boundaries. That way, when she got out of bed in the morning, she was coming to work to make him breakfast. Not rolling out of bed to make breakfast for her lover.

Boundaries.

Mac looked up from the log he was getting ready to split and watched Lucy walk up the porch steps and into the house. And he watched her ass in those tight black pants she was wearing.

Boundaries. Freaking, stupid boundaries.

She was working, which meant going into the house to instigate a little bit of foreplay would be a violation of those boundaries. It was part of the unspoken rules they'd slowly sunk into over the past two weeks.

Lucy slept in her house, and when she was working, they hardly spoke. Then, at dinner, the rules started to relax. They ate together, talked. Then Lucy did the dishes. Sometimes he did them because, since dinner was more relaxed, the moments after always felt like a gray area in terms of Lucy's responsibilities.

Then, after that, they went upstairs to his room, and all professionalism and boundaries ceased to exist. So did clothes. There was just the two of them and a day's worth of tension to burn off. Sometimes it required half the night to burn through it. And they used half the night if necessary.

They were both a little sleep-deprived.

But it was worth it. He brought the axe down on the top of the log, putting his sexual frustration into the motion. Because it was the only way he was burning through anything in the next few hours. All he could do was exhaust himself.

Although he needed a break. Definitely. He set the axe down and stripped his shirt off, using the fabric to wipe the sweat off his chest. He slung it over his shoulder and headed down toward the house. Surely Lucy would have some lemonade or iced tea for him. Which was all he wanted from her. Honest.

He pushed the front door open and walked in. Lucy was dusting. It was very domestic and weirdly sexy all at the same time, and he wasn't sure what he was supposed to do with the onslaught of feelings that tumbled down on his head.

"Hi," he said.

Lucy turned, her eyes widening. She was good for his ego. "Hi yourself."

"I'm thirsty. I was wondering if there was anything to drink?"

"Lemonade," she said, turning back to her dusting.

He walked into the kitchen and opened the fridge, a completely surreal feeling shrouding him in a fog. Even without kissing, there was some weird domestic vortex that seemed to be surrounding them both.

Strange, because it wasn't something he'd ever had, and yet he recognized it. And a strange part of him wanted it. Which was even weirder because he knew that this was a lie. This kind of quiet, sweet union. And forget one existing that could be this companionable and also be filled with crazy hold-on-to-your-hat sex. Nope. Wasn't possible.

Of course, there were Lucas and Carly. Mac didn't know about their sex life, and he didn't want to, but he knew they were happy. So happy it made his gut hurt to look at them. He was happy for Carly. Thrilled for his sister, and for his best friend, that they'd found some happiness after having had such tough childhoods.

But they were two in a million. That kind of thing just wasn't out there for him.

Especially not with Lucy.

"What do you want for dinner?" she asked.

He froze. That sounded like a wife question. Not a housekeeper question. Which was stupid, because it was her job to cook for him. But the lines were so blurred and the boundaries just weren't helping right that second.

"I thought I might go out," he said—not a lie, because he was thinking he might right now.

"Oh." He could tell by the tone of that single syllable that she wasn't very happy about it. But that was too bad. They weren't in a domestic partnership, no matter how things might feel. And that meant he could go out if he wanted to.

"That frees you up tonight," he said. "You can work on more plans for Carly's deal."

"The fundraiser for the school district," she said, her tone waspish.

"Right, the fundraiser. Well, you can work on that."

"Great. I will. When do you think you'll be back?"

"Late." He was shooting himself in the foot and he knew it. Pushing himself straight into a cold, womanless bed for the evening. Because he was being an ass and he knew it. But he also needed to remind her, and himself, what this was.

He wasn't accountable to her. She wasn't accountable to him. They were just having sex. That hot, sweaty sex they both needed.

Of course, he wouldn't be having it tonight, but he was doing his part to maintain the status quo.

"Late late?" she asked.

"Yep."

"Great. Well." She set down her dust cloth. "I'll see you in the morning, I guess. I'm going to go work on *Carly's thing*," she said, the phrase dripping with disdain.

"I'm sorry," he said, not able to leave things quite so bad. "I didn't mean to minimize it." Especially since that was what her ex had done. All the time.

She nodded. "I know. Thanks."

"See you."

"Yeah."

Lucy turned and walked out, and Mac waited for a feeling of right to settle over him. For a sense of accomplishment to hit. He had done what needed to be done. If only he felt more triumphant. He just sort of felt like a douche. A douche who was going to bed alone tonight.

Lucy tried to ignore the hurt that had lodged itself down deep in her chest. But it was hard to ignore because it just . . . hurt.

She could sense when the tide had turned in the house earlier. It was when she'd asked what he'd wanted for dinner. And suddenly he'd gotten this frozen, wide-eyed look, like a buck in the headlights. And then he'd said he was going out.

She snorted and flipped open the notebook she was using to keep track of her expenses for the barbecue. Thankfully, Carly had managed to get the PTA and the city council on board with the concept, and now it was just a matter of making it all work.

Using an outdoor venue, one that was being provided free of charge by one of the students' parents, went a long way in reducing costs. But they were still going from an exclusive formal affair to an inclusive event that was still supposed to maintain an element of luxury.

No big deal.

Yes, thinking about this was way better than thinking about Mac and his attitude problem. She didn't care about Mac like that anyway. She was just disappointed because sleeping with him was the highlight of her day. She'd found out she liked sex a lot more than she'd thought she had.

And she refused to feel bad about it. With Mac, she got everything she wanted without having to risk anything. If only the lead weight in her chest agreed with that.

She scowled and picked up the phone that was installed out in her house. One day, when circumstances improved, she would get a computer for her event planning, and a cell phone.

She paused. Was she really thinking about a career? A future? She smiled in spite of the hurt feelings. Because she was. She had a goal. One that went past survival. It felt like a huge step.

She sighed and dialed Sarah's number. The other woman had become her sounding board, and even though she was sure Lucy shocked her prim friend now and again, she was also sure it was good for her. Everyone needed to be shocked sometimes. Mac managed to shock her every night.

"Hello?" Sarah picked up on the first ring, something Sarah often did, since she seemed to always be at home in the evenings.

"Why aren't you out?" Lucy asked.

"Nowhere to go. What's up, Lucy?"

"Nothing. Something. I think I'm messing things up with Mac."

"How?"

"I think I might feel something for him."

"And that's bad?"

"Yes. It's very bad. It's not what either of us wants. I want to get over this thing with my ex and find a real job and some independence. I need to figure out who I am."

"And you want to be happy?" Sarah asked.

"Well, yes. Who doesn't?"

"So, what will make you happy?"

She sighed. "I'm afraid to try for happy."

"Why?"

"Because I don't know if I've ever really had it. I'm afraid to want it because if I do . . . if I do and I can't have it . . ."

"What makes you happy?"

"Mac does."

"You were the one who told me a woman should go for what she wants. You're kind of my hero, Lucy. You fought your way out of a horrible situation; you've fought to get back on your feet on your own terms. To find out who you are apart from what that . . . that horrible man you were married to said you were. Don't stop fighting now."

Lucy swallowed hard. "I think I love him."

"I know," Sarah said.

"And if he doesn't love me back?"

"He's an idiot. He should love you back. He should be beyond happy and honored that he has you."

"It wasn't supposed to get this complicated."

"I know. Why should you be happy with okay? Why not go for great?"

Lucy chewed her lip. "I have nothing left to teach you, grasshopper. You've become the master."

Sarah laughed. "Not really. It's a lot easier to say than it is to do."

"So, let's both do it. Let's both shoot for amazing. How about that?"

"I . . . yes. Yeah. I think . . . that's a good idea. Let's do that."

"Then it's a deal. No more okay for either of us. We both deserve more."

"It's not that late, Mac. I think you're becoming a lightweight in your old age."

Mac stopped in the doorway, his hand paused on the light switch. He could see Lucy's silhouette, see where she was sitting on the couch. He turned the light on, and his breath caught.

She was wearing a red dress. Red lipstick. She looked . . . out of his league. She looked like the woman he'd imagined she'd grow up to be. Confident. Cool. Sophisticated and sexy all at the same time.

She definitely didn't look like the kind of woman who should be working for him. She didn't look like the kind of woman he could ever hope to hold on to.

"I have to get up early," he said. It was a lame response, but there wasn't enough blood left in his brain to help him come up with a better one.

"Well, that's too bad. Maybe I should let you go to bed then?"

"No," he said. "No." Because he'd come to some kind of conclusion while he'd been out at that stupid bar. He didn't know where the conclusion would lead him, but it was there nonetheless.

A blonde had bought him a drink. And then she'd come over to make conversation. And she'd made it very clear that with little effort on his part, the two of them could have ended up, if not in bed, at least horizontal in the cab of his pickup truck.

But he hadn't been tempted. Not even a little. Because all he could do was obsess about Lucy and the issues from earlier. And about how much he wanted her to be in his bed tonight. The idea of sex didn't seem that appealing when the woman wasn't Lucy. And that was almost unheard of.

He was faithful to the women he dated, always. But if a random woman flirted with him while he was out, he turned her down with a little feeling of wistfulness. There had been no wistfulness tonight. Nothing but the desire to get back home and fix things with Lucy.

For whatever reason, she was the only woman he wanted right now. So that meant, until that changed, he intended to keep her as close as possible.

"If you don't want to go to bed, what do you want to do?" She draped her arms over the back of the couch, thrusting her breasts into prominence.

"I have a feeling you have something in mind?"

A half smile quirked her cherry-red lips. "Why yes. Yes, I do. Take off your shirt."

She didn't have to ask him twice. He tugged his T-shirt over his head and stood in front of her, waiting for her next command.

"Boots. Pants. Underwear. I want you naked," she said.

"Oh, Lucy, you really are the perfect woman," he said, working to comply with her wishes.

"Not perfect," she said, standing up. "But not as bad as some people have made me out to be."

"You seem like a pretty bad girl to me," he said.

Dark eyebrows shot up. "Do I?" She sounded intrigued by the thought.

"Right now? Oh yeah."

"You like bad girls?" she asked.

"Hell yeah." Her eyes flickered down to where his cock was unashamedly announcing just how much he did.

"I spent an awfully long time being good. Sit down."

He took a seat on the couch, obeying her command. A little turned on by it.

"And I think being good is highly overrated," she continued. "Highly." She reached around behind her and tugged on her zipper, her dress loosening, falling down to her waist, revealing her lacy red bra that did nothing to conceal the dark shadows of her nipples beneath.

"You won't get an argument from me."

She pushed her dress down her hips, and then it was just her in a red bra, panties and black stilettos. His mouth went dry, his stomach muscles so tight they hurt.

She sauntered to the couch, her expression intense, her eyes not leaving his. She put her knee up on the couch, reveling in her dominant role. He liked it too, but he had something else in mind he liked even better.

He took hold of her thigh and tugged it up so that her high-heeled foot was on the couch, the other on the ground, and the very tempting heart of her was right within his reach.

He extended his finger and let it drift beneath the seam of her panties, sliding his finger through her folds, finding her wet and ready. "Bad or good, Lucy Ryan-Carter, I just think you're perfect." He slipped a finger deep inside of her and her head fell back, a sharp curse on her lips. He liked seeing her like this. Liked seeing the woman she was becoming. Not prim or proper. Not nervous. Confident in herself. In the woman she was.

"You're pretty perfect yourself," she said.

She put her knee back down on the couch and put her other one on the other side of his thigh, so that she was straddling him. "I came prepared." She reached into her bra and produced a condom packet, an impish smile on her face.

"You just got more perfect," he said, kissing her deeply, taking the condom from her hand. "I didn't think it was possible."

After taking care of the precautions, he pushed her panties aside and she moved over him, sliding down onto his length, her lips shaped like a perfect *O*.

He put his hands on her hips and thrust up inside of her, and she matched his movements, meeting him. Challenging him. Pushing him. It was building too fast. His arousal peaking too far, too fast, clashing with the emotion that was raging through his chest.

He was nearly blind with it, the blood roaring through his ears, blocking out the sound. There was nothing but Lucy. Her skin. Her scent. The way she felt, so tight and hot and perfect around his body.

The way she made him feel.

"Mac," she breathed, release shuddering through her, fingernails digging into his skin.

And that was enough to push him over into the abyss. He felt like he was burning alive, like the fire would consume him. There was no way anyone could survive so much heat.

But he did. And when he came back to himself, Lucy was there.

And he found he couldn't breathe. Because she made him crave something he'd vowed he would never, ever need.

Not because he didn't want it. But because he was afraid of what might happen if he did.

CHAPTER

Ten

Lucy's world was officially rocked. And it was all Mac Denton's fault. But she wasn't upset about it. She didn't have that kind of floating, hazy feeling she often had after release. Not this time. Instead, she felt this incredible clarity. Everything seemed sharper. More real.

Everything made sense.

"I love you," she said.

She hadn't meant to say it. Hell, she hadn't realized she'd meant it until the words had come out of her mouth. But she did mean them. She meant them with every newfound piece of herself.

He went stiff beneath her, his muscles locking up, his whole body tense. "What?"

"Do I really have to repeat myself?"

"You had better."

She moved away from him, suddenly feeling very exposed where before it had all felt so natural. So right.

Now she just felt stupid and awkward. Laid bare. And it didn't have much to do with her nudity.

"I said I love you," she said, cold dread winding itself around her stomach, making her feel like she couldn't breathe.

"Lucy . . . no. This isn't what this was supposed to be."

"I know that," she said. "Don't you think I of all people know that? I just got out of this . . . miserable marriage and I'm trying to put the pieces of my life, pieces of myself, back together, and the last thing I need is a committed relationship, or strong feelings of any kind for someone, but . . . but I have them. Because you've been a part of this process. You've supported me."

Mac's eyes were blank, his expression cold. "Don't confuse that with love, Lucy."

Anger spiked in her veins, hot and unreasonable. "I'm not confused about love. Not now. I used to be. I used to think that love was there because I'd made vows to a man, so it didn't matter how he treated me. Didn't matter that he thought I was stupid and worthless, and that he told me so. I thought just because he was my husband, it meant he loved me, but I was wrong. He didn't love me. He didn't even like me. He owned me, and that's what he loved. He loved having me in his power. And I didn't know that possession wasn't love. But I know that now. You've never once tried to put me down, or put me in my place, and you of all people had a reason to. I earned your disdain, and still you had too much decency to."

"Listen to yourself, Lucy," he said, standing. "Your husband was an ass, so you're confusing common courtesy with something deeper."

"I'm sorry, is that what you consider screwing a woman on your couch? Common courtesy? Silly me. I thought it might be more than that."

"Don't. You were the one who said it could be all physical. You were the one who said you could handle it."

"Yeah. I can handle it. I'm pretty strong, in case you missed it. Look, still standing. But you know what? Just because I could handle it doesn't mean I didn't develop feelings."

"That's not handling it."

"You're the one who doesn't seem to be handling it," she said, not sure where the calm tone of voice came from. Not sure why she was able to stand him down, feeling totally strong and justified.

He looked down and it suddenly struck her as almost funny that they were having an argument with her in her underwear and heels and him completely naked. Almost funny.

"I'm not handling it. You're right. It's not the time. Just . . . get your stuff and let's go upstairs."

Her mouth dropped open. "Excuse me?"

"Get your clothes and let's go upstairs," he repeated.

"After this? I don't think so."

"Everything was going great, Lucy. Let's just forget this happened."

"No," she said. "No, I'm not going to forget it just because it's inconvenient for you. I'm not going to go upstairs and just go on with the 'sex only' thing when I want more. I am so damned tired of taking half, Mac. I took it for far too long in my marriage and I will not take it from you, or from anyone else, ever again. I want it all. I want a man who loves me—more than that, I want a man who isn't too afraid to let himself love me."

"You think I'm afraid?"

"Yes, I think you're afraid. No, I know you are. Because your parents are such a disaster. Because you've seen love play out badly. I've lived it. I have walked that road myself."

"So why the hell would you ever do it again? Why would you risk a good thing for something I'm not even sure exists?"

She swallowed and looked down at the floor. "Did you ever think that maybe what I had, what you saw, wasn't love? Maybe it's not that love doesn't exist, it's just that very self-ish people misidentify it. They say they love someone, but what they really love is themselves. Their own comfort. Maybe that's what we've experienced. But that's not what we have. Not what we could have."

Mac shook his head. "If you have to believe that, Lucy, I understand. But I don't. I just think it's asking for a life filled with a bunch of fighting and pain. And my parents brought kids into it. They made us be a part of it. I'm not doing it."

"I didn't think you were a coward, Mac."

A muscled jerked in Mac's jaw, and his teeth clenched tightly together. She could tell he wanted to say something. That he wanted to yell, even. But he didn't. Instead, he backed away. "I bet you'll be wanting to find another place to work."

"Maybe eventually," she said. "But I'm not just going to quit working here."

"Oh, really?"

She crossed her arms beneath her breasts. "I need this job. I'm not walking away from it over some hurt feelings. I'll get over it. I've learned enough about myself over the past few months to know that. And to know that I survive heartbreak pretty well."

Not this kind though. Her love for Daniel had eroded slowly over time. A casualty of his behavior. His harsh words.

This was a sharp break in her heart. The loss of a man who had given up before they'd ever really tried. The loss of something that could have been amazing.

"If you're staying anyway," he said, "why don't you stay with me?"

She shook her head. "No. And I hate that I have to say that. But it's time I lived on my terms, and not just someone else's. It's time I asked for what I want and actually expect to get it. I love you. If you decide you love me, if you decide not to be scared, if you decide you want more than just sex and common courtesy, then you run to me, and don't wait. But until then . . . until then it has to be done."

She bent down and picked up her dress, sliding it back over her curves and zipping it. She put her hand on her chest. The throbbing in there, around her heart, was physical, so painful it blindsided her.

She had done what she needed to. She'd made a decision for herself. She'd demanded more. Demanded what she deserved.

It sucked a whole lot more than she'd imagined it would.

Because part of her just wanted to run back to him and say, *Hell yeah, let's keep having the sweaty sex.* But there was something new inside of her, a core of strength that she couldn't ignore, didn't want to ignore. And that strength wouldn't allow her to bend.

Not anymore. She'd spent too many years so bent, she'd nearly broken.

And if she just bowed down and let go of everything that mattered to her, she wouldn't even be the kind of woman Mac would care for. More importantly, she wouldn't be a woman she could care about.

But it still sucked.

Mac didn't want to get out of bed. He couldn't remember that ever happening to him. Not even after an all-night bender. Because he was a rancher, and that meant getting up at the ass crack of dawn. It meant putting on his boots and his hat and getting in gear.

Daylight was precious, and his land was his livelihood.

But right now, he figured daylight and his livelihood could go to hell. He was already there.

How could the absence of someone feel so miserable? He was used to the presence of a woman making him miserable. It was why God had invented breaking up.

Usually, after a breakup he felt light and free. Now he felt hungover, and he hadn't even gotten that drunk.

The simple truth was, when he thought about love and

marriage, he was filled with bone-deep terror. It was why he'd generally avoided thinking about it. It was why his relationships always ended early. So he never had to face it. So he never had to deal with the fact that he was afraid. Lucy was right—he was a coward.

He was afraid of being the callous bastard his father was. Afraid of being stupid like his mother. He didn't know which thought scared him more. But he'd never seen it go another way. And when he thought of being locked in that endless hell with someone . . . he just couldn't even entertain it.

No matter how much it hurt now, it would hurt worse later. For both of them.

Which meant no matter how much he wanted Lucy, no matter how much he wanted to tell her whatever she needed to hear to keep her in his bed, his life, he had to let her go.

He growled and threw the covers off, planting his feet flat on the floor. He had things to take care of. He didn't have time to wallow. And still, all he wanted to do was wallow.

"Sad sack," he muttered, forcing himself to stand up.

He'd always assumed his life experiences had just beaten the ability to love right out of him. But it turned out that wasn't true. He could love. He was just too damn afraid to do anything about it.

Anything other than hurt.

CHAPTER

Eleven

Lucy felt proud of herself. She'd made it through two weeks of working at Mac's house without falling into his bed or falling apart. And neither was any mean feat.

The man was gorgeous and frequently walked around shirtless looking like a dessert. He was visual cake, and she wanted to lick all the icing off.

And then there were the moments when the pain of not being with him, of not having an emotional connection, hurt so bad she thought she was dying a little.

They barely spoke. He barely looked at her. They were almost worse than they'd been when she'd first shown up on his doorstep. Because they'd been enemies then. But they were strangers now. At least enemies had evidence of passion. This was . . . it was like he was pretending nothing had happened between them.

The upside was that she wasn't hurting over her marriage anymore. She just felt . . . past it. She felt new, and different.

She also had the barbecue project to fling herself into,

and now, with less than a day to go before the big event, she was up to her neck in planning, so pining was a little difficult.

"Almost done!"

Lucy turned at the sound of Carly's voice, straightening from where she'd been tying a bow on the back of a chair. Not a stiff linen bow on a crisp white chair cover like she might have done at a formal party. She, Sarah and Carly had been tying raffia bows around wooden chairs for hours. But everything was getting close to completion.

They'd also spent time prepping mason jars by putting sugar on the rims, perfect for the strawberry lemonade that was going to be served. And the people who had volunteered to man the grills had already started prepping the beef—high-quality, highly sought-after beef provided by Mac Denton, of course.

Lucy sighed. All right, so she might suck at love, but she was good at planning events. And she didn't need anyone to tell her so.

Well, it wouldn't hurt. But unlike when she'd been married to Daniel, she wasn't pinning all of her hopes and dreams on someone else's response. She wasn't putting all of her self-esteem in someone else's hands.

"Yes." Lucy planted her hands on her hips. "We are. It's really looking great."

"And you're frowning because . . . ?" Carly asked.

"Because?"

"Does this have anything to do with my brother?"

Lucy and Sarah exchanged a look. Sarah's cheeks were bright red. Subtle the other woman was not. If there was ever a need to cover up a crime, Sarah would not be her first choice as accomplice.

"Why do you ask that?" Lucy asked.

"Because while the rest of us were devouring chocolate cake a couple of weeks ago, he was devouring you with his eyes."

"Oh." All things considered, that was a hideously embarrassing observation for Mac's sister to have made.

"Was that a confirmation?" Carly asked.

"If it was," Lucy said slowly, "then . . . let's just say that we want different things. There's just no way that we can make other things work right now. Because of the different things we want."

"Because of your marriage?"

"What does my marriage have to do with anything? I'm free and clear legally. I can do what I want with who I want."

"Legally . . . but emotionally?"

Lucy frowned. "It's not me. It's him. I love that sorry jackass and he's way too scared to accept it."

Both Sarah and Carly looked at her, open-mouthed. "You love him?" Carly asked.

"I didn't mean to," Lucy said.

"I'm sure you didn't!" Carly said. "My brother is a bad bet. I love him, but when it comes to women—"

"I know," Lucy said. "I know. And I thought I just wanted to have some fun after the divorce, but then . . . it turns out there's a lot more to Mac than it seems like at first. He's a good guy. I don't know if even he realizes how good."

"I'm sure he doesn't," Carly said.

"I can kind of relate because, until recently, I thought I was pretty worthless. But Mac showed me something else. He made me see myself differently. You both did too. Maybe I need to help him with a change of perspective too."

Because she hadn't been wrong about his fear. It was there, as real as her own. And it was easy to walk away, to say she needed to stand on her own feet. She did need to stand on her own feet, and she was standing on them, but Mac, and her feelings for him, didn't have to compromise that.

He was in the woods. Just like she'd been. Lost, blind. Unable to find the path out.

No, she couldn't go on sleeping with him, wanting more

and getting nothing. But she couldn't leave him to wander the wilderness forever either.

And if there was nothing, if he wouldn't come with her, she'd have no choice but to leave him, even though it broke her heart.

But she'd be damned if she'd abandon him to his anguish, like her parents had done to her. She and Mac had always been left to their own pain. Well, he'd helped her step out of hers.

She had to at least try and help him do the same.

Mac couldn't shake the strange tightness in his chest. He hadn't been able to shake it since that disastrous fight and subsequent breakup with Lucy. Was it even a breakup? They'd just been having sex, hadn't they?

A sharp twinge in his chest mocked that little lie he'd been telling himself.

He took a deep breath and looked around. The fundraising barbecue looked like it was a huge success. There was something magical about it, something unique. From the paper bag lanterns that lined the walk, to the lights strung overhead, the live band and the candles on all the tables.

It was both country and classy at the same time. It was so very Lucy.

He suddenly wanted to be anywhere else. Or stay here forever, in this place that had the imprint of the woman he loved all over it.

Love? Damn. When had it come to that?

And what the hell was he supposed to do about it?

Just not be afraid?

Or maybe be more afraid of life without her than of taking a chance at life with her?

Yeah, that hit close to the truth. In a big way. Because the simple fact was that if he didn't have her, he would never be happier than this. And this was not happy. This was miserable. This was "climb into the bottom of a bottle of Jack Daniel's and never come out" miserable.

And sure, marriage, commitment, all of that, were scary as hell. But on the other side, he had this. This howling void of pain, and honestly, no amount of unknown was scarier than feeling this forever, and ever, and ever.

It was true what they said. Love, perfect love, demolished fear. At the very least, it made it seem small.

"Hi, Mac."

He turned and his heart just about stopped. Lucy in a simple white sundress was enough to make him lose his mind. And it turned out Lucy just being Lucy was enough to make him lose his heart.

"Hi. Things look great."

"Thanks," she said.

"Look, I—"

"Eh. Don't start a sentence that way. No one ever says anything good when they open with 'look.' 'Listen' is the same."

"I was going to try to make a half-assed, lame apology."

"I was right then. I really don't want to hear it, so . . . why don't you try something else?"

"Like?"

"Ask me to dance."

"I don't think it's a good idea."

"It is."

"How do you know?"

She smiled, her dark eyes glittering. "Because it was my idea." She studied his face for a moment and her expression turned serious. "What?"

He let out a breath he hadn't realized he was holding. "Sometimes, when I look at you, I feel like I just got punched in the gut."

A short laugh escaped her lips. "Is that a good thing?"

"I don't know. It makes it impossible to pretend like I don't feel anything, that's for sure."

"Then it is a good thing. Come on, come dance with me."

She took his hand and led him over to the raised wooden dance floor. He pulled her into his arms, and his knees shook. It felt so good to have her near him again. After so many days of pretending like he'd never touched her, never kissed her, never made love to her.

"So let's talk about that feeling that makes it feel like you got punched," she said.

"I don't know what to say about it."

"You feel something for me," she said.

"I never said I didn't, Lucy. I just said it was impossible for us to have more."

"It's not though," she said. "Do you see all this?" She waved her hand around.

"Yes. It's amazing."

"I know. I know it is. And it's amazing because of me. Do you know how great that feels? I have confidence in that. But I wouldn't if it wasn't for you."

"I didn't give you the job. Carly did."

"I know. But you gave me my first job. You didn't laugh at me when my pie turned out to need a log splitter to cut it—you just ate the filling. You didn't push me down further when I was at the bottom— you pulled me up. You got angry for me when I told you about my ex. No one else had done that for me. No one else had listened. You made me see something new in myself. You made me see something of value." A tear slid down her cheek. "I want to do that for you."

"Lucy," he said, his heart squeezed tight. "I'm fine. It's not that. It's just . . . relationships . . ."

"You're afraid of messing it up, I know. But do you think I would do anything to hurt you?"

"No."

"So you're afraid you would hurt me," she said.

"Maybe," he said, feeling like his throat was about to close up.

"You wouldn't. I wish you could see what I see. I wish you saw the man who helped a woman who treated him like dirt. The man who gave that woman her self-confidence back. Because that's the man I see. A man completely worthy of giving and receiving love. A man I wish would love me. Because I really do love him."

"I do love you," he said.

She stopped dancing, her mouth falling open. "You do?"

"But . . . I don't know how to be a husband. My parents had a horrible marriage. I've never thought about being a husband or a father. I don't know . . . I don't know if I would do right by you, and after what your ex did, I can't stand the thought of hurting you."

"I told you I didn't need your protection. Anyway, you hurt me in your effort to not hurt me."

"I hurt myself too," he said.

"That's a little bit gratifying," she said. "Okay, a lot gratifying even. I'm glad to know I haven't been suffering alone."

He took her hand and squeezed. "Let's move this somewhere else."

"Okay." There was no missing that they were drawing interested looks from the other dancing couples. And he had no doubt this would be serious town gossip by morning.

He took her over to one of the barns and around to the side. It was dark there, quiet. And he was done talking.

He pulled her into his arms and kissed her, with every ounce of emotion—all the pain, love, desire—he had in his body. When they parted, they were both breathing hard. He pushed a hand through his hair and discovered it was shaking.

"I don't know how to say all the right things," he said. "I don't know how to do all the right things or be all the right things, but I know that I want you. I want you with me, by my side. And it's not because of your cooking."

She laughed. "No kidding?"

"Not even a little. It's not because of anything you can do for me, really. It's just because of . . . you."

Another tear slid down her cheek, silver in the moonlight. "What do you mean you don't know how to say and do the right things? In one sentence you just showed me love in a more profound way than my husband showed me for eight years."

Something expanded in his chest: a depth of emotion he hadn't realized was possible for him to feel that made his eyes sting. "Wow, Lucy, just think what I could do with that kind of time."

"I'd love to find out," she said.

He felt like he was standing on the edge of a cliff. And he had two choices. He could go back and he could live the same way he always had. Or he could jump. Forget fear. Forget everything but Lucy.

If he was lucky, he would land in her arms and nothing else would matter.

"That's the best idea I've heard in a long time," he said. He found there wasn't room for doubt anymore. And that he'd left fear behind, back up on the ledge.

"Mac . . . I've been in love. I've seen what it's like when it withers. But when I fell in love the first time, I believed that I had to make myself into the wife my husband wanted to see. What I'm offering you is me. Me the way that I am. I can promise you that I won't always conform to what you'd like me to. And I can promise I'll fail in some things. But I can also promise that I'll love you through all that. I promise that if you can love me, *me*, and not the idea of me, then I'll give you the same."

Mac cupped her cheek, his heart pounding so hard he thought he might pass out. "I don't want you to change. You're so strong. And when you told me where to shove it, you were right to do it. I deserved it. Because you deserved more than I was giving, and I'm damn proud of you for that. Don't take less, Lucy, not from me or anyone."

"I won't. And the very fact that you asked me not to compromise shows me I won't have to."

"My parents," he said, his throat tight, "I think they were in love once too. But they forgot to give to each other. They were so caught up in their own shit, they didn't look at each other, they didn't look at their kids. I'll remember."

"I will too," she said. "I promise."

"It helps that I know you're a strong woman who won't put up with that kind of stuff."

"It helps that you're a strong man who won't put me through it."

For the first time, he felt like he was strong. Strong enough to make a change. Strong enough to promise love, and to know he would honor that promise.

"I love you, Lucy," he said. "The kind of love that changes a person."

"This is the first time anyone has ever changed for me," she said.

"It's a change for the better. I owe you for that."

"Do you?" she asked, arching her brows, pressing her breasts into his chest.

"I truly do. Good thing I have a long time to make it up to you." He kissed her, long and deep, and when they parted, they were both breathing hard. "Starting right now."

Epilogue

Mac leaned over and put his hand over Lucy's. "You really did a great job planning the wedding."

Lucy smiled. "Thanks. Most of it was Carly's idea, of course. I just executed it."

"But you did it perfectly."

Lucy's heart expanded, love for Mac, for her life, almost overwhelming her. He had been so supportive of her over the past months, encouraging her as she got her new event coordination business up and running. And until she'd started making decent money, she'd quit her job as his housekeeper and worked at Delia's Kitchen in town, in spite of Mac's insistence he would take care of her.

He *had* taken care of her, and then some. But after moving into his house, she'd been uncomfortable with just living off his income, or cleaning the house she lived in and getting paid to do it . . . from her boyfriend's bank account. So diner work it had been.

And extra work, cleaning houses other than her own, while she'd worked at getting accounts for her business.

Mac's support had never wavered. And he'd more than made good on his word about respecting who she was. Though he didn't seem to respect her pie-baking skills.

Still, she knew she couldn't win them all.

Though lately she was winning quite a bit. Even her parents seemed more accepting of her choices, ever since she'd marched back to her childhood home and explained that she wasn't going to live the life they wanted her to. That she had to live on her own terms, and they could accept that or not have her in their lives.

The thaw had been slow, but it was happening. So many good things were happening.

"It means so much to me to hear you say that."

"I mean it."

Lucy sighed and leaned back in her seat. Then the music started and the guests stopped talking, and all attention turned to the head of the aisle, where Lucas stood, ready to greet his bride.

Mac leaned over again. "I know you've done this whole wedding thing before."

"Yes," she whispered. "I have."

"Do you think you'd ever want to do it again?"

Her eyes opened wide and she forgot to whisper. "With you?"

"I was hoping so."

"Yes, Mac. Yes. I want you to be my husband. I want to be your wife."

Mac smiled and leaned in, kissing her lips. And Lucy kissed him back.

With Mac, she wasn't the queen bitch of Silver Creek. And she wasn't his doormat. With Mac, she was just Lucy. And just being Lucy had never felt so good.

"How long were you planning on it lasting?" she asked, swallowing the lump that had risen in her throat.

"A lifetime sound about right to you?"

"A lifetime sounds just about perfect. You sure you won't get tired of me?"

"Not as long as you keep being you."

UNWRAPPED

One

What was a girl to do when she was too afraid to take a shot of liquid courage? Sarah Larsen had never let any alcohol touch her lips, unless you counted cough syrup. And even her grandmother hadn't counted cough syrup, which meant it officially didn't count at all.

Sarah pushed the shot glass away from her, then turned it. She should have ordered something with an umbrella. Or at least something with more sugar than booze. But filled with false bravado and a feeling of utter claustrophobia brought on by the way she lived her life, she'd walked into the bar in the tightest—skimming her figure, not hugging it, but still—shortest—an inch above the knee, but whatever— black dress she owned, strode right up to the counter and ordered a shot of whiskey.

That she was too afraid to drink.

And if she couldn't get even a little drunk, then there was no way she was going to be able to find the courage to re- alize the night's ultimate goal: Finding a man. A hot, sexy man. And cutting loose for the first time in her life.

And by "cutting loose," she meant "having sex."

She winced internally. Yes. Sex. She wasn't backing down now. She wasn't going to spell it mentally anymore either. She could think it. She could even *say* it. She wasn't going to be repressed tonight. No, she was not.

Of course, she'd been in the bar an hour and she knew every guy who had come in. Not that that was a bad thing, except it meant that she just sort of blended into the wood paneling when they scanned the room.

Typical. Sarah Larsen, kindergarten teacher, was not the woman the men of Silver Creek called for a good time.

That line of thinking had her feeling decidedly morose. Which was just another reason she shouldn't drink the alcohol. It would probably make that feeling worse.

The door to the bar opened and a rush of cold air spilled in. Sarah looked, and nearly choked. The man standing in the door was a stranger. Tall, broad shouldered, wearing tight jeans and some very expensive-looking boots. He was backlit by the porch light, snow falling behind him across the black sky.

If she'd been drunk, she could have blamed the whiskey for the sheer drama of the moment. But she still hadn't touched her drink.

She blinked as the man walked in and let the door swing shut behind him. And . . . and he was coming toward her. She almost stopped breathing. Then she almost took the whiskey shot because she really did want to find the courage to at least talk to him.

Except if she tried alcohol for the first time right now, it would probably put her on the floor, and that wasn't the idea either.

He rested his forearms on the bar beside her, not noticing her at all. Typical. There was a group of women standing by the jukebox, wearing skirts so short that they were in danger of showing London, France and their underpants. Assuming they were wearing any.

They presented a much more enticing picture to the male of the species. She was sure. Not from experience, but because it was why her grandmother had always made her wear skirts that went mid-calf or longer. Because anything else would tempt men, and her along with them, to sin.

Well, she was looking for sin tonight, and she wasn't having a lot of luck finding it.

She should ask those women where they'd bought their skirts.

She looked out of the corner of her eye, just enough to get another peek at the stranger. He drew his hand over his beard. Not a full beard, but a couple days' worth of growth maybe.

As if she had any idea of how quickly men's facial hair grew. She'd never lived with a man, not even a male relative.

Still, that was her guess. She also guessed it would feel rough on her skin. And she was surprised to learn that she didn't find the thought off-putting in the least. Oh, no, the idea of a little rough stubble against her skin seemed altogether too enticing, really.

"I don't actually . . . want this," she said, her voice way too mousy and shaky and not at all vampy. She pushed the shot in his direction. "So if you were going to order one . . . you could always have mine."

He arched one dark eyebrow. "I was after a beer. I have to drive."

"Oh." She looked back down at her glass. "I could . . . I could drive you . . . if . . . if you wanted to . . . Never mind."

He raised his other brow and pulled the glass toward himself, lifting it to his lips and knocking it back. "Thank you. For the offer and the drink."

"It seemed like a nice thing to do. I don't . . . Where are you from?"

"Texas," he said. "Austin."

"Oh. I hope you weren't planning on driving back to Austin. My offer wasn't . . . really meant to extend that far."

He laughed, and a flush of heat spread over her skin.

She'd made him laugh. She took a breath and tried to banish her nerves. She wasn't totally failing at this.

"I'm staying here tonight. I have a room at the lodge over by the lake."

"Those are . . . nice. I hear. I've never had an occasion to stay in one, since I live here and all."

"Local girl, huh?"

"Very."

"And what brings you out tonight?"

Did she just say it? Did she just say, "The desire for hot sweaty sex brought me here; would you oblige me?" How was the game played? How did one pick up a stranger? Did they talk for a while? Did they just get down to it? She had no idea.

"Dancing?" he asked, a smile quirking his lips. Wicked lips, she noticed. And she thought "wicked" because they made her think of him doing wicked things with them. Kissing her mouth. Her neck. Her . . . oh, boy.

Thirty years of fantasies. Thirty years of virginity. It had to go, and it had to go now. Tonight. She hoped she didn't mess it up. Because if she lost hold of her stranger, she was left with the local boys . . . and that meant there would be no action for her.

"Sure. Dancing sounds much better than what I was going to say."

He stood and held out his hand. She took it, heat surging through her when his rough fingers closed over her skin. "What were you going to say? Now I'm intrigued."

He led her out to the dance floor, such as it was, a little space carved out by the jukebox. The women in the tight skirts were still there, and they were looking on—with envy. *She* was being envied. And she could see why.

This man, this stranger, was tall and lean, handsome to an almost ridiculous degree, and—she discovered the last part when he tugged her up against his body—all hard muscle.

He laced his fingers through hers and wrapped his other

arm around her waist, holding her close. "Come on, now, Red, I'm curious."

"Red? Really? That's the best you have?"

"I would have better if you gave me a name. And if you hadn't given me a shot of whiskey."

"Sarah," she said, first name only.

"Walker." First or last name, she didn't know. It didn't matter. She'd already made her decision. This was the night. This was the man.

If he wanted her, this was most definitely the man.

"Now you have better, so you may ask me again," she said, knowing she had her teacher voice on a little bit. But it helped. It helped her feel confident.

"Sarah," he said, his voice husky, a whiskey-coated dream, "what were you going to say?"

"I—" He started moving in time with the music and her brain just sort of stopped sending signals to her mouth. She'd never been held this close by a man before. Had never danced with one. Had never danced at all. "Would it be too convenient for me to say I don't remember?"

"Yes. Much too convenient. And you're only making me more interested."

"Oh." She sucked in a deep breath and closed her eyes. She couldn't look at him, not while she said this. "I was sort of here to . . . to see if a nice man might take me back to his . . . lodge. For the night. And it's especially nice that I met you since you're staying in a literal lodge and I've never been to that particular lodge. Also, point in your favor, you're a man."

The silence on his end was thick. And awkward. And Sarah thought she might die of humiliation then and there.

"Tough night, baby?" His thumb brushed the corner of her lip, and her eyes flew open, meeting his startling blue ones, glittering in the dim light.

"What makes you say that?"

"You don't seem like the kind of girl who comes here for this kind of thing on a regular basis."

"What gave me away?"

"The pantyhose, for a start. The blush, for another."

"It's cold. And anyway, I'm not in the habit of going out with bare legs."

"That's another indicator."

"All right, so I don't usually, but . . . but"—she looked at him, at his impossibly handsome face—"but it's what I'm here for now."

He nodded once. "There was a time in my life when I was the kind of man who came to places like this and did this kind of thing. Not for years though. But I'm thinking I might make an exception tonight. For you."

Her heart climbed into her throat and sat there, making it hard to breathe. Hard to speak. But she had to know one thing.

"You don't have a wife, do you?"

He shook his head. "Nope."

"Then . . . okay. Yes. I want . . . to go back to your lodge. For . . . *that*."

"Want to finish the dance?"

"No." She might lose her nerve if they waited too long. She didn't want to lose her nerve. She wanted Walker. He was so much better than the fantasy she'd conjured up. And it had taken weeks of heated fantasies to bring her to this point, so that was saying something.

"Then let's go. You drive."

"You aren't drunk, are you?" she asked.

"No."

"Good. I don't want to . . . take advantage of you."

He laughed and she realized how silly she sounded. Like she, mousy Sarah Larsen, who came up to the middle of his chest, could take advantage of him in any way.

"Got a coat?"

"Oh, yeah." She would have forgotten it, because she felt so hot. She took her coat from the back of the bar stool and followed him out of the bar and into the cold night.

She could feel the eyes in the bar following her, following them. She wondered, for a brief moment, if everyone in there knew what they planned to go do.

And then she dismissed it. Because she was Sarah Larsen, the patron saint of celibacy, and no one would ever believe she was off to have sex in a stranger's hotel room. They probably thought she was the designated driver for the evening. That she was taking care to see this poor, debauched soul made it back to his lodgings without encountering any hedonistic temptations. That was much more like her.

Well, showed what they knew. She was the evening's hedonistic temptation. So there.

She started walking toward her car, the snow crunching under her feet.

"Wait."

She turned back to face him, her heart stopping. He wasn't going to back out, was he? "Why?"

He approached her, his eyes burning into hers. Then he cupped the back of her head with his hand and pressed his lips to hers. His tongue slid along the seam of her mouth and she opened for him, her hands sliding up, palms pressed flat to his chest.

She'd never, ever, ever experienced anything like this. Her heart was beating so hard, she thought it was going to explode. She curled her fingers, his shirt balled up tightly in her fists.

Then he raised his head, breaking the kiss. Too soon. Way too soon.

"Just wanted to show you what you were getting into," he said, his voice rough. "Give you time to back out."

She blew out a long breath that lingered in a cloud between them. "Thank you. I feel informed."

"Change your mind?"

"No. But I might be inspired to drive a little faster."

CHAPTER

Two

Walker didn't know what the hell he was doing. He was in Silver Creek to finish up looking at the ranch he was about to move in to. He was not here to hook up. It had been so long since he'd hooked up, he'd basically forgotten how it went.

And since he'd decided hooking up was a good idea, he had no idea why he hadn't picked the buckle bunnies hanging by the jukebox. Why on earth was he being driven back to his lodge by this little redhead in the dowdiest black dress he'd seen outside of a wake?

He didn't know.

But there was something about her. Something that called to him, and made him hungry. Divorce and other circumstances had compromised his appetites, and he'd been without and fine with it for quite a while.

Suddenly, being without it for the next ten minutes seemed impossible.

That was the thing. The reason he hadn't gone for the buckle bunnies. He had been after a drink. He hadn't been after sex. Not until the little redhead had pushed the whiskey in front of him. Not until she'd confessed her reason for being in the bar.

She was the reason he wanted it. The reason his body was suddenly out of hibernation.

She pulled her car into the lodge parking lot. The roads had been plowed, leaving them all pretty easy to navigate, thankfully. The lot was mostly empty. The few people who came to Silver Creek in the winter were, he'd heard, hard-core sports enthusiasts and mainly opted to stay at the ski resort, not the lake.

She put the car in park and left the engine on. She looked at him, her pale green eyes huge.

"Second thoughts, baby?" he asked.

She shook her head. "No. Nope. No."

"That's a lot of nos."

"Because it's true. I'm not."

"Then maybe you could kill the engine and we could go inside."

"Okay. That . . . uh . . . that works."

He leaned in and kissed her again. Her lips were so soft; a taste of everything he'd been missing.

"Yes," she said. "That really works. Let's go."

She opened the car door and scrambled out and he followed, amused and flattered by the enthusiasm. The last time he'd had sex, his bed partner had just given him an eye roll and a "whatever." Like a punch straight to the ego. But then, she'd always been good at that. He felt bad thinking about his ex-wife in an unflattering light, especially since she'd passed away, but their marriage had not been a happy place.

And the fact that she wasn't around at all anymore didn't change that.

It was nice to be wanted. Nice to be treated like a man. He couldn't deny that.

"I'm this way," he said, getting out of the car and heading toward his cabin. It was about two hundred yards from the lodge, down near the lake. She followed, biting her lip and in general looking nervous, and not like a woman who had experience with this sort of thing. Which she'd said, but he hadn't necessarily believed her.

Women didn't often admit to being the type who frequently picked up men in bars, but in Sarah's case, it was pretty believable. The fact she was wearing pantyhose and her concern over the hemline on that dress being Exhibits A and B.

He took the key out of his pocket—an actual key, not a card. It had been a while since he'd stayed in a place that had keys. He shoved it into the lock, turning it and pushing the door open.

"It's pretty nice," he said, holding the door while Sarah made her way into the living area.

The bed was upstairs, on a loft floor that offered great views of the lake. Maybe he could use the views as a selling point to get her up the stairs quickly. Of course, it was dark. And if Sarah was really after what she claimed to be after, he shouldn't need a line.

"Not at all." She sucked in a deep breath, her petite shoulders rising and falling with the motion. Then she turned to face him. "Is there any point in making conversation or will it just compound the awkward?"

"What's your theory?"

"I find it all less awkward when you kiss me. Which means maybe we should head that direction rather than conversing."

He wasn't going to turn down a request like that. Because she had the pinkest, ripest lips he'd ever seen, and they tasted like a little bit of heaven. Funny, since the thoughts they gave him most certainly put him on a downward slide to hell.

He leaned in and tasted her, tracing the outline of her perfect mouth with his tongue. He felt her shiver beneath him, a little sound escaping. Shock. Arousal.

When he pulled away, she was looking at him, her eyes glittering and round. Yes, shock was definitely a part of the sound she'd made. And right now, her eyes were telegraphing a hell of a lot of emotion. Emotion he wasn't ready or able to deal with.

He didn't want to talk. The only way he wanted to connect was physically.

He was an asshole, and he knew it. But he was way too tired to have anything more than this. And this—this felt like a lot to him. Two damn years without sex. And in the years before the total sex ban, he and his ex hadn't exactly been burning up the sheets. She would humor him on occasion, and some of the time . . . he was just doing the same for her.

Sometimes making an effort to touch someone you didn't like anymore was worse than having no sex at all. More disconnected than a one-night stand and about a million times more depressing.

This at least felt fresh and new. Didn't feel stained by the same kind of ugliness that had tarred his marriage.

As long as he looked at her mouth and not her eyes, everything would be okay.

He kissed her again, deeper this time, pulling her into his embrace, against his chest, running his hands down over her curves, down to her ass. Round, perfect. The dress was a crime against humanity. It hadn't given him a hint that her butt would be this nice.

He wondered what lies it was telling about her breasts. And he decided to find out. This was a one-night stand, after all, which meant it was about one thing. It was about getting what they wanted, what turned them on. It was about getting off.

And he was so ready to get off.

He slid his hand down her leg, to the hem of her dress, and gripped the fabric, bunching it upward and tugging it up over her head in one smooth motion.

She stepped back, eyes bigger now, cheeks flushed. Her red hair was tumbled around her, her breathing ragged, full, creamy breasts, breasts that hideous dress had done a good job at concealing, rising with the motion.

She was soft. Curvy. Her stomach was slightly rounded, her hips generous. But those panties had to go. Black, plain, and hitting just below her belly button. They were, to the part of her he wanted most, what the dress had been to the rest of her body.

"Take your bra off, baby," he said, his voice rough. The bra first—there was an order to this. Like saving the very best bite of a rich dessert for last.

She flushed a deeper shade of red, one that nearly matched her hair, and wrapped her arms around her waist. "That's weird," she said.

"What?"

"Baby. No one has ever called me . . . baby."

"You don't like it?"

"No, I . . . I do. It makes me feel . . . like not me. I like that. You make me feel like I'm not me."

She still didn't make a move toward taking off the bra. "Do you want me to do it?"

She bit her lip and nodded. "Everything is better when you touch me."

So he did. He bent and kissed her, cupping her chin in his hand as he reached around behind her and undid the clasp on her bra, letting it all loose.

"Let me see you," he said, releasing his hold on her and pushing the garment down her arms and to the floor.

Ms. Sarah-Just-Sarah slowly lowered her arms and stood before him, blushing like an innocent. And it was the sexiest damn thing he'd ever seen. Pale, soft skin, tight raspberry nipples. Two years since he'd seen a pair of bare breasts in person.

It had been worth the wait.

"Do you need me to do your panties too?"

She nodded, silent, her eyes on him, big and bright and unblinking. As if she was afraid she might miss something. He'd never had a woman look at him like that. Like he was a foreign entity. Fascinating and maybe a little terrifying.

For some reason, it stoked the fire burning in his gut. Made the flames go higher.

Sarah's heart was beating so fast, she thought she was in potential danger of some kind of medical episode. She was topless in front of a man she'd just met a half hour ago. And she was about to be naked in front of him.

Walker advanced on her again, his big hands moving around her, pulling her into his embrace, fingers sliding beneath the waistband of her underwear, cupping her bottom as he pushed the cotton down her legs and to the ground.

They were the sexiest pair of underwear she had. And mainly they were sexy because they weren't white or didn't have pink rosebuds on them. She was suddenly very conscious of how unsexy everything she'd been wearing was, as if blinders had been torn violently from her eyes. And she had to face the reality of what she was presenting to him: a modest black dress and panties cut to match.

But Walker didn't seem to have a problem with her. In fact, he was staring at her, his dark eyes intent on her breasts and now . . . lower. *Oh gosh. Oh gosh.*

Now she really wanted to cover up. But at the same time, she never, ever wanted him to stop looking at her. Because the way he was looking at her . . . it was the strangest thing. She felt different. She felt beautiful.

She felt *wanted*. Not tolerated. Wanted.

So she didn't cover up. Instead, she looked right in his eyes. "Your turn."

He smiled. Oh Lord, that was a wicked smile. Just one side of his mouth quirked upward, a dark brow mimicking the motion. The man was walking, half-smiling temptation.

And he obliged.

He tugged his tight black shirt up over his head, his muscles shifting with the motion. And there were lots of muscles. Lots and lots.

His chest, his stomach. It all rippled.

She'd never given much thought to chest hair. She'd never considered herself for or against. But looking at Walker's lean physique of muscles dusted with dark hair, she was now firmly in favor.

His jeans sat so low on his hips, it was indecent, showing lines that led down to a part of his body she was getting increasingly nervous about. She could see the bulge in his jeans, see clear signs of his arousal.

She took a deep, shaking breath. It was for her. The arousal was for her. That realization helped to offset any nerves.

And heck, not only was the arousal for her—this whole night was for her. He was for her. Merry Christmas to Sarah. A bit in advance, but it was kind of fun getting a package early.

She nearly laughed at her own double entendre. She never made jokes like that. Her friend Lucy was starting to influence her in quite a few ways. Without Lucy, and her edict that they deserved more out of life than "just okay," she wouldn't be standing here now.

He put his hands on his big belt buckle and she forgot how to breathe. That was most certainly a big, big . . . belt buckle.

She couldn't take her eyes off of those hands, so large and masculine. He undid the buckle, then the snap on his jeans, and slowly drew the zipper down. She'd never seen a naked man before. She'd seen diagrams. Drawings. Not of erect men, though.

She was so innocent, it was horrible.

But then, this was why the virginity had to be lost.

And then he was pushing his jeans and underwear down, his body on display for her, his arousal on display for her.

And she forgot to be nervous. She forgot to be afraid at all. Because this man, this man who was more beautiful than any other man she'd ever seen, was hard for her.

"Now let's go to bed," he said.

Sarah took a deep breath and started up the stairs that led to the loft bedroom. She was very aware of Walker's eyes on her, on her naked body, as she climbed the stairs.

She was suddenly wishing she had less pie in her life and more sit-ups. Because Walker clearly had the sit-ups. She had a little layer where marionberry tarts went to stay and insulate her from the harsh Silver Creek winters.

Practical, but not sexy.

Still, she persevered.

She could hear his steps behind hers, but she couldn't bring herself to look at him. When she made it to the bed, she put her knee in the center of it and climbed on, then slowly turned to face him, propped up on her knees.

He was advancing toward her now, a predator, his dark eyes locked on hers.

And for the first time she seriously questioned her sanity.

"Condoms," she said.

"What?"

"I have them down in my purse. I left them downstairs.

Unless . . . do you have them?" He must. He was a paragon of male sexuality—surely he did the condom-in-his-wallet thing. Even *she* knew men did that.

"I don't have any. I'm damn glad you do," he said. He shook his head and turned, moving quickly down the stairs.

And she watched the view. Acclimated to seeing a man naked. This man.

He returned with her purse in hand, and the sight of this muscular, very masculine man carrying her little black purse out in front of him like it might bite him forced a giggle up her throat and through her lips.

She clapped a hand over her mouth. "Sorry."

"What?"

"For laughing."

"Laughing during sex is half the fun." He put her purse on the bed and she approached it, digging for the little makeup case she'd stuffed four condoms into earlier.

"Oh. I didn't know," she said, spreading them out on the blanket.

"You've been having the wrong kind of sex," he said. "Clearly. No laughing. And only four condoms?"

"Only four?" she sputtered.

"Baby, if we only have one night, it's gonna be a good night." He climbed onto the bed, kissing her lips, and she followed his lead, lying back against the pillows.

His body was over hers, his hands roaming over her bare curves, his erection hot and hard against her hip. She put her hands up over her head and let them lie there while he kept kissing her. Her lips, her neck, lower . . . lower.

Oh.

He sucked one nipple deep in his mouth, then traced a line around it with his tongue. "Touch me," he said, his tone commanding.

And she obeyed. She laced her fingers through his hair while the other hand roamed over his back, following the lines of those hard, amazing muscles.

He moved, shifting his attention to her other breast, the sensations rocking her, from point of contact to down between her legs. She could feel herself getting damp, an ache building deep inside her.

She stretched her toes, wiggled beneath him, trying to find some way to release the building tension deep inside of her.

Then he abandoned her breasts and kissed her mouth, slow and deep, his tongue sliding against hers, the friction sending a shiver through her, a bolt of pleasure so intense, it sent a flash of white light streaking behind her eyelids.

He kept kissing her, his hands exploring her body, the touch not overly intimate. And yet, that in and of itself made it seem more intense.

He put his hands on her lower back and pulled her tightly against him so that her naked body was flush with his, so that every inch of her was touching every inch of him. Every. Impressive. Inch.

She kissed him back, and she didn't care if she was clumsy, or that she didn't know what she was doing. She felt hot all over, her face burning, but not with embarrassment. And she ached. Like nothing she'd ever felt before. She felt empty, like she was desperate to be filled by something.

By him.

He gripped her harder and tugged her gently, rolling onto his back so that she was partly on top of him, her legs draped over his, the position opening her to him. His thigh came into contact with the part of her most desperate for his touch, and lightning streaked through her, along with a surge of embarrassment. Because of course he could feel how . . . how wet she was. How much she wanted him. Wanted this.

It was wanton and wicked and a whole bunch of other things she'd always tried her best not to be.

Be them tonight. Just tonight.

She closed her eyes tighter and kept on kissing him. Shut out the shame, chased the pleasure.

He shifted his hands to her hips and she was suddenly being tugged upward.

"What—"

He had repositioned her so that her . . . that her . . . that she was right above his mouth, her thighs bracketing his face. "Hang on to the headboard, baby."

She obeyed, her hands shaking, her whole body shaking. She looked down at him, at their position, and closed her eyes. And tried to suck in her stomach.

"Damn," he said, fingertips sliding up her inner thigh, to the heart of her, brushing against her clitoris. She arched her back, clinging to the headboard, trying to hold position with her legs shaking.

He gripped her hard, pulled her forward, his tongue traversing the path his fingers had just taken and then delving deeper.

A shocked cry escaped her lips, and she warred with the urge to jump up and run in horror, or cling to the headboard and push herself closer to his wicked, wicked lips. She'd known that mouth was wicked. Even she, the world's most sheltered virgin, had known.

But she'd had no idea just how wicked.

And she'd had *no* idea just how much she would like it.

Her indecision had her frozen, which meant she was just submitting to the pleasure. To him. To his lips, his tongue, so good. So wrong. So right. He held her bottom with one hand, the other moving up to cup her breast and tease her nipple as he continued to taste her.

And suddenly the earth moved and she found herself on her back with him over her, his dark eyes intense on hers.

"You have no idea," he said, his words coming in sharp bursts of breath, "how much I needed that."

"You?" she asked, completely breathless, shaking and unsatisfied. She was very unsatisfied, considering how good all of that had felt.

And she knew why. She wasn't stupid. More than once,

she'd very quickly and quietly given herself an orgasm to help herself get to sleep. She'd always felt vaguely ashamed, but she'd at least felt sleepy and able to drift off.

And she knew she hadn't had one with him. But at the same time, what he'd done had felt better than anything she'd accomplished with her own hand.

He put his hand between her thighs and kept stroking her, pushing one finger deep inside of her. She bit her lip, trying to hold back the cry of pleasure, unsuccessful the moment he started to slide his finger in and out of her while brushing his thumb over that needy bundle of nerves.

A little ripple ran through her, the beginning of release, so sharp, so intense. The rest of this might kill her.

He left her for a moment, sitting on the edge of the bed, a condom packet in hand. He tore it open quickly and rolled it onto his length before joining her again, his lips crashing down on hers, something about his actions changing.

He seemed desperate now. Less controlled, less smooth.

And she liked it. She liked that he was coming undone, because she was. She liked that she made him swear, because he made her want to. He made her want things she'd never wanted. Made her hungry deep inside for things she'd never known would matter to her.

She parted her thighs for him, and he settled between them, the blunt head of his arousal pushing against the entrance to her body. She was wet, and she was grateful for it now, because it seemed like it would help everything go smoother.

Still, she should have bought condoms with lubrication. Or brought a bottle of it. Anything to make this easier. Her planning had fallen short on that end.

But he lowered his head, his tongue sliding over the line of her collarbone and down to her breast, sucking her nipples while he pushed home, and she couldn't think.

She was torn between the pleasure brought about by his mouth and the sharp, wrenching pain as he entered her body.

She pressed her face into his shoulder and clung to him, her eyes squeezed shut as she tried to get used to the feeling, to the intense sensation of being filled and stretched.

It didn't hurt so much now, but it didn't feel good either.

"Sarah?"

She shook her head against his skin. "'Baby' works." She didn't want to be Sarah again yet.

"What's wrong, baby?"

"You know."

He nodded slowly. "Yeah."

"It doesn't matter. Please. Just please."

He didn't need a lot of encouragement. A harsh groan escaping, he pushed deep inside of her, and waited. Slowly, the discomfort began to recede.

She moved against him, the action producing some pleasurable results. So she did it again. And again. And a little moan worked its way up her throat.

"Good?" he asked.

"Yes. Yes," she said, "it really is."

He flexed his hips at the same time as she arched against him and her mouth dropped open, pleasure shooting through her like a star, leaving a trail of sparks in her bloodstream. He moved again, harder, then again.

And now she knew what all the fuss was about.

She was lost. In this, in him. She ran her hands over his back, wrapped her legs around his hips, letting him go deeper. And everything in her built, built until she thought she would break. Until she didn't know where he began and she ended. Until she didn't know herself.

Because she was lost. In this. In pleasure. In Walker.

In sex. She was Sarah Larsen, and she liked sex, thank you very much. And she was not, not, *not* a virgin.

That was her very last thought as the pleasure that had been building in her crashed over her and shattered like a sheet of glass. Devastating. Altering. Impossible to put back together.

It never seemed to end, the release going on and on. Dimly, she was aware of Walker stiffening above her, thrusting hard into her one last time as he found his own orgasm.

She clung to him then like he was the only thing keeping her on earth. Because she thought he might be.

They were both breathing hard, and a sheen of sweat was on his chest. She didn't care. He wrapped his arms around her and held her against him, rolling them both to the side. She rested her head on him, listened to his heart beat against his cheek.

She'd never been so close to another person before.

Sex had been something her grandmother had preached heavily against. That it would make a woman fall. That all a woman could be expected to get out of it was hurt and condemnation. That it was a shameful thing. That sexual desire was sin.

Because of that, she hadn't realized what sex could do emotionally. Sarah hadn't realized what it would make her *feel*.

She'd been so focused on the physical want, on not denying her needs anymore, on not being ashamed of them, that she'd missed the fact that there *was* a spiritual element to sex—the one part of it her grandmother hadn't warned her about.

But as a stranger held her in his arms, the full horror of what she'd done crept over her, along with a terrifying, awful feeling.

A feeling that she wanted to stay in his bed, in his arms, in his life, forever. That parting with him would tear away a piece of her.

No. No. That wasn't what this was. This was her taking control of her life. Forming her own opinions and morals. Giving herself excitement. Shooting for more than okay.

This had nothing to do with him. Nothing to do with emotion.

But she wanted to cry. Not just cry—sob. Her heart felt

too big for her chest. And she was shaking. What was happening to her? Why did she want to hold on to him forever?

She sat up, her teeth chattering, her hands shaking.

"I have to . . . I have to go," she said, getting out of bed and looking around for her dress. *No.* It was downstairs.

She picked up her purse. "Keep . . . keep the condoms. I have to go."

"What the hell?" he asked, swinging his legs over the side of the bed.

"I just . . . I can't. I have to . . . I'm sorry." She went downstairs and started pulling her clothes on as quickly as possible.

"What are you doing?"

"I made a mistake," she said, her heart squeezing. "I made a mistake," she said again, to herself this time.

"My truck is at the bar."

"Sorry."

She put her coat on and rushed out the door, the cold air hitting her like a wall. She got into her car and jammed the keys into the ignition, starting it and pulling it away from the lodge. Away from Walker.

She focused hard on not crying. On not regretting. She wasn't going to regret this. She wasn't. She'd made her choice. She'd taken control of her life.

No one ever had to know. And she would never see him again.

Sarah was ready for the day to be over. But it was ten minutes after most of the children had left, and her newest student, Kayla Callahan, was still there, looking at her with overly serious eyes.

"Who's supposed to get you, Kayla?" Sarah was riffling through the paperwork on her desk, hoping she had the slip with Kayla's information on it. But she was starting to think it was still in the school office.

"My daddy," she said, barely meeting Sarah's eyes.

"Does your daddy always come and get you?"

She nodded slowly. "Yes. He does."

She sounded so sad, and Sarah knew there was a story. It was helpful when this information was passed on to her so she knew what she was dealing with.

"Is he usually late?"

She shook her head, her blond curls swinging over her shoulders. "No. But he said the school was hard to find in this blizzard. And he said another word, but I'm not supposed to say it."

Sarah could imagine. "Okay, I'm sure he's just lost. Does he have a cell phone number we can call?" She would just take Kayla down to the office to get the information if she had to.

"Sorry I'm late."

Sarah looked up and froze. Suddenly, that night last weekend when she'd been in a bar and looked up to see a man standing in the doorway, snow falling behind him, looking dangerous and sexy, superimposed itself over the here and now.

Because there he was. Standing in the doorway of her classroom.

She blinked, but he was still there. It was still him. Black hair, dark stubble on his perfectly square jaw. He was in torn, dirty jeans today, a work jacket zipped up with snow on the shoulders.

He looked . . . he looked the same, but different. Real. Today he looked real. Not a larger-than-life fantasy, but a mortal man. And it almost made him seem even more dangerous.

"I . . ." She reached up and touched her hair, such a stupid, girly reflex, and rued the fact that it was in a bun. "It's fine," she said, standing from her desk. She couldn't acknowledge that she knew him. Not now. Oh Lord, not now.

Heat crept over her face, and she knew she was bright red. The full horror of it all was dawning, slowly, horribly.

"She's fine, she was just . . . we were just . . . about to go and call you."

Kayla brightened a little when she saw her dad, a smile on her little face. "I told her you didn't forget. I told her you just got lost in the blizzard. And I didn't say that word."

"Good, Kayla, thanks." Walker smiled—a very forced smile, but his daughter clearly didn't know that.

His daughter. He was a father. He was the father of one of the kids in her class. Oh. Oh no. *Oh no.* She needed a paper bag to breathe into.

Or that shot of whiskey she'd surrendered to him a week ago. Or if she could go back that far, maybe she'd just reclaim her hymen. Stay home. Sit on the couch. Watch cute cat videos on YouTube. She could have bought a cat. She could have skipped men and bought a cat.

Hindsight. Stupid hindsight.

Instead, what she'd had was one blistering sexual experience that haunted her nights and that she had flashbacks to in the middle of class. In the middle of teaching five-year-olds, she would suddenly remember what it had been like to have a man's face between her thighs and . . .

Oh. Now she was blushing. Good.

Just great.

"I . . . So. You don't live in Texas," she said, the words slipping out without her permission.

"No. I'm *from* Texas. Just moved here."

"Excellent. How are you liking it?" she asked, clasping her hands in front of her and smiling a smile to rival his fake smile.

"My welcome was . . . very friendly."

Oh, she could have cussed. But his daughter was there. And she never cussed. "Good," she bit out. "Happy for you. So, in future, the school hasn't moved. This isn't that much snow, and we're done at two thirty. Not two forty-five."

"I'll bear that in mind." He looked down at Kayla. "There are some things I'm going to need to discuss with you," he said, his eyes flickering back to Sarah. "If we could have a meeting? And . . . is there a way she could be here, but not in the room? I don't have anyone to watch her."

"We can arrange something." She really did need to hear about Kayla's home situation. The girl was quiet. And sad. This was her first day, but that much was clear to Sarah. "The sooner the better." Time to be a teacher and not an insecure little girl. "Tomorrow? Maybe after class. I'm sure Mrs. Jones in the office will be happy to help with Kayla."

"Great. Tomorrow. Two thirty?"

"Yes. Blizzard or shine."

He nodded once and put his hand on Kayla's shoulder. "See you then."

"See you then."

Sarah collapsed when Walker walked out, a groan escaping her lips. Of course. Of course her indiscretion would come back and bite her like this. Her grandmother had warned her.

Of course, her grandmother had been slightly over the top and incredibly ridiculous. Obviously sex worked out fine for a lot of people. Like her friend Lucy, who was deeply in love with her boyfriend, Mac, and was, by all accounts, having fabulous sex with him on a regular basis.

Lucy.

She had to call Lucy.

She started to run out to the car, locking the classroom behind her and pulling her phone from her purse. She dialed as soon as she was in the privacy of the vehicle.

"Hello?"

"Lucy, it's me." She put it on speakerphone and started her car—the car that had been her grandmother's for ten years before passing into Sarah's possession. The car that certainly looked like it belonged to an old woman: brown with a tan stripe, and roughly the size of a small yacht.

"Sarah! I haven't heard from you in forever. You didn't answer when I called last week."

"I know." She was a bad friend who was avoiding confessing her transgression. "I . . . I have a lot to tell you, and I'm going to be skimming over what you would call the juicy bits so I can get to the part that's making me panic right now."

"Ohhhh-kay."

"I met a man last week. At a bar. No, that sounds like it was chance; it wasn't. I went to a bar because I wanted to lose my virginity."

"You're a virgin?"

"No. But that comes later in the story." She'd never wanted

to confide in her new friend that she'd never had sex. So she'd just made vague allusions to being inexperienced. But the cat was out of the bag now. Although she had no cat. She'd had sex instead. Because she made terrible decisions.

"What?"

"I went to the bar to find a man to take my virginity because I was tired of being the way I was. Am. You said we needed more from life than being just blah and I agreed when it was you and Mac. And, well, I agree for me too. I thought, go grab life and seize . . . stuff. So I did. And then after we had . . . we did the . . . that, I left because I got this weird swelling feeling in my heart and I think I wanted to keep him and that's so stupid"—she took a breath—"and then this afternoon he showed up. At my kindergarten class."

"He came to get you?"

"He came to pick up his daughter! He's one of the dads!"

"Is he married?" Lucy asked, her tone murderous.

"No, no. Thank God. No. But what am I going to do? Can you die of awkward?"

"I don't think so, or I would have died when I showed up at Mac's house to take a position as his housekeeper."

Sarah let out a long breath. "Okay, that gives me hope. I was concerned for my health."

"Let's get back to the fact that you picked up a stranger at a bar, please?"

"That's all there is to tell, really," Sarah said, her cheeks burning as she pulled her car into her driveway.

Her little house looked like it always had. Neat, clean, tiny. It was part of the oldest neighborhood in Silver Creek. The home her grandmother had lived in for most of her life. The home Sarah had been raised in from the time she was a baby, when her mother, who she didn't remember at all, had left her there with her grandmother.

"Lies," Lucy said. "All lies! Tell me. And why didn't you tell me you were a—"

"Because. Gosh. It's humiliating." Sarah turned off the

car and got out, walking quickly inside, ignoring the chill in the air. "And anyway, okay, all there is to tell is that I went to a bar, looking for . . . that. Excitement. Whatever. And I met Walker. And it was perfect because he was a stranger, only he's not a stranger, he's someone I'm going to have to see! Lots."

"Okay, you have a dilemma. And you owe me details, but first, your dilemma."

She thought of the details. Of her whisker-burned inner thighs. "Oh, sure. Later." She cringed. "But the dilemma?"

"You have to decide what you're going to do. How you're going to be with him."

"Parent/teacher," she said. "Strictly."

"All right, then next time you have to see him . . ."

"Tomorrow."

"Tomorrow . . . just . . . act like you're meeting him for the first time. The man you were with that night isn't the same man. How about that?"

"Great. Perfect."

She'd known Lucy would have a solution. She would just pretend that Walker was a stranger. Again. And she would pretend that night had never happened. Easy. Totally easy.

Walker tried, and failed, to listen to his daughter talk about the fairy movie she was going to watch when they got home. It didn't really surprise him that she wasn't talking about her day, or the other kids in her class.

Kayla just wasn't interested in friends. Not anymore. Not since his damn wife had had the guts to leave. And then the nerve to die.

Yeah, he was pissed at her for both. Hard enough to tell your daughter that Mommy might come visit again "someday." Harder to have to tell her there was no chance Mommy would come back at all now.

Maybe it wasn't fair to be mad at Elise for dying. Okay,

he knew it wasn't fair. But it had just compounded the abandonment Kayla had already felt. The abandonment *he* felt.

Grief. And that was probably what it was, which was weird since in the end he'd hated that woman. Losing her, every single way he'd lost her, had hurt like hell.

But he wasn't focused on any of that. Not now. It wasn't, for once, dire thoughts keeping him from hanging on to Kayla's every word.

It was the thought of one impossibly sexy redhead. Who was so soft beneath his hands, she put silk to shame. An impossibly sexy redhead who had left the lodge while his head was still buzzing with his orgasm. And had left him to get a cab back to his truck the next morning.

She'd sent him on a walk of shame.

Oh yeah, and she'd been a damn virgin. Who the hell was a virgin? Not him, not for nearly twenty years, that was for damn sure.

To recap, he'd picked up a stranger for a one-night stand, his first night of sex in more than two years. An attempt at recapturing a moment lost in time. One when he'd just been a man who did what felt good. And she'd been a virgin. She'd left him stranded. And then a week later he'd walked into his daughter's kindergarten class and his old life and new one had collided viciously. Head-on. No survivors.

He'd come here for a new start. A new life for him and Kayla.

Oh well, she wouldn't be in kindergarten forever. All he had to do was grit his teeth and make it through the next few months.

There was no other option. He was in no place to have a relationship, no position to have an affair. He'd pretty much resigned himself to intense bouts of celibacy potentially stretching out for years at a time. But he was not going to be the dad who left his child with a nanny while he picked up random women down in the bar. It had been different the night he'd met Sarah, because he'd been away from home anyway. But he wasn't going to abandon his daughter in search of sex.

And he most certainly wasn't going to be the dad who banged the kindergarten teacher.

At least he was not going to sleep with her again.

No, that wasn't going to happen again. This was his new life. And now his life was all about Kayla. She was all he had left, and he would make sure that wasn't as much of a tragedy as it might be.

If he had to spend an hour freezing his balls off in a snowbank before every school function? So be it.

"She's down in the office." Walker closed the classroom door behind him and looked around for a seat. Sarah was sitting in a blue plastic chair at a table that was low and shaped like a semicircle.

"Have a seat," she said.

"Where?" He looked around at the miniature orange chairs that were set up around the table.

"Here," she said, indicating the chairs.

He arched a brow and kicked one of the little seats away from the table and sat down, his knees getting acquainted with his chest. "Nice classroom you have here."

"Yeah, um, thanks," she said, leaning back in her chair, as if the table and height disparity hadn't already put enough distance between them.

"I wanted to give you some background on what's going on with Kayla," he said. Which he suddenly realized amounted to giving his one-night stand the rundown on most of his dirty laundry, which was . . . not ideal. But it was what he had to do. He had to be a father right now, not a horny lecher who was looking with lustful intent at a sweet, innocent, recently devirginized kindergarten teacher.

He shouldn't look at her as a lover at all. She was the teacher. End of story. His life was about Kayla, not about his dick.

"Kayla's mom . . . we divorced a couple of years back. But Elise still came to visit sometimes. She lived out of town, but she did come for Thanksgiving and Christmas. Anyway, she died a few months back. And even though she wasn't a big part of Kayla's life anymore . . . she was her mom. And you can't replace that. I can't replace it. I've tried. I try to do the best I can, but I never saw myself doing the kid thing by myself. Now I am. And now I'm what she has, so . . . somehow she has to get through this. The new-school thing. Christmas. I don't know what the hell I'm going to do about Christmas break."

Sarah frowned, her brow creasing. "She doesn't have anyone to watch her?"

He shook his head. "No. But I guess I'll figure it out. Maybe it was a dumb move, coming here. But I couldn't stay in Austin. I couldn't stay where we'd been anymore. Too many pieces of the old life . . . they keep you from finding a new one."

Sarah swallowed hard, pressing her hands flat on the desk. She knew exactly what he was talking about, because she was on that journey too. Because she lived in the same town, in the same house, that she'd always lived in. Because she had aged, but her life had felt so much the same.

Like being stuck in mud, unable to move forward. So yeah, she was well acquainted with those issues. And that was lame, because she didn't want to find a point of connection with him. Already, being near him was making her insides feel all shaken up and funny. She'd already experienced that overwhelming desire to cling to him. To hold him. To have him rattle the headboard in the modest home she grew up in.

Ahem.

She didn't need to find things in common with him.

"I appreciate your telling me," she said, keeping her voice as neutral as possible. "It will be helpful going forward."

"How is she in class?"

"Quiet, but she's very sweet. You're doing a good job with her, Walker," she said. She regretted saying his name almost immediately. It left a funny feeling on her tongue, her lips. Somehow, it conjured up the way he tasted. Left his flavor lingering.

Or maybe it had been lingering for the past week.

"Appreciated."

"And . . . and . . ." she said, feeling her face turn red even as she formulated the sentence. She had to say it though. Had to make sure he didn't do anything to compromise her position at the school. "I need . . . I need for no one to know that we've . . . met before."

He arched a dark brow. "That we've met? We've done more than that."

He stood up, and she found herself eye level with his . . . yeah. That. She stood too. "Yes," she said, keeping her voice even. "I know we have. But there's no place in my life for that kind of thing right now and—"

"Are you really brushing me off? As if I have . . . tons of vacant space in my life? I wanted a fuck, babe, that's it, and I got it. There's no reason to talk about it again."

His language, the hard words, were so incongruous in her bright, cheery classroom covered in construction paper and glitter that she would have laughed if they hadn't cut so deep.

"Well," she said, biting the inside of her cheek, knowing her face was bright red, hoping he didn't notice the stupid, useless tears that had welled up in her eyes, "good, because I don't want to talk about it. And I don't want you to talk about it to anyone. So . . . I'm glad we're on the same page."

"Good."

"*Good*. So . . . I won't see you probably because . . . I don't stay out there for the whole parent line and you'll be on time from now on. Two thirty."

"Two thirty." He tipped his hat and walked out the door.

Sarah folded into her chair. "Oh . . . oh no." Her stomach hurt. All because he'd said *that* word to talk about what they'd done. Because he'd said it was all he wanted. It was supposed to be all that she wanted. What was wrong with her? She was such a stupid virgin.

And she didn't have time to worry about her own drama. Walker had drama. Kayla . . . poor Kayla had drama. She knew what it was like to lose your mother. Her mother had walked away too. And Sarah didn't know what had happened to her.

Sarah knew what it was like to be that little girl. To be so lost and sad. To miss someone you could hardly remember. Someone who maybe didn't even deserve for you to miss them.

That was going to be her focus then: Kayla. Because she was a teacher, and a darn good one. It was what she did and it was who she was. She was not going to let her feelings about Walker affect that.

She planted her hands firmly on the table and pushed herself up. No, she was not going to let this affect her. So she'd had a one-night stand and she was going to have to deal with said one-night stand for a while. Big deal. She was a woman. She could handle it.

She had nothing to be ashamed of and no reason to regret the orgasm he'd given her.

She'd wanted to grow up a little. So now she was going to have to act like a grown-up.

Walker was running late, because the damn nanny interview had run late, and in the end it hadn't even mattered, because this woman hadn't been able to start when he needed her to, and he hadn't liked her very much anyway.

This was what he got for not arranging a nanny before coming to Silver Creek. This was what he got for having to work all the time to get his ranch up and running when he should have been spending time with his daughter.

This was what he got for being such a lousy husband he hadn't been able to keep his wife around. So she'd left, and as a result had been driving on an icy road in Houston too quickly.

Yeah, so this was what he got. For failing at everything. At least, that's what it felt like he was doing.

He left the truck running in the school parking lot and headed toward the kindergarten class, ready to get banshee-screamed at by Miss Prim and Ginger.

He opened the door and stopped when he saw Kayla sitting at her desk, her head bowed low. Her shoulders were shaking. And Sarah was crouched down next to her, her hand over her arm.

"I'm sorry. It was the . . . the nanny and the snow and . . ." And he was drowning here.

Sarah stood up and shot him a steely glare. "We're glad you're here. Kayla was worried."

His daughter jumped up from her desk and flung herself at him, her arms wrapped around his waist. "I thought you died," she said, her voice thick.

"Oh, no." He put his hand on her back, held her close, guilt tearing at him. "No, honey, I should have called."

"It's just that you said you wouldn't be late again. You promised."

He was shit at promises too. He should just add that to the list. "I'm sorry, baby girl. Some things happened. I should have called, but when I realized"—he looked up at Sarah—"I just wanted to get here."

"It's okay," Sarah said, the fight draining out of her. "Just a second and I'll walk you out."

She grabbed her coat from the peg by her desk and put it on. It was a strange coat. Floral and square. Both old fashioned and a little bit ill fitting. But then, that seemed to be Sarah. Unless she was picking up a stranger at a bar, going back to his room with him and holding on to the headboard while straddling his face. That was less old-fashioned. And a memory he did not need right now, thank you very much, horny subconscious.

His body hadn't appreciated its reintroduction to celibacy this past couple of weeks. It was like a horse resigned to its fate, then let out of the gate to run for just a little bit. Reminded of how good it could feel. Then put back in a tiny stall.

He felt like a douche worrying about his dick while he'd made a huge parenting mistake, but then, he was a man, and he was always worried about that part of his body. At least, now that he'd been reminded he was a man and not a gelding.

The truck was still idling, the heater on so it would be a comfortable temperature for Kayla. He opened the door to his truck and Kayla got in, climbing into the backseat and into her booster. He shut the door and turned to face Sarah.

"Lecture coming?" he asked.

"No. Actually, I was wondering if there was something I could do to help." The cold air was making her cheeks pink; the tip of her nose too. And her lips looked redder. The cold had a similar effect on her skin as arousal, and he found it pretty damn interesting.

"You want to help?"

She shifted in the snow, crossing her arms. "Well, yes. Look, I would offer this to anyone in your situation, and I feel like not offering it to you just because we had a bit of a . . . rocky start isn't right. I'm a teacher first, and for me, that transcends the classroom when necessary. Kayla is a sweet girl, but . . . fragile."

"Yeah. Obviously." And he wasn't good with fragile things. Sarah didn't have to say it for him to know it was true.

"I want her to have the extra support she needs over the winter holiday."

"So do I. That's why I've been searching for a nanny, but I don't have one. I've been overusing my housekeeper, but it's not what she does, and I knew that I was really asking too much during the holiday when she wants to head back home for a bit to be with her own family."

"So you need someone to watch her during the day."

"Only for the hours while I'm working. I'm on the property, but I won't leave her in the house by herself. And I can't bring her with me for a whole day when it's this cold. It's a recipe for a sick and crabby kid. Plus she'd be miserable."

"And ranch work doesn't wait. I wasn't raised on a ranch, but I do know how that goes."

"So what exactly are you offering me here?"

"Temporary nannying. I can keep her busy and this will give her some consistency on top of it. She knows me, and she feels comfortable with me. And . . . and you won't be there."

He leaned against the truck. "Important to you."

"I'm not a glutton for punishment. Frankly, I'm not a glutton for much. I think you have the wrong idea about me."

He could have laughed. There was no way he had the wrong idea about her. She had to be nearing thirty, and he knew for a fact she'd been a virgin. Yet she seemed to be under the impression he believed she was some kind of town tramp.

He knew exactly what she was.

Trouble. She was sweet, heart and soul, and she was the kind of woman who deserved to be offered forever. And he only had that one night to give instead. A damn sorry thing.

"I don't think I do, Red," he said.

"Sarah. Better still, Miss Larsen will do."

Miss Larsen. Well hell. That made him hard instantly. He could picture calling her that in bed. Miss Larsen. He wasn't the kind of man who did the taking-orders thing, but he could get on board with asking permission from Miss Larsen.

He was a sick puppy. And he was in no position to indulge it. He needed her help, not her body.

"Well, Miss Larsen," he said, trying to will his hard-on into submission even as he said it, "I'm in no position to turn down an offer of help. If you can give it, I'm going to take it. And I'll pay you a fair wage, I promise."

That statement felt a lot more layered, a lot more dangerous, than he'd intended.

If she blushed, he couldn't see it. Her cheeks were too red from the cold. And it was just as well. His body didn't need any more encouragement.

"I trust you. Shall we plan on Monday?"

"Works for me."

"What time?"

"Sometime after eight is fine. Laurie is still around for part of the week, and she won't mind feeding Kayla breakfast."

"Great," she said, and he was sure her enthusiasm was as fake as Astroturf. "I'll see you then."

"Yep." He tipped his hat and watched her face closely. The cold was still keeping him from seeing a blush. Dammit. He wanted her to blush.

She took a step away from the truck. "So. Yes. See you. Then."

Yes, he would. And he could only hope he had better luck with keeping his body under control by then. If not, he was going to be spending Christmas with his balls on ice.

Sarah screwed up her face and got out of the car, scrunching even more when the cold, dry air hit her straight on. It was eight a.m., the first Monday of winter break, and she was at Walker's ranch just outside of town with a bag full of activities for Kayla.

She was dressed warmly for the weather, and in a pair of floral granny panties for her own protection. Because Walker had magic panty-removing powers, and if she wasn't careful, she'd end up with them stripped off again.

As if he wants to . . .

Well, yeah, there was that. Because she'd run like a cat being chased with a hose. It wasn't like she'd stuck around to get his take on it. There had been no "Oh, baby, that was the best I've ever had." Not that she was expecting that. She would have been happy with a "Pretty good for your first time."

But for all she knew, it had been bland, boring *meh* to him. Certainly not world-rocking or earth-shattering like it had been for her.

Still, the granny panties were on, which meant he wasn't getting any of her clothes off. Because, please. How embarrassing.

She blew out a breath and watched it linger in the air before heading up the steps and onto the porch, ringing the bell and bouncing up and down a bit before the door opened. It wasn't Walker. And that sharp, punched feeling in her stomach wasn't disappointment. No. It was just an adrenaline explosion or something, because she'd been prepared to deal with him again.

It was a middle-aged woman, who smiled and invited her in. "I'm Laurie," she said, taking Sarah's coat. "The housekeeper."

"I'm Sarah. I'm Kayla's teacher. I don't know if Walker explained things to you or—"

"Mr. Callahan gave me a brief overview of the situation. I'm glad you agreed to help him. He really needs it."

Mr. Callahan. Of course. She ought to call him that. Not Walker. It was far too telling.

"Oh . . . good. Have you been with the family for long?"

"Since his wife left."

Sarah nodded slowly. "Well, it's nice that Kayla has you. Nice that you came with them."

"My family doesn't live in Texas anymore anyway. A plane ride is a plane ride. Besides, the Callahans are a part of my family."

"I'm glad they have you."

Laurie smiled. "I'm glad they have you for the time being. I don't mind taking care of Kayla for a while, but I do have a lot of household chores to see to, and I can't exactly keep her entertained."

"I understand."

"She's just in here, having breakfast."

Sarah walked into the cozy kitchen and saw Kayla sitting on a bench at the little breakfast nook, eating pancakes. When she saw Sarah, her eyes lit up and she smiled. "Miss Larsen! My dad said you were coming today. I didn't know if you would."

Sarah's heart did a little flip. This poor girl. She'd been let down so many times already. It made her hurt. Well, for her part, she wouldn't let her down. She would spend this time with her. Make her feel valued.

"All right, Kayla," Sarah said, sitting down, "what do you want to do today?"

CHAPTER

Six

Sarah managed to go two days at the Callahan ranch without seeing Walker. She was in after he left and out before he got back, thanks to Laurie.

But by the third day, Laurie was getting ready for her trip and was at her little house on the property packing instead of coming back to relieve Sarah at dinnertime, which meant she had no choice but to wait for him to come home.

She sat down at the dinner table with Kayla, their plates already piled with chicken, potatoes and green beans. "Is your dad usually late for dinner?" she asked, looking out into the blackness.

She was hungry, but she'd been planning on skipping out so she didn't end up intersecting with Walker's meal and causing any awkwardness. But now it was getting to where it would be more awkward if she didn't eat. Also, obvious.

"Sometimes." Kayla shrugged a shoulder and took a bite of her potatoes. "But he doesn't like me to wait until my dinner is cold."

"Okay." Taking a cue from Kayla, Sarah took a bite too.

Just then, right when she was wholly committed to dinner and unable to back out, the front door opened and she felt a rush of air come through the short hallway and into the dining room.

Darn it all to heck!

"Laurie? Kayla? I'm home." She heard boots stomping on the rug, probably getting rid of caked-on snow and mud, then the door shutting and heavy footfalls on the wooden floor.

Kayla jumped up and ran out of the room. "Daddy!"

The whole thing made Sarah's heart feel suspiciously tight. And when Walker came in holding Kayla's hand, she thought her ovaries would explode.

God bless her granny panties. For they would steer her clear of temptation and lead her not into Walker's bed.

"Sarah," he said, pausing. "Miss Larsen. I didn't expect you to be here."

"Yes, well . . . Laurie had to pack. So . . . so since she's leaving tomorrow to go and visit her children, probably this will be . . . normal."

Except nothing felt normal. She felt all sweaty. And her lips were tingling.

He took a plate out of the cupboard and sat down at the head of the table, serving himself. And she suddenly felt extremely out of place.

"I should probably go," she said.

"No," he said. "It looks like you took one bite of your dinner. You should finish it."

"I'm not hungry."

"Sure you are," he said, his eyes never leaving hers. "And unfinished . . . dinner is about the worst thing I can think of."

"Unfinished dinner?"

"Sure. You sit down to eat and you want to enjoy it. Sit for a while after. Maybe have dessert."

"Yes, well, sometimes a bite is enough."

He arched a dark brow and took a bite of potatoes, savoring it with far too much . . . carnal enjoyment for her liking. "Not of something this good."

"Too much of a good thing is never . . . good. These potatoes, for example, are amazing. But butter filled."

"And?"

"And butter isn't good for you. It just tastes great. But it . . . makes you . . ." She looked at Kayla, who was looking at her. "It's bad for your heart." Which was too close to what she was afraid they might actually be talking about for her own comfort. But she didn't want to talk about things making you fat in front of a little girl either.

"Fair enough," he said, taking another bite of the potatoes. "But you should still stay and finish dinner."

A challenge. And she didn't want to back down. Because she felt like she should have transcended childish fear and angst. Like she should be past that, because she was supposed to be different. Not because she'd had sex, but because something in her had changed enough to decide she wanted to have sex. To decide she wasn't going to live only to please other people and to meet their expectations.

Tonight, though, she had to meet her own expectations and not be drawn in by talk of butter and of lingering for dessert.

"I can do that."

And she did.

Fortunately, five-year-old girls were pretty good at filling silences left by two somewhat awkward adults. Or maybe Walker wasn't awkward so much as trying not to bust out the inappropriate innuendos.

She'd been all set to concede the fact that their night together hadn't been so great for him. As he'd said . . . he'd just wanted a . . . well, that word he'd said. And he'd gotten it. So there was no reason for him to look at her like she was . . . buttered potatoes.

"Hey, sprout," he said, looking at Kayla. "It's bedtime."

She frowned. "I don't have school tomorrow."

"I know, but you want to stay on a good routine so you can be ready to wake up Christmas morning, right? Seven days until Christmas."

She brightened at that. "Oh, yeah!" She got down from her chair and gave Walker a kiss before trotting up the stairs.

"Can you hang out a minute?" he asked Sarah. "I want to talk to you after she's in bed."

Come into my den, said the wolf to the lamb . . .

"Sure. I can do that." And she could. She had granny panties. They were her modern-day chastity belt.

She lingered at the table and waited while Walker did, presumably, the bedtime routine with Kayla. She tapped her fingers on the solid oak surface while she waited, eyeing the partially full bowl of potatoes and trying not to think of them as a metaphor for decadence.

She'd had one little taste of decadence. And it had been a gorgeous, perfect disaster.

If only she'd just never seen him again. No, even better, if only she'd felt nothing but a post-orgasm buzz after they'd had sex. If only she hadn't felt that intense swelling of emotion in her chest after they'd finished.

Then she could have stayed all night and sated her lust for him. And she would have been able to see him in her classroom and not feel . . . sad and yearny. She wouldn't be feeling yearny now, or counting on dowdy underwear to be her last guard against total ruin.

She heard his boots on the stairs and her heart leaped into her throat. He probably just wanted to talk about Kayla. That was all. He was a wonderful father and of course he wanted to know how she was spending her days. It was only natural he should.

"Come into the living room," he said, not bothering to stop by the dining room on his way in.

She got up and wandered through the entryway and into the living area. Vaulted ceilings with exposed beams, along with large windows that, during the daytime, surely offered a magnificent view, gave the space an open feel.

And yet, in spite of that, she felt like the walls were closing in on her.

He went to a cabinet and took some keys down from high up on the top of it, then unlocked it and produced a bottle of Jack Daniel's and two tumblers. "Drink?"

"N-no." She still didn't have the nerve.

"I'll pour two anyway. We'll see if I get to the second one. I keep it under lock and key now. And I only drink after she goes to bed. Which means I usually drink alone. So that's its own kind of sad." He poured a measure of butterscotch-colored liquor into both glasses and set them on the coffee table in front of the leather couch. "Sit."

She gave him her frostiest glare. "Do most women follow your one-word commands like that?"

"Sorry, I'm out of practice," he said. "Please sit down."

She complied, her eyes on the alcohol, rethinking her earlier no. "Kayla was really great today. She's a fun kid. We did some crafts and reading. And she actually asked to work on her letters, so we did. But of course, this is break, so I'm not going to force schoolwork on her if she doesn't want it."

He picked his glass up and took a drink, moving to the far side of the room. "Great. You feel like everything is going well then?" He paced in front of the windows, his reflection following his movements. "No concerns?"

"I can tell she's been hurt."

He grunted. "Yeah."

"I just want to make sure I keep my word to her. She's been let down too many times."

"Yeah. My damn ex."

"She has you though. And that's good."

"Yeah." He looked at her, his dark eyes glittering, and then he walked to the couch and stood in front of her. "Stand up."

"I just sat down."

"Then I'll sit down." He did, putting his glass on the table, and then he cupped her cheek with his hand, his gaze never leaving hers. "I want you."

"Oh no . . ."

"You left before I was done."

"You said you only wanted a . . . a . . . sex."

"Well, it was all I wanted. But I wanted more than I got. And don't go playing the wounded maiden here—it was what you wanted too, and we both know it."

She shifted. "Well, yeah, but that's the thing. I kind of was a, uh . . . maiden. So there was some irrationality on my part. Both in my desire to, uh . . . off-load my maidenhead and in the actions that followed that resulted in the loss of said . . . you know. So . . . I don't . . . I didn't know what I wanted."

"Bull. Shit." He drew closer, and she could almost taste the alcohol on his breath. "You knew what you wanted, and I gave it to you."

"I . . . n-no . . . I . . ."

"Shut up."

"Okay." And then he was kissing her, his tongue getting things good and slick before he slipped his lips over hers in slow, maddening friction. His mouth was barely pressed against hers. Nothing more than a tease.

She found herself leaning in, gripping his shirt, pulling him to her as she leaned into him, deepening the kiss. Crushing his lips to hers. Because she needed more. Needed to taste the slow burn of the Jack Daniel's on his lips.

She was afraid to drink it herself, but she wasn't afraid to take it from Walker's lips. Maybe because, like that first night, things just seemed clear when he kissed her. Completely focused.

Because when he kissed her, she knew only one thing: that she wanted him. That she wanted to be as close to him as possible. That nothing, not the future, not fat rolls and

not granny panties, mattered more than getting naked and
getting him inside of her.

It was amazing. He took her from outraged near virgin
to scarlet woman with just the flick of his tongue. The man
was magic. The kind you should stay away from. But never
did. Because it was too seductive. The lure too strong, the
power too intense.

Damn Walker Callahan and his black magic kiss. And
yeah, *damn*. Not darn. It was that bad. That deep. That
desperate.

She released his shirt when she was sure he wasn't going
anywhere and wrapped her arms around his neck, and then
suddenly found herself on her back, her head on the armrest
of the couch.

He was kissing her deep, his tongue tracing patterns
against hers. He put his hands on her stomach, fingers edg-
ing beneath her shirt as he abandoned her lips and pressed
kisses to her neck, her jaw.

"I haven't made out on a couch like this since I was six-
teen," he said, his voice rough, his mouth hot on her skin.

"I"—she gasped for breath—"haven't made out . . . on a
couch . . . ever. With anyone."

"That's a shame. It's fun," he said, his teeth scraping her
collarbone.

"Unf!" she said, the closest thing to articulation she could
get with his hands making their way upward and his kisses
burning through her system. "I . . . yeah. Well . . . I can see
that."

"Why weren't you out kissing all the boys?" he asked,
his lips hovering at the edge of her shirt collar.

"I wasn't allowed to," she said, gasping as he flicked open
the top button of her blouse.

"Well, I wasn't allowed to get frisky in the back of Denise
Jameson's Camaro, but I did."

"I did what I was told."

"I'm going to file that away for later," he said, undoing

another button, "because it's very interesting. But for now"—he pressed a kiss between her breasts—"I think we should take this upstairs."

"Kayla?"

"Asleep." He hesitated. "You can't stay the night though. If that's a problem . . . well, I don't see why it should be. It didn't bother you last time."

The accusation burned, but it was true. She'd been the one to run out. But the thing was, she didn't want to get booted out of his bed and into the cold. It wasn't rational, because she knew why he had to get rid of her before morning. She knew she couldn't be here when Kayla woke up and it wasn't meant to be insulting to her in any way.

It was life. She couldn't be a part of confusing or disappointing that little girl any more than she already had been. So that meant that she had to either leave now, or deal with the fact that she was going back home tonight after she and Walker . . . made love.

Though it wouldn't be making love. She looked at his dark, glittering eyes, at the intent there. Oh, no, making love wasn't on his mind. And she didn't have to know much to realize that.

She didn't want love . . . maybe a little more experience? *A chance to be wanted.*

Okay, that thought wasn't the most appropriate. It shouldn't be about how she felt. Not emotionally. But she could admit that it was nice—more than nice—to have a man who was looking at her like she had something to give him.

Something he craved desperately.

She had no idea what to do. She only hoped that, for once in her life, she would be enough.

"Let's go upstairs," she said, her voice shaking.

"I bought condoms," he said. "If you didn't."

Her face burned and she felt something hot in her stomach. Anger. Jealousy. At the thought that he'd bought condoms, because it meant he was probably planning on using them with someone else. Well, of course he had been, because they were only supposed to be together once. And the idea of him with other women . . .

Get a grip, Sarah!

Yes. A grip needed to be gotten. She should be thankful he had protection, because she didn't. And she wanted sex, but without a pregnancy, thank you very much, so that meant one of them needed to be in possession of condoms.

"I didn't. Yay for preparedness. I would give you a gold star if you were in my class."

"You would give a kindergartner a gold star for buying condoms?" he asked, a dark brow arched.

"I . . . No." She slapped his bicep, and he laughed. "You know what I meant. Stop making my witty banter sound stupid."

He pulled her off the couch and up against his chest. "Is that what we're doing? A bit of witty banter before the main event?"

"Yes. It's just one of those things you do."

"Says?"

"Common knowledge, Walker. Don't you read, or watch British television?"

"Nope." He scooped her up into his arms and headed toward the stairs. "Do you know what I have done? Had sex. So you can trust me when I say witty banter isn't part of the necessary repertoire."

"Verbal foreplay, they call it."

"Nope, baby, no one calls it that." They came to the top of the stairs and he pushed his bedroom door open with his shoulder, crossing the room quickly and depositing her on the center of the bed.

He tugged his black T-shirt up over his head, and the air rushed from her lungs. "They . . . they do," she said. "Because it's invigorating."

"You know what's invigorating?" he asked, tugging his

belt through the loops and pushing his pants and underwear down to the floor.

She swallowed hard, "What?"

"Actual foreplay."

"Well, sure, I guess so. If you want to be base about it."

"Oh, baby, I intend to get very base here in a second."

He got onto the bed and kissed her, hard and deep. She held him close, returned the kiss, felt his erection, hot and hard against her hip. And she didn't feel nervous. Except . . .

"Oh crap." She scrambled away from him and scurried into the bathroom that was off the bedroom. "Just a second!" she shouted, stripping all of her clothes off, most especially those panties, those faulty, useless panties that hadn't done anything to keep her from hopping into bed with Walker, and then she went back into the bedroom, leaning against the bathroom door, naked and trying to look casual.

"What was that about?"

"I was not . . . dressed for the occasion."

"What the hell did you have under your clothes? A wet suit? Bondage gear?"

"Ack! No. I don't even really know what that would look like."

"Crotchless panties. And you lost your nerve."

"No. I wasn't trying to seduce you. Anyway, less talking, more kissing."

"You were the one who wanted verbal foreplay, Miss Larsen," he said, leaning back on the bed, his legs spread, his erection jutting up against his flat stomach. He looked completely indecent, and wholly tempting. "This isn't working for you?"

Oh, it was working. And it made her feel wicked.

"I'm just ready for kissing," she said.

"Mmm. I see. And if I don't comply, Miss Larsen?"

She crossed her arms. "Do I have to punish you?"

His smile turned wicked and something pitched in her stomach, sharp and hard. "You might." Her brain didn't quite know what to do with those words, but her body was all over them.

"And what would be a fitting punishment?" she asked, not sure where the confidence was coming from. Not sure what rabbit trail she was following now.

"I think you should tease me," he said. "Until I'm begging you to take me."

Her cheeks got hot. "I couldn't do that."

"Why not?"

"Because I don't think I could make you beg for me."

"Oh, baby, that's where you're wrong."

"I'm not. I'm just a . . ." Suddenly she felt like a fraud. Like an idiot, standing there, totally naked with Mr. Tall, Dark, Muscley and Chest-Haired staring at her like she was going to deliver him some sweet dessert. She had no sweet dessert. She barely had carrot sticks.

"Miss Larsen, I'm begging you right now. Come here and kiss me."

"Walker . . ."

"Please, Miss Larsen," he said, lying back on the bed. "I need your mouth on me."

She let out a slow, unsteady breath, uncertainty coursing through her. She didn't know how to do this kind of thing. Didn't know how to play sex games, or make a man want her.

But he seemed to want her already. She got onto the bed and leaned in, her lips hovering over his. "This is what you want?" she asked, boldness hitting her square in the chest. Because he was hard. For her. This man who was so impossibly gorgeous. He was begging—for her.

And how could she not feel powerful? How could she not feel beautiful?

How could she not feel wanted?

"Yes," he said, his voice rough. "This is what I want."

"You're going to have to say please," she said.

"Kiss me," he said. "Please."

Walker waited for Sarah to make her move. Her lips were so close, a tilt of his head and he could have them. Could take them and claim her mouth for his own.

But he was going to wait. He was going to make her choose it. He was going to let her have the control, and for some reason, the prospect of that got him even hotter.

Now that he was committed to this little piece of debauchery, he was all in. Yes, it was a bad, bad idea for him to keep sleeping with Sarah. But the simple fact was, avoiding her for the past few days had been torturous and awkward. Their only hope was to have sex until they didn't want to anymore.

Which, he was dimly aware, was somewhat faulty logic. Convenient, penis-led logic. But dammit, it was the line of logic that got him laid, and he was following it.

"Since you asked so nicely," she said.

Sarah dipped her head and swept her tongue between his lips, quickly, a touch so light he might have thought he'd imagined it if it weren't for the intense ache of need it sent firing along his veins.

"More," he said, his voice rough.

"More?"

"Miss Larsen," he said, between clenched teeth.

"And ask nicely."

"Please," he said. "Please, Miss Larsen, do something about this." He took her hand and guided it to his cock. Her eyes met his, wide and filled with . . . wonder, of all things. Like his dick was the most amazing thing she'd ever seen. And damn if that didn't go a long way in soothing his battered ego.

He hated to admit that his ego was battered, but it was the truth. You didn't spend years feeling like your touch was an inconvenience without those feelings getting buried under your skin. Like getting hit by a porcupine. And every movement he'd made to try and fix it had driven the barbs in deeper.

Every time he'd tried to touch his wife, seduce his wife, and gotten rejected, they'd sunk in farther. Now they were there just beneath the surface. Not easy to remove.

This was like balm for those wounds. This woman who was taking her time with him. Who was looking at him like he was God's gift. And yeah, the fact that he was the only man she'd ever been with probably had a lot to do with that.

But then, if the sex had been crap the first time, she wouldn't be looking at him like that. And she wouldn't have wanted a repeat performance.

"I . . . Can I . . . ?" She leaned forward, the slide of her tongue over his shaft like the strike of a match.

"Oh . . ." He swore. "Sorry, baby."

"It's okay," she said, tasting him again. "You did this for me. And I liked it. I thought you might like it. I mean . . . I know men like this, but . . . I don't really know what I'm doing, so I was hoping you might still enjoy it. But you don't seem opposed."

"Not in the least," he said, his hands tightening on the sheets, holding fistfuls of material, trying to keep himself from doing something out of line. Like grabbing her hair and tugging hard, holding her to him.

Yeah, that was something you probably shouldn't do with a woman who'd been a virgin roughly two weeks ago.

But he wanted to do it. Later. Next time. Oh yeah, next time.

Except one of his hands released its hold on the sheet and migrated to her hair without his permission. He sifted his fingers through the strawberry strands, flecks of deeper red and gold catching the light from his bedside lamp.

Then she took him into her mouth, a low, long moan from her vibrating through his body. He tightened his hold on her, tugging at that gorgeous hair. And he half expected her to get mad at him, or wonder what the hell he was doing. But instead she took him in deeper.

And he pulled her hair harder, flexing his hips in time with her movements. This felt like the first time. He couldn't remember the last time he'd gotten a blow job—sad but true. Years. Seven years, maybe. His wife had quit giving those about the time he'd popped the question. As if the rock he'd put on her finger was her Get Out of Jail Free card for foreplay.

But he wasn't going to think about the past now. Not when the present was so damn perfect. Not when Sarah's mouth was so wet, warm and attentive on his skin. Not when he had a woman lavishing him with attention, a woman who didn't yell at him for pulling her hair or for wanting to play a game where he took orders. A woman who seemed wholly in tune with what he wanted, and more than happy to give it to him.

And then he was lost. Completely. His mind blank of anything but her lips and tongue on his cock and how good it felt. He let her take him to the edge, let her take him to where his blood was like molten rock in his veins, before he tugged her hair hard and pulled her away from him.

"I don't want to finish like that."

She sat up, pushing her fingers through her hair. "Was that okay?"

"More than okay." He reached out and touched a piece of her hair. "Did I hurt you?"

She smiled, a shy, sweet, wicked smile. "A little. I didn't mind. I kind of liked it, actually. Is that normal?"

"Anything you like is good, baby; don't ever feel embarrassed about it."

"I liked it when you pulled my hair," she said, her smile getting wider, her face flushing. "I liked the way you . . . tasted. I don't even know who I am right now . . . I like me though."

"I like you too."

She laughed and leaned forward, kissing him deep and hard, pushing him back onto the bed. "I like when you call me Miss Larsen, because it feels naughty. I like feeling naughty."

He smoothed her hair and kissed her, reveling in the feel of all that soft, bare skin against his. "You do naughty very well."

"I need naughty underwear to match."

His throat tightened. "I wouldn't say no to that."

"You don't say no to much, do you?" she asked.

"Are you calling me a slut?"

She laughed and leaned in, pressing her breasts hard up against his chest. "Maybe."

"For *you*, yeah."

"You have no idea how hot that is," she said, kissing him again, straddling him, her thighs on either side of his, her wet heat pressed against his cock.

She started to move against him, so slick and perfect. He gripped her ass, holding her to him, letting her find her rhythm. She braced her hands on his chest, threw her head back, the view of her breasts enough to make him come then and there.

But he gritted his teeth. Held back. Because he wasn't

going to let things end until she was satisfied. Until he was buried in her tight body, with her surrounding him completely.

She shifted her hips and the tip of his erection slid inside her. So perfect. Better than anything he could ever remember feeling. Her body surrounding his naked shaft . . .

"Dammit." He pushed her off of him, his heart beating fast.

"What?" she asked.

"Condom." He fished around in his bedside drawer and produced a packet. "These were for you, by the way," he said. "I was hoping I would be able to seduce you into my actual bed, and not just a hotel bed. I had a weak moment the other day and bought them. Just in case. Which was when I knew I was a total goner."

"Oh," she said. "That's . . . good to know."

He rolled it onto his length and kissed her, tugging her back over him. "As you were."

She smiled and he gripped his cock, guiding it into her body. She had a look of such fierce and beautiful concentration on her face as he slid home.

"Okay?" he asked.

"Oh, just . . . absolutely brilliant, actually," she said, her voice like a purr.

"Brilliant?" He flexed his hips upward and she gasped.

"Yes."

"You really are good for me, baby."

And then she started moving and he couldn't have spoken again if he tried. He was completely lost in her. Her movements, her beauty. The way her hair slid forward and covered them like a curtain, shielding them from everything but this. The way he felt stronger, and weaker, than he ever had in his life, all at the same time.

His orgasm rushed up to meet him too soon, and he tried to hold it back, tried to hold himself to earth with his hands on her hips. But then she closed her eyes, her mouth falling open, her body tightening around him, as her climax shook her and called his forward. There was no willpower on earth that could keep it from happening.

So he let go. Gave in.

It was like an earthquake deep inside of him, and when it passed, when he opened his eyes, he was shocked to find out the house hadn't fallen down around them.

"Damn," she whispered, collapsing onto his chest.

He wrapped his arms around her and withdrew, turning them so that they were on their sides, facing each other.

She looked at him, her red hair tangled around her face. "That's the first time I've ever said that word out loud before."

He kissed her lips. "I'm honored."

What was it about her? She made him horny, which didn't really concern him. But the other stuff he was starting to feel was more concerning. The tenderness. The connection. Again, he had to blame her inexperience.

And, hell, his own serious bout of celibacy. She was his first lover who wasn't his wife in nearly a decade, which made it even more likely that the feelings were down to his own sex life.

Or lack thereof.

"I guess I should go," she said, her voice muffled.

He didn't want her to go. Not for any soft or tender reasons, but because he wanted to spend the rest of the night deep inside of her, easing this constant ache he'd felt in his body from the moment he'd first laid eyes on her in that bar.

"In a minute," he said.

"Yeah, okay. In a minute."

"Why were you a virgin, Sarah?"

"Kinda beating a dead horse there, Walker."

He tightened his hold on her. "Indulge my dead-horse beating."

"I was raised by my grandmother. And she was . . . protective. And very traditional. She used to make me wear skirts all the time. Skirts that came down to my ankles. And turtlenecks that itched. I had to keep my hair long. Wasn't allowed to pierce my ears. Even in high school. And the thing about living in a town like this is that no one forgets that stuff. I was completely invisible then, and even as I became an adult, I was still invisible, because to them I'm that same girl who wasn't allowed to date and lived with that crazy old lady."

"Yeah, that's a tough one. But why wait until now to find someone?"

She shifted and propped her head up on her elbow. "I don't know." She blew out a breath. "I do know. It's just . . . she always made sex sound so *dirty*. She made it seem like women who wanted it were dirty. My mom . . . she was really young when she had me, and single. She dropped me off with my grandmother and I never saw her again. My mom was this scarlet standard to my grandma. She held her up and said, 'This is what happens to loose women. This is how they are. They get pregnant, get their lives ruined by men. Abandon their babies.' And I . . . I knew it wasn't that simple, but it was hard not to feel like my own . . . like anything sexual I felt was wrong. Or dirty. She was just such a strong influence on my life. But she died last year, and I've had some time to think. Really think."

"And your conclusion?"

"I knew I needed to find out how I felt about life. What I thought was right and wrong. I knew I needed to figure out how I felt about sex. I knew I wanted sex, actually, and that was something that was always a struggle when I was younger. I had a sex drive, and didn't that make me wicked?"

"She wanted you to wait till your wedding night?"

"That's not even it." She sat up, her breasts bouncing a little with the motion. And hell yes, he looked. "There was no provision for that. I mean, yeah, I think she knew I'd get married someday, but it was more like . . . good women endured sex. It was the bad ones who wanted it. Here I was this horribly sheltered, mousy girl who knew nothing about sex except that . . . I liked men. I liked to look at them. And I knew I wanted to be with one . . . and what did that make me? Shaking that . . . It's hard. I don't know if I really have."

"Do you regret being with me?"

"No," she said. "And I want to be with you again."

"That's good. I want that too. But . . . but you know what this is, right? This isn't going anywhere. Nowhere but the bedroom. My life is a hell of a lot more screwed up than yours."

"That's saying something."

"So I gather." He touched her hand. "I have Kayla to worry about. And my last try with commitment was a nightmare, so I'm not anxious to repeat it."

"Yeah, I get that." She looked sad though, and that made him feel like a prick.

"But I want this," he said.

"Me too."

"And I want you to know I'd let you stay the night if not for . . ."

"Yeah . . . I get it. I do." She stood up and made her way back into the bathroom. He watched her round, perfect butt the whole way.

"Why exactly did you hide in the bathroom?" he called from the bed.

"I had on granny panties!"

Her response tugged a short, sharp laugh out of him. "Granny panties, huh?"

"They were supposed to keep me chaste."

He really laughed that time. "Oh, sorry. You going down on me like that wasn't exactly chaste."

"Hardly," she said, her tone dry. She appeared a moment later, all dressed. "But you don't need to highlight my failures."

"Baby, from where I'm sitting, that was a big success."

"Yes, well."

"Is that one of the things you always wanted to do?"

She looked away from him. "What?"

"You did, didn't you? You used to fantasize about that. About sucking a guy off."

"Walker," she said, her voice a whisper, her cheeks red.

He stood up. "You don't have to be ashamed about wanting sex, Sarah. Not with me. I don't think any less of you for having desire. It's sexy."

She looked at him. "You think?"

"Yeah, but who the hell cares what I think? What do you think? Did you like what we did?"

"Yes."

"Then don't be ashamed."

She nodded slowly. "Okay. I'll do my best." She headed toward the bedroom door. "I'll see you tomorrow, Walker."

"Give me a second to get dressed and I'll walk you out."

"You don't have to."

"This is something I want to do. So let me, okay?"

"Okay." She stood there and watched him while he dressed. There was something really hot about that fascination of hers. There was nothing coy or practiced in her eyes. It wasn't a finely tuned look, practiced on lots of men before him. It was just Sarah, doing what she wanted to do. And what she seemed to want to do was ogle him.

He opened the bedroom door and she followed him down to the living room. It seemed like such an asshat move. Sending her out into the snow right after accepting a blow job from her. *Thanks for the orgasm, now drive yourself home on the black ice.*

But she couldn't stay, because he had Kayla to think of.

And it has nothing to do with the fact that the idea of a woman sharing your bed all night makes you feel like the walls are closing in?

Oh yeah, well, maybe a little of that too. But given the weather, he would have ignored that feeling in favor of letting her stay warm in his house. He was sure he would. But he couldn't test the theory because of Kayla.

So it saved him from uncovering what a bastard he actually might be. Which suited him.

"Good night," he said, pulling open the front door and wincing when a wall of cold air broke through over the threshold and into the room.

"Night," she said, putting her coat on, and her scarf and hat. She was in all black, her hair a bright shock of color against the dark.

She turned to go, then stopped, and flung herself into his arms, kissing him, hard and clumsy on the lips. Then she smiled, a kind of giddy, sweet smile he'd never been on the receiving end of. One he was pretty sure he didn't deserve to be on the receiving end of.

"Good night," she said, walking outside and closing the door behind her.

He watched her go, watched her get into her car and pull out of the driveway. And he had to stand there, with his head spinning and his body buzzing, wondering what the hell had just hit him.

"How old are you?"

"What the hell kind of question is that?"

Walker was lying behind her, tracing patterns on her stomach with the tips of his fingers. They were naked and tangled together, breathless and both a little sweaty. Walker had been doing a very good job of helping her deal with her remaining inhibitions over the past few nights.

And now, post-orgasm, she just felt warm and sleepy. Not ashamed.

Although she wasn't looking forward to driving back home either, so that meant a little bit of delay by pillow talk was on her agenda.

"It's a getting-to-know-you, normal kind of question," she said. "I'm sleeping with you, I ought to know things like that."

"To make sure I'm not too old for you?"

"To make sure I'm not being a cougar."

"Not even close, Miss Larsen, but it's an interesting idea."

"How not close am I?"

"Why does this matter, Sarah? Honestly."

"Because." She sat up and looked down at him, at his perfect face, his perfect chest, his perfect . . . everything. "I want to know the man that has made me one heck of a gleeful fallen woman. Is that so weird? I want to not be sleeping with a stranger."

"I'm not a stranger," he said, tucking her hair behind her ear, "am I, baby?"

"Fine. Not as such. Since we're sitting here naked and you were just inside me."

"Yeah, that's pretty friendly where I come from."

She blew out a long breath. "The point is, Walker, I told you about me, and now I want to hear a little about you."

"Boring shit. I'm thirty-six, I was born in Texas, I grew up in Texas, I got married in Texas and I got divorced in Texas. Then I moved here."

"How old were you when you got married?"

"Twenty-nine," he said, short and fast, like he was resigned to answering questions, but only if he could behave like he was being interrogated.

"And when you met her?"

"Twenty-seven. I was young, dumb and kinda naive. I'm now old and not in the least naive. Possibly still a little dumb though."

"And what happened with your wife?"

He let out a harsh breath. "It's not important."

"I'm curious. Look, I told you about my draconian grandmother and my sex shame issues. And I have done things with you I'd never even imagined before. So, all things considered, I think it would be nice if you shared some of your issues with me."

"Fine. Everything was fine. I mean . . . it's not like we had sex all the time, it's not like we were perfect. But we were fine. She was . . . fine. And then she started to drift away from me. She didn't want me to touch her. Didn't want to talk about it. She started not taking very good care of

Kayla. I would go out and work on the ranch and come back and find Elise sleeping and Kayla crying because Mommy hadn't fed her lunch. But I thought we'd be okay. I thought she was having a hard time. Depression even. But she didn't want to talk about it, so I didn't either. Then one day she left. I came home and Kayla was napping in her crib, and Elise was gone. Her stupid girly shit was gone. She packed up her shoes, her makeup, her dresses. She forgot her kid," he said, his voice rough, "but I have to say I'm pretty damn pleased about that."

"It sounds like she couldn't cope."

"No, she couldn't. And . . . and sometimes I wonder what would have happened if she had taken Kayla. If Kayla had been with Elise when she'd had her car accident. And then I just want to throw up. As hard as it's been, just me and her, losing her would have been impossible."

"You're a good dad," she said, her heart clenching tight. She was glad that Kayla had Walker. But she wished Walker had someone. In that moment she realized how alone he'd been. And her being naked in bed with him didn't make him less alone. Not really. Not when they didn't share anything other than their bodies. No when their connection didn't go any deeper than skin.

"Thanks, but I think I do a pretty crappy job half the time."

"You love her," she said. "You love her enough to do the hard things. That's not doing a crappy job at all."

"Kids are little, but you have no idea how tight of a hold they can get on your heart."

She nodded. "I know." She had a vague idea, because she loved all of the kids that came through her kindergarten class. She felt invested in them, in their futures, but she knew it wasn't the same as the kind of love a parent felt. Where every worry, every responsibility, rested squarely on you.

Suddenly, she felt a strong, intense need to feel it. To

know what it meant to love like that. To have love like that. To belong to a family.

A real one. Not the cold, sparse upbringing she'd had.

"You know," she said, "you might not feel like love is enough, but . . . my grandmother was punctual. She always got me from school on time and got me out the door on time. She dressed me neatly, and she was an incredible cook. But she didn't love me. At least, if she did, she didn't show it. She didn't have any warmth to her. Any give. She was so angry all the time. So stiff and cold. She took care of me, but she didn't make me feel loved. And I missed that, Walker. I still miss it, every day of my life. And maybe Kayla will be late for school, or you'll be late to get her, but when she's grown and she looks back on her life, she won't remember those days. She'll remember what it was like when you hugged her. Just like I remember every hug I ached for, but didn't get."

He sat up, his dark eyes fierce. "She didn't hug you?"

"No."

"She made you afraid of sex, your body, your own desires. Made you feel like there was something wrong with you. And on top of all that, she never even hugged you?"

"Nope."

"Sarah," Walker said, his voice ragged, "I'm going to hug you now."

And then he was hugging her, crushing her to his chest, his skin hot and bare and sexy. It wasn't an easy friendship hug, which she got often enough from her friend Lucy, or one of those little half hugs that touchier people seemed to be inclined to give on greeting you. It was something fierce and tender at the same time, gentle and rough.

It was everything she'd ever craved in a hug. But it was even more. Because it was Walker. And he smelled like spice and skin, sweat and sex. She never wanted him to let her go. Ever. And just then, the full feeling in her chest didn't scare her. The need to have him forever didn't seem frightening. Because it felt too right.

She clung to him, her fingers curled into his shoulders, her face buried in the curve of his neck. She was falling in love with this man. This wounded, ridiculous man who hadn't even wanted to tell her how old he was.

This man who was giving everything to raising his child. This man who'd had his heart broken so badly.

In this moment, she could almost believe there was hope for them. She could almost believe he felt something too. That she wasn't alone in this feeling.

He released his hold on her, his hands bracketing her face, his eyes intent on hers. The expression on his face was one of wonder, then, suddenly, fear. Then he looked away, took a deep breath and let her go. And she felt his absence so sharply, it was near pain.

"You should go," he said.

She nodded, feeling numb. "Yeah, I know."

And this time, he didn't get up and get dressed. He didn't walk her out. He rolled over and closed his eyes like she was already gone.

"Sarah!"

Sarah turned around just in time to see a loosely packed snowball sailing toward her, shedding snowflakes as it flew and hit her in the thigh. Kayla grinned, impish and gleeful.

It was the first time Sarah had seen her look so happy. Part of her knew that she shouldn't encourage Kayla to call her by her first name. Knew that she should try and keep some distance. Keep it like a teacher and a student. She wasn't Walker's girlfriend; she wasn't potential stepmother material.

But she wanted to be. That was the bottom line. The longer she spent in this house, the longer she spent with Kayla, the longer she spent in Walker's bed, the more she wanted this to be her life. The more she wanted this to be her family.

But Walker was clearly not on board with the idea. There had been no more talking and sharing during their nights together. And no more hugging. Kissing, yes. Sex, yes. But not hugging. No more tenderness, no more sweet understanding.

No. Walker had put a moratorium on the feelings.

Too bad she still felt them. Too bad she couldn't just turn them off, even though she knew they were utterly futile.

She got hit with another snowball, this one on her stomach, and she looked at her attacker. "You're in big trouble, young lady."

Kayla looked nervous for a second. "I am?"

"Yes, because I have an excellent snowball arm." She'd thrown snowballs exactly once in her life. She'd gone outside on a Saturday morning, in a skirt and a heavy woolen coat, black tights covering her legs, and played with some of the neighborhood boys. They'd chased each other, and they'd thrown snow, and made snow angels.

Until her grandmother had found her.

Young ladies don't behave that way. And they certainly don't play with boys without proper supervision.

She shook her head and dismissed the memory. That didn't matter anymore. It didn't matter that she hadn't been allowed to play then. She was allowed to now. Because she made her own choices. Because she could have the life she wanted, if she would just aim for it.

Right now, she would settle for aiming at Kayla's shoulder, very gently. She threw a ball of loosely packed snow at the little girl, who shrieked and ran out of Sarah's throwing range to gather more snow.

"What's going on?"

Walker was standing in the distance, looking like spilled ink on the snow, dressed all in black, from his hat down to his boots.

"I'm getting Sarah!" Kayla said, laughter making each word jiggle.

"I got her back," Sarah said as Kayla ran up on her and flung another snowball at her.

Walker bent down and started slowly forming snow into a tightly packed ball. "Walker," Sarah said, her tone warning.

"Looks like fun," he said, smiling in a way that spelled doom for her. Complete and total doom.

"Have mercy," she said.

"There is no room for mercy in times of war, Miss Larsen," he said, cocking his hand back, his expression downright wicked. And then she was hit with a hard-packed ice ball that exploded against her well-cushioned shoulder, right on her down coat. The snow sprayed up onto her face and she sputtered, melted droplets running down her neck, under her jacket and scarf.

She shook her fist at him. "You fiend!"

"You're hit!" he shouted back.

Kayla laughed and Sarah staggered forward, falling to her knees for maximum drama. "I'm mortally wounded. Avenge me, Kayla!"

Kayla flung snow at her father, who promptly rushed her and grabbed her, flinging her over his shoulder like a sack of potatoes, a smile on the little girl's face. "I win," he said.

"You cheated," Sarah said.

"How?"

"You play dirty! If I'd been packing my snowballs like that, I could have done serious damage. But you ambushed us." She stood up and brushed the snow from her knees. "And I'm pretty sure you're not supposed to pick your enemies up."

"What, this?" he asked, indicating Kayla. "Prisoner of war."

"I am not!" Kayla said.

"Fine then, a prisoner of dinnertime. Why don't we go in and wash up? I can make you some cocoa."

He set his daughter down and she ran for the porch, her boots clomping on the deck. Sarah was still grinning when she looked back at Walker, and their eyes clashed. And something on his face changed. From happy and light to heavy and closed-off in a split second.

"Don't look at me like that," she said.

"Like what?"

"Like I'm holding leg irons. I'm going to be nice to Kayla when I'm with her, and it's inevitable I'll get close to her, but I'm not planning on trapping you, Walker, so please don't look at me like I am."

"That isn't what I was thinking."

She shook her head. "I don't believe you."

"Go in the house."

"Maybe I'll go home."

"You won't."

She crossed her arms and cocked out her hip. "Oh, really?"

He took her arm and hauled her against him, dropping a hard, short kiss on her lips. "You want me too much," he said.

"I . . . I could go to a bar and pick up someone else," she said, biting her lip, the cold stinging her skin. "I'm good at it."

"You suck at it. I didn't take you back to my hotel room because your pickup lines screamed that you were the hottest lay. And your clothes were ridiculous."

"Then why did you take me back to your room?"

He shook his head. "Damned if I know, Sarah, but I couldn't leave you there either."

"Is that supposed to be flattering?"

"I don't know, but it's the truth."

"Well, there's that, I guess."

He let out a long, slow breath, and it lingered in the air like smoke. "Sarah, I can't explain why I wanted you, because I hadn't wanted a woman in a long time. Sex seemed like way too much work to me after going through what I did with my wife. But I saw you there, and you offered me your whiskey while looking like the most timid little mouse I've ever seen. And then I asked you to dance and you didn't run. Far from it—you propositioned me. I couldn't say no to that, and . . . I didn't want to."

Warmth bloomed in her cold cheeks, beneath the surface of her chilled skin. "So you . . . wanted me even though you could tell I wasn't . . . good at all that?"

"I could tell you weren't a pro at it, but I was pretty sure you'd be good."

"Really? Why is that?"

He shrugged. "Just expected it, considering how hot you made me from the moment you offered me your drink. I hate to disappoint you, darlin', but the Sunday church dress you were wearing wasn't doing it."

"Oh."

"You took your clothes off and made me think I ought to burn that dress because it was hiding all your beauty."

Sarah's throat tightened and she could feel tears stinging her eyes, threatening to fall. Stupid tears she couldn't go shedding because they would betray the fact that what she felt for Walker was so much deeper than sex. And then he really would see visions of her standing there with leg irons.

She had feelings for Walker, yes, but she wasn't stupid enough to think that he'd return them.

She curled her hands into fists, her fingernails digging into her palms. No, Walker couldn't love a woman like her, and why would he? He might be attracted to her, and that in and of itself was a shock. But he'd lived life. And he'd been burned by it. She was just sort of emerging from her shell, a little bird with wet feathers who didn't know how to fly yet.

For both of their sakes, she had to get her feathers dry and learn how to leave the nest, so to speak. She didn't need to attach herself to someone else. Someone else's life and expectations.

Anyway, he wouldn't want her to.

So, there was that settled. No love business or anything remotely resembling it.

"Thanks for that," she said. "I'm pretty thrilled you like the way I look without clothes on, actually."

"I know it."

"I'm pretty fond of you naked too."

"High praise."

"Well, yes, all things considered. I was sort of brought up to fear penises, so I found it a refreshing surprise that I actually think they're rather enjoyable."

He laughed, each note of it punctuated by a puff of frozen air. "I'm glad you've found my penis enjoyable."

"Oh, gosh, yes. More than. Aesthetically, athletically . . ."

"Athletically?"

"It's kind of a workout, actually."

"I think that's why they call it the devil's cardio."

It was her turn to laugh. "They do not call it that. If they did, my grandma would have. And I most definitely would have heard it."

"As in, beware the devil's cardio for it will give you the abs of hell?"

"Something like that," she said.

They smiled and their eyes met—another companionable moment. Two in a very short space of time. It was enough to make a girl forget herself completely.

"Dinnertime," he said.

"Yes," she said, nodding. "Kayla will wonder what became of us."

"So you'll stay?"

She should say no. She really should. She should walk away now while she could do it without being wholly devastated. She should recognize the fact that she was being stupid and predictable and falling for her first lover when that wasn't what she wanted at all.

She should walk away and leave him to an empty bed and go back to her own. Do what she should have already done: consign him to the bin of new experiences had and be done with him.

But instead she nodded. "Yes, Walker, I'll stay."

And then, after her traitorous mouth spoke those words, her traitorous feet carried her to the house and inside. Another night playing at a strange version of family. Sitting around the dinner table with him and Kayla. Sneaking up to his room when Kayla was in bed and letting him make love with her, holding her until both of them were on the verge of sleep.

A window into a life she wasn't sure she could ever have. At least not with Walker. Not with Kayla.

It was heartbreaking, painful. She knew she should stop it. But she didn't have the strength to walk away. And she didn't have the courage to name the feeling that was pounding through her, in her.

Because if she acknowledged how deeply she felt for him, she really would be in trouble.

"I don't know if we're getting a Christmas tree," Kayla said, looking down into her cereal with a grumpy expression on her face.

"Did your dad say that?" Sarah asked.

"He said he didn't know if he had time."

"Well . . . that's not right. We can make time. I'm sure we can." If nothing else, she could get the tree and Walker could decorate it in the evening with Kayla. But there was no reason for them not to go get one. In fact, she was pretty sure she could get John, who owned Silver Creek's mercantile, to bring one from his store if she played her cards right.

It was a bold move for her, but darn it, she was feeling bold lately. She'd gone shopping and gotten some sexier panties the other day, and they just made her feel different. She was a new woman beneath her clothes, and this woman was an action taker. She wasn't going to wait for permission to get things done.

She was going to get Kayla her Christmas tree. "Yes," she said again, "we can absolutely get a tree."

This earned her a "Yay!" and a big smile from Kayla. Sarah smiled and picked up her phone, putting in a quick call to John. With any luck, by the time Walker got home, they would have a tree to decorate.

It looked like Rudolph had vomited on his porch. That was Walker's first thought when he got home that evening. There were white icicles hanging from the roof, with white-and-red-striped lights wrapped around the support beams.

And there was a fresh wreath on the door.

He just stopped, standing there in the snow like an idiot, staring at the decorations, his heart frozen with the rest of him. It was a moment out of time, a taste of life as it should have been. Not a memory; better than the memories of his life at the holidays with a wife.

This felt so right for a moment that it damn near knocked him to his knees. And then—then he felt angry. Because this wasn't reality. It wasn't Sarah's job, it wasn't her place, to take his house and put her stamp on it.

To take Christmas and wrap herself around it like tinsel. Wrap herself around his life that way. All glittery and decorative. And bright. So damn bright. She was like a shot of glitter into his surroundings, and he knew it wasn't going to last. But Kayla didn't.

He stomped up the porch steps and into the house, gritting his teeth, twisting his face into a scowl. He pushed the door open and then froze.

It smelled like apples and cinnamon, and there was mistletoe in the entryway to the living room. And there Kayla and Sarah were, sitting on the floor surrounded by boxes, a tree behind them, rich, green and bare of decorations.

"You're home!" Kayla shot up from where she was sitting and raced across the room to give him a hug. "I was so sad because we didn't have a tree, and I told Sarah you said we didn't have time, but Sarah got a nice man to come and bring all of the stuff, and then I helped her find our old decorations."

"Really?" he asked, his throat tight.

"I just thought it wasn't right for you to not have a tree," Sarah said, standing up. "Do you want some cider? It's in the slow cooker."

"Oh, why not?" he grumbled, kicking his boots off and going into the living room.

Sarah walked into the kitchen and he followed her. "Why are you so grumpy?" she asked, whirling around to face him when they were out of earshot of the living room.

"What do you mean, why am I grumpy? Give me some cider."

She grabbed a mug and ladle and held them against her chest. "I don't know if you deserve any, Mr. Bah Humbug."

"Cute. But you look like you just opened the Silver Creek location of Santa's Workshop, so excuse me if I'm a little surprised."

She scowled and ladled cider into a mug, handing it to him and crossing her arms, her expression dark. "Well, your daughter wanted a Christmas tree, so I wanted to make sure she got one. Your panic seems a little overboard, considering it's over twinkle lights."

"Unauthorized twinkle lights."

"Oh . . . good heavens, Walker, take the stick out of your butt."

His eyebrows shot up. "Did you just say . . ."

She crossed her arms, her lips turning down. "Yes. Yes I did. You're acting like you . . . have one up there. Your daughter wanted Christmas to look familiar and it didn't, and I went out of my way to make sure she had some cheer. I don't think that merits being on the receiving end of your angry eyebrows."

He set the mug down on the counter. "It's a little too close to domesticity, don't you think?"

Worse, it had made him ache. Made him long for something that he'd never wanted to long for ever again. Because he knew how marriage gone bad looked. He'd lived it. And he never wanted to put himself, or his daughter, through that again.

"That wasn't my intent," she said. He could tell she meant it, and he could also tell he'd hurt her feelings. Which he hated, but dammit, she knew what this was. He knew what it was. There was no point wanting more or pretending, even for a second, that it could be more.

"I know," he said, his voice rough.

"I could go," she said, "while you decorate the tree."

And then he'd have to explain to Kayla why Miss Larsen had left. Because of her mean old dad. And that didn't seem fair at all. Especially when he'd been such an ass about the decorations.

Sarah was right; Kayla needed normal, and he was too busy being pissed that the holidays were daring to come. He'd been worried about dealing with a Christmas without Elise, and what that would mean for Kayla, and he hadn't accounted for the fact that not getting a tree wouldn't make Christmas stay away.

They had to deal with it. He had to deal with it, whether he wanted to or not.

"Stay," he said.

She nodded. "Okay."

Walker did the lights, Sarah wrapped the tinsel, and Kayla hung ornaments until she fell asleep in front of the tree, completely wiped out.

"I'll carry her to bed," Walker said. He scooped his daughter up and his eyes met Sarah's. It was another of those moments—the ones that filled him with hope and anger all at the same time.

The kind that made desires long dead stir back to life inside of him.

It was all fine and good when the only thing she'd woken up was his cock, but now she was starting to get to his heart.

He was pretty sure he'd signed a DNR for his fricking heart. But she was doing it. Damned woman.

He sighed heavily and deposited Kayla into her bed. He looked at his daughter's face for a long time. So peaceful. And he prayed that she was young enough that she wouldn't carry the scars her mother had left forever. The fact that Elise had died would never be easy, but in some ways the purposeful abandonment would always be harder to deal with.

It had destroyed his trust. He only hoped it hadn't destroyed hers. He wanted more for her than that. More than this angry, dark feeling swirling inside of him all the time. More than the intense, gut-wrenching longing, married to a fear that was so strong, it threatened to destroy him.

Yeah, he wanted more than this for her. But he didn't want more for himself, because he was too damn scared. So there was that. And he'd admitted it.

He rubbed his hands over his face, weary down to his bones.

What a mess. He started back down the hall, back down the stairs, with the intention of sending Sarah home. He needed distance, and he needed to get his head back on straight.

But then he saw her sitting in front of the couch looking at the lights. And he wondered who she was going home to tonight. If her house was warm. If she had a Christmas tree.

"Do you have a tree yet?"

"What?" She turned to look at him, and his heart skipped. "No, it's just me. I don't see the point. I'm only a block away from the town tree, and the lighting is at the end of the week. I walk down there and enjoy it, but then I don't have to vacuum up pine needles."

"Smart. But I have to vacuum up pine needles."

"I can help you with it, Walker."

"I didn't hire you to be the housekeeper, Sarah."

"I know." She stood up and stretched, the move so unconsciously sexy that it sent a bolt of lust straight to his gut. "So, I should probably go."

"Not yet," he said, regret and warning warring in his stomach. She should go. He knew it. She knew it. But he didn't want her to.

"What am I waiting for?"

"You can't buy mistletoe and expect I won't want to make use of it."

He wandered over to the doorway and stood beneath the mistletoe. Waiting. She moved to him, confusion and desire visible in her eyes, and he knew, beyond a shadow of a doubt, that he should turn her away. Tell her to go home. Never touch her again.

But he couldn't.

He needed her too badly. And he was, it turned out, all out of selflessness.

"I've never been kissed under the mistletoe before," she said.

"I don't expect you have been."

"You're the only man I've ever kissed, Walker."

He felt like he'd been punched. "Shit, baby, you have to stop surprising me with things like that."

"Sorry." She looked down. "It's kind of embarrassing, really."

He took her chin between his thumb and forefinger and tilted her face up. "Don't be embarrassed."

"Kind of hard not to be."

"You're brave, Sarah. To try and change your life and find out who you are. Most of us are just content to let the status quo stand."

"Well, I didn't like my life. And I realized I was living it for someone else. Someone who's dead, actually, which I think is extra lame."

"But you aren't living for her now. You're living for you."

"I suppose so," she said, but she didn't sound very excited. Or very convinced.

"Can I give you your first under-the-mistletoe kiss, Miss Larsen?"

Her eyes drifted closed, her lips parting, like she was expecting him to feed her a decadent dessert. "Please."

And he obliged her. He dipped his head and kissed her. She tasted like apples and cinnamon, fruit and spice mingling with the flavor of Sarah. A flavor that was unique, that he knew down in the deepest parts of himself. That he was sure he would never forget.

It would haunt his dreams, and he knew it. A craving that could never be satisfied. Like the milkshakes from an old diner in his hometown. It had closed when he was a kid, and there had never been anything else like them.

And even now, he remembered the way they tasted. And sometimes, for no reason at all, he would crave one. A craving that would always go unmet.

That's how it would be with Sarah.

But he couldn't keep her. Because he couldn't offer her marriage or love. All he could offer was sex. Half the night in his bed, and then a boot out into the cold.

That was nothing. That was balls.

And he wasn't going to insult her by asking for that.

When Christmas was over, this would be over too.

So for now he was just going to keep kissing her under the mistletoe. Like he was a teenage boy with a date. Like there was no time limit. Like his body wasn't roaring for more. For her to be naked, for him to be inside of her.

He tilted his head and deepened the kiss, slid his tongue against hers. Her lips were so soft, her kiss so generous. She was a damn good kisser for a woman who'd only learned how recently. Or maybe skill didn't really matter. Maybe the only thing that mattered was how much he wanted her, how much she wanted him. And how that made him feel.

He tightened his hold on her, pulling her body up against his, feeling her breasts pressed so perfectly against his chest. She wove her fingers through his hair, holding him to her, kissing him harder.

"I think we should take this upstairs," she said.

"You do?" he asked, his stomach tightening, blood rushing south of his belt.

"Definitely. I have plans for you, Walker Callahan. Naked plans. And they need to be done where we won't get walked in on."

"I'm all for seeing how these plans work out," he said.

"You'll like them." She pulled away from him and started to walk upstairs. He had a flashback to their first night together, to when she'd walked up to the loft ahead of him. She'd looked timid then, so different from the woman she was now. She had a sway in her hips, the confidence of a woman who knew that she was wanted. Who knew she was driving him crazy.

He hadn't been able to imagine then that that woman could become this one.

To an even greater degree, he couldn't have imagined that she would still be in his life. That she would be in his home. Or that she would make his chest feel like it was going to explode.

He should go roll around in the snow and get himself under control. He should send her home. He should stop whatever madness had taken him over.

But he didn't want to. He couldn't. He could do nothing but follow her up the stairs, because his need for her transcended logic. It was more basic than that. Completely and totally undeniable.

And he sure as hell wasn't going to waste time denying it when he could be embracing it, and her.

When they got into his bedroom, she started taking her clothes off. She pulled her shirt over her head, slowly, and revealed a bra he'd sure as hell never seen on her before.

Red satin, pushing those glorious breasts up high. And when she took her jeans off, he could see she had matching panties.

"Damn, woman," he said, advancing on her, pulling her into his arms and kissing her until they both ran out of breath.

"Do you like?"

"I more than like. But I didn't think I was supposed to get such pretty presents, since I'm sure I'm on the naughty list."

She chuckled, throaty and seductive. "I know you are, but I wouldn't ask you to be any different."

"No?"

"No. You make me feel pretty naughty too."

"You might not get any presents this year, baby," he said.

Her lips curved, her smile nothing short of wicked. "As long as I get this"—she put her hand over his cock, her fingers caressing him through his pants—"I don't really mind."

"Sarah Larsen, I believe I've corrupted you."

"Maybe so."

"Think you can handle a little more?"

"Is there any more?"

"Get on the bed, Miss Larsen," he said. She obeyed, a questioning light joining the mischief in her eyes. "I like it when you give orders," he said, taking off his shirt. "I like it a whole lot." He loosened his belt and pulled it through the loops on his jeans. "But I like to give them too. On your knees."

"What?"

"Do as you're told, Miss Larsen, or you don't get your present." She nodded slowly and rose up onto her knees. "Turn around," he said, his voice hoarse. And she obeyed again.

He finished undressing and joined her on the bed, putting his hand on her stomach and kissing her shoulder, sweeping her hair to the side and kissing the back of her neck. "Yes," he said, "I like this view."

He unhooked the clasp on her bra and admired the line of her bare back, her hips, the little dimples above her ass. He couldn't have created a more beautiful woman in a dream.

"These have to come off," he said, running his fingertip beneath the waistband of her panties.

"Do they?"

"For what I have in mind? Yeah." He pushed them down her hips, and stopped where her knees bent. "On second thought . . . leave them like that. And bend over."

"What?"

He traced a line over her back. "Was something confusing about my command, Miss Larsen?"

She shook her head, her hair cascading over her shoulder like a copper river. And she obeyed, bracing herself on her hands.

"Better." He swallowed hard, his hand going to his erection, squeezing himself because if he didn't do something he was going to go off now. She was far too erotic a picture for him to keep his cool.

He had a perfect view of that perfect ass, with her red panties halfway down her thighs. His for the taking.

"Wait just like that," he said.

He got a condom out of the bedside drawer and rolled it on quickly, his hands shaking, his heart pounding so hard, he was sure he was on the verge of a major cardiac incident. But it wasn't going to stop him. He couldn't stop. Not now.

He leaned forward and kissed her on her rear-end cheek, following it up with a light smack of his open hand. She let out a short, sharp sound, but didn't change her position.

"Okay?" he asked.

"I don't think you could do anything I wouldn't like," she said, lowering her head, her hair spilling over to cover her face.

"You're going to make my ego explode," he said, sliding his hand down between her thighs and pushing two fingers inside her, one hand braced on her lower back as he tested her, making sure she was wet and ready.

She rocked her hips back and forth against his hand, setting the rhythm. He withdrew from her and placed his cock against her slick entrance, going in slowly.

She breathed in deep, her hands curling around the blankets.

"I'm not hurting you, am I?" he asked.

She shook her head. "No. Oh, no. So good. I didn't realize."

"I'll bet this is a first for you too," he said, his voice rough.

"Yeah. This is something else I've never done. Under the mistletoe or not."

He gripped her hips and pulled her back hard against him. "You feel so good."

"Mmm."

"I take it that's good?" He took one hand off of her hip and slid his fingers over her clit. Her ass hit him hard as she pushed against him, a harsh groan on her lips. "I take that as a yes." He repeated the motion and was rewarded again, her slick body holding him tight as she moved against him.

And then he was lost. In her. In the emotions and pleasure that were pounding through him, in his blood, so deep he didn't know if he would ever be free of it. Didn't know if he wanted to be. She was everything in that moment. So right, so perfect.

She was pleasure and she was pain. Happiness and perfect sadness. Because while he wanted it all to last forever, he was so very aware that the clock was counting down. That the closer he came to orgasm, the closer he was to his last time with her.

Each measured thrust, each passing second, was closer to the end.

But he couldn't hold on anymore, couldn't stretch the moment out, no matter how much he wanted to. He felt her tighten around him, and it pushed him over, his blood roaring through his ears as his climax overpowered him. Left him numb and shaking.

He withdrew and lay on his back next to her, trying to catch his breath, his chest heaving with the effort. Sarah was beside him, on her stomach, looking at him.

"Wow," she said.

"I agree."

"Walker . . . I . . . Walker, I love you."

Sarah knew she'd said the wrong thing. She'd known for days it was the wrong thing. So wrong she'd never even said it to herself. She'd never even said those words to another person.

She'd lived with her grandmother all her life and had known that while the older woman had cared for her out of duty, she hadn't loved her. And so Sarah had never said the words. Sarah knew that blood ties and time weren't a guarantee. And that was one of the many reasons she was so confident that, regardless of the fact she hadn't known him long, what she felt for Walker was love.

And now she'd admitted it. To herself and to him. And he looked . . . like he'd been hit in the head with a hammer.

Which was maybe not the thing a woman wanted when she confessed she loved a man. But how would she even know? In this, as with everything else, she was woefully inexperienced.

But something had changed in the past few seconds. All of her thoughts about how Walker should be a milestone in her new life, a stopping point on her way to true independence and liberation, suddenly seemed so ridiculous.

Because she realized that she was still trying to live someone else's life. She was trying to fit a vision of what her life *should* look like without her grandmother's influence, without asking what actually made her happy. She was after an ideal, not after what *she* truly wanted.

She wanted Walker. She wanted to be his wife. She wanted to be Kayla's mother. This was the life that she was meant for, the man she was meant for. This broken rancher who had felt so unwanted in his marriage, who didn't know how to trust. Who had taught her what it meant to be confident in her desires, who had told her she never had to be ashamed.

Yes, she was meant for this man. Most of all, she was meant for him because she loved him, and when she realized that, she'd also realized that she couldn't hold back her feelings because of fear.

Because her whole life had been her obeying fear.

But she was over that. Because she really was a new person. And she was ready to prove it.

"I love you," she said again.

"Oh . . . shit, Sarah, don't do this." He sat up, his muscles shifting and bunching. Strange that she would notice how beautiful he was, even now. Strange that it should still be so prominent in her mind even while she was starting to break apart inside.

"I'm not doing anything," she said. "I'm telling you how I feel. I'm not . . . I'm not doing the obligatory 'I'm a virgin so I fell in love' thing. I didn't want to fall in love, Walker. I wanted to kick-start a new, independent life. I wanted to find out who I was and what I wanted. But . . . but I found out that what I want is you. So no matter what my vision was for the future . . . it doesn't matter anymore. Because you're the man that I need. The man I want. I'm braver because of you—if I wasn't braver, I couldn't do this. I'm more myself because of you. I bought red underwear because of you. I like this version of me better. I like this life better."

"I told you," he said, his voice low, "that this isn't what I wanted. I am not putting myself, or Kayla, through the marriage thing again. Not ever."

"Can we at least have a relationship?"

"Why? So I can tell you in six months that I don't want marriage? I'm not changing my mind, Sarah."

"Why? Why are you so opposed to it? I'm not your ex. I'm not—"

"You know what, Sarah? She wasn't my ex either, in the beginning."

"Obviously not. She was your wife."

"That isn't what I mean. What I mean is that she wasn't the woman who would leave her husband and child when I married her. She became that woman, and I never saw that change coming. She became the woman who didn't want me to touch her anymore. The woman who didn't even like to look at me, or at her own child. When I married her, she was beautiful, and happy, and she liked being my wife."

"What happened with her . . . it doesn't mean it would happen with me."

"There are no guarantees in life, and at this point? With Kayla? I need a guarantee."

She swallowed hard, her heart aching, her throat burning. "I . . . I wish I'd had a guarantee before I told you I loved you, Walker, but the thing of it is that me loving you was more important than your response. The chance that we could have something? It's so much bigger than the pain I'm feeling right now. It was worth it. It's still worth it. And if you don't feel that way about me, then maybe I am better off."

He stood up, pacing the room, naked, unconcerned.

"You are, Sarah," he said, every word hitting like a bullet. "Because you want everything, and I'm not willing to give it. You know what I said I wanted. I got it. And for longer than I imagined I might. That's it. We're done."

"Yeah," she said, anger building in her. "I remember, Walker. You just wanted a fuck." He drew back like she'd slapped him. "But you know what? You never made me feel that way. You never made me feel like you were using me.

Not really. Until now. Until you reverted back to the man you were a few weeks ago, a man I know you're better than. Until you ran and hid like a coward. You're so afraid of the past, you haven't dealt with the fact that you have a future. Kayla has a future. And you can have more than this half-life. More than no Christmas tree because you can't deal with your issues."

"Listen to you, little girl. You hadn't had so much as a kiss before I came into your life and you think you can tell me what I should want? What I should do? Everything you know about sex, I taught you. And that's what you seem to think love is."

"To quote you, Walker? Bull. Shit. I might have learned about sex from you, but I already knew what love was. I knew it because I didn't have it. I felt the hole in me where it should have been. Where someone should have loved me. Where I should have loved them. And it's gone now. Because you filled it. Because I love you. I love Kayla. And I don't need you to teach me how to do that. I just need you to calm the eff down and let me love you."

"Sarah—"

"Stop looking at me like that. Like you feel sorry for me. Like you're so superior because you know things I don't. You've been through stuff, I'm sorry about that. My mother left me with an old woman that never saw me as anything but a living, breathing cautionary tale against fast living, and she made sure I knew it. I know what it's like to feel like no one wants you. I know what the hard parts of life look like. What they feel like. Sex isn't the be-all and end-all for life experience. My life didn't start the night you broke my hymen."

"I never said that."

"But it's what you think! Like I'm Virgin Barbie and you just took me out of my box, all new and unplayed with."

"You make it sound like I'm being dismissive."

"You are! You think because I was a virgin, I don't know

my own emotions. You think it's why I fell in love with you. And you know what? That's what I was afraid of too. Then I realized that if I didn't let myself love you just because you were my first, then I was being dismissive of myself. I had a list, Walker. Of things I would do. Of the woman I would be. And nowhere on that list did it say, 'Marry that dumb angry rancher you picked up in a bar.' But it's what I want. And I'm not too afraid to say it. I'm not afraid like you."

Walker looked away from her and swallowed hard, his Adam's apple bobbing up and down. "Baby, you think I'm afraid, but the fact is, I just don't want forever with you. I never told you different, so don't go acting surprised now."

A tear slid down her cheek, and she didn't bother to brush it away. "Dammit, Walker. Now you're making me cry."

"I never wanted to do that. But it's better if I make you cry now than pretend that it could be something else and make you do it later."

"I don't think there's a better." She started to collect her clothes, feeling stupid because she'd bought red underwear for him. Feeling stupid because she'd thought it made her different.

She froze while she was putting on the red panties. No, she hadn't bought these for him. She'd bought them for her. And she hadn't bought them to make her different, she'd bought them *because* she was different.

So he was taking himself from her, and that was horrible. Awful. Heartrending and painful. But he couldn't take this change from her. He could break her heart—and oh, he was—but he couldn't take away everything he'd given her, everything she'd found out about herself.

She was determined that her grandmother wouldn't be proven right. Determined to stand behind the choices she'd made.

Because she couldn't regret Walker. She wouldn't.

"Do you need me to come back tomorrow?" she asked, when she'd gotten completely dressed. He'd just stood there watching the whole time, and she'd done her best to ignore him.

"No. We'll manage."

Just like that. Out of his bed. Out of his life. Out of Kayla's life. Like she'd never mattered.

"Fine. I'll . . . I'll see you sometimes still, Walker. I hope it's not uncomfortable."

It couldn't be anything but. Still, she was going to pull herself together now. She would fall apart later. She would keep it together now, drive home, then throw herself on the bed and cry for three days straight.

"I can handle it."

"So can I," she said.

"Great. I'm sorry, Sarah," he said, his voice rough.

"Oh, please don't apologize. Like you have no control over any of this." One final surge of anger, of adrenaline, shot through her. "Because between you and me? I think you're lying to yourself. I mean . . . good Lord, Walker. I seduced you in a funeral director's dress with all the skills of a thirty-year-old woman who'd never been kissed. If that's not love? I don't know what to tell you."

And on that note, she walked out of his bedroom, and out of his life.

Ten

Bah fricking humbug. That was about the best Walker could do for Christmas Eve. At least on the inside. On the outside he had to smile and make sure he plugged in the damned Christmas tree, because he was doing this holiday for Kayla, and not for himself.

Wasn't that what Sarah had reminded him of?

Oh, Sarah.

Just thinking about her sent a wave of emotion, of pain, over him. And this pain wasn't centered in his dick. It wasn't about sex or desire, or the fact that his bed felt empty and cold and he kept waking up with a hard-on, although that was all true.

No, this pain was mainly centered in his heart. And it was bad.

Not that it really surprised him. Because he'd lied to her. He'd just flat-out lied. He'd told her he didn't love her. He'd told her he wasn't scared. And none of that was true.

He was petrified. Because she made him care. She made him want. She made him love. She'd torn open the locked doors that had barred off places in his heart and soul that he'd never wanted to visit again. And she'd left them that way, then left him.

Of course, he'd made her leave. With his stupid, angry words. And all that fear. That overwhelming, choking fear.

That she would love him today and stop tomorrow. That she would decide one day that he wasn't worth it. That Kayla wasn't worth it.

She was right; he'd wanted a guarantee. So he'd guaranteed himself a life of sad and horny misery instead of taking the chance on anything else. At least it was a sure thing.

Some consolation.

"We're going to the tree lighting tonight, right?" Kayla said, her blue eyes huge and pleading.

"I don't know, squirt. Why don't we stay home? You can open a present and we can watch *Rudolph*."

"But Sarah . . . I mean, Miss Larsen, is leading the kindergartners in Christmas carols at the lighting and I miss her and I really want to go. We practiced the songs before we left for break and they're really fun. We have one about Santa on a skateboard."

"Real traditional, huh?"

"Yeah," his daughter said, clearly not getting his meaning.

"And Miss Larsen is going to be there?"

"Yeah. I miss her. Don't you miss her?"

He missed her like he would miss air if he were pushed underwater. He missed her so much, he didn't know how he was supposed to keep going.

But what was the option? Just . . . forget how hard his marriage had been? Forget how much it hurt when Elise left him?

To just stop being a coward?

Was it really that easy?

"Having Miss Larsen here made me happy," Kayla said.

She'd made him happy too. Having her here had been like having little glimpses into a kind of perfect, beautiful life he'd thought far beyond him.

Well, it's too far to reach now, dumbass, because you pushed it away. Because you're afraid. You're just what she said. A scared little boy who doesn't want to get hurt again.

But he was hurt. It was too late to be anything else.

He was in love too, and he'd promised himself he'd never do the love shit again. Because love was horrible.

No, that was wrong. Love was wonderful. Loving Sarah, when she was in his home, in his arms, her eyes shining at him, that special smile on her lips, was wonderful. Losing love was horrific.

And he hadn't lost love. He'd tied a millstone around it and chucked it in the river.

He was an idiot.

He did love her. He loved her more than he'd ever loved a woman before, and that was where the fear came in. Losing Elise had been hard. Losing Sarah, losing her right now, was killing him by inches, killing him with grief, and he'd known it would.

But he'd thought maybe if he did it now instead of later—now, when he had control, when he could say to her face he didn't love her—that it might spare him.

Well, that was damn funny now, as he sat in his living room in front of a Christmas tree he wouldn't have if it weren't for her, drowning in sorrow while trying to smile for the sake of his daughter.

"It's easy to be happy when Miss Larsen is around," he said, his voice rough.

"Can she come over?"

"No," he said, leaning his head back on the couch. "No, she can't."

"Oh. Because she's busy?"

"Yeah," he said, his throat tightening. He closed his eyes and pictured her like she'd been on that first night, her hair back, in that horrible dress. She was right. That tug that he had felt had gone beyond lust. It always had.

Oh, there was plenty of lust, but it was deeper. Like he'd

known from the first moment that she was special. That she was her own brand of woman, unique in every way.

And yet you're trying to make her pay for someone else's sins.

No. That wasn't it. He was trying to make himself pay. He leaned forward and put his head in his hands. Because it was his fault. Because she'd left because of him—that's what he was afraid of. Afraid that changing the woman would never matter because he wouldn't be able to change himself enough.

He felt a little hand on his arm, and he looked over at Kayla. "Are you okay, Daddy?" she asked.

"I think I made a mistake, Kayla," he said.

She frowned. "Then you should say sorry. You can always say you're sorry."

He laughed and planted his hands on his thighs. "Yeah, I suppose I could."

It was simple. But then, that's how kids saw life. Without all the garbage adults piled onto it. Kayla knew hurt, but she'd attached herself to Sarah without hesitation. To Kayla, fixing mistakes was still as easy as saying sorry.

Another one of those funny aches took over his chest. It made him long for more things he couldn't have. For a time when things had been that simple.

Just say sorry.

Why not? Why the hell not? He didn't have anything to lose.

He looked around the room, at the Christmas decorations, at the warmth that Sarah had brought into his life.

No, he sure as hell didn't have anything to lose. Except for that crushing fear. And once he lost that, he had everything to gain.

Sarah wrapped her arms around herself and bounced up and down in place, trying to keep her blood flowing to all her extremities. It was below freezing and she was herding a bunch of chilly kindergartners around a roped-off parking lot, trying to get them in place in front of the Christmas tree for the big ceremony.

Walker wasn't here. Neither was Kayla. That she wanted them there seemed seriously silly. And a little masochistic. But she did.

She just wanted to see Kayla's sweet little face. She wanted a quick glance at Walker. At the man she loved. Still. She loved him so much.

Stupid lame heart. She had half a mind to cut it out with a spoon.

"Sarah!"

Sarah looked across the parking lot, which was still covered with snow, and saw a little figure in a pink hat and jacket running toward her, blond braids swinging with the motion.

"Kayla!"

Kayla flung herself at Sarah, her arms like a vise around her waist.

Sarah squeezed her eyes closed, tears threatening to fall. "I'm glad you made it," she said, her throat too tight to let out anything much louder than a whisper.

"Me too. Where do we sing?"

Sarah shook her head and did her best to get herself back on track, and to get over the disappointment that Walker had gone out of his way to avoid her. "Right over here."

After a few run-throughs of the little music program, the kids were antsy, and the lunch lady, Ms. Mckenna, brought cocoas over to help keep them still while the crowd started to fill up the parking lot and the area around the tree.

First came an introduction from the mayor, then the kindergartners were on. They were adorable—and off-key. Their rendition of "Silent Night" was all over the place, their "Joy to the World" only half remembered.

And it was the first thing to make Sarah really smile in days. As they sang the last notes of "We Wish You a Merry

Christmas," the lights on the tree came on, bathing everything in a colorful glow.

When they were through, everyone clapped. Sarah turned to face the audience, and froze when she saw him. Backlit by the tree, snow falling behind him, was Walker. Just as sexy, just as imposing as he'd been that first night she'd seen him.

But he was more now. He was so dear to her. So perfect.

And he didn't just make her heart race; he made it ache.

"I need to borrow Miss Larsen for a second," he said to the class, and then he held his hand out. Like he expected her to do something other than stand there and look dumb. He was going to have to be disappointed on that score. Ms. Mckenna stood behind the line of kids, making a shooing motion, her eyes wide.

She moved away from the kids, but she didn't take his hand. And she wasn't blind to the fact that the whole town was watching mousy Miss Larsen wander into a shadowy patch with a dark stranger.

Well, fine. They should know that she was a little surprising. That she had mysterious qualities. She wasn't *just* mousy Miss Larsen.

Though that didn't matter as much as she'd thought it would. She didn't really care what they thought. Not when she was brokenhearted and miserable. Not when her mystery man was the one who'd done it. The whole scenario was less glamorous than she'd thought it might be. Sure, people might see her differently if they knew she'd had an affair with Walker, but did any of it matter if she didn't have Walker?

"I need to talk to you," he said.

"Right now?" she asked. "Because there are people everywhere, and if you want to make me cry again, I'd just as soon we not do it in front of the whole fricking world."

"I don't want to make you cry," he said. "You might cry. Hell, baby, I might cry, and I don't want to do it at all, in private or in front of people, but I can't make any guarantees."

"Why is that?"

"I'm a coward. You're right about that. I was afraid. I am afraid. I'm shaking, inside and out." He held his hand out and she could see how unsteady it was. "But I have to do this. Because . . . because I need you."

"You need me?"

"Yes. I had no idea how much until I tried to live the past few days without you."

"You've lived thirty-six years without me."

"But it wasn't the same."

Hope bloomed in her chest. And she tried to suppress it, because she really didn't think she could take being let down by him again. "You're not about to tell me you missed that silly ginger you were sleeping with, are you?"

"So much. And not just sleeping with her. I missed not coming home to her. I missed the fact that my house felt warm. That there was someone sharing my space with me. Mostly, though, I just missed you. I thought . . . I'm scared, Sarah, because I chased Elise away and I don't want to do that to you. So I lied to you. And I told you I didn't love you because I thought . . . somehow, losing you now would hurt less than losing you later. But that wasn't true."

"Rewind. You love me?"

"Yes. But I don't want to repeat the same mistakes I made. And she didn't tell me what they were. What I'd done. What I could have done differently. I don't know if I've done enough to become a better husband now, but I want to be. I want to . . . to date you," he said, "to find out. If you really want me. If I can really do this."

Whether or not she had experience in love, she knew her love for Walker was true. And no, she had no idea how to have a relationship. Had no idea how to be a good girlfriend or, eventually, wife. Had no idea how to be a mother.

But she was choosing Walker and Kayla. She wasn't going to stay with them out of duty, like her grandmother. And she would never leave, like her own mother had done.

Like Walker's first wife had done. She just had to trust that love would cover all the things she didn't know how to do. That love would fill in all the gaps.

"I don't think the problem was you, Walker."

"But if it was?"

"Then we have time to find out. And if I have a problem, I'll tell you. Because I'm going to fight for us. For this. I've never had a boyfriend before. I might be a terrible girlfriend. And pretty much everything I'm about to say . . . well, I'm just making crud up. But it's crud I believe in. Everything worth having is worth a fight. Is worth tears. And dammit, man, I've shed buckets these past few days. It's worth pain, and fighting, because the good stuff is better than all of that. Because love is better than all of that. Love is worth staying for."

"Your love is," he said, pulling her against him and kissing her. Hard. Deep. Filled with emotion. This wasn't simple lust. It wasn't the promise of a one-night stand. It was so much more. They parted and he rested his forehead against hers. "Yeah, Sarah, your love is better."

"Walker . . . I can't even begin to tell you what you mean to me. What you've changed in my life."

"You changed your life, Sarah, not me."

"Maybe. But you're the best thing to come from the change."

"So are you willing to take a chance on me? Even if I'm not perfect?"

"Are you willing to sleep with me even when I'm in granny panties?"

He kissed her again. "No question."

"Then yes, Walker. Yes, I will take you. Imperfections and all. And it won't be a hardship. Do you know why?"

"Why?" he whispered, his lips against hers.

"Because your imperfections fit mine just right."

"Well, Merry Christmas to me," he said.

"Not just yet," she said, extricating herself from his hold. "I have a tree lighting to finish."

"And after that you're coming home with me. And staying the night."

Her heart fluttered. Honest to goodness, it fluttered. "Really? All night?"

"Well, we need you there Christmas morning."

Her cheeks warmed, in spite of the cold air. "Oh."

"And the next morning. And next night, and . . . You get the idea."

Sarah reached over to the table next to them and grabbed a Styrofoam cup fill with hot chocolate. "Here," she said, handing it to him, "you deserve cocoa."

A smile curved his lips. "I gave her my heart, she gave me a cocoa."

"And *my* heart."

"That makes it better." Walker leaned in and dropped a kiss onto her lips, his smile turning wicked. "I guarantee that you'll be my very favorite present I unwrap this year."

She laughed. "Oh, the feeling is definitely mutual."

Epilogue

It had been a beautiful wedding. Carly had been radiant, Lucas the most glowing groom on record. Lucy and Mac had gotten engaged just before it started, and Sarah and her friend had spent the first half of the reception gazing at her ring and talking about wedding venues.

Until Mac stole Lucy for a dance, anyway.

Sarah sighed and sat back down at her table, watching Kayla run barefoot in the grass with the other kids, her smile a mile wide.

The past six months had been the most blissful of her life. She'd gone from having never told anyone she loved them to telling two people she loved them every day. Life with Walker and Kayla was more than she'd ever dared to hope for, more than she'd ever known she could have.

At first, her relationship with Walker had been the subject of some serious gossip, but it hadn't bothered Sarah at all. Quite the contrary, she had reveled in the fact that Silver Creek's least scandalous resident had finally made waves.

After a lifetime of good behavior, she'd been due.

Walker came to the table, dressed all in black, a glass of punch in his hand.

"Why don't you sit?" she asked.

"Maybe in a second," he said. "I was thinking."

"Uh-oh."

"Hey, I'm serious."

She laughed. "So was I."

"I've been a bad influence on you," he said.

"That's for sure."

"And you've been a good influence on me."

"I've tried."

"You've succeeded. And it's not only me; it's Kayla. Your presence . . . your love and support have meant everything to her. I'll never forget the terror on her face that day I was late to the school. She was so afraid of loss, afraid of things a child shouldn't ever have to think about. But you've replaced that fear with so much love. You've changed both of our lives. You've changed us."

She smiled up at him. "Oh, Walker. No more than you've changed me."

"Sarah, you complete my family. Because we're so different, but like you said at Christmas, our imperfections seem to fit just right."

Sarah's throat tightened, emotion overwhelming her. "You're going to make me weepy in front of everyone. Why don't you sit? We'll have a drink."

"All things considered," he said, "I'd rather kneel." He got down on one knee in front of her and her heart stopped for a second. "Damn Mac stole my thunder."

She put her hand over her mouth. "No," she said, talking through her fingers. "He didn't, Walker. He really didn't."

"You haven't seen the ring yet."

"I don't need to see the ring to know that. To know my answer. I only need to see the man."

Walker swallowed, his dark eyes glistening. "And what is your answer?"

"Yes."

Keep reading for a preview
of Maisey Yates's

UNBROKEN

Available now!

"It's bad form to get drunk at your sister's wedding, right?"

"Since when has that ever stopped you, Cade?"

Amber Jameson leaned back in the folding chair and then checked to make sure the little purple bow tied to the back hadn't fallen off and onto the grass. She'd spent too many damn hours tying those things on yesterday.

They were finicky. Finicky flipping ribbons. Almost as finicky as the bride, who, while cute as a button under normal circumstances, had had a bridezilla flare-up during the decorating yesterday and had gone around micromanaging said ribbon tying.

And placement.

She'd demanded ribbon curls in lengths that were impossible for mere mortals to achieve. If Lark weren't the little sister Amber had always wanted, she would never have gone along with all of it. Not without attacking her with the scissors she was using to curl ribbons, at least.

But then, Lark's life had been short on frills. Being raised by two brothers and a dad. So Amber supposed she was entitled.

But then, Amber's life had been short on this kind of thing too, and she didn't feel at all yearny for it. Nope. Marriage and men and bleh. Not her thing. Not these days.

"It doesn't usually," Cade said, leaning back in his chair so that they were sitting at the same angle. "But I thought, since this is for Lark, maybe I should behave."

She looked at her friend's profile. Strong, handsome. Square jaw, roughened with dark stubble. Brown eyes that always had a glint of naughty in them. And today he was wearing a suit jacket and a tie, along with a black cowboy hat.

Damn, damn, *damn*, he was fine. Sometimes it hit her. Like a shit-ton of bricks, that her best friend was the best-looking guy in a five-hundred-mile radius. Or possibly the world. And it made her feel . . . things she didn't want to feel.

Then he turned to face her head-on and offered her his very best smart-ass Cade smile, and the moment faded out as soon as it hit. Like driving on one of Silver Creek's fir-lined highways and seeing a sunbeam peek through the trees. A brilliant shaft of light that colored the world gold for just a moment before racing back behind the dark green branches. Just a glimpse, an impression of something she didn't want to explore.

Like, ever.

"When did she grow up?" Amber asked, looking over at the dance floor, where Lark was currently holding on to her new husband, both of them swaying to the music without displaying any particular dancing skills. Quinn was a rough-and-tumble-cowboy type, though he seemed to have a little more rhythm than his new bride. "It makes me feel old," she continued. "Like an old cliché. Sitting here at her reception looking at this grown-up woman in a wedding gown and thinking . . . how is she not eight years old still?"

"Imagine how I feel," Cade said, his voice rough.

"Yeah, I know."

The Mitchells were a part of Amber's cobbled-together family. She didn't have a lot in the way of people who loved her, so when she found people who were willing to accept her, she clung to them as best as she could.

In her younger years that clinging amounted to some very poor decisions, but she'd matured past that. Especially after she'd realized that her grandma and grandpa weren't going to just ship her straight back into the system. That they were going to let her stay in Silver Creek.

That she could stay, with them, in their home.

Since then, she'd built herself a solid foundation for her life. And Cade was the cornerstone. Had been since she was fourteen years old. She would never, ever do anything to jeopardize that.

Though there was nothing wrong with infrequent, secret ogling.

"Are you having empty-nest syndrome, Mitchell?" she asked, nudging him with her elbow.

"Me? Oh, hell no. This nest isn't getting emptier. Maddy runs around like hell on pudgy feet. That little beast cut holes in one of my work shirts the other day with those little plastic-handled scissors. And now Cole and Kelsey have the other baby coming in January. Nope, it's just filling up over here."

"But Lark's gone."

"She's been gone. She's been shacking up with that asshole I now call a brother-in-law for a year."

She patted his thigh and didn't notice how hard and hot and muscular it was beneath those thin dress pants. "I know. But now it's official."

"Yep."

"Emotions don't bite, Cade. Don't run from your feels," she said dryly.

"That's pretty rich coming from you, missy."

She made a face at him and earned a smile. "I don't have to take advice to give it. I'm emotionally stunted and I know it."

"That's why we get along so well."

"I thought it was because I'm such a good pool player," she said, lifting her beer up from the table and taking a long drink.

"That's not it. I'm a lot better than you are."

"Uh-huh."

"What do you think?" he asked. "Wanna dance?"

She eyed Cade. More specifically his leg. The one she hadn't just patted. "Um . . . really?"

He lifted a shoulder. "Okay, maybe not." The grooves around his mouth deepened and Amber felt an answering chasm deepen around her heart.

She hated that he couldn't dance anymore. Hated that the man she knew as being so totally vital and energetic was hobbled because of a rodeo accident four years ago.

For a long time they'd all blamed Quinn, Lark's husband, but they found out they'd been mistaken. Hard for Cade to process, as evidenced by the fact that he frequently referred to his new brother-in-law as an asshole.

They were getting there, but they weren't exactly best friends yet.

The dude-bonding process was not yet complete.

Now they didn't know quite who to blame, except for a poor kid who'd been paid to sabotage the ride. The spike he'd put beneath Cade's horse's saddle had only been intended to end the ride faster, not send Cade to the hospital and cause life-changing, career-ending injuries. Getting hung up on your horse was never a good thing, but when the horse was that spooked? You didn't walk away. You got carted away on a stretcher.

Quinn got to move on from it all. His name was cleared. He was reinstated into competitions. And the question of who'd sabotaged Cade was left unanswered.

And Cade would never be fixed. Even if they did find out who was behind it, Cade wouldn't magically be healed, damage undone by justice. That hurt her. Always. Every day.

Because whenever she had a problem, Cade was there.

He was always trying to fix things for her. Had been since they were in high school. But there was no fixing this for him. And she'd give her own leg to do it. So he could go back to doing what he loved.

She only used her legs to wait tables and help around her grandparents' ranch.

She didn't do anything like Cade. Watching him ride? It had always sent a flash of light down her spine. A spark that lit her up everywhere and sent tingles to places.

It was art with him. Athletic grace, and sheer masculine willpower. Straining muscles, gritted teeth, dirt, sweat and mud flying in the air.

Yeah, that flipped her switches like whoa.

Cade Mitchell on the back of a bucking horse was a truly orgasmic experience.

When he was through with a ride, he always shook. From his hands down to his boots. Adrenaline, he said. She shook too though, and it wasn't always that.

He scared the hell out of her. Watching his accident during the Vegas championships, on TV in her living room, had been the single most painful moment of her life.

Her best friend, her family, dragged around the arena like a rag doll, white as death and knocking on that door.

In those moments, she'd gotten a look at life without Cade. And it had been a yawning vacuum of empty cold. She'd always known he was important. Right then, she'd realized just how much.

Ironically, she would still give it all to get him back in the saddle, so to speak. Because he loved it. Even though she knew that after that accident she'd sweat off three pounds during those precious seconds he was on the back of one of those beasts.

Small price to pay for allowing him to have his passion. For giving back the ability to dance, however badly, so they could go out on that wooden floor together on his sister's wedding day.

But there was no going out on the dance floor for Cade. So they sat at the table and drank beer until the sky turned purple and the candles, strung over the tables in mason jars, lit everything with a pale yellow glow.

"Last dance," Amber said, knowing that Quinn and Lark would be leaving soon. Off on their honeymoon. "Wanna get out of here?" she asked.

"Are you hitting on me?"

"Hay-ell yeah. What do people come to weddings for but to hook up? Certainly not to see their BFF's little sister tie the knot with a ridiculously handsome cowboy."

"You think he's handsome?" Cade asked, eyes narrowed.

She looked back at Quinn and Lark, who were still twined around each other like vines. "Uh, yeah. Have you checked that tat he has on his shoulder? Meow."

"Hey, he's my sister's husband," he said, grimacing slightly when he said the words.

"Don't worry, I'm out of the game."

"I thought we were gonna hook up."

"Did I say hook up? I meant, 'Let's get out of here so I can whup your ass at pool.' How about that?"

"Sounds like more fun anyway."

More fun than watching his little sister ride off into the sunset with a guy that Cade still had a tough time with in some ways. He didn't say that, but Amber could read Cade's subtext pretty well. Most often, said subtext was: "cheeseburger" or "breasts." But every so often it was a real, deep emotion that he was never, ever going to show to the public.

Or even to himself.

Which was when she made sure she was on hand to help him out.

"Yep. I'll even buy you a beer because you look so damn pertty," she said, tweaking his hat.

"Well, shucks," he said, that lopsided grin tilting to the left, tilting her stomach along with it. "Let's get on with it . . . Can you play pool in that dress?" he asked, indicating her very abnormal and feminine attire.

"If you can play in a tie."

He reached up and grabbed the knot at the base of his throat and loosened it. "I think I can handle it."

"But can you handle me?" she asked, quirking her brow.

"I guess we'll see."

The Saloon, so named because it had been around since that was the usual name for a place where drinking and carousing occurred, was packed. Not so much because it was a Sunday night, but because there was no other nightlife in Silver Creek. Nothing beyond a music festival that ran through the summer and attracted mainly the gray-hairs who only lived in town seasonally.

Not that Cade needed much of a nightlife. Not considering he hadn't done any real "going out" since his accident. Not considering that, even if he did, he couldn't dance.

He didn't know why he'd asked Amber to dance at Lark's wedding.

Ah, shit. Lark was married. That made him feel . . . well, it made him feel. And that was just something he hadn't been prepared for.

But she was his baby sister, and dammit, no matter how unsentimental he wanted to be about it, he and Cole had practically raised her. Which really made Amber's words closer to the truth than he wanted to admit.

He had empty-nest syndrome. A thirty-two-year-old single man with commitment issues . . . and empty-nest syndrome. As if he wasn't dysfunctional enough already.

He wandered up to the bar behind Amber and settled in next to her, his forearms resting on the wooden surface. Scarred from years of use and misuse. Bottles broken in brawls and Lord knew what else.

There was a story on the menus about a shoot-out between a sheriff and an outlaw that had resulted in the outlaw giving up the ghost on that very bar top.

The Saloon was filled with history. And Cade had spent too many nights in it over the past four years. Just soaking in the alcohol haze and absorbing the hormones of those more up to the challenge of getting laid than he was.

He'd become pathetic. And he didn't have it in him to change it.

"Two Buds, please," Amber said, leaning over the counter and catching the bartender's attention a lot quicker than Cade would have.

"I wanted a hard cider," he said. In truth, he would really like to have something that would knock him on his ass, but he tried to save the pitiful drunk trick for the privacy of his own home. In case he got maudlin.

"Too bad," she said.

He was glad she was here. Because there was nothing she hadn't been there for. Every hard thing he'd ever had to cope with. Finding out about his father's affair, his mother's death, his father's death . . . his accident. Lark's wedding.

Amber Jameson had been there for every-damn-thing.

"Beer me," he said, once she had the bottles in hand.

"Try again. I don't speak frat bro."

"Amber," he said, giving her his very best plaintive look.

"Fine. I pity you. Drown your sorrows in the way society has dictated men ought. Much healthier than expressing genuine emotion."

"Can I interest you in a friendly game of pool wherein I use your sad, pathetic skills at stick handling to make me feel more like a man?"

She arched a brow. "Sure, honey, if you think hitting balls into a pocket will make you feel more like a man."

"I do," he said, getting up from the bar and heading to the table.

Amber picked up a cue and started chalking the end.

"Your balls are mine, Mitchell," she said, the light in her eyes utterly wicked.

"Whose balls haven't been yours?"

That taunt didn't come from Cade's mouth, and it had him on edge instantly.

Mike Steele. Standard, grade-A douche who worked at the mill. They'd all gone to high school together, but he'd never been too big of an ass. He was drunk tonight though, and hanging out with two other guys from high school who fell on the wrong side of the douche spectrum.

And for some reason, they were interested in letting their asswipe flags fly.

Cade opened his mouth to tell them to back down but Amber had already whirled around, the end of the pool cue smacking sharply on the floor, the tip held up by her face.

"Can I help you, Mike?" she asked.

"Just saying, is all," he said, his words slurred.

"Maybe you should just say a little clearer," she said, "because I didn't quite take your meaning."

"He's just sayin'," douche number two said, "you're like the town mare. We've all had a ride."

Cade saw red. Death and destruction flashed before his eyes, but Amber barely blinked.

"Come on now," Amber said, her tone completely cool, "official rules say there's no score if the cowboy can't stay on for a full eight seconds. And if I recall right . . . you didn't."

"You stupid slut . . ."

And then Cade did step in, his fist connecting with the side of the other man's jaw. And damn it felt good. He hadn't punched anyone since . . . well, since he'd broken his brother-in-law's nose a year ago.

He was worried the other two goons might round on him but they were too drunk to maintain a thought that went in a straight line, so they didn't seem to key into the fact that Cade had just laid their buddy out flat.

"Hey!" Allen, the bartender, shouted. "Cade, could you not bust faces in my bar?"

"Tell these assholes not to run their misogynistic mouths in your bar." He looked around at all the people who were staring at him, agape. "Yeah. Ten-dollar word, I just raised the IQ of the entire room," Cade shouted.

"Oh, Cade, for heaven's sake," Amber said. "Knock it off."

"He said—"

"Like I haven't heard it before?"

"I'm not going to listen to it."

"There's no point. And I don't need you to step in and save me. I just wanted to play pool. Now you punched him and we have to go so he doesn't call the cops on you."

"I know the cops."

"So what? Now I'm a spectacle, so thanks."

"Are you . . . are you pissed at me for punching a guy who called you a—"

"Yes! I am pissed at you! Outside," she said. "Now."

They walked out the swinging front door of the bar and into the dirt and gravel parking lot. Dust hung in the air, clinging to the smells of hose water and hay and mingling together to create their own unique scent of summer.

"What did I do? He was the one . . ."

She turned to face him, her cheeks red, her brown eyes glittering. "He's not worth it. He's got half a brain and a tiny peen. And all you needed to do was just let it go. I don't need attention called to shit like that, Cade."

"What do you mean 'shit like that'? As in, it happens frequently?"

"Yes."

"I've never—"

"Because they're normally too sober to do it in front of you. Why do you think I have no friends other than you?"

"Because I'm all you need?" he asked, knowing full well that wasn't true.

"Because I came into town with a bang, no pun intended, seventeen years ago and no one can forget it. Because a lot of the guys from high school I . . . And now as far as the women are concerned, I'm that skank their husband screwed under the bleachers during free period."

The blood was pounding in his ears, his heart racing. "I don't think of you that way."

"I know. But I didn't have sex with your husband."

A laugh rushed out of him, awkward and angry. "Obviously that will never be a problem I have with you. And it's not like you slept with their husbands after they were married."

"Granted. But it doesn't seem to matter."

"Who cares about that high school BS anyway?"

"Everyone," she said. "Everyone but you. Which is why we're friends."

"I did a lot of stupid things in high school. Nobody gives me crap."

"That's because you were never naked with them. Guys are dumb about that stuff," she said, the lines around her mouth curving downward. "Anyway, it doesn't matter, Cade."

"It does."

"No. It doesn't. And don't go punching people for me anymore."

"Come on . . . you liked it a little."

The previously noted grooves at the corners of her lips turned up a bit. "Fine. A little bit. But only because he so had it coming."

"He really did."

"I wonder if any of your former flames are going to come up and accuse you of being a manwhore."

"Nah," he said, "they won't. But only because they don't want anyone to know they slept with me. That guy's just pissed 'cuz he's not going there again."

"I'm going to go ahead and take that as a compliment."

"I would never mean it as anything else."

"I know," she said, looking down at her thumbnail. "I'm not the same person I was then."

"Sure you are. You're just more emotionally well-adjusted."

That earned him a smile. "Is that what you call this? Shooting pool, drinking beer, bar fights?"

"If it's not well-adjusted, then we're both screwed."

"I think we're screwed."

"Good thing we're screwed together then." He slung his arm over her shoulder and they started walking back to her truck, the gravel shifting underneath his boots with each step.

"I guess so." She pulled away from him and rounded to the driver's side, climbing up inside the cab and turning the engine over.

He got in after her, slowly. Pissed that just climbing into a truck made him conscious of his limitations. Made him see the bad kind of stars, not the orgasmic kind, lightning bolts of pain shooting up his thigh and crawling up his back, stabbing right at the center of his spine.

He settled into the seat and let out a long breath. For a second there he'd felt ten foot tall and bulletproof. Punching that jackass in the face.

He didn't want to know what that said about him. But maybe it didn't matter since he was back to feeling roughly six foot three and vulnerable to being trampled on by a horse.

Which he was.

He held on to the handle just above the passenger window and leaned out, shutting the heavy truck door.

"Do you feel like a man now?" she asked, maneuvering the truck out of the lot and onto the cracked two-lane road that led back to Elk Haven Stables.

"I'm riding bitch in your Ford, how much of a man could I possibly feel like?"

"Would you like me to throw you a raw steak when we get back to your place?"

"No. Tuck me in and read me a bedtime story."

"Aw, poor baby." She leaned over and put her hand on his thigh. Second time that night. Weird, but he seemed to be keeping a ticker on "number of times her fingers caressed him" that evening.

"She's married and off on her honeymoon," he said, resting his elbow out the truck window.

"Yeah. What do you think they're doing right now?"

He whipped his head around to face her. "Playing Scrabble."

"Is that what the kids are calling it these days?"

He had no frickin' idea what the kids were calling it these days. He hadn't had it for four years. Four. *Years*. He half expected the League of Players to come and confiscate his dick after so much time off.

He grimaced. His thoughts had taken an unsanctioned turn. He didn't like to think about his celibacy. His sister on her honeymoon was honestly preferable.

"Word games. In flannel pajamas," he growled.

"Fine, Cade, whatever works for you." She cleared her throat. "I bet Quinn got a triple-word score."

"No!" he said. "I punched a guy for you, don't torment me."

"You deserve it. You've given her enough hell."

"I have not," he said. "I've been a steadying and wonderful influence. Godlike, in many ways."

"In what way?"

"I have to think of examples."

"No, I believe you."

"She turned out in spite of me," he said, letting out a heavy breath. "I'm well aware of that. Kind of amazing that Cole and I were able to turn her into a functional human being. Or maybe she just did . . . anyway."

"Either way, you should be proud."

"Damn. I am an empty-nester."

"As you pointed out, you still have Cole."

"Oh, yes." Never mind that living in his older brother's domain was suffocating as hell. Cole was a great guy, but when it came to the ranch, which they all owned equal stakes in, he could be a control freak.

And Cade had usually been happy to be in the backseat on decisions, because he liked to be a silent investor, so to speak. He'd put money into the ranch from his wins on the circuit, reaped profit in return, had had a place to crash at when he was home and mainly got to live on the road.

Now he was home. All the time. And having a brother who thought of himself as his boss didn't really do a lot to help with their sibling rivalry.

Cade had been fine for a while, playing the dumbass and in general drifting along with whatever Cole said.

But now that this was starting to look like it was going to be his life . . . like he was never getting back in the saddle in a serious way . . . well, now he was starting to realize he was going to have to make a new success for himself.

Otherwise his glory days would be perpetually behind him. And never in front of him. Ever again.

What a nice thought that was.

"I only drank half a beer and I'm starting to get philosophical and shit," he said.

"Uh-oh, better get you home then. I wouldn't want to embarrass either of us by being present for this."

"You really are a good friend," he said.

She looked at him and smiled. "The best."

"Pretty much the only one I have."

"Because you're surly."

"Am I?" he asked.

"You just a punched a guy in the face for offending you, so yeah, I'd say."

"I think it was noble of me," he said.

"'Noble' and 'godlike' in one conversation. If this is your version of being a sad drunk, then I'd hate to be exposed to your ego when you're feeling sober and upbeat."

"You'll be around me in that state tomorrow. Because now I owe you a game of pool."

"I don't know, I think I owe you for defending my honor. I didn't need it defended, but nonetheless, I appreciate you risking bruised knuckles for me."

"Anything for you," he said. "You know that."

"Oooh, dangerous promise, Cade Mitchell. You never know what I might ask of you."

"I've known you for seventeen years and you haven't shocked me yet."

"That smacks of a challenge," she said, giving him an impish smile. "You know I can't resist a challenge."

Ready to find
your next great read?

Let us help.

Visit prh.com/nextread

Penguin
Random
House

UNBUTTONED

"I loved *Unbuttoned* by Maisey Yates in a big way. . . . I love a feisty heroine and a charismatic hero, especially when they clash. The scenes where they duked it out verbally, all the while undressing each other mentally, were so delicious. . . . Lots of fun."   —Smart Bitches Trashy Books

"A sexy, compelling read. . . . It's a great start to what looks to be a promising new small-town contemporary series and has introduced me to a new-to-me author who writes enjoyable characters with great emotional depth, witty dialogue and steamy love scenes."   —Ramblings from This Chick

"A lot of fun to read. . . . I look forward to reading the next installment. She provided humor, tension, smexy times, twisted family dynamics and a re-enjoyment of life."
     —The Book Pushers

"Maisey Yates is a very talented author and has created the perfect small-town romance about two people that found love once they learned to take a leap of faith. . . . I can't wait to see what is in store for the residents of Silver Creek."
     —Books-n-Kisses